CW01209951

Wyvern of Wessex

Millie Thom

SONS OF KINGS:
BOOK THREE

To Mike,
Very Best Wishes,
Millie

Copyright © 2018 by Millie Thom

The moral right of Millie Thom to be identified as the author of this work has been asserted in accordance with the Copyright, Designs and Patents Act 1988.

All rights reserved. No part of this publication may be reproduced, stored in a retrieval system, or transmitted, in any form or by any means, electronic, mechanical, photocopying, recording or otherwise without the prior consent of the publisher.

Contents

Dedication

Wyvern of Wessex is for my grandson, Kieran, a great history lover who will be heading off to university in September (2018) to study Military History.

About Book Three

Wyvern of Wessex was intended to be the third and last book in my *Sons of Kings Trilogy*. Unfortunately – or perhaps fortunately – the story has since expanded and I am now writing the fourth and final book in what has become the *Sons of Kings Series*. I felt that Alfred's story needed finishing off and that Eadwulf, Bjorn and the rest of their 'associates' still had so much more to do and say…

Wyvern of Wessex starts where Book 2: *Pit of Vipers* ended, and we join Eadwulf, Bjorn and their friends in a quest to discover whether Eadwulf's father, Beorhtwulf, is still alive. Their adventures in the first part of the book take them to a kingdom known as al-Andalus, now the modern-day Andalusia, in southern Spain.

While Eadwulf and his friends are engrossed in their search, the newly crowned King Alfred begins his reign in Wessex. It is a perilous time for the kingdom and Alfred's many battles to stop the Danes from conquering it form a major part of the book. Many years after Alfred's death, his efforts would earn him the title of 'The Great'.

In this book, we share Alfred's victories and his defeats, his highs and his lowest of lows… How he rises from the depths of despair has since given rise to many well-known stories, including his burning of the cakes.

A white wyvern on a red background was the flag/banner of Wessex, carried into and proudly displayed during battle. It inspired courage, determination and strength in the warriors. In this book, the title, *Wyvern of Wessex,* refers not only to the banner, but to Alfred himself: the man who refused to give in when all seemed lost. Such determination earned him the respect, trust and love of his people. Like Robert the Bruce of Scotland four centuries later, King Alfred has also been an inspiration to numerous storytellers and novelists over the years. And rightly so.

Although each of the three books so far can be read as single units, or 'one-offs', it is true to say that the story is ongoing throughout, and the books would ideally be read in sequence to gain full appreciation of the characters and events, and how they develop over the years.

Characters

In Wessex:

King Alfred: fifth son of King Aethelwulf (deceased)

Ealhswith: Alfred's wife

Aethelflaed, Edward, Aethelgifu, Aelfthryth and Aethelweard: Alfred and Ealhswith's children

Agnes: nurse to Alfred and Ealhswith's children

Ethelred: Archbishop of Canterbury

Hunlaf: royal reeve at Wilton

Erwig: royal reeve at Wedmore

Garth: Aethelred's friend at Athelney

Wessex ealdormen in the story:

Radulf of Hampshire

Aethelnoth of Somerset

Brihtnoth of Wiltshire, succeeded by Wulfhere on his death

Odda of Devon

Paega of Berkshire

Unwine of Sussex

Anlaf of Kent

In Mercia:

Eadwulf (Ulf to the Danes): Mercian ealdorman at Elston (near Nottingham) and son of Beorhtwulf, former king of Mercia

Aethelred and Leofwynn: Eadwulf's children with his (now deceased) wife Leoflaed.

Aethelnoth, Eadwulf's long-term friend

Odella: Aethelnoth's wife.

Burgred: King of Mercia

Aethelswith: Burgred's wife and Alfred's sister

Mildrede: Burgred and Aethelswith's daughter (and only child)

* * *

The Danes:

Bjorn: eldest son of the deceased Ragnar Lothbrock. Once Eadwulf's master, now his firm friend

Freydis: Bjorn's sister

Hastein: husband of Freydis and cousin of Bjorn

Leif: Bjorn's trusted old steersman

Dainn and Aguti: Hasten and Freydis' sons

Halfdan: one of Ragnar Lothbrok's sons, Bjorn and Freydis' brother and bitter enemy to Eadwulf / Ulf. One of the principal invaders of the Anglo Saxon kingdoms in 865

Ubbi: another of Ragnar's sons

Guthrum / later Aethelstan: Norse invader and Alfred's nemesis

Thorgils: Guthrum's right-hand man

In Cordoba:

Jamil: chief advisor to Emir Muhammad

Ameena: Jamil's daughter with his (now deceased) wife, Karima

Hamid: bastard son of the emir

Muhammad: Emir of al-Andalus and Hamid's father

Britain in the 800s

Wessex Shires 880s

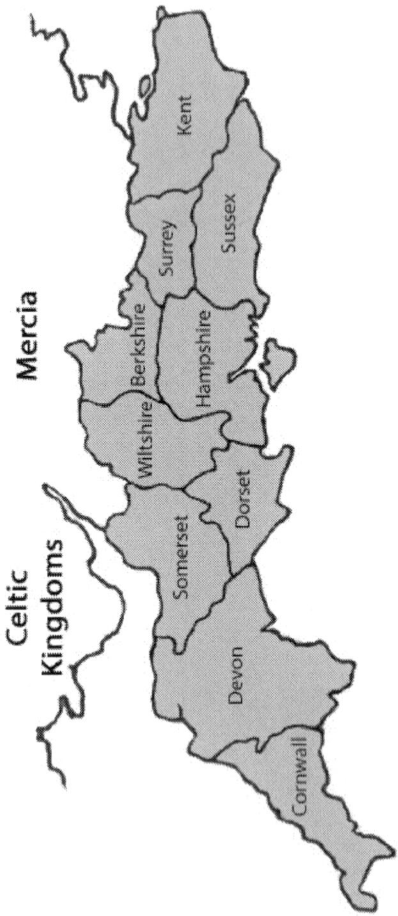

One

Cordoba: Early June, 871

Sweat trickled between his shoulder blades as he heaved yet another lump of stone onto the cart. His dust-clogged hair, tied at the nape with a length of twine, clung to his skin like a soggy clump of moss. He swept his sleeve across his brow, squinting into the blazing sun, considering how this crescent-shaped quarry with its shimmering white rock seemed to magnify the heat.

Around him men were flagging, earning them a lash or two from their masters. He'd had more than a few lashings himself for time-wasting in this God-forsaken place. But there'd be no respite until they'd sent enough stone to keep the masons in the city busy for another few weeks.

He leaned against the cart, running his tongue over parched lips and longing for a mouthful of cooling water.

The stinging lash caught him across the shoulders, cutting through his tattered tunic and reopening a livid wound from a recent flogging. But what did he care about the sting of a whip, or his scarred back? He had nothing left to live for and longed for death to claim him…

Ameena knelt before his chair and reached up to touch his cheek. 'You've been dreaming again, Father. But it's over now and, as you see, you are home with me.'

The ageing man smiled at his flame-headed daughter. For her fifteen years she had a wise head on her shoulders. 'Pay no heed to me. The dreams are no more than I deserve for nodding off instead of attending to my papers. Your mother would often chide me for it. Besides, you are right when you say they pass.'

Ameena rose and poured him a mug of goat's milk. 'Hamid should be home by now,' she said, placing the mug in her father's hand. 'He's been out a long time today. Work must be going well.'

'Your brother's aiming to become a master of his trade, which does him credit. There's little about carving stone he doesn't understand.'

Ameena nodded. 'Hamid's a fast learner, that's true, but without a good teacher even he could not have gained such skills. I'm told the Byzantine's a real master and is teaching all our craftsmen a thing or two about carving stone. And from what I hear amongst the women at the Alcazar, the emir is not only pleased with Theophilus but impressed with Hamid's progress, too.'

'Your mother would have been so proud, had she lived to see him grown. As for the emir, he owes it to Hamid to see he makes a name for himself. I just hope his eminence remembers to pay him in silver dirham and not just effusive praise.

* * *

Bjorn whooped as the newly risen northerly smacked into the *Sea Eagle's* sail. The sleek dragonship pitched forward over the shimmering brine, gliding effortlessly ahead of the dozen longships and two knarrs in his small fleet. Tall and proud at the ship's prow, he scanned the open seas ahead, his arms reaching up to the blindingly blue sky. As he turned, Eadwulf grinned at the look of pure exhilaration on his face. Bjorn would never lose his passion for life aboard his beloved ship.

It was almost twelve years since Eadwulf had sailed in a longship and he could barely contain his own joy. Oars redundant now the wind was in their favour, he twisted round to face the prow and enjoy the antics of the *Eagle's* master as he shared some jest with Hastein. Eadwulf had almost forgotten how much he'd missed the banter between the two cousins.

He inhaled deeply, filling his lungs with the briny air, as though its very presence would leave no room for the feeling of dread that had settled like a boulder deep inside. How could they possibly expect to find Beorhtwulf alive after twenty years? He would be almost sixty by now; an old man who would have endured the hard life of a slave to the Moors. The more Eadwulf thought about it the more he convinced himself that his father would have long since died.

In front of him now that he'd turned, Jorund was gazing absently at the Frankish coast, his once fair skin a radiant pink after several days at sea. He grinned as he realised Eadwulf was watching him and tugged at the neck of his tunic. 'I'd never have thought the sun could be this hot. How much longer before we reach the river?'

'Bjorn reckons another day to reach the northern coast of Iberia, where we'll pull ashore for the night. After that it could take another three days to reach the mouth of the Guadalquivir.'

Jorund nodded and Eadwulf ruffled his brother's fair hair,

a picture of their mother suddenly filling his mind. Jorund's colouring and almond-shaped blue eyes were so like Morwenna's. He wondered whether Beorhtwulf would see that, too – if he was still alive.

A warm westerly favoured their sails as the longships pulled away from the Iberian coast the following day. For two days, oarsmen savoured the respite from rowing; taking turns at catching up on much-needed sleep. But with the calm, windless nights came the need to pick up the oars, since Bjorn was reluctant to make camp too often and waste vital travelling time.

The lightening dawn of the third day brought with it a low mist. It hovered over the still water as though daring the wakening breeze to hurry it on its way, the only sound the regular dipping of the oars. But slowly, the mist bowed obeisance to the rising sun and began to dissipate.

It was then that Eadwulf saw them, rearing out of the mist no more than a hundred yards landward: a small fleet of sturdy ships, each looming tall in the water and already turning to give chase to the Norsemen.

Hastein had spotted them, too. 'Moors landward!' he yelled, causing a scurry as men heaved their shields from the *Eagle's* strakes and gathered their weapons. The Moors were closing in on them fast and Eadwulf knew they had no other option than to stand their ground and fight. He counted nine ships and thanked the gods that at least the number of vessels was in their favour. But the ships were bigger than their own, with taller hulls, and how many men were carried on each was difficult to tell.

Fire arrows flew and one or two struck home. Hit in the sail, one longship was soon engulfed in flames and men dived into the sea to swim for their lives to their closest comrades' vessel.

The attacking ships were moving so fast Eadwulf feared they'd be rammed, but Bjorn's men were well trained for sea battles and had no intention of becoming sitting ducks. The longships swung deftly to meet them broadside.

Moors leapt onto the decks of the Danish ships with practised ease, their clash of combat ringing out as battleaxe and sword met deadly scimitar, or found their way through to bare flesh. Anguished cries were drowned out by the yells and shrieks fuelled by bloodlust.

Bjorn's men fought for their lives, their gods and their ships, and it soon became clear that most of the fallen were Moors. Though fierce and skilled with their scimitars, on unfamiliar decks and outnumbered, their attack was soon quelled. An ululating voice rang out in Arabic and as one, the remnants of the Moorish attackers aboard Bjorn's fleet stood still, their scimitars pointing skyward.

The *Eagle's* crew watched, weapons poised, as Bjorn moved towards the ululating Moor, his sword aimed at the man's throat. Eadwulf took in the dark skin and brightly coloured dress of these seagoing Moors compared to the plain-coloured flowing robes and headdresses of those he'd seen on land. The baggy breeches and turban-like hats gave them a roguish rather than a sinister look.

'We've had better welcomes to countries we've visited,' Bjorn growled, eyeing the sour-faced Arab. 'We're here to trade, nothing more. Are foreign traders so unwelcome in your lands? Many Moors come to trade in ours.'

The Moor let his scimitar fall to the deck and pushed the tip of Bjorn's sword away from his throat. 'Traders we welcome,' he declared, 'but not pirates and raiders. Your people take what is not theirs. We make them think again.'

'I can only repeat that we're here to trade. What we take from your country will be rightly ours.'

Eadwulf almost smiled at Bjorn's words. Taking Beorhtwulf from Cordoba could hardly be called stealing.

The Arab bowed stiffly and gestured to his men, who stood still with scimitars raised. 'Weapons down,' he ordered, and scimitars clattered to the deck. 'Failure shames us, so now our lives are yours. Kill us now.'

Eadwulf watched intently, knowing that Bjorn would be thrown by such a request.

'The thing is,' Bjorn started, scratching his head, 'we usually do our killing in battle or when our lives are threatened. And this little skirmish can hardly be called a battle. Besides, you've lost a lot of your men today, so I'd say there's been enough killing.'

The Moor gaped at the *Eagle's* master as though he were talking in riddles, but eventually gave another stiff bow. 'Then we are free to return to our ships…?' he said, his voice matching the expression on his face.

Bjorn nodded slowly. 'But before you reboard, you will swear to me on your god that you will return to the coast and leave us to continue our journey.' He gestured to the bodies strewn on the deck. 'And take your dead with you.'

'You are lenient. I would not be. And I swear by Allah we will let you sail on.'

'I haven't finished yet,' Bjorn snapped, glowering at the arrogant Arab. 'I said *you and your men* could go, both the living and the dead, but you will leave your scimitars with us. Just a precaution, you understand, in case you decide to attack a second time.'

The Moor's mouth opened to voice objection then snapped shut as he seemed to think better of it. Bjorn grinned. 'As I said, we only take what is rightly ours. Those defeated in conflict forfeit ownership of their goods. Be grateful you have your lives and be gone from our ships.'

* * *

Sailing was good over the next two days, the light breeze remaining steady, and by the time the sun hovered over the western horizon they had reached the mouth of the Guadalquivir. The *Sea Eagle* veered towards the wide delta as the rest of the fleet sailed on south.

'This is it,' Bjorn yelled to the *Eagle's* crew as he headed toward the helm. 'From now on, it's just us.' He stopped beside Eadwulf and Jorund and squatted down next to them. 'A couple of weeks should be enough to find out what we want to know in Cordoba, then we head for home, hopefully with an extra passenger aboard. I've given the rest of our fleet up to three or four weeks, if they need it, to trade at ports around the Middle Sea. If all goes well, the *Eagle* should be back in our homelands by then – after we've taken you and Jorund back to Elston.

'But now we head inland as far as we can before sunset,

when we'll pull ashore for the night. Two days after that should see us at our destination. If we push out at first light tomorrow we could reach Seville by midday and spend the rest of the day around the city. I've heard there's a sizeable market there and we've heaps of goods to barter before we dip into our silver to pay for food. We'll stay overnight, then sail on upriver to Cordoba.'

He gave a mock grimace. 'I hate to say this, but we'll taste no ale till we're away from this kingdom – which, I'm told, the Moors call al-Andalus. Their religion bans all ale and wine, so we take no chances. We're here to find Beorhtwulf, and do some trading when we can.' His eyes moved between Eadwulf and Jorund as he heaved himself to his feet. 'What happens when... if... we do find your father, we'll just have to play by ear.'

* * *

Eadwulf had never seen anything like the Moorish city of Seville. The great, stone buildings with their elaborate architecture were awe-inspiring. It was truly a beautiful and colourful place, with the hot sun glinting off the wide river that flowed through the middle of it. Beyond the city the fertile coastlands stretched out, the low hillsides covered with rows of the same type of trees they'd noticed as they'd sailed from their night's resting place some forty miles downstream.

The bustling market place teemed with people in flowing robes, many of the women concealed behind head veils and loosely fitting gowns down to ankle and wrist. Eadwulf gawked at the sites of this exotic place. But Bjorn and Hastein were intent on trade and took little time in exchanging some of their decorative Rhineland pottery for food.

'What's in the jars?' Eadwulf asked a swarthy-skinned stallholder in Moorish dress whose stall displayed jugs and jars of various sizes, each containing some kind of liquid. Baskets of small, green, oval-shaped fruit also decorated his stall. Jorund moved to take a closer look and Eadwulf followed.

Smiling widely, the vendor picked up a jar. 'This is olive oil from our finest orchards, my friend.' His hand swept out to indicate the hillsides beyond the town before gesturing at the baskets of the little green fruits before him.

'Olive oil we use, and can buy on our own markets,' Eadwulf said, picking up one of the fruits and rolling it between his fingers. 'I take it these odd-looking things are the source of the oil?'

The stallholder scowled at the insult to his wares. 'Odd as they might look, the olive has been a much prized fruit in al-Andalus since before the Romans came. The Phoenicians brought the first olive trees to our shores, but the Romans planted them extensively. Well,' he said, evidently deciding against regaling them further with history, 'the oil is pressed out of the olives and, I might add, our olive oil is the finest you will find anywhere.'

Eadwulf winked at Jorund. 'Then we'll take a small jar to sample.' He pulled open the cord to his small pouch and gave the vendor a silver coin, which he knew was far more than would have been asked for the jar. 'For your patience and gracious explanation,' he said, picking up the jar and heading off to the sound of the stallholder's profuse appreciation.

They made camp for the night on a stretch of open land outside the city but within easy reach of their ships, ready to sail at first light. By the following day's dawn they were back on the river and by late-afternoon they had covered the almost ninety-mile journey to berth at the most important city in al-Andalus.

Two

Cordoba's main dockside was downriver of an unusually shaped bridge, which Eadwulf guessed to be Roman, and beyond which navigation of the Guadalquivir looked to be impossible. The quayside backed onto a large market area which stood outside the remnants of the old city walls, the design of which was so similar to the city walls at York that Eadwulf decided they also must be Roman. Daunted by the enormity of the place, his hope of finding his father plummeted still further. It all began to seem like a fool's errand, though he could not allow Jorund to know how he felt, or Bjorn, who had organised this whole venture just for him.

He suddenly felt very humbled that Bjorn still prized the friendship that had started so long ago.

Eadwulf had thought it best that he and Jorund take a look at the city alone to start with while Bjorn and his men stayed in the outer market, trading and browsing for the rest of the day. A mass entry of thirty men into the city could arouse suspicion, which was the last thing they wanted to do.

The architecture inside the city dazzled Eadwulf. Many buildings displayed ornate carvings and statues, and fountains stood in open plazas. The sight of the Great Mosque left them in awe, as did the huge Alcazar, the palace of the emir, the ruler and most powerful man in the country. The narrow streets were crowded with people about their business, most dealing at the many establishments selling wares of every description, from exotic cloths and jewellery to finely decorated pottery and glassware. There were also stalls offering a variety of freshly cooked foods.

'I wouldn't have thought they'd need an outer market with all these trading places in here,' Jorund remarked. 'But whatever's being cooked over there smells too good to be true. I don't suppose we could eat now, could we?'

Eadwulf grinned at his brother, who was almost salivating at the sight of a stall offering an array of steaming foods. 'The outer market is probably intended to satisfy most foreign traders and keep them from pouring through the city gates. But there'll always be some who want to take a look inside those walls. And right now,' he added, 'eating sounds like a good plan while we decide what to do next.'

Eadwulf's stomach gurgled at the tantalising aromas as they sat at one of the tables provided for customers. It had been many hours since daybreak when they'd broken their fast.

'If Beorhtwulf's here, he'll most likely be working,' he said, glancing round once they'd eaten their fill. He thought of umpteen places where they could begin their search and swallowed the last dregs of goat's milk from his cup. 'But we've got to face the possibility that he's been dead for years. He was brought here as a slave, after all.' He stared down at the chicken bones on the pottery bowl before him, hoping his words would be proven wrong. But the last thing he wanted was to build up Jorund's hopes, only to have them shatter like eggshells later on.

Jorund glared back at him. 'Do you think I don't know all that? But to see the father I've never known would mean a lot to me, although he doesn't even know I exist. If his hair's the same colour as yours, he shouldn't be too hard to pick out.'

'If he's not already bald as a coot, his hair will likely be very grey.'

Eadwulf heard himself saying the words, but his mind clung to the image of his father in his prime: tall and broad, with a mass of thick red hair and alert green eyes. He swallowed hard, trying to control the surging anger as old memories resurfaced. Someday he'd find his treacherous uncle. And when he did, by all the gods, he'd make the man suffer for the way he betrayed his family. He couldn't help a grim smile as he imagined Burgred's face when he eventually realised his executioner was Eadwulf.

'The only thing we can do for now, Jorund, is look around, perhaps ask a few questions –but nothing too obvious. We need to find out if anyone knows of a slave brought here twenty years ago.' He rubbed his head, realising just how stupid that sounded. 'To be honest, I've no idea what we should ask. If we mention red hair, mine is likely to get people jumping to conclusions. Whichever way we put it, people are going to wonder just why we want to know, and I don't want word of our questioning getting back to anyone in command here.'

Jorund nodded. 'Just what I was thinking. We've little time left today, anyway, and if we aren't back by dusk, Bjorn'll be out looking for us. Perhaps we should just poke our noses into a few more corners and head back to camp.'

Eadwulf could only agree. It was too late in the day to begin questioning people. Early morning would be a good time to start that, when there was a likelihood of slaves being out and about. In his experience, slaves were often sent out to buy fresh foods at that time. And if anyone here remembered, or knew anything at all about a particular slave, it would more than likely be another slave.

They wandered around the narrow, paved streets, taking in the layout of the expansive city. Eadwulf was amazed at how clean the streets were compared to northern towns like Hedeby, Ribe and York, where fly-infested muck and waste caused a nauseating stench. This city was well loved and well cared for.

It also became clear that Cordoba was a rapidly growing place. New buildings were going up in every available space, most of a bright, golden stone. Workmen's sweating bodies glistened in the afternoon heat. Many of these newer buildings were large villas surrounded by high stone walls over which colourful plants peeped. Homes of the wealthy, Eadwulf decided. Sounds of running water caught their attention, and when a tall wooden gate swung back to allow admittance to a young man and woman in Moorish dress, they stopped to take a look inside.

Inquisitive as ever, Jorund stepped closer to the gateway, determined to get a better view. The young man suddenly yelled and launched himself at him, his dagger thrusting out menacingly. Jorund darted sideways, narrowly escaping a gash to his upper arm, just as Eadwulf stepped up to land a blow on the man's jaw, sending him reeling and his dagger clattering to the ground. Jorund deftly scooped it up and pressed it to the young man's throat.

The young woman screeched and hurled herself at Eadwulf, long arms and sandaled feet flailing, managing to deliver a sharp blow to his shin before he caught hold of her, twisting her arm behind her back to keep her still. She was a wildcat indeed, and continued to kick backwards and screech until Eadwulf was forced to yank her arm more sharply to make her cease.

'Do you promise to keep your arms and legs still if I release you?' he said, over the top of her veiled head. 'We mean you no harm, and apologise for peering into your private domain. We are strangers to your city, and were just intrigued to see such beauty behind these high walls. Sorry for the blow to the jaw,' he added, his attention fixing on the young man, a grin spreading across his face. 'But I really don't want to lose my brother just yet.'

Eadwulf could feel the woman's shoulders relaxing, and eventually she nodded. 'Lower the knife, Jorund,' he said, gently releasing her arm and easing her forwards as Jorund backed away from the young man.

She spun round to face him, rubbing her assaulted right arm, and Eadwulf realised she was little more than a girl. Her eyes flashed at the insult and humiliation she had suffered, but as she glared at him, her smooth brow crinkled with what appeared to Eadwulf to be puzzlement.

'It seems we have misjudged you,' the young man said, breaking the silence. 'We mistook you for would-be thieves and, I admit, I acted on impulse. Thieves have gained entrance to some of our neighbours' homes by simply waiting for gates to be opened.'

'Then we'll remember not to get close to opening gates in future,' Jorund assured him, warily handing back the dagger and joining Eadwulf, ready to move on.

'Your hair is so brightly red,' the young woman suddenly remarked, taking Eadwulf by surprise. 'The only people I've seen with red hair before have been slaves.' She gestured at the young man. 'Most people who were born here have hair black as night, like my brother, Hamid.'

'It would seem so,' Eadwulf agreed, wary as to why she should make this observation. 'But where we come from, red hair is not so unusual, and I can assure you, we are not slaves. We've come here to trade.'

'You are right, red hair is not so rare in people from the northern lands,' Hamid said. 'Nor is fair hair, like your brother's. We have many slaves here in Cordoba, but few are permitted to walk around, taking in the sights.'

Eadwulf's eyes briefly met Jorund's but he nodded at the young man's words. 'I've seen slaves in most lands, my friend, but they're generally sold into different households. Most are trusted outside of the house – at least, after a while. Is that not the same here?'

The young man's face became thoughtful. 'Some captives are bought at the slave markets by our people, of course, and some of those are free to walk in our streets as they pursue errands for their masters. But many foreigners are captured or bought elsewhere and brought to al-Andalus to be of use in the service of Emir Muhammad. Most of them are put to work in the mines or quarries a little to the north,' he explained, pointing to the line of mountains to the north of Cordoba. 'Others stay here to work as builders. At night, they are locked in the building next to the Alcazar and allowed no freedom to explore the city.

'Al-Andalus is a growing country,' he went on, 'and Cordoba is her most populous and important city. You may have already noticed that much building work is being done?' Both Eadwulf and Jorund nodded. 'We need new homes for the many people moving here, and for mosques and other public places like baths. Our magnificent Great Mosque is our pride, although by no means is it finished. The emir has recently ordered still more extensions, so building work will continue for some time.'

'Where have you come from?' Ameena asked, again taking them by surprise. 'I mean, where is your home?'

Eadwulf looked at her earnest face and suddenly caught the flash of green eyes. He wondered what colour her hair was, hidden beneath that veil. 'The Saxon lands, far to the north,' he replied, imagining she would have no idea where that was.

'Which of the kingdoms would that be?'

'We're from Mercia,' Eadwulf replied, impressed by her knowledge. 'We're looking for goods to take home to our people – perhaps some fine cloths and leather, as well as household goods like glassware and pottery. I'm sure we'll find most things in the market beyond the walls.' He suddenly stopped, realising this pair might just wonder why he and Jorund were inside the city whilst their comrades were trading outside. 'But now we should be heading back to camp. Tomorrow our shipmates will want to see the city for themselves, especially once we tell them of the many goods on offer here.'

'Good fortune with your trading,' Hamid said, as Eadwulf and Jorund moved away. 'Perhaps we'll see you around our city another day.'

'You might just do that,' Jorund called back cheerily. 'Although I hope not,' he added under his breath.

* * *

Ameena could hardly wait to speak with her father. That men from Mercia were trading in Cordoba would surely be of interest to him and, hopefully, lift his spirits. Since her mother's death three years ago, he'd shown little interest in anything and she often found him asleep, locked in some unpleasant dream.

Hamid went off to bathe and change his sweaty clothes, and Ameena discarded her head veil before making her way to the spacious garden at the heart of the opulent villa. Advancing age had brought the bulk of her father's work at the Alcazar to a close and he spent much of his time in his beloved garden, often sitting on one of the wooden seats in the shade of the leafy trees and shrubs he'd had planted for the purpose. Her father always became tetchy during Cordoba's hottest months, but he loved to watch the fountain shooting its cooling spray high into the air before it fell, tinkling like raindrops on the water of the pond beneath. He said it reminded him of the rain that so often fell in his homeland.

Ameena could only wonder about a land where it rained so much and the sun constantly hid behind dark clouds.

She found him sitting on a high-backed bench along one of the winding garden paths, gazing at the ornately carved fountain, seemingly lost in thought. But he must have sensed her approach because he turned, a smile brightening his lined face as she came to sit beside him.

'I was remembering the days when your brother was learning his craft with a stone worker's knife,' he said. Ameena nodded and leant across to kiss his cheek. This was one of her father's favourite memories. 'You were such a little thing then, eight years old and wanting to do whatever Hamid did. This fountain was the first thing he ever created on his own – and he barely a lad of twelve. But your mother adamantly refused to let you handle a knife, or any other sharp sculpting tool. So you skulked about for an hour or two before deciding to simply sit and pester Hamid.'

Ameena willingly joined in her father's memory, watching him as he surveyed every finely chiselled crevice on the fountain's surface, every swirl of the flowers and creatures that adorned it.

'Sometimes it is hard to believe such beautiful sculptures were once just lumps of rock. And that fish sitting at the base of the pedestal is, of course, simply magnificent,' he said, grinning at her again. Karima never did guess that such a handsome creature was your creation. How I kept that secret from your astute mother, I'll never know. I watched Hamid giving you the lump of stone, probably to keep you quiet while he worked. Neither of you knew I was there. I found it amusing, and I admired the way Hamid only gave you hammer and chisel. He would never have risked an accident with a sharp knife.'

That time was still vivid in Ameena's memory and she nodded. She had always been close to her brother and would miss him once he needed to spend more time at the emir's palace. 'Hamid is just bathing, Father,' she said, changing the subject. 'We had a little tussle at the gate today. We mistook two men for thieves, trying to get in and…' She trailed off, not wanting to relate the humiliating details. 'Well, they weren't thieves, Father, but I do have something interesting to tell you.'

Ameena twisted to face him and took his hand. 'You have been in al-Andalus for many years now, and in all that time I know you have seen no one from your own homeland.'

'So what are you saying… that there are Mercians here now?'

'Yes, Father. The two men at our gate came from Mercia, and they said they were with others, too. They'll all be coming into the city tomorrow to look around for goods.'

The old man gave her an amused smile. 'Cordoba's a big place, Ameena. Besides, I'd probably not recognise any of these men if I saw them, even though they're unlikely to be in Moorish dress. We get so many foreign traders wandering the streets.'

'I suppose you're right,' she agreed, 'but one of them would stand out in any crowd. He's as tall and broad as you are, and shares the same colouring as you and I – at least, the same as yours was before it became streaked with grey.'

She paused as he chuckled at that, and considered how to phrase the next part. 'There's something about him that gave me a start. When he looked at me with that amused expression, he reminded me of, well, of someone I know.'

'And do I not get to share this part of the information?'

'There, that's it! The way your lips twitch at the edges when you're amused. His did exactly the same.'

'Ameena, many people's lips do that when they find something funny.'

'Hmmm,' she agreed with a nod, 'but there's something intriguing about this particular twitch.'

* * *

Eadwulf and Jorund headed for the western gate in the Roman wall, beyond which the outer market and their camp were located. The sun had already dipped behind the buildings and dusk would soon fall. The streets were gradually emptying as traders packed away goods on their stalls and Eadwulf absently wondered whether the night-time city would remain quiet in a country where ale and wine were not permitted. Or, could it be that the Moors found other sources of entertainment?

The Alcazar loomed ahead of them as they walked. A number of armed guards patrolled the outer palace walls while others clustered at the entrances, and Eadwulf considered how it would be impossible to enter unseen. He couldn't help wondering if Beorhtwulf had been put to work in constructing parts of this impressive building. There were signs that it had been rebuilt and extended at some stage in recent years. The bases of many of the walls were far older than their upper halves, again reminding Eadwulf of York, and the way the Angles had built their homes over the ruins of old Roman remains.

Four men suddenly hurtled into them, seeming in a desperate hurry to be somewhere else. Jorund was sent flying and instinctively his fists flew in the direction of the nearest man, connecting with his chin and rendering him sprawled on the ground. Eadwulf groaned as the other three turned and closed in on Jorund. Having no other option, Eadwulf leapt to his aid.

Three against two was an easy fight for Eadwulf and Jorund and it took little time for all four men to be overcome. By this time a small crowd had gathered, most cheering as they witnessed the outcome. It seemed the four men were not too popular. Eadwulf saluted in mock thanks of their appreciation and grabbed Jorund's arm, intent on making a hasty retreat from the city.

But too late…

Palace guards shoved their way through the crowds, dispersing them without a word. Half a dozen swords pointed at Eadwulf and Jorund. A scowling guard in a flowing black cloak stepped forward, gesturing with his sword for Eadwulf and Jorund to move towards the nearest doorway into the gardens of the magnificent Alcazar.

* * *

The night in the dungeon was both uncomfortable and worrying, the stench of the fetid straw making it impossible to sleep even if they had been able to. Eadwulf fretted throughout the long hours, not only about how this predicament would play out but of the anxiety they would cause Bjorn, Hastein and Leif. The echoing silence so deep underground was unnerving, adding to Eadwulf's feelings of great unease. This was the worst thing that could have happened on their supposedly discreet look around the great city. All he could do was hope that Bjorn and his men didn't make such a commotion looking for them, they'd get themselves arrested, too.

Torches flared on the walls of the long, narrow passageway

visible through the grille on the heavy door of their cell, but they had no way of knowing whether it was night or day in the outside world. A guard appeared at intervals, peering through the grille before disappearing without a word, so it came as a surprise when three armed men arrived and placed mugs of water and a platter of bread on the floor. Eadwulf recognised the man in the black cloak amongst them and it was he who spoke.

'Your turn soon,' he said, his clean-shaven face expressionless. 'I wouldn't dally with your food if I were you. It could be some time before you eat again.'

Jorund shot to his feet. 'Our turn for what? We've done nothing wrong! We were just protecting ourselves, so you should be setting us free.'

Jorund's tone was a mix of petulance and indignation and Eadwulf cringed. His brother would do them no favours by annoying their captors. But surprisingly, one of the two bearded guards grinned, his white teeth gleaming in the flickering light coming through the open door.

'You'll have time to explain yourselves soon enough. Believe it or not, our emir can be quite lenient in these matters. More lenient than I would be, I promise you that.'

'What did he mean, their *emir*?' Jorund asked when they'd gone.

Eadwulf didn't answer immediately; he'd wondered the same thing himself. That the most powerful man in al-Andalus should deal with petty fights and brawls seemed unlikely.

'Maybe he meant we'd be dealt with in the usual way,' he said, at length. 'You know, as in rules laid down by the emir's counsellors for dealing with such matters.' He gave a half-hearted shrug. 'I can't see the emir himself being involved with such things, somehow.'

They finished off their meagre offerings and it wasn't long before the door swung open and they were invited to step out.

Three

Bjorn fretted and cursed alternately as to the possible whereabouts of Eadwulf and Jorund, and after a night largely devoid of sleep he was in no mood for waiting to see whether or not they'd return. Every instinct told him they'd met with trouble during their venture into the city and he struggled to push that thought to the back of his mind. At sunrise he and Hastein gathered a dozen of their men and headed for the western gate, leaving Leif to take charge of the camp and the day's trading.

They had no trouble getting into Cordoba. By the time they reached the gate, the city had already opened for trade. At Bjorn's side as they stood close to the walls of the great Alcazar, Hastein gazed at the maze of streets ahead of them, pulling on his earlobe as he thought.

'We could spend days wandering round this place and still never see them. Any ideas on where we should start?'

Bjorn shrugged. 'Not a clue. And I imagine that's just what our two friends thought once they'd come through that gate.' He glanced behind at the impressive building, noting the presence of patrolling guards. 'This place must belong to someone important, perhaps even the emir. I think we'd best move on before we're suspected of plotting something we could be arrested for. He gestured toward a wide thoroughfare leading further into the city. 'You take half the men and head in that direction and I'll take the rest and try that winding street going the opposite way. Meet up back here at noon.'

Many of the stallholders were still setting up when Bjorn

headed along the unfamiliar Moorish streets with his half-dozen men, and it wasn't long before customers began arriving, most of them locals, aiming for the food stalls. Bjorn found it hard not to stand and stare at the elaborate architecture around them. Beside these buildings their own wood-planked homes seemed like mere hovels. Yet somehow, despite Cordoba's soaring heat as the day got underway, he couldn't help feeling that such buildings had a coldness about them. But, he reasoned, thick, cold stone would keep out this blazing heat far better than any timber structure. He thanked the gods that their home was in a place where the sun was far less fierce – just as he'd done when he and Hastein had ventured to the Middle Sea thirteen years ago.

By mid-morning, the group of Danes were still no wiser as to Eadwulf and Jorund's whereabouts. They'd stopped to ask several people, describing the two men as best they could. Bjorn even gestured to his own red locks when describing Eadwulf, yet no one knew anything helpful. By this time the streets were teeming with shoppers and Bjorn was beginning to feel the hopelessness of this task. They sat down to break their long fast at one of the stalls when he noticed a serving girl in Islamic dress staring at him. A thought crossed his mind and he gestured for her to come over.

'You must have enjoyed my father's chicken yesterday to be back so soon,' she said, managing to speak before he did. 'But I'm afraid it's fish today. Want to try some?'

His men guffawed as Bjorn pulled a face. 'Our master hates fish,' Thorolf said. 'Never touches the stuff. The rest of us will have some, though, with plenty of good fresh bread.'

'Pity', she said, addressing Bjorn. 'I think we have some soup –'

'Soup would be good,' Bjorn cut in, reluctant to discuss the details of his preferences in foods. 'You say you remember me eating here yesterday?'

'I thought I did, but…' She hesitated, frowning, her eyes ranging over Bjorn's face and hair. 'Now that I think on it, it couldn't have been you, after all. You look very like him, but I see you are a little older. Besides, we saw *that* red-haired man and his friend being arrested later on yesterday, and the palace guards wouldn't have let them go so soon.'

Bjorn raised his eyebrows, hoping she'd say more, and she seemed to take the cue.

'My father,' she continued, tilting her head towards a rotund man coming towards their table, 'said they could be taken into slavery for causing such a disturbance. The emir won't have trouble-makers in his city.'

'It must have been my brothers you met yesterday,' Bjorn lied. 'The older one looks a lot like me. They wanted a look around before the rest of us came in to trade today. But they didn't come back to camp, so we're here to search for them.'

The serving girl shook her head. 'And now you know why you haven't found them. They'll be locked away inside one of the emir's dungeons.'

The girl's father was now standing at her side. 'That's right,' he said. 'The emir's chief counsellor sits in court today, which means he hears accusations against anyone arrested before sentencing them to appropriate punishments. If the crime was some kind of theft, the sentence will be to pay the sum back, plus its worth again. Anyone convicted of more serious crimes, such as plotting against the emir and his household, or opposing the Islamic faith, are tortured almost to death before they're eventually beheaded. And that punishment will be dealt to anyone who commits this crime, whether he's a local man or not.'

Bjorn felt his stomach lurch. If Eadwulf and Jorund had been heard asking too many questions, it could well have been seen as plotting against the kingdom, or the emir himself.

'But your brothers weren't arrested for that,' the man said quickly, halting Bjorn's imminent question. 'They just gave some thieving tax collectors a good thrashing. Those rogues had it coming for taking coin from people too poor to feed themselves. The crowds loved it and cheered them on. They'll probably be charged with breaking the peace and taken into slavery, which usually means they'll be sent to the quarries to start with…

'But I'll tell you, your brothers were provoked into fighting when the scoundrels ran right into them. The younger man was almost bowled right over. I'd say he had every right to lash out. And when the rest of them set on him, the redhead came to his aid. Bested them, too. It was just a pity some of the guards from the Alcazar were close by. '

Bjorn patted the man's arm as he rose. 'We thank you for your help, er…?'

'I am Isaac,' the round-faced man said with a curt bow of his head, 'and this is Esther, my daughter, who's been helping me on my stall since her mother died.' He suddenly threw out his hands as in a gesture of helplessness. 'I'm not sure I've helped you much. I know of no way in which you can reach your brothers while they are held in the Alcazar, and when they leave it will be on a wagon surrounded by guards. That's usually a day or two after sentencing.'

Isaac gestured to the mountain range some distance to the north of the city. 'It's a good two days' journey to reach the quarries, and they'll be there for many weeks before they come back to perform other duties in the city, such as building work. But slavery is for life, my friend, unless a man's family or friends can buy him out with much silver.'

Bjorn stared at Isaac as he said all this, trying to decide whether he had some ulterior motive for helping them. 'And why are you a telling us all this?'

'My wife, Rebecca, was a slave in the Alcazar when I met her,' Isaac said with a sad smile, 'taken from her family in payment for their debts. They were Jews, you see, as am I, and Jews have few rights in Cordoba. The emir might claim to tolerate Jews and Christians in his Islamic city, but our taxes are unfairly high and we must abide by strict rules to be permitted to stay.

'But I won't bore you with such details. Enough to say that I met Rebecca shopping at the market for her wealthy mistress, and I knew I wanted her for my wife. For two years I thought my dreams would never come true but the death of my beloved father changed things. Since I was his only son, all he possessed came to me. Once I recovered from my father's loss some weeks later, I used every dinar to buy Rebecca's freedom.

'I tell you all this simply to explain that buying your brothers' freedom could be a possibility, provided you have the coin.'

At that, Isaac gave a quick nod and moved on about his

business, leaving Bjorn feeling at a loss as to his next move. He cursed Eadwulf and Jorund for getting into this plight, but by now, his anxiety for their safety was rapidly turning into dread. Not knowing what they were accused of, he prayed to Thor that it was something minor. But, if Isaac were to be believed, foreigners of any kind in this city faced a harsher system of justice than Islamic citizens.

After meeting with Hastein at noon and relating what he'd learned, they headed back to camp with their men. As they walked, Bjorn mulled over the facts as he knew them. Yet, with no idea what the sentence would be, it was impossible to take anything further. Their friends could well walk back into camp later today, found to be innocent of any crime. But, if they did not, Bjorn knew he'd be prepared to hand over every piece of silver they had in order to secure their freedom.

* * *

The great hall to which Eadwulf and Jorund were escorted was more magnificent than anything Eadwulf could have imagined. Vast in size, it appeared square in design, with its intricately patterned high ceiling painted in vivid colours and edged by coving in spiralling gold relief. Around the outer sections of the room, rows of lofty arches formed a corridor, each decorated in bands of deep reds and golds in the upper half. Eadwulf and Jorund passed through a section of this corridor and were ushered across the superb floor of colourfully patterned tiles to the centre of the room. A group of five men, all prisoners from the positioning of guards around them, already stood waiting, glum-faced. At intervals around the room, more guards in Islamic dress stood to attention, their elaborate, ceremonial spears held upright.

A few yards from the group stood a wide wooden table on which a selection of scrolls and quills had been arranged. Three high-backed chairs behind it were evidently awaiting their occupants. Either side of the table and a few yards away from it, a row of benches had been set.

The nerve-racking silence was broken by the blast of a horn, and three white-robed men emerged through the columns to take their places on the vacant seats. Two were dark-skinned and swarthy. The other was an older man whose heavily creased skin was of a bronzed hue, more likely due to the effects of the sun than birth. A fourth, dark and officious-looking man followed, coming to stand at the table's side, a chest-high, stout wooden staff held upright. Following him, another dozen men in variously coloured Arabic robes and skin tones ranging from ebony to bronze came to take their places on the two benches. All the men wore beards, most of them long and straight.

Eadwulf glanced sidelong at his brother, but whatever Jorund was thinking, he was hiding it well. He just stared ahead, his features impassive. Perhaps, like him, Jorund was considering whether or not holding such a formal ceremony boded well for them receiving a fair hearing. After all, they had been provoked into the fight.

The three seated men were raking in the details of the unfortunate huddle of accused men, and Eadwulf became aware that the older man, who had taken the centre seat at the table, was focusing on him a little too long. Perhaps he'd never seen such bright red hair before. Eadwulf shuffled beneath the constant appraisal until one of the guards prodded him sharply in the ribs and the officious-looking Moor standing beside the table suddenly rapped three times on the tiles with his staff.

'High Counsellor Jaleel,' he intoned, 'we are honoured that you grace our courtroom with your presence. Your counsel is wise and just; your knowledge of the Law extensive. The sentences you pronounce on the accused before us will be accepted and revered. Our esteemed Emir Muhammad has set you in his stead for this task. His trust in you is echoed by our trust in you.'

The older man murmured his thanks and unenthusiastic applause followed. Eadwulf had the feeling that this same announcement was made every time prisoners were tried.

A new voice suddenly rang out from the entrance. 'It seems all is in readiness for the session, High Counsellor.'

Courtroom officials fell from their seats to crouch low on the floor with their noses to the tiles and guards knocked the prisoners into the same position. From his position at the edge of the prisoners, Eadwulf peered up to see a tall man with a long, pale-coloured robe and heavy gold belt gliding across the floor towards the central table. His head was covered by the usual flowing Moorish headdress. He was flanked by two bodyguards.

'Rise,' the lordly man said, and waited until the court was on its feet. 'Sit.'

Whoever this man was, he wasn't a person to waste words, nor did he expect to wait for his orders to be obeyed.

'Most holy Emir, we are humbled by your appearance in

our court,' the high counsellor said, still on his feet. 'Will you stay to hear the cases today?'

'I think not,' the emir replied, twisting a ruby-studded gold bangle around his wrist. 'It seems you have several cases to hear, so I won't keep you. But I need your opinion on a new building when you finish here. I'll expect you then.' And after waving a heavily ringed hand to the court he silently glided out again.

After a moment, the big Moor continued from where he'd left off: 'Counsellor Jaleel, on your command we will call the first prisoner.'

At the curt nod from the high counsellor, the guards hustled the first prisoner forward. Questions were repeatedly hurled at him regarding his name, his whereabouts and activities at the time in question. The accused man responded with plausible replies. But it took little time for those who sat in judgement to expose them all as lies.

It seemed the accused, a man of middling years named Nizar, had stood before them on several occasions, and on each, Counsellor Jaleel had chosen to be lenient. Today, Nizar was charged with being a cunning thief, who had used a combination of flattery and cajoling, together with his strikingly dark good looks, to win his way into the home of an extremely wealthy young widow and steal a number of small but costly ornaments and several pieces of exquisite jewellery from under her nose.

On this occasion the high counsellor was not prepared to be lenient and Nizar's sentence was an indefinite period in the quarries.

The other four were prodded to stand forward. Eadwulf

watched with increasing anxiety, knowing that he and Jorund would be next. These four men were brothers, each admitting to be of the Jewish faith when specifically asked. They stood accused of refusing to sell several skeins of fine cloth from their stall to Yasir, a high ranking member of the Islamic community.

The brothers' case was debated between all who sat in judgement. Most were in favour of revoking the men's rights to trade in Cordoba; a few thought they should also forfeit their homes. Eadwulf was shocked that such a harsh sentence should be given without even hearing the brothers' side of the story. The only question asked concerned their religion.

Then the word 'Jews' hissed around the room and he wondered why that was of such importance to these men. He focused on the four, staring silently at the tiles. None dared to look their judges in the eye.

Eadwulf was on the verge of shouting out at the injustice of this, when the Counsellor's voice boomed across the hall, silencing all in a moment.

'I have personally looked into this case,' he said, causing more than a few intakes of breath. 'It so happens that my daughter has traded on this stall. Yes, a young woman who has our great emir's favour…' He let that thought hang. 'The girl has always found these men to be fair in their dealings. In fact, more often than not, they are inclined to give her an extra length of cloth quite free of charge. And I can truthfully say that this is not because of who she is. These men are also known to my servants, and my daughter's friends, to be fair and generous with everyone.'

Eadwulf and Jorund shared a glance. This was becoming interesting.

'Moreover, my enquiries led me to find something else,' the counsellor added. 'There were witnesses to this so-called altercation over cloth. Two customers, waiting at nearby stalls, have now come forward. The testimonies of both men – completely unknown to each other –agree that at no time did any of these four men refuse to sell cloth to their accuser. Nor did they ridicule the Islamic faith, or Yasir himself. Rather, it was Yasir who shouted and slandered these men and their faith, threatening to see them hurled out of Cordoba without a dinar to their names.

'Both witnesses are of the Islamic faith,' Counsellor Jaleel continued, encompassing all present in his sweeping gaze – a gesture that tugged at something familiar lodged in Eadwulf's memory – 'and are honourable men. Both men have been known to me for many years and I know, without doubt, they would not lie in this. They have written and signed their statements and personally handed them to me. Both now wait outside should they be required to give testimony in person. I leave that to you, fellow counsellors, to decide.'

The dark-skinned Moor at Counsellor Jaleel's right rose to his considerable height, instantly halting the buzz of comments from around the room. In his hand was a piece of parchment. 'In situations such as these, it is our duty as members of the emir's court to abide by the wisdom of the esteemed high counsellor. I have before me the names and sworn statements of the two witnesses.' He gestured to the smaller, gaunt-faced man at the chief counsellor's opposite side. 'Both Usayd and I know these men, and accept their statements as true. We see no need to prolong this case further, and await our counsellor's final decree regarding those accused.'

'My thanks, Rashid,' Counsellor Jaleel replied, rising from his seat. 'I pronounce these four men innocent of the crime laid at their feet. They are free to go about their business... and I, for one, hope it continues to prosper. As for the accuser, he will be called to account for his lies at a later date.'

With that he sat down as the jubilant brothers were led from the court murmuring words of heartfelt thanks.

Jaleel was staring at Eadwulf again and Eadwulf could not help staring back. There was something familiar about those eyes, and the turn of the mouth. The grey-bearded face and wrinkled skin was that of an old man, and Eadwulf imagined that even the hair beneath the headwear would be grey. But he had no time to deliberate further. The stiff official uttered words to the guards and he and Jorund were shoved forward.

The official reeled off the charges: that of brawling in the street and showing disrespect to the Islamic city that had graciously allowed them to visit.

Questions from Rashid determined their names, their homeland, their reason for visiting Cordoba and who accompanied them. Eadwulf could not miss the start from high counsellor when he gave his name, or the confused frown when Jorund gave his and the fact that they were brothers was revealed. Then the questions were opened up to the room, targeting Eadwulf first.

'Do you deny you were caught brawling, and within sight of our esteemed emir's palace?'

'No, lord.'

'Do you deny you used undue force in rendering a man unconscious?'

'Yes, lord. We were only two men against four. If we had not used all our wiles in our defence, we would have likely been killed.'

'Are you a trained warrior?'

'Self-trained mostly, lord.' Eadwulf looked directly at Counsellor Jaleel. 'Except when I was a boy and had arms training with a warrior named Ocea.'

Jaleel's sharp intake of breath was not missed by Eadwulf, though he covered it well by an immediate cough.

'This Ocea taught you to brawl well, it seems,' the same questioner said, lowering himself to his seat, his sarcastic remark requiring no answer.

Then it was Jorund's turn.

'You were seen to strike the first blow, effectively starting this brawl. Is that true?'

Jorund's face darkened. "I did strike the man, lord, but only because he sent me reeling and went on his way without saying he was sorry. He barged right into me! How would you feel if–'

'Silence!' Rashid's voice boomed across the room. 'Answer only what you are asked.

Eadwulf inwardly groaned. If Jorund couldn't play by their rules in this he would ensure they went straight back into that dungeon.

'Are you a trained warrior?' was the next question thrown at Jorund.

'I fight when I have to, lord, but I've had little training at all – just a few lessons from my brother here and our friend, Aethelnoth.'

Again the counsellor's gasp was rapidly followed by a small cough. By now, Eadwulf was convinced this man was Beorhtwulf, though how that could be possible was beyond his wildest imaginings. Across the room they stared at each other, while Jorund struggled to defend himself against charges of instigating the fight. Eventually, the room fell silent and the big Moor stood.

"Honourable Counsellor, we have heard these two foreigners admit to starting a fight in our city. In doing so, they showed great disrespect to Islam. I motion that the usual punishment be administered. But, as always, the final verdict is in your hands and we will abide by your judgement.'

Eadwulf could see that Jaleel looked troubled as he rose to his feet and he feared the worst. As chief counsellor, the old man could hardly be lenient when the usual punishment was expected by all in the court. He prayed to all the gods that it wouldn't be too harsh.

'I have listened to both the questions and answers in this case and confess to having difficulty in laying blame for this brawl entirely on these two.' The counsellor gestured to Eadwulf and Jorund to stress his point before sweeping the room with his commanding gaze. 'Yet it is they who stand before us on trial and, as they are foreigners, policy decrees they pay a heavy price for disturbing the peace of our city. But I motion that at a future date, the tax collectors should also be called to task for their part in the skirmish.'

Heads were nodding agreement and Eadwulf knew what

was coming next.

The old man looked directly at Eadwulf as he drew breath to speak, the shake of his head so slight that Eadwulf wasn't sure whether he'd imagined it. 'I therefore decree that these two brothers from the Mercian kingdom be taken into slavery in the service of our gracious emir, Muhammad. Two days from now they will be taken to the quarries in the Sierra Morenas for an indefinite period of time.'

Jorund's yelp of outrage was drowned by the applause and shouts of approval from the court. Eadwulf's eyes again locked with the old man's and he did not miss the plea for patience in his green eyes or the barely raised palm.

The guards duly surrounded them and escorted them back to the miserable dungeon.

Four

Jorund continued to rant and grumble in equal proportion about their unjust treatment and the fate that had befallen them. It was getting on Eadwulf's nerves, and he was now on the verge of revealing his suspicions about Counsellor Jaleel being their father just to quieten him. The only thing stopping him was the possibility that he was wrong. Such suspicions could simply have been triggered by the similarity of the half-remembered voice, the mannerisms and gestures, and those trust-inspiring green eyes. And if he were wrong, Jorund's disappointment would be harder to bear than his constant whinging. So Eadwulf held his peace.

The day seemed to drag by unrealistically slowly, though they knew it must be well into evening by now. Already they had been given two offerings of bread and some kind of hard cheese that counted as meals. The prospect of another night on the stinking straw was putting them both on edge and they continuously snapped at each other, each blaming the other for all that had gone wrong before eventually sinking into a sullen silence.

Eadwulf's thoughts ran riot, swinging from complete trust in Beorhtwulf having some plan for setting them free, to thoughts that, after all these years, he just didn't care. And always there, writhing between them was the possibility that the esteemed counsellor wasn't Beorhtwulf at all.

As the night moved on, the silence and inactivity lulled them into an uneasy half-sleep and the sound of a commanding voice outside the door made them both start. They were not expecting to be visited, or fed again, until morning. The rattling of a heavy bunch of keys was followed by further forceful words and the swinging open of the door.

Outlined in the glow of torchlight from the passageway behind, the shapes of two men loomed. Eadwulf instantly recognised Counsellor Jaleel, but the other man moved back beyond the cell, shutting the door before Eadwulf got a clear view of him.

Moments of uneasy silence passed as Eadwulf's heart pounded in his chest, not daring to ask the question heavy on his lips. His gaze was locked with the counsellor's, but he sensed Jorund at his side and reached out to touch his arm. It was Jorund who broke the silence.

'There must be something we need to know for such an important man to be visiting prisoners so late at night.' Eadwulf could hear the tremor in his brother's voice. Jorund evidently feared further bad news.

'Jorund, you do not know me, nor I you, but I sense you to be a good man, young as you are. I have no worse news for you, other than the sentence I was forced to lay upon you earlier.

'Eadwulf...' The counsellor's voice cracked and he forced back a sob. 'Can it really be you … my son? Every fibre of my being tells me it is, yet logic denies the possibility of that.'

Eadwulf's emotions threatened to overwhelm him and his voice refused to work. He moved into the old man's outstretched arms and wept, clinging to the still strong body of the father he'd believed to be dead for so many years.'

'My heart leapt the moment I saw you,' Beorhtwulf murmured into Eadwulf's hair. 'No other man could look so like me, but I feared I may have simply been willing you to be him. But I believe you recognised something in me, too, despite the ageing body and unfamiliar apparel. I could tell by the way you watched me. I have been unable to rest all day, waiting for this chance to see you.'

Eadwulf pulled back, suddenly jolted to the reality of the situation. 'Yes, I knew – or perhaps I just hoped – you were Beorhtwulf, from the moment you entered the hall and stared at me. Your green eyes are hard to miss and I recognised the shape of your face and the tone of your voice. I confess, the wrinkles and Moorish garb threw me, but not as much as did the position of influence you hold in these lands.'

'We have much to explain to each other, Eadwulf, but now is not the time for that. It is enough for me to know that you are alive. That you have a brother confuses me, but that must wait for another time. I cannot stay much longer or the guards will become suspicious. They believe I'm here taking details that were forgotten in court. My son...my adopted son,' he added before Eadwulf could question, 'stands guard outside.

'I need to think carefully how we can stop you from reaching the quarries. There's no chance of escaping once you're there, and we'd never get you out of these dungeons – alive, that is. Too many guards. So it has to be done while you are on the way to the Sierra Morenas.' He paused momentarily in thought. 'Tomorrow, I'll think of some reason for sending for you. You will be escorted to my chambers in the palace where we can make plans.'

At the sharp rap on the door, Beorhtwulf turned and said

something in Arabic through the grille before continuing. 'Before I go, tell me the names of some of the people you came to al-Andalus with. They will need to help us in this, and be ready to sail the moment we get back to Cordoba. My son out there will be the one to approach them.'

'The men we sail with are Danes, Father. They are our friends and I owe them more than I could ever repay: my life for one thing. Our camp is outside the city walls and your son must ask for Bjorn or Hastein. They could well be somewhere in the city looking for us, but there'll be someone left in charge - probably Leif.'

'So it's Bjorn, Hastein or Leif,' Beorhtwulf said, repeating the names he needed to remember. His strong hands clamped on Eadwulf's shoulders. 'Until tomorrow, Eadwulf. I have no choice but to leave you in this reeking hole for the next two days, but at least you'll see daylight for a while tomorrow. No one will disturb us with my son and a few of my own men standing guard.' He glanced at Jorund. 'You can explain to me how you came to be brothers then, too...

'You're a sparky young man, Jorund, and perhaps a little too headstrong for your own good. No,' he said quickly, raising a hand, 'I mean no insult by that. I was young once and remember well how it felt. But you were definitely winding up the court members today with your answers.'

He reached for the door and left, leaving Eadwulf to face Jorund's questions, and why he had not told Beorhtwulf that Jorund was also his son.

* * *

The changing of the guards in the passage beyond their cell signalled the start of a new day. The usual meal of bread, hard cheese and water was brought, and Eadwulf and Jorund waited expectantly to be sent for. But time slipped by and Eadwulf guessed it to be well past noon when the sound of voices made him peer through the grille. A group of four men was approaching, joined by two of the dungeon guards, one of them rattling the keys. Once again the door swung open and a young man, whom Eadwulf instantly recognised as Hamid, stepped forward and raised a piece of parchment. He read out something in Arabic and the two guards replied and stepped aside.

No one spoke as they were hustled out and along the same route they'd taken to reach the great hall where the court had convened the previous day. After ascending a couple of flights of stone steps, dazzling sunlight assaulted them. The route now veered and they headed across a courtyard bright with greenery and vivid blooms, through a couple of opulent, high-ceilinged chambers and across yet another courtyard. This one was paved, with a fountain sculpted in the likeness of some large bird at its centre. Huge potted plants stood sentry around the edge. A flight of steps took them up to an outer balcony where they halted beside a heavily carved door. One of the men rapped on it with his sword pommel and they were admitted into a pleasant but not overly opulent room.

Sunlight streamed through windows of brightly coloured glass to splash in vivid pools on the patterned tiles. Half a dozen silken red cushions were positioned beneath the largest window to their left; another six at the opposite side of the room. Since no chairs were visible other than those along either side of a long table in the centre, Eadwulf decided the cushions must serve as somewhere his father and any guests could relax.

Beorhtwulf appeared through an open-arched entrance opposite the outer door. He wore a simple, white, Moorish-style robe but, on this occasion, no headdress covered his greying hair.

Eadwulf could barely contain his emotion as he stared at the father he had thought he'd never see again, despite his feigned optimism on the voyage – which he confessed to himself was for Jorund's benefit more than his own. Yet here was Beorhtwulf, looking fit and well, and holding a position of influence at the emir's court. It was too much to take in, and he decided to let his father tell his story in his own due time.

But one glance at Jorund and he knew his impetuous young brother would find it hard to do the same.

'Welcome to my chambers, from which I conduct interviews of those accused and deal with matters pertaining to Emir Muhammad's Court of Law. On this occasion, our business applies to both.'

Beorhtwulf's words were stiff and formal, his face impassive. 'Leave us,' he added curtly, addressing his four men. He gestured to two of them. 'You two stand guard outside on the off-chance the prisoners should attempt some foolish move. But since Hamid is here and armed, and they are not, I see little point in you remaining. You two,' he went on, his hand specifying the men in question, 'will prepare the documents regarding my next court attendance. Have them ready by sunset.'

The men glanced uncertainly at the two prisoners before saluting their master and leaving.

Beorhtwulf moved to clasp Eadwulf in his arms, eventually stepping back to look him up and down. 'You've grown into a fine man since we last clapped eyes on each other –'

'A time I will never forget as long as I live!' Eadwulf heard himself snap and felt his father's eyes bore into him.

'Nor I, and I want to know what happened to you and your mother once you have both eaten. Some explanation regarding the relationship between you and Jorund here might also be useful.'

Eadwulf could not help a grin. 'Some explanation regarding the relationship between you and Hamid would be useful, too – and the little vixen who was with him the other day. I recall her referring to Hamid as her brother…?'

'I'll prepare the food for carrying through, Father,' Hamid said, heading rapidly for the arched doorway.

'We have so much to say to each other, but little time at present,' Beorhtwulf said, indicating they should seat themselves at the table. 'I suggest we each give each other no more than a quick summary and leave the details for a later date. Right now we need to finalise arrangements for your escape. Suspicions will be roused if I keep you here longer than I normally keep prisoners I call for questioning.'

'Our escape, but not yours...?' Jorund's question had been on the tip of Eadwulf's tongue, too, and he stared at Beorhtwulf, dreading to hear the answer he feared.

'I haven't yet decided whether I will go with you. I know,' he said, looking from Eadwulf's stricken face to Jorund's, 'and if it were just a question of me sailing away with you, I wouldn't hesitate. But there are others to consider, which we'll talk about later.'

'You mean Hamid and the girl?'

'Yes, Jorund, I do. Hamid and Ameena are my responsibility since their mother died.' He rubbed his brow, suddenly looking tired and old, and a wave of sorrow shot through Eadwulf. He'd missed so much of his father's life.

'I ask you not to press me on this until I've discussed the possibilities with them. And before we begin to fill in the gaps of the past twenty years, I need to say something about arrangements for your rescue.

'This morning, Hamid and a couple of his men spoke with your friends at their camp. They had already learned you'd been arrested, but knew they would never get into the Alcazar. Bjorn and Hastein were seriously worried and feared for your lives, as well they might. Many of those arrested never leave the palace alive. And foreigners are rarely treated fairly, much as I try to temper the sentences.'

'So what did Hamid arrange with them... anything?' Jorund's impatience was wearing thin and Beorhtwulf reached over to pat his arm.

'Yes, my young friend. They mulled over the plans that Hamid and I sat up most of last night making. And if this plan works, we may manage to get you away without alerting the palace.'

'Did Bjorn and Hastein agree to your plans?'

'They agreed it was the best anyone had come up with yet,' Hamid responded to Eadwulf's question as he carried a large platter of meats, fruits and flatbreads to the table. A huge watermelon sat in the middle and Hamid proceeded to slice through it with a curved knife he pulled out from beneath his striped robe. 'I'll explain everything to you when I come to you tonight.'

'Now you must eat,' Beorhtwulf insisted, 'while I tell you something about my life here. Then I'll hear a little about yours. Eat as much as you can and take your fill of goat's milk. I've seen the pitiful offerings the prisoners get.'

Beorhtwulf's story began, as Eadwulf knew, with Egil's ploy to earn himself coin by selling the Mercian king to the Moors instead of killing him as Rorik had ordered. 'I arrived in Cordoba a broken man, believing my beloved wife and son to be dead,' Beorhtwulf continued, his eyes meeting Eadwulf's as he bit into a slice of melon and wiped the juice from his lips. 'I prayed for death to take me, and for two years I thought it would do, many times over. I worked in the punishing Iberian heat from dawn till dusk, willing the next harsh flogging to finish me. But somehow, each time I lived to face another gruelling day.'

'Something must have changed, or you'd not be here, living the life you do now,' Jorund remarked, before Eadwulf could voice the same thought.

Beorhtwulf smiled. 'You're right. That something was a visit of Emir Muhammad to inspect his quarries. At that time, he'd been emir for a single year, a young man with visions of making Cordoba the most splendid and prosperous city in al-Andalus. Many new beautiful buildings featured in his long-term plans, and the attractive stone was important to him.

'The point is that he came to the quarries with no shortage of bodyguards. But what happened while he surveyed the rock face seemed to have been missed by them all...

'Perhaps I had become attuned to the grating of stone on stone, but something caused me to glance up. I saw the huge boulder teetering on the edge of the clifftop, right above where the emir stood. Instinctively I hurled myself at him, landing both of us a mere yard or two from where the boulder crashed to the earth.

'Despite the ensuing pandemonium, those responsible for the attempt on Muhammad's life were taken. They turned out to be three of his own bodyguards, angry he hadn't shown enough tolerance to the Mozarabs – the Christians living in the city. Somehow, they'd managed to enlist in the emir's army for the sole purpose of assassinating him.

'Muhammad ordered them crucified upside down outside the walls of the Alcazar as a lesson to any other would-be assassins.

'I was rewarded for my deed by being taken to the emir's palace as his chief bodyguard. My life of slavery was over, and Muhammad came to rely on me for advice on everything from matters of state to the designing of new areas of Cordoba. And two years ago I was given the role of chief counsellor and must officiate at the law court.'

'Where do Hamid and Ameena fit into all this?'

Beorhtwulf nodded. 'I'm about to come to that, Eadwulf, but I ask you not to judge me harshly. At the quarries I had thought my life was over, yet the emir offered me a chance to start anew and put the past behind me. I grieved for a long time for the loss of you and your mother, but eventually accepted you were gone and that my life had to go on.

'I met Karima in the Alcazar during my first year there. She was one of Muhammad's concubines and I met her simply because it became my duty to escort her from the harem and back again later on. Whilst she was with Muhammad, I was tasked with standing guard outside the door, ensuring that no one entered. By this time, Karina had already borne Muhammad a son; a chirpy child of five when I first met him.'

Hamid came to stand at his side and Beorhtwulf smiled up at him. 'Over the months I came to love both Karima and Hamid. As we walked, Karima spoke of her life back in Frisia, before she'd been taken by Norse raiders and sold to the Moors. We were so alike in that.'

Beorhtwulf looked levelly at Eadwulf and added, 'Forgive me for saying this, but she reminded me of Morwenna. She was tall and fair and very lovely. Hamid, with his olive-coloured skin, is the product of her union with the darker-skinned emir.'

'There is nothing to apologise for, Father. I understand.'

'The following year, I discovered that the Muladi – the Muslims in the city who were of Iberian origin – were planning an uprising against the emir. I sent out troops to capture the six leaders as they were in the process of rallying their supporters.' He shook his head, his face reflecting his sadness at the memory. 'They met the same fate as the men who made the attempt on Muhammad's life at the quarries. I take no pride in knowing that I was responsible for that, but I owed the emir my new existence, for which I had pledged to protect his in return.

'Muhammad rewarded me by granting anything I wanted.'

Beorhtwulf smiled at those words. 'He is a very generous man and would have given me silver or jewels, had I asked. But he can also be utterly ruthless to anyone who defies him or threatens his Islamic faith or al-Andalus.

'I didn't crave riches, just the companionship of the people I had come to love. I asked for Karima. After an outburst of outrage and three days of thought, I was granted my request and Karima and I were married, in the style of Islam. Where and how we were married mattered nothing to either of us. The Christian God had deserted us years ago… just as Burgred had said He would.

'I see my brother's name still stirs great anger in you, Eadwulf. I hope whichever god he believes in now forgives his sins.'

Eadwulf held his tongue on that issue. His vow to kill his traitorous uncle once he was back in Mercia was his own affair. 'Then Ameena is your daughter?' he said, instead.

Beorhtwulf nodded. 'And your half-sister.'

'Then she is my half-sister, too,' Jorund blurted, unable to keep his secret any longer.

'*Your* sister...?' Beorhtwulf gaped at Jorund, his face revealing his confusion. 'You need to explain how that can be possible.'

Jorund glanced pleadingly at Eadwulf, and Eadwulf took his cue. 'On the day of the raid on Thrydwulf's hall, my mother and I were both taken captive by the Danes.' He paused at his father's stunned reaction. 'We both survived that day, Father. Mother was taken by the Danish leader, Jarl Rorik as… I can't say this in any other way, Father, other than to say that he wanted her as his concubine. I was taken by a group of Rorik's men, to be sold as a slave at Hedeby. But my story can be continued another time,' he declared, sweeping it away with a flick of the wrist. 'It is Mother's story you need to know now.'

Beorhtwulf was by this time looking very distressed; tears for his beloved wife streamed down his face. But he motioned for Eadwulf to continue.

'I didn't know whether my mother had survived during my years as a thrall at Aros. I'd seen, or thought I'd seen, her being hustled into a wagon as Thrydwulf's hall smouldered behind us. Yet I had no means of looking for her until Bjorn took me as one of his crew. He promised to sail to Rorik's hall one day so I could be certain, one way or the other. And when we eventually did, six years later, it was to find her alive, with two healthy children in tow.

Beorhtwulf said nothing. His head was bowed as he wrestled with his thoughts, but he motioned to Eadwulf to continue.

'The younger of these two children was a pretty little girl, not yet a year old: Morwenna's child by Rorik. But there was a boy of six, with hair and eyes just like Morwenna's, but with a jawline the same set as mine. And yours, Father.'

'And that boy was Jorund,' Beorhtwulf said, his gaze fixing on his newfound son. 'I can see that now I look closely. You have Morwenna's beautiful blue eyes and little nose. And the square jaw is similar to Eadwulf's and mine.' He halted as the meaning of Eadwulf's words hit, his eyes opening wide at the thought.

'Father, Jorund is your son, just as much as I am. Morwenna was with child when Rorik took her. She swore that was true, and I have no reason to disbelieve her.'

'Are you saying Morwenna still lives?'

Eadwulf shook his head. 'Mother died not long after out reunion; some kind of lung disease, we heard.' Eadwulf almost choked on the lie, but to tell the truth would be too unkind a blow to strike. 'Rorik's wives didn't want the children of his concubines in their hall, so Bjorn's sister agreed to take them off their hands and they were brought to Aros. The rest of our tale can be told at another time.'

Beorhtwulf rose and pulled Jorund to his feet. 'I grieve for all the lost years when I could have known you, my son. I'm sure your mother loved you dearly.' He pulled Jorund to him in a firm embrace, and Eadwulf could hear his father's stifled sobs.

The sharp rap at the door made them all start. 'Lord Counsellor, the dungeon guards are approaching to take the prisoners back to their cell.'

Beorhtwulf picked up a pile of parchments, a ploy to impress on the dungeon guards the need for the long interview with the prisoners. 'Hamid has been a good son to me,' he said as they headed for the door, 'and I urge you to accept him as you would your own brother. He will come to you later with the plans we have made for your escape. If we are to succeed, you must do exactly as he says.'

The arrival of the guards put an end to further conversation.

Five

Ameena paced the tiled floor of her family home, willing her father and brother to be back soon. The words of a conversation she'd had earlier with Rani, one of the handmaids to the emir's principal wife, still rang in her head, and she desperately needed to relay them to Beorhtwulf and Hamid before she went mad with worry. But, for the first time in weeks, both were late home tonight.

Rani had always been a nosy young woman who managed to overhear many a conversation that was none of her business. But Ameena was very glad she'd heard this one.

She accepted the cool, fruity drink offered by one of the household servants and forced herself to sit as she mulled over Rani's words...

'When I arrived at my mistress's quarters to ask if she was ready to bathe, she and her sister were discussing the emir's plans to take another concubine into his harem. I darted behind one of the pillars to see if they would mention the name of this new woman. And it was lucky I did. Now, you and I, Ameena, both know that Muhammad often takes new concubines.' Rani shrugged quite nonchalantly to emphasise the ordinariness of that. 'But it seems that Salihah's objection to the girl is due to the fact that she has a half-brother who is one of Muhammad's bastard sons. A highly favoured one at that…

'My mistress became very angry,' Rani added with a giggle. 'I thought she might even have a seizure! She is so jealous that Muhammad favours the bastard over her own precious son.

I'm not surprised at that, mind you, Rajiv is a lazy, good-for-nothing who will never make a wise emir.'

Ameena could only agree with her about that. Unless Rajiv changed his idle ways, the lands of al-Andalus would not prosper under his rule.

'The bastard's sister is very pretty,' Rani rambled on, 'and her mother was once the emir's favourite concubine. But Salihah was not really concerned with that. Yet she repeated many times over that she would not tolerate the girl's brother around the palace for much longer.

'You know that two of Muhammad's bastard sons have already met with unfortunate accidents, don't you, Ameena? Well, if I were that young man, I'd be very worried for my life. You'll have to tell him before it's too late!'

It had taken Ameena a few moments before she realised what Rani had been telling her. She, Ameena, was the intended new concubine – and Hamid's life was in danger! 'Accidents' could be made to happen anywhere. The thought that Muhammad was planning to have her in his harem was of no importance compared to what Salihah was planning for Hamid. The thought of anything happening to her brother struck terror in her heart.

Swallowing down the last of her drink, Ameena resumed her pacing of the tiled floor.

* * *

The morning for the journey to the quarries of the Sierra Morenas arrived. Eadwulf and Jorund had seen no more of

Hamid following his brief visit to their cell two nights ago and they were ready to play their part in the escape plan. Unfortunately, in reality, there was little they could do. It was a question of relying on others to set them free. Hamid had explained things briefly, his visit, ostensibly, to relay the news that following the extended interview, the high counsellor was satisfied the sentence he'd decreed in court was just and fitting for the crime committed. They would leave for the quarries in two days' time.

For most of the first day, the mule-drawn cart trundled on. They sat, cramped between an assortment of boxes that Eadwulf could see contained food for the journey and what appeared to be furs for their night-time camp. Water was passed to them at intervals and they made one short stop to eat the meagre scraps offered and relieve themselves. Their wrists remained bound at the front throughout. The Iberian sun beat down with a vengeance and Eadwulf was thankful for the pieces of old cloth the dungeon guards had given them to drape across their uncovered heads and shoulders.

Distinctive in long striped cloaks and flowing headdresses, six guards rode alongside the cart on sleek Arabian stallions. Two others sat at the front of the cart, sharing control of the reins of the brace of mules.

Eight. Not too great a number to deal with, Eadwulf decided, scrutinising the riders as the miles passed slowly by. The guards were silent and vigilant, continuously scanning the open land for movement that could signal attack. Beneath their voluminous cloaks their great curved scimitars would be concealed. Hamid had told them there were always bandits on the lookout for easy pickings.

Daylight was fading as they pulled to a halt close to an outcrop of rocks and Eadwulf could hear running water somewhere nearby. It was a sheltered place to sleep for the night and replenish the near-empty waterskins, and he had no doubt that the guards would organise a number of watches throughout the night.

A small campfire was lit, but since no food was cooked, the flames were probably to keep the prowling wolves and lynx at bay that Hamid had warned them about. They were each given a slice of cold mutton and more of the same flatbread they'd had earlier. Eadwulf welcomed the food. His stomach had been growling for hours and he knew that if a rescue attempt was made during the night, it would be many hours before they'd eat again.

It would have been impossible to sleep, even had they wanted to. He and Jorund were securely trussed, the ropes binding their wrists now stretched down to secure their ankles. And, on top of everything else, they had no idea of when the rescue attempt was likely to be made. It might not be tonight at all. Hamid had simply said it would be some time before they were within ten miles of the quarries. Yet somehow Eadwulf had the gut feeling it would be in the darkness of night, or perhaps in the dim light of the pre-dawn.

He leaned back against the rocks, alert to every sound. On the outcrop above them, he sensed the movements of two of the guards, and in the light from the campfire he could make out two others guarding either side of the camp. Round the campfire, four of their companions slept beneath their furs.

So, four men were on guard whilst four men slept, and from the length of time he'd sat here, Eadwulf guessed it would soon be time for a change of watch.

Several yards away along the rock face, Jorund was also awake. Eadwulf could hear his constant shuffles on the gravelly scree beneath the rocks and his occasional over-loud sighs. Like himself, his brother would be tuned in to every sound: the cries of the night birds, the scurrying of small creatures and rustling leaves in the undergrowth of the nearby scrubland. The howl of a distant wolf sent shivers down his spine. As pack animals, wolves were rarely alone.

The long dark night seemed to drag on forever. The guards kept the campfire burning, its low flames enough to deter any wild creature with intent to kill. An owl screeched from somewhere close by and from further away came the answering call from a possible mate. Movement around the camp eventually signalled the change of watch. He could make out the shapes of two men heading towards the rocks to relieve the lookouts up there, and the sleeping men were roused to let others take their place.

Suddenly there was pandemonium. Men screamed from on top of the rocks; a body landed close to Eadwulf's feet. The sound of swords being drawn rang out and voices yelled in Arabic. The clash of metal indicated that the swords were being wielded. But many men had come and the outnumbered guards were swiftly overcome. Then two men in Islamic dress were cutting away Eadwulf and Jorund's bindings and Eadwulf recognised them as the two men who had been driving the cart.

'Your handiwork?' he said inclining his head to the corpse

close to his feet. The man nodded. 'First watch or second?'

'We were first watch. We had to be – others may have detected your friends' approach. And I needed to answer the owl call. But now we need to work quickly', the man added, removing the final length of rope from Eadwulf's ankles. 'High Counsellor Jaleel will be waiting for you and we need to bury the bodies in the scrub over there before we leave. We also need to bury the cart once we've finished with it and release the mule to fend for himself. Unfortunately for him, he won't last long out here with the wolves.'

By the campfire, Bjorn and Hastein were loading the bodies of the six guards onto the cart with four of their men.

'Are we glad to see you two!' Bjorn said, coming over to embrace first Eadwulf then Jorund as they approached. 'You had us at our wits' end until young Hamid came to tell us what was going on. But we'll talk about it all later. There are spades on the packhorse over there and we need to bury the bodies deep so no wild animals can dig them up or buzzards give away where they lie.'

Two separate graves were dug, well into the scrubland, three bodies in each. Both were deep and solidly packed, with a layer of large stones a foot or so from the surface where they couldn't be identified as grave markers. But it was enough to stop any animals digging through. More soil was piled on top and branches hacked from the scrubby trees to disguise them. The cart was chopped into pieces and also buried and all signs of a camp and campfire were removed from the rock face. Should anyone from the palace come looking when news got back that the new slaves did not arrive, they wanted no sign of what happened, or where they could be found. Let them think the party had been taken by one of the many bandit groups.

Sunrise sent a ribbon of pink shooting across the eastern horizon as they set off for Cordoba. Soon daylight would brighten the land and Eadwulf thanked the gods that Hamid had not only sent horses for Jorund and himself, but Islamic cloaks and headdresses as a precaution to disguise their arrival back in the city.

'The rest of us will circle round Cordoba to get back to camp,' Bjorn said as they neared the city in the late afternoon, 'but you two will enter the city through the north gate and head for your father's house. I just hope you know how to find it again from that direction. If you don't, you'd best head for the Great Mosque or the Alcazar and find your way as Hamid told us you did before. And before you ask, these are Beorhtwulf's orders, and as for what happens after that, we're as much in the dark as you are.'

Eadwulf couldn't argue, but he had the sinking feeling that his father would tell them he was staying in al-Andalus.

* * *

Beorhtwulf was seated in the garden at the front of his opulent villa when Eadwulf and Jorund rapped on his gate, ready to let them in quickly. Bjorn had taken their horses back to their camp with him in the hope that Hamid would collect them with the rest he'd supplied, leaving them to enter the city on foot. They'd had little trouble finding their father's house again, having simply headed straight for the Great Mosque, whose towering dome could be seen all over the city.

The late afternoon was still stifling, and Eadwulf and Jorund were relieved to be able to remove the restrictive cloaks and head coverings once they were inside. Beorhtwulf led them through the villa to a chamber with a high ceiling and magnificently tiled floor where food and cold drinks had been laid on a marble-slabbed table. Eadwulf savoured the room's delicious coolness as he admired the view of a courtyard garden through the opened doors, in the centre of which was a pond with an elaborately carved marble fountain. But his thoughts were focused on his father, and whether he'd want to leave a place such as this.

'Thank God everything went to plan,' Beorhtwulf said, once they'd relayed the events of their rescue and eaten their fill. 'Things could have gone very differently and I'd never have forgiven myself if I'd lost you both. Your friends Bjorn and Hastein have my sincerest thanks for what they did.'

Eadwulf was too emotionally strung in his belief that Beorhtwulf would not be leaving with them to speak, so it was Jorund who replied. 'My brother and I owe more than we can say to those two, Father.' He hesitated, looking away, embarrassed at using that word for the first time. 'But we can talk about such things once we're all on our way home.'

Eadwulf's eyes met his father's and for a moment, no one spoke. Then Beorhtwulf said, 'Hamid reported that if all went to plan, Bjorn wants to sail at first light. So we must leave the city before the gates close for the night.'

'Where is Hamid?' Jorund suddenly blurted in his usual direct way, while Eadwulf contemplated the use of 'we' in what his father had just said. 'Will we see him before we leave, or our half-sister, whose name I don't remember?'

'Ameena,' Eadwulf supplied. 'Are they here, Father? We owe great thanks to Hamid and would like to wish them both well.'

Beorhtwulf stared down at his fingers on the table before him. 'There's so much I need to explain to you both, but I assure you, you'll see Hamid and Ameena again soon. Right now we need to head for the west gate. Get your cloaks and headdresses back on, making sure no stray hair is visible, and I'll do the same.'

* * *

Streams of people were leaving as they arrived at the gate, many of them strangers to the city, come to trade for the day. Others were in Arabic dress, so the three of them blended in well with the moving crowd, none of whom were given a second glance by the guards. Night-time was rapidly closing in and the guards seemed keen to lock the gates and get back to their homes.

As they reached the Danish camp, many of the crew were traipsing back and forth to the *Sea Eagle,* loading the goods they had traded or purchased before daylight faded. Bjorn and Hastein came to greet them with bear hugs and much back-slapping. Beorhtwulf stood aside, looking a little bemused, until Eadwulf drew him forward to introduce him to his friends.

'I feel I already know you, my lord,' Bjorn said, clasping Beorhtwulf's arm. 'Eadwulf talked about you often when he was a lad.'

Beorhtwulf nodded. 'I know that both my sons think highly of all of you, and that Eadwulf owes you his life. But that's all he's managed to tell me so far.'

'I don't suppose he told you that *he* saved my life, in such a way that I will be forever in his debt.' Bjorn grinned and Eadwulf could see that his father could not help grinning back.

'I can tell there is great fondness between you, and you've likely been through much together. I'd dearly love to how you came to save each other's lives at some stage but, for now, I'm sincerely grateful to you all for the way you risked your lives to save my sons.'

He turned to Jorund and held out his arms. 'To know that I have another son is a greater blessing than I could have asked. Some good things have come from the tragedy that engulfed our lives and we have much to catch up on once we're away from here.'

'We should finalise things before we clear the rest of the camp and head for the *Eagle*,' Hastein put in, gesturing towards the tent flap. 'It's not often we can surprise our friend Eadwulf, but I think this might just do so.'

In the glow of a few small oil lamps, Eadwulf recognised the four people waiting inside the tent. The two drivers of the cart bowed as a gesture of greeting, while the other two waited, seeming uncertain of Eadwulf's reactions on seeing them.

Then Hamid came to clasp Eadwulf and Jorund's arms in turn. 'So we meet again,' the young man said, 'though I know you were not expecting to do so. I'm sure you both remember our sister, Ameena…'

Ameena came from the shadows to stand at Hamid's side

and smile at Eadwulf and Jorund. Eadwulf gaped at her flowing red hair.

'I can see we have startled even you, Eadwulf,' Beorhtwulf said, 'but Ameena's mother was fair, like Morwenna, and I am her father, who once had red hair.' The others laughed at his small jest. 'Like you, Eadwulf, it is my colouring that Ameena took.'

'It just took me by surprise,' Eadwulf blustered as the others hooted.

'I am relieved and happy that the rescue went well,' Ameena said, 'or I would have lost two brothers I have only just found.'

'Our friends saved us from years of hard labour at that quarry,' Jorund put in. 'Something neither of us will ever forget. But now I must ask what the four of you are doing here. Won't it be risky getting back into the city? The guards could recognise you, which could prove dangerous once our escape becomes known.'

'We'll leave you now so they can explain things further,' Hastein said. 'But make it snappy because we need to strike camp soon and head for the ship. We sail at first light.'

'I can think of only one reason why you four should be here,' Eadwulf started once Bjorn and Hastein had left and they were seated on the furs of the tent floor. 'You'll be sailing with us, right?' Hamid nodded and Eadwulf continued, 'I'd already guessed Father had decided to return to Mercia when he came here with us tonight, and that his two men should need to get away from here makes sense,' he added, turning his attention to the cart drivers. 'Once Beorhtwulf was known to be missing, you two could be questioned until the emir got what he wanted to know, and still probably end up dead.'

'And I'm guessing that's why Hamid and Ameena are coming with us, too,' Jorund concluded. 'The emir isn't likely to believe they didn't know where Beorhtwulf had gone, especially as they all live together.'

Hamid nodded. 'You're both right in everything you say, but Ameena and I have other reasons for wanting to leave here.'

Ameena explained to her brothers what she'd heard from the handmaid.

'So you see, Hamid's life is doubly at risk if he stays in Cordoba,' Beorhtwulf added, 'and Ameena will find no favour with the emir when her father is proven a traitor. The only thing both of them can do is leave with us. Bjorn has no objection to us aboard ship, so it's you and Jorund, Eadwulf, who must decide whether you want them with you in Mercia.'

'How can you doubt that we would, Father? We have a hall in Elston where all will be welcome, including your two men.'

'We thank you, Eadwulf, but all we ask is passage to the north of Iberia,' the older of the two men said. 'We are from these lands and wish to stay. Counsellor Jaleel has given his permission, and your friend Bjorn has agreed to put ashore close to Santiago de Compostela, where we can stay with some old friends.'

The tent flap opened and Bjorn stepped in. 'Time to move. We've still got the tents and bedrolls, and some cooking pots to get aboard. Then we stay on the ship until we sail. If there's the merest hint of the palace guards heading our way, we row – even if it's still dark. I don't expect that, of course. It could be days before anything is known about missing quarry slaves.

That's right, isn't it Beorhtwulf?'

'Yes, unless the emir sends for me tonight, and I can't be found. And if it should be noticed that Hamid and Ameena are also missing, Muhammad could well order a search.'

'But even if that happened, surely they wouldn't search out here?'

Beorhtwulf shrugged. 'I hope you're right, but there's always the chance that one of the palace guards saw or heard something connected with the rescue.' He turned to his men. 'You two are certain you told no one what you were involved with, or that no one heard you talking about it? Abdul?'

'We saw no one around, Counsellor,' the older of the two men replied. 'But, as Ameena recently discovered, the palace walls have eyes and ears. The emir has men patrolling the palace, watching and listening to everything that goes on. If we were followed or overheard, we are ignorant of it.'

'So,' Bjorn concluded, 'we stick to our plan and get to the ship as soon as possible. I'll not feel safe until we're out on the open sea.'

* * *

The night sky was paling as Eadwulf and Jorund's watch neared its end. Just a fraction lighter and they'd waken the rest of the crew in order to pull out. It was Jorund who picked up the first distant sound of voices. Then he caught the glimmer of torchlight close to the palace wall.

'Guards!' he yelled, causing a mad scramble aboard ship as men took to their oars.

The *Sea Eagle's* crew pushed away from the bank as the palace guards lined the quayside. Arrows rained down on the river around them, some striking the hull of the ship. A crewman yelled as one skimmed his arm. Another slumped, dead, across his oar. Beorhtwulf's two men stepped in to replace them. Then another oarsman collapsed as an arrow pierced his back and Hamid moved to take his place. An arrow struck deep into his thigh and he sank to the deck. But the ship sped on, the distance from the Cordoba quayside continuously widening.

'No let up until we've some miles between us!' Bjorn yelled. 'The emir may send ships after us.'

The first fifty miles was fraught with fear of falling into the emir's grasp. Though no ships had appeared in pursuit, thoughts of Moorish tortures and methods of execution were enough to make the crew ignore strained muscles as they rowed. The men were fit, their bodies well-used to rowing for hours, but the pace needed to distance themselves from Cordoba was gruelling. The westerly breeze was also contrary to their desperate needs.

Once west of Seville, efforts were relaxed a little as it became clear they had accomplished the mission they'd set out to do. The emir's guards had seemingly given up the chase, and no Moorish ships were following them. But fear of the possible consequences of pulling ashore still hovered like a menacing black cloud over them and they rowed on without stopping, oarsmen alternating shifts to allow rest for overworked muscles.

The first sighting of the open sea brought a sigh of relief to all and the *Eagle* sped on, veering northward towards home.

Six

Winchester: Late June 871

The Winchester hall suddenly fell silent. Alfred waited for one of his ealdormen to speak, to ignite some ray of hope in his fading spirits. Sounds of his armies preparing their evening meal beyond the palisade carried through the open shutters, intensifying the suspension of movement within. He dare not contemplate their numbers just yet. Though recently swelled, he feared they would still fall dangerously short.

The dread of failure knocked against his skull. Since his coronation a month ago and the arrival of the fresh horde of Danes at Reading, Alfred had felt keenly the weighty pressures of kingship – and had come to doubt his ability to rule. His unreasonable mind yelled abuse at Aethelred for leaving him on his own. Then the grief at the loss of his beloved brother would overwhelm him, and he'd vow yet again to fight to his dying day to keep Wessex free from Danish control.

Each day of the past two weeks had seen the Norsemen advancing deeper into Wessex, and Alfred knew there was only one way of stopping them: by mustering an army large enough to match them. The depleted remnants of the Wiltshire, Somerset, Hampshire and Sussex fyrds were already here at Winchester; Alfred had insisted on their continued presence on receiving news of the arrival of the Great Summer Army at Reading immediately after Aethelred's funeral. Only the Berkshire fyrd had been permitted to return and remain in their shire, in view of the huge Norse presence at Reading.

Alfred's ealdormen had ridden back to their respective shires to organise the enlisting of more men into their armies. There would doubtless be some ceorls who'd failed in their duties the last time they'd been called, perhaps some through injury or illness. There would also be those who'd simply refused to fight, or feigned illness. Such men must be found. The future of Wessex depended on his army's ability to keep the Danes at bay. And at present, the Wessex army consisted of a mere few hundred.

Now those ealdormen were seated around the table, ready to discuss their success – or failure – in raising more men. Cornwall still refused to give aid to Wessex, as Alfred had known it would. Kent too, was unable to help. Shiploads of Norsemen were mustering on Thanet and raids were frequent and violent. Kentish armies were needed where they were.

Alfred breathed deeply, knowing he must appear strong, whatever the news. His gaze moved from one man to the next, eventually coming to rest on Unwine, the Sussex ealdorman who had fought beside him at Ashdown.

'My lord,' Unwine responded, his arm sweeping round as he gestured to his fellow ealdormen. 'We've done our best to enlist as many men as possible but there were few men left in most of our shires to find. Those who hadn't already been summoned were mostly too old, too young, or infirm.' Around him, several ealdormen were nodding agreement. Then Daegmund of Dorset spoke up.

'My thegns have raised almost a hundred men, lord – could've been more but we've had to leave an army along our coast in case the Danish bastards who plagued us last summer come back from Wales!'

'We've raised a few more than a hundred,' Odda of Devon added. 'Like Daegmund here, we're expecting those pillaging swine to try their luck along our coast again now its spring.'

Alfred inwardly thanked God for at least this ray of hope. Two hundred men would be a good boost to his army.

'But, as Unwine pointed out, the rest of us have met with little success.' Radulf, the burly Hampshire ealdorman shook his head and gestured to Aethelnoth of Somerset and Brihtnoth of Wiltshire. 'Between us we've raised little more than a hundred and fifty men.'

Alfred nodded, adding up numbers as he did. 'I'm convinced that with the numbers you've just given me, Radulf, plus the three hundred or so men here since Meretun, we have a good chance of victory.'

Radulf shrugged. 'I'd say that depends on the size of this Summer Army, my lord. We know Halfdan's army suffered heavy losses at Meretun, but we've no way of knowing how many more of the heathens have landed in Reading recently, have we, Brihtnoth?'

The Wiltshire ealdorman shook his head. 'Nothing certain, but my scouts estimate anything between eight hundred and a thousand, so who's to know which end of the scale's closer to the truth? And more Danes are arriving each week. So even with these extra numbers, we're still a long way short, even of eight hundred.'

Alfred swallowed down his rising anger. The odds may be against them, but Wessex would not give in so easily. 'We prepare to move out at first light the day after tomorrow, and I pray we're not too late to make a stand.'

* * *

Ealhswith gazed down at her four-month-old son, sleeping soundly in her arms, drawing comfort from knowing that nothing in life could change the love in her heart for either of her children. At her feet, two-year-old Aethelflaed played with her building blocks, intent on building a tower as tall as herself. In a chair opposite, her round-faced nurse, Agnes, kept a watchful eye on the little girl while continuing her embroidery.

Satisfied after his feed, little Edward would now sleep contentedly for a few hours and Ealhswith rose to lay him in his cradle. She recalled how this very act would have so easily woken Aethelflaed when she was a babe. How different her two children were. Aethelflaed still slept little and her energy seemed boundless. Ealhswith smiled at that, knowing too well that her own parents had said the same thing of her on many occasion.

'Surely we'll hear something today, Agnes,' she said, her anxiety suddenly returning to sweep away all other thoughts. 'Five whole days, and we haven't heard a word.'

'No news usually means there's nothing to report,' the nurse replied with a reassuring smile. 'Don't you go fretting again, my lady. If anything had happened to the king, the whole of Wessex would have heard by now. Besides, we don't know when the battle took place – or even if it has happened at all. But King Alfred did say he expected to reach Wilton the day after they set out. If the battle was later that day, it would mean there's been plenty of time for messengers to get back here with any news.'

Agnes said no more and Ealhswith was relieved the nurse hadn't spelled out the possibility of the entire Wessex army being either wiped out or taken captive. This 'Great Summer Army' of the Danes was reported to be vast, and Ealhswith knew only too well how depleted Alfred's army was by comparison.

Her heart pounded wildly at the mere thought of such a one-side battle; the very suggestion of losing Alfred was simply too hard to bear. And should her husband survive, but the battle lost, Wessex nobles would not look kindly on a king who failed to win the first battle of his reign. The kingdom's crown may not be Alfred's for much longer.

* * *

On a grassy plain, a mile outside the royal vill at Wilton and thirty miles west of Winchester, Saxon forces faced the newly arrived Norse Summer Army for the first time. Noon was approaching and although banks of persistent, hazy cloud masked the sun, the air hung still and humid. Beneath his mailshirt, Alfred's tunic clung to his sweaty skin, though he knew the sweat was as much a product of his heightened anxiety as the cloying heat.

His stomach churned as he took in the enormity of the Danish forces. Spread out across the plain in their battle lines, they were a boundless and ominous presence, their pounding on shields and jeering starting as the Wessex army had neared and formed its own lines, ready for combat, some twenty-five yards from the foe.

From the centre of the front line of his shield wall, Alfred gauged the enemy lines, the clamouring and jeering of the two armies ringing out across the hillside: a sound to instil immeasurable dread or raging battle lust into the hearts of the bravest warriors. He adjusted his helm as he sought out places of weakness in the Norse defences. But their lines seemed tightly formed, each a hundred men wide, and perhaps eight, or even nine lines deep, though he couldn't see clearly.

His spirits took a further pounding as he noted the Danes' mail byrnies and metal helms. Well protected against sword and spear thrusts in their impressive armour, the fresh army of Norsemen looked an unbeatable force. In Alfred's own army, only his nobles were suitably armed. Most of the Wessex fyrd wore helms and gambesons of simple leather as body armour, both little safeguard against sharpened spear heads and battle axes, or well-honed swords. Few villagers had coin for metal armour and good weapons. When called for, the fyrd made do with whatever they could find.

Alfred recognised Halfdan along the Danish front line but having never met, or even glimpsed, the three new warlords, he couldn't pick them out. Several warriors in the front line were imposing enough to offer a commanding presence, but during the deafening clamour, none claimed more attention from their men than any other.

Soon the taunts and insults would begin and this time, Alfred intended to be first to ridicule the enemy. He stepped forward, raising his sword arm, holding his weapon high, and his men instantly ceased their hammering. Gradually the Norsemen quieted.

'If you think renewing your forces can daunt Saxon warriors, Halfdan,' he yelled, 'you'd better think again! We can't be cowed by heathens. Each of my men is worth two of yours.'

Pounding on shields from the Norse lines halted Alfred's flow, the clamour ceasing only when a tall, broad-shouldered warrior stepped forward, a short distance to Halfdan's left. He held his sword and shield out wide, as though offering a deadly embrace. Alfred took in the striking figure and arrogant stance and, although his face was obscured by the nose guard of his helm, Alfred had little doubt that this man was one of the three new warlords.

'I have just one piece of advice for you, Alfred of Wessex,' the warrior boomed. 'Surrender!'

The Wessex army responded with raucous jeering until Alfred raised his arm. 'And why would I do that?' he threw back. 'My men are itching for the fight. But should your armies be afraid to meet us, I'd gladly offer the same advice to you.'

Mocking cheers from the Saxons and jeers and hammering on shields from the Danes followed, until Halfdan stepped forward, followed by two other warriors who emerged along the front line.

'So we meet again, Alfred. Pity, I'd hoped you'd have come to your senses by now.' Alfred sneered at the Dane's derisive tone. 'You must know that we intend to take Wessex, and it would be much more sensible in the long run if you handed it over now. As you see, I've been joined by my three comrades, each a mighty king.' He gestured to the imposing warrior who had spoken first. 'Guthrum you have already met, and these two,' he added gesturing to the others who had stepped forward, 'are Anwend and Oscetel. You must realise that your feeble resistance won't take our strong, fresh army long to quell, and you'll be left with hundreds of bodies to dispose of.'

'Enough talk!' Guthrum had evidently lost his patience with Halfdan's rambling. 'Now we fight.'

This time, Alfred's men were ready, and gave as good as they got. Volleys of spears flew across the twenty-five yard gap, some soaring wildly overhead, others slamming into shields or sinking deep into exposed flesh. Men from the front line dropped like stones and, no time for sympathy, those from behind stepped over the bodies to replace them.

The assault of spears gradually lessened and stopped, and the two armies momentarily faced each other in silence...

Then, bellowing like wild beasts, the Danes charged.

Alfred's army launched itself forward, the clash of shields deafening as the two armies met. Warriors lent their weight to the push, grunting with the effort of moving the other side back. Spears and swords thrust out, seeking unprotected parts of their opponent's body.

And as Alfred had expected, he was face to face with Halfdan.

Though no taller than himself, the Danish leader was strong and Alfred needed his wits and agility to avoid being wounded, or worse. Halfdan's every thrust and stab met with resistance from Alfred's shield or sword, and Alfred retaliated with slashes and stabs of his own. But it soon became clear that Halfdan was not a warrior to be defeated with ease and, unless one of them was caught momentarily off guard, the fight was likely to drag on.

After the best part of half an hour, Alfred knew he wouldn't be able to keep up this pace for much longer. The constant ducking and dodging to fend off the Dane's lethal thrusts, together with the inhibiting weight of his mailshirt, was sapping his strength far too quickly. But somehow, as he jerked to one side to avoid another lunge, the Dane lost his balance and his vicious strikes momentarily ceased. In that briefest of pauses, Alfred struck out, his sword cutting deep into Halfdan's thick thigh.

Halfdan fell to his knees and Alfred raised his sword for a killing strike to his neck, only to have it deflected by a quick-acting warrior at Halfdan's side. The warrior stepped in front of his lord, giving him time to drag himself back through his lines.

Alfred could do nothing but face his new opponent and continue the fight. But this man was no Halfdan, and it took little time for Alfred to thrust his sword between the loosely joined side seam of his byrnie and finish him off.

The battle raged on, with neither army dominating the field for long. Bodies of the dead and wounded were trampled and the grass had become thick and greasy with blood. Men lost their footing, enabling a swift and deadly reaction from the enemy. Each time the Saxons held sway Alfred's hopes rose, only to plummet when the Danes retook control. But as the sun touched the western horizon, he sensed a renewed strength welling in his men and the Danes were being pushed back.

The Norse shield wall was suddenly crumbling. Warriors fled across the plain towards a stretch of dense forest at its edge. Cheers rang out from the Saxon lines and Alfred watched the retreat with his men, murmuring his thanks to God who must surely have been on their side this day. Defeating the huge Summer Army had seemed an impossible task, and the battle ending this way was surely a gift from God.

Around him, the Wessex shield wall had broken up as the men celebrated their victory and, high on elation and pride a few score of them gave chase to the fleeing Danes. Alfred made no move to stop them; he'd felt keenly that the Saxon failure to pursue the defeated army at Meretun had enabled the Danes to reform their lines and ultimately defeat the Saxons.

Alfred watched, hoping the pursuit would be enough to keep the Danes running. But before his men could reach those trailing behind, the Danes stopped, as though the sight of the paltry numbers chasing them had rekindled the possibility of their own victory. Fear slammed into Alfred's chest as the Norse shield wall rapidly reformed and charged at the disorganised groups of Saxons. A huge roar went up from the remaining Wessex army as men watched their comrades being brought down like swatted flies... and the Danes heading back towards them.

Alfred tried frantically to reassemble his lines, but with his unpractised fyrd it was hopeless. His already shrunken shield wall was still loose and ragged as the Danes slammed into them, cutting them down with remorseless precision.

His men fled towards Wilton with the Danes hard on their heels; the slow and injured at the rear falling victim to Norse sword and battleaxe. Alfred's horse – as well as the mounts of his nobles – was inside the vill and he prayed the Danes would abandon the chase before then.

Dusk was closing in as they reached Wilton and the Wiltshire ealdorman pounded on the barred gates. 'Hunlaf, it's me, Brihtnoth. In God's name, open for the king!'

Arrows flew from over the palisade, keeping the enemy at bay as the gates swung back and Alfred's battered army streamed in. Norse warriors hovered in the distance, out of range of the archers. But Alfred knew better that to take any chances. 'Brihtnoth, Radulf, set up a rota for a night watch. Our men will join those already set by Hunlaf here.' He gestured at the ageing reeve. 'There are few young men left here at Wilton.'

'That's true, lord, Hunlaf agreed. 'Our warriors were all with Brihtnoth in your army. We only had the old, the young and the ailing here. But it's enough to keep our palisade guarded and even the young lads can fire arrows.'

Alfred nodded. 'I hope you're right. But right now we make sure we all survive the night. I hope your men are well supplied with arrows, as well as spears. If the Danes get near, it will be spears they need,'

'We've been making plenty of arrows since the Danes came to Wessex over a year ago, and our smith's been kept more than busy making spears.'

'That's good to hear,' Alfred responded, wondering whether all his reeves were as vigilant as Hunlaf before turning his attention back to Radulf and Brihtnoth organising the watch.

'Pick none of the wounded, and ensure those chosen understand the need for total vigilance. It wouldn't surprise me if the Danes launched an attack once it's dark. I'll be part of the first watch and others of our nobles will take their turns throughout the night.'

At long last, Alfred was relieved from his watch and headed for the hall. He slumped in a high-backed chair, weary to the bone and too sick at heart to speak of his army's defeat. He'd lost several of his bravest thegns during the battle, as well as scores of his fyrd. But, despite his exhaustion and grief at the losses, he needed to think, and he needed to plan.

Two things were foremost on Alfred's mind, the first being what move to make before the Danes succeeded in taking Wessex completely. The second was whether or not he'd still be accepted as king on his return to Winchester.

He almost cried out at the shame he felt at having lost the first battle of his kingship, especially as it had seemed the Saxons had won. Now was not the time for analysing what had gone wrong, but he knew that the deciding factor in their defeat had been the lack of an organised pursuit.

And for that, he could only blame himself. At Meretun, there had been no pursuit whatsoever. On this occasion, the pursuing Saxons had been mere straggling groups. No threat at all to the Danes. It had been his responsibility to send the men out as an ordered unit, one that the enemy would not wish to meet–

Unless… just unless… the Norse flight had been a trick, a ploy to draw the Saxons out, just as it had done. The more he thought about it, the more he was certain. At the end of the battle, Danish forces had still far outnumbered those of the

Saxons, so why had they turned and fled?

The retreat, which had seemed like a gift from God, suddenly became a clever and devious ruse, which had worked.

Alfred knew his defeat would not bode well for his reign in the eyes of his ealdormen. The possibility of them ousting him in favour of someone else – likely someone older and more experienced in battle – hung over him like a storm cloud. For now, he could do nothing about keeping his kingship, but he knew a way in which he just might be able to save Wessex or, at very least, delay the Danes taking it for a time.

Yes, time was the very thing he needed. Raising more men for the fyrd would be impossible in a matter of days, perhaps even weeks. But given a few months or, better still, a year, he just might be able to do so. And tomorrow, he'd start putting his plan into motion.

His decision made, Alfred eventually gave in to his exhaustion, closing his eyes as crashing waves of slumber overwhelmed him.

* * *

No raid came during the night. By late morning Alfred and the remnants of his army set off on the thirty-mile journey back to Winchester. The pace was slow, due to the many wounded, and some of the men with severe leg wounds were given the use of noblemen's mounts. For others, they made simple stretchers from tree branches which could be carried by their comrades.

After a night's rest in a stretch of woodland, it was mid-afternoon the following day when Alfred's army limped through the palisade gates at Winchester. Spirits were low. Losses had been high and the many wounded were in immediate need of treatment. The remains of the fyrd set up camp, this time within the confines of the palisade. Alfred had a mere moment to spend with Ealhswith, who was too relieved to see him back to speak of his defeat. She'd hear about it soon enough after the evening meal, when he would call his ealdorman to inform them of his plans. He'd need all his wits about him, yet again, to convince them of the wisdom of that course of action.

Tomorrow, Alfred would send out his scouts to discover the whereabouts of the Norse army. Until that was known, he could do nothing.

Seven

Halfdan glowered at Guthrum as they rode at the head of their exhausted army. The new arrival was not a happy man, despite their victory over the Saxons at Wilton. It was Guthrum's idea to head back to their stronghold at Reading to plan their next move, and none of the leaders seemed inclined to argue with him, least of all Halfdan.

As though feeling the heat of Halfdan's glare, Guthrum suddenly twisted in his saddle to face him. 'I think we've got more than we bargained for with the West Saxons,' he said, before twisting himself forwards again.

Halfdan inwardly fumed. Guthrum had a habit of dropping the odd thought, observation or criticism then clamming up, leaving his listeners to figure out his point. By Odin, the man had only been in Wessex for a couple of weeks, but it was more than enough to make Halfdan take a dislike to him. Besides, Guthrum was steadily asserting himself as overall leader, just like Bagsecg had done before the fool got himself killed, and the men seemed happy with that. Guthrum certainly had an air of authority that let everyone know he wasn't a man to be messed with. His dark-haired good looks and pleasant smile could rapidly turn into a venomous glare that could wither a man of lesser standing than Halfdan.

And Halfdan already had his own opinion to add to this particular remark. 'It's not the Saxon scum themselves we need to worry about but that young king of theirs. There's more to Alfred than meets the eye.' He let the thought hang, smiling to himself. Two could play at Guthrum's game.

But Guthrum nodded. 'I think you're right. I could tell his men were right behind him. He must have done something in the past to win their approval, young as he is.'

Halfdan cringed, remembering his army's humiliating defeat at Ashdown. And it was Alfred who had killed that bull of a man, Bagsecg. He reached to touch his bandaged thigh. The gash was deep and he'd lost a lot of blood, but at least he was still alive.

He could sense Guthrum watching him and refused to make eye contact, but it didn't deter the man from speaking his mind. 'The young king can fight, too. I'm told few men could inflict a wound on you, Halfdan.'

Halfdan wasn't sure whether that was praise for him or for the whippersnapper of a king. He had a sudden longing to have Ivar here beside him. Guthrum wouldn't be trying to rule the roost if his strange and powerful brother were around. Ivar could put any man in his place.

'Alfred doesn't lack confidence either, and makes a good show of himself in front of his shield wall,' Guthrum went on. 'But he's still much to learn as a leader in the battlefield.'

After another long, infuriating pause, Halfdan eventually asked, 'Why do you say that?'

'Look at our army, Halfdan. What do you see?'

Halfdan glanced back, beyond Oscetel and Anwend riding behind them. 'Exhausted men, wounded men – but all look happy enough that we won and we're all still alive.'

'But that's just my point, Halfdan. We're not all still alive. We've lost well over a third of our army in a battle against a force little over half the size of ours to start with. The Saxons fought well today, and very nearly won. If we hadn't used that old trick of retreating, they just might have done. Our shieldwall had begun to collapse and the Saxons knew it. Any longer and we would have been fleeing for real.'

Halfdan sighed and nodded. He'd known that himself, but could never have forced himself to openly admit it. 'So we head back to Reading to give our army time to recover and hope that a few more shiploads of men soon arrive up the Thames.'

Guthrum just grunted.

* * *

Two days later, Alfred's scouts were back, with news that the Danes had returned to Reading. Alfred had expected as much. The Norse army had lost as many men as his own, and would need time to recover. Building up their numbers again would be dependent upon more shiploads of Norsemen coming to join them, and he prayed to God that none would come.

Tonight he would meet with his ealdormen and thegns to discuss his intentions. Fortunately, none of the ealdormen with him at Wilton had been killed but four Saxon thegns had been lost and would need replacing in their respective shires: all tasks that Alfred wasn't ready to face just yet.

So far, none of the nobles had put voice to his failure at Wilton. Radulf of Hampshire and Unwine of Sussex even praised the valiant effort made by Wessex forces in the face of such vast numbers. But still, Alfred's unease would not abate and he knew that the outcome of tonight's meeting would be the deciding factor in whether or not he still had the throne.

* * *

The tables for the evening meal had been cleared of leftover food and the women, children and servants had departed the hall, leaving the men to their meeting. Thirty-odd Wessex noblemen sipped their mugs of ale and waited for their new king to speak. Alfred was silent as he focused on what he needed to say. Anticipating opposition from most of them did little for his composure. But, at length, he knew he could prevaricate no longer.

'My lords,' he started, rising to his feet and sweeping the room with his amber gaze. 'I won't dwell on our army's defeat at Wilton. We lost many men from our already meagre numbers and the wound is still raw with each of us. We were in no position to face such a huge force to start with, but now, should the enemy strike again we would not stand a chance.'

No one spoke, though he noted a few flickers of eye-contact amongst them. He could sense them weighing him up rather than any outright disapproval, and was thankful for that.

'But, my lords, our army was not alone in losing so many men. I'd say that Danish losses were higher than ours.' He paused, glad to hear the murmurs of agreement. 'Our men fought like lions for our kingdom and, had our numbers been greater at the start, I have no doubt we could have won.'

'But we did win, lord!' a young Hampshire thegn called out. 'The Danes retreated, and if we'd made an organised pursuit, we would, surely, have retained the victory.'

There it was, the first criticism of Alfred's organisation and control of his army, and he had his response well-planned. 'At the time, I would have agreed with you Osrid. But I've since had the opportunity to think things through. Now I'm certain that what happened was all part of a plan by the Danes, should the battle start to go against them. And we all know that at the point before the retreat, we had the upper hand and the enemy shield wall would have soon been completely broken up.'

Allowing no one to interrupt, he ploughed on. 'This is the second time we've fallen for that trick. The Danish retreat at Meretun resulted in our defeat.'

'Then why, if you suspected a trick in the enemy withdrawal, did you allow some of our men to make pursuit?' Daegmund, the ealdorman of Dorset, looked down at the table as though embarrassed by his own boldness in speaking out.

'Shall I answer that, my lord?' Radulf's concern for him touched Alfred, yet again, but he knew only he could deal with this question.

'I'll answer the question myself, thank you, Radulf. It's directed at me, after all.'

His eyes locked with Daegmund's. 'I accept all blame for such a grave error, and can only say that, as God is my witness, I'll never make the same mistake again. I now have the measure of Danish trickery. But, at the time I was being carried on a wave of elation at our unexpected success, like the rest of you. I confess to recalling how our men pursued the defeated Danes at Ashdown, and the comparison filled me with pride. The events at Meretun seemed to have been temporarily blocked from my mind.

'So, what I'm saying is this: what's done is done, and we… I…will learn from this mistake. But for now, I am convinced that the Danes are no more in a state for battle than we are, and will welcome time to recover and rebuild their forces. What I'm about to propose should take them out of our kingdom and give us time to build our own army up again, too.'

He waited, pleased to see that Unwine, Radulf and Brihtnoth were nodding. They must have guessed what he was about to suggest and approved of it.

'My lords, I propose we try something that worked for Charles the Bald for many years while the Danes were at liberty in West Francia. He succeeded in keeping them from ravaging his people and lands, and even managed to build up his fortifications against the Danes for some time. This, my lords, he managed by paying them tribute.'

The buzz of animated voices rose as men expressed their thoughts on this proposal. Alfred waited for a while, allowing them to vent either objections or support amongst each other. Then he raised his hand and gradually the hall quietened.

It was Radulf who spoke first, choosing to address the whole gathering. 'I can see no way forward other than following through with King Alfred's plan. He's right about Charles the Bald. What Charles was buying was time. And that's exactly what we need to do: buy ourselves time, not only to recover, but to build up our army, bigger and stronger…'

'…so that when the Danes return,' Unwine continued in Radulf's stead, 'and make no mistake, they *will* return when they want more tribute, we'll be ready to make sure they never take Wessex.'

Nods and murmurs of agreement around the room brought a silent sigh of relief from Alfred and he felt truly humbled to have supporters such as Radulf and Unwine. He flashed a grin around the room and said, 'I couldn't have put it better myself.'

* * *

At daybreak the following morning, Alfred sent messengers to the Danish fort at Reading and three days later they returned. Silence fell in the Winchester hall as the spokesman for the trio knelt before Alfred, who had been speaking with his ealdormen.

'Good news, my lord,' the Hampshire thegn reported. 'The Danes accepted your request for a meeting, and agreed that it take place at Basing on Wednesday next, that's in five days' time.'

'Then I thank God for that, Sigmund, and I'm equally relieved to see the three of you back. Approaching an enemy stronghold is a risk in itself, yet you and your men freely volunteered for the task. Which of the leaders did you meet with?'

'Halfdan was there, and the three who'd arrived with this Summer Army. Halfdan wasn't happy with the idea of a meeting but the big, dark-headed one who called himself Guthrum just overrode all his objections. The other two seemed to agree with everything Guthrum said so, in the end, Halfdan just kept quiet.'

Alfred nodded as he thought about the implications of that and Sigmund added, 'If you ask me, lord, I'd say Guthrum's the one really in charge of the Norse army now. He's got that look about him… the look that says he's not to be trifled with. And whether we can trust him or not remains to be seen.'

Alfred harrumphed. 'In my experience to date, I wouldn't be inclined to trust a single one of them.'

* * *

The royal vill at Basing had been Alfred's choice for the meeting to take place. It was almost centrally sited between Winchester and the Danes' stronghold at Reading. Alfred had stipulated that two leaders from either side should be accompanied by no more than a dozen men and he prayed that the Danes would be true to their agreement to that. He'd also arranged with Eadred, his Basing reeve, that the Norsemen would meet no resistance on their arrival.

As the Saxons approached the vill on the appointed day in mid-July, it became clear that the Danes were already there. Horses were tethered outside the hall and Norse warriors sat along the enclosing palisade, waiting for their leaders. On entering the sizeable hall, Alfred and Radulf were greeted by the sight of two Danes sitting comfortably at a trestle table with a mug of ale. Their helmets and swords lay beside them on the table-top.

Alfred instinctively knew the dark-haired one was Guthrum, despite never having seen his entire face before. He was a handsome man with a short dark beard and moustache and, without his mail byrnie and under-padding he was not as burly as Alfred had thought at Wilton. His calculating dark eyes fixed on Alfred as he and Radulf crossed the room, while at his side, the steely eyes of his older, greying companion glowered at them both with sheer contempt.

“So you want to pay us off, Saxon,’ the seasoned warrior started before Alfred and Radulf had even seated themselves. ‘You think a little geld can send us packing and leave this prosperous-looking kingdom in your oh-so-capable hands?’ A sneering grin shaped his face and he chuckled at his own derisive words. Alfred just watched him, his face fixed into an impassive gaze. ‘Your offer had better be worth our while,’ the warrior continued, ‘or Wessex will be ours sooner than you can blink – and your piddling little army won’t be able to do a thing about it.’

Alfred had no intention of rising to the bait and his reply was simple. ‘I’m sure we can come to an agreement that will suit us all.’

‘We’ll be the judge of that,’ the older man snapped, ‘but I doubt that a king who fails as a battlelord will be respected enough by his people to raise silver enough to satisfy us. They’re as likely to kick him up the arse as–’

‘Enough, Oscetel,’ Guthrum warned, with a rapid flick of his wrist. ‘We’ll never know that until the young king has the opportunity to try. His lords might just forgive his greenness on this occasion.’

Alfred inwardly fumed at the reference to his age and newness to the throne, but his need to buy peace for Wessex overrode his pride. Still, he had no intention of being ground into the earth by these men. ‘We’re here to discuss terms for peace,’ he said, ‘which means that the conditions of our agreement must suit both sides.' Alfred's gaze swung from one man to the other. 'Exactly what you swear to uphold in return for a sizeable sum of tribute will determine whether or not we agree to raise it.'

Guthrum was watching him with interest and Alfred found it hard not to shuffle under the scrutiny. 'Then we'll be gracious on this occasion and hear your proposals first.'

Oscetel grunted, leaving little doubt as to his opinion on that. 'And just what do you think you'll do, *king,* if we don't come to an "agreement"? Another battle and you'll have no army at all!'

'We can offer you enough tribute to make it worth your while to leave Wessex for somewhere you can glean further goods and coin,' Alfred said, ignoring the remark. 'Your own army suffered heavy losses at Wilton and I doubt it could stand up to another engagement so soon. My army was defeated by a mere trick which, I assure you, will never catch us out again.'

Alfred suddenly thrust out his hand, thumb and forefinger almost touching. 'Your army was *this* close to becoming the loser, despite your superior numbers. I'd say, best to go somewhere with easier pickings than Wessex.

'We'll need a few months to collect the coin, of course.' He glanced at their expectant faces, knowing they wanted more than vague promises of payments. They wanted to know *how much.* He glanced at Radulf at his side, eyebrows raised.

Radulf's brow creased in thought. 'If we have long enough, we should manage to raise twenty large bags of silver coin.'

Guthrum and Oscetel shared a look and Alfred sensed he'd hit the mark concerning heavy losses in the Norse army and the need for time in which to build them up again: time in which he intended to do exactly the same in Wessex.

There was nothing more to be said, other than to arrange a date for payment of the tribute at Basing in a month's time. Alfred just hoped he wouldn't be the one unable to fulfil his side of the bargain, particularly in so short a time.

* * *

By September the exhausting task of collecting tribute from the nobles and clergy of the Wessex was still by no means complete. Alfred reluctantly admitted to his closest advisors that more time was needed and messengers were again sent to Reading.

Alfred seethed at the audacity of the monastic orders, as well as more than a few of his nobles, for claiming they were unable to give anything towards this tribute. Equally worrying for him was their attitude to paying the Norsemen anything in the first place.

'They're still not convinced I'm a fit ruler for Wessex!' he ranted as he and Ealhswith eventually reached their bed after Alfred had finished totalling the last few bags of coins to have come in with Unwine and Radulf. 'That's what all this is about. They still think I should have won the cursed battle at Wilton, so paying off the Danes wouldn't have been necessary.'

He hung his head and Ealhswith wrapped him in her arms as he vented his thoughts and fears.

'The most infuriating thing,' he murmured into her neck, 'is that most of those who refuse payment are the nobles and clergy from shires that provided very few men for our army at Wilton. How did they expect me to win with such limited numbers? They'd all heard of the size of the new Summer Amy.'

'I know, Alfred,' Ealhswith soothed. 'Your advisors have told me the same. Radulf says his journey to Kent yielded little tribute. The ealdorman there joined him and his men on their trek across his shire, and even he couldn't persuade some of the Kentish religious houses to contribute, or his thegns come to that. They all claimed they hadn't enough coin to spare.'

Alfred leaned back against the wicker wall behind their bed. He was weary to the bone after days of riding across the surrounding shires – shires that had provided the bulk of the Wessex fyrd since the Danes invaded. It had been difficult enough persuading the thegns and churchmen from those regions that tribute was vital to their kingdom's survival, so what chance did he stand with more distant shires?

'Kent's had its problems with the Danes camped on Thanet,' he explained, as Ealhswith rested her head against his chest, 'but they've had nothing compared to the likes of this Great Army to deal with. They seem ignorant of the desperate fight in our kingdom's heartlands.'

Ealhswith nodded. 'Radulf found the same in Devon and Dorset. Although those shires did send us a few men, they held many back in case the Danes struck along their coasts again, as they did last year. It seems the nobles and clergy there claimed to have their own fight with the marauders and saw no reason to pay geld to any other cause.'

Hearing all this through the lips of his wife caused Alfred's temper to flare. 'For the love of God, don't they understand they're as much a part of Wessex as Wilshire or Berkshire?

Their own shires aren't isolated units, independent of the rest and answerable only to themselves. Can't they see that if no tribute is paid, very soon the Danes will take *all* Wessex shires?'

Ealhswith was used to hearing Alfred rage and he knew she'd just wait patiently for the flames of frustration and anger flaring inside him to burn down to a lingering smoulder.

'Fortunately for us,' he said after a short silence, 'only a few more Norsemen arrived at Reading over the summer, so Guthrum and the other "kings" will have to curb their impatience for the tribute. If they'd built up their forces, we could have been facing more battles – and we wouldn't have stood a chance.

'The messengers I sent to Reading will ask for another few months, and I can't see the Danish leaders refusing. They need time to recover as much as we do, and they're living well enough off the fertile lands of Berkshire. Even if they have to overwinter there, there's plenty of game in the forests. And no doubt they'll continue to raid abbeys and monasteries as well as any unfortunate villages they come across.'

Alfred rubbed his aching brow, the anguish he felt for his people too hard to bear. 'To have the Danes ravaging Wessex grieves me more than I can say, Ealhswith, but until we pay them enough danegeld to move elsewhere, they will stay where they are.'

Ealhswith gently turned his face towards her own. 'There must be something we can do to convince these stubborn lords to look more closely at their needs and see if cash can be spared? You are the elected king, Alfred. Can't you order them to pay?'

Alfred shook his head. 'If I'd been king for some years and

earned their trust and respect, things would, perhaps, be different. But at present, those same stubborn lords could refuse to acknowledge me as king. A meeting of the witan could well see them doing just that. All I can do is have my loyal ealdormen stress the desperate situation we're in and the consequences of failing to dig deep into their coffers. As for the abbeys and monasteries, I may have a way forward there. I just need to think it out more clearly before I leave.'

Ealhswith gasped. 'Leave? Where are you going?'

'Once we hear back from Reading, we start all over again. My ealdormen will ride out with their men in a final attempt to collect tribute and I'll be heading to Kent to speak with Ealdorman Anlaf, since Radulf found him supportive. We'll revisit some of his most stubborn nobles and clergymen in an effort to make them see sense. Hopefully at least some of them will, especially when they realise the size of the army we're dealing with and what the future holds for their shire if the tribute isn't forthcoming.'

Alfred closed his weary eyes. He longed for sleep. But the worry that another few shiploads of Danes would arrive before the treaty with Guthrum was well and truly sealed, would probably keep him awake for most of yet another night.

* * *

Ealdorman Anlaf of Kent was a genial enough man who welcomed Alfred and his party graciously into his hall. Even from the outside, the Canterbury hall looked just as Alfred remembered it: a handsome structure, the lower half of which had incorporated the stone ruins of an old Roman villa. As he stepped through the door, memories flooded back.

It was seven years since he'd last visited this hall. He remembered well the time when the Danes wintering on the Isle of Thanet had broken the treaty and invaded Kent. The ealdorman at that time, along with Ceolnoth, Archbishop of Canterbury, had sent to Alfred's brother, King Aethelberht, for help and Alfred, then a mere youth of fifteen, had requested to accompany them here. This was also the hall in which his father had spent his last days. King Aethelwulf"s death had hit Alfred hard…

'I'm glad you decided to come here yourself, my lord,' Anlaf started, interrupting his thoughts as they sat by the hearthfire sharing a mug of ale. 'Ealdorman Radulf couldn't reason with some of my thegns when he was here, and the clergy was even more defiant – despite knowing I had already given tribute myself. I would have thought they might follow my lead. They all know the size of the army you face in mid-Wessex.'

'I'd hoped they'd see that, too, but we might get somewhere if they hear from me the likely consequences of not paying. I'm convinced that delivering the Danes silver to leave Wessex is the only way we can buy time to rebuild our army and strengthen at least some of our defences. I don't doubt they'll be back. The experience of other kingdoms tells us that paying tribute once leaves us wide open for repeated demands. I'm praying that by the time they return we'll be ready to stand against them and get rid of them for good.'

Throughout the following two weeks Alfred and Anlaf rode out to Kentish halls and religious houses. On being confronted by the King of Wessex himself, many of the thegns took a closer look into their monetary matters and decided they could manage to contribute to the tribute if it meant keeping Wessex from the hands of the bastard Danes. Unfortunately, the religious houses, monasteries and abbeys in particular, were reluctant to demean or impoverish themselves by paying the huge sums demanded. Alfred soon realised it was time to visit Ethelred, the new Archbishop of Canterbury.

'Greetings, Archbishop Ethelred,' Alfred started with a curt bow as a household servant led him and Anlaf into the spacious Canterbury hall. Although Ethelred had been appointed archbishop a year ago by Alfred's brother, King Aethelred, this was the first opportunity Alfred had had to meet the man. And his first impression was not favourable.

Ethelred was a tall, wiry man, whose simple dark tunic contrasted sharply with the arrogant stance and facial expression that had been absent in his predecessor, Archbishop Ceolnoth, whom Alfred had truly revered.

'I realise why you're here, of course,' the archbishop remarked as they moved to sit opposite each other at a trestle table in the middle of the hall. 'I've heard nothing but complaints from my bishops and abbots for days. Your requests for coin are not only excessive but in no way are they conducive to the wellbeing and livelihood of our Church.' He paused, his glowering gaze shifting between Alfred and Anlaf. 'And I imagine you expect me to request them to capitulate… which I have no intention of doing.'

By this time Alfred was seething. 'You have no choice in this, Archbishop, and if you continue to refuse, *I'll* have no other choice than to call the witan with the intention of having you dismissed from your office. My ealdormen fully support my decision to pay off the Danes. It's is the only way we can buy the time needed to rebuild our army and fortify some of our defences. Furthermore, I'll remind you that Kent is as much a part of Wessex as any other of our shires.'

The archbishop rose and walked towards the window, the shutters thrown back to allow the mellow October sun to stream in. He stood there for a few moments, silently staring at the outer walls of his cathedral barely forty yards away, and Alfred hoped he was mulling over his words. But, as he returned to his seat, hostility still shaped his face.

Alfred snapped. 'Do you realise what will become of this kingdom if the Danes don't get the geld? No… I don't believe you do,' he said, before Ethelred could reply, 'or else you simply don't care for the people of Wessex. The Danes won't be content until they've beaten us into submission – and that will involve the deaths of hundreds of Wessex people. I had hoped that my chosen clerics would be willing to do anything to prevent that.'

Alfred headed for the door, Anlaf close on his heels. 'You have until mid-January to ensure the tribute is collected. If Ealdorman Anlaf sends word that you still refuse to support our kingdom, the glorious role of Archbishop of Canterbury will be handed to someone I know I can trust.'

* * *

The efforts of Alfred and his closest ealdormen gradually yielded fruit. Over the winter, the tribute poured in and the last day of January eventually arrived: the date fixed for handing over the danegeld. Alfred cursed the Danes and everything they stood for as he considered how such an enormous sum could have been used in the interests of Wessex. There were so many things he wanted to improve during his years as king. He cast such thoughts away, knowing that until Wessex was freed from invaders, this coin would keep his people alive – at least for a time.

Guthrum had reluctantly agreed to Alfred's request for a later date, Halfdan and the two other kings accepted his decision.

'I'll expect you to honour our agreement and leave Wessex by the end of the month,' Alfred said, watching his men carry the sacks of silver into the Basing hall. The four kings each gave a curt nod.

'We'll be gone sooner than you think, Saxon. Your kingdom has paid us handsomely, for the present. And it's time we paid some old friends a visit.'

Alfred wanted to wipe the stupid grin off Halfdan's face, but he held himself in check. 'Do that,' he said, turning to leave. 'But I doubt those "friends" will welcome you with any more enthusiasm than we have.'

Eight

Ribe, Danish lands: Late July 871

The sun hovered over the western horizon as the *Sea Eagle* veered east from the Northern Sea into the estuary of the River Ribea in the Danish homelands. Eadwulf sat at his oar port as the great dragonship sailed on toward the port of Ribe. Although Hastein had successfully removed the arrowhead from Hamid's thigh, the wound remained red and angry and was in desperate need of stitching. Had Hastein been equipped with needle and silk – as he had been all those years ago in Francia, when Eadwulf had taken an arrow to his shoulder – he would happily have done so.

Eadwulf focused on Beorhtwulf and Ameena at the stern with Hamid. His father and half-sister had barely left the young man's side since they'd fled from Cordoba and Hamid was struck. Emir Muhammad had been ruthless in his attempts to kill them all, and rapidly deployed archers along the river bank for almost half a mile downstream of Cordoba. If not for the skill of Bjorn's crewmen, sending the *Eagle* speeding along the river, he would have succeeded. Eadwulf thanked the gods they'd lost no more than two men as the arrows rained down on them. It was fortunate for those aboard that only one fire arrow hit the ship, and that had been quickly extinguished.

The journey was fast and tiring, a mix of rowing and sailing as always, with only one overnight rest along the northern coast of Iberia, where they'd bid farewell to Beorhtwulf's two men. Sailing was steady along the coast of Francia and now, six days after leaving Cordoba, they were almost at Ribe.

It was Hastein's suggestion they should sail to his hall rather than straight to Mercia. 'The south-westerly wind will give us fast sailing to our lands,' he told Eadwulf as they left the Iberian coast behind. 'And I know of no two people better able to take care of Hamid than Freydis and Yrsa. There isn't much those two don't know about herb lore and soothing salves. And Yrsa works wonders with a needle and thread. I taught her myself.'

Eadwulf laughed at that image, but he'd never forgotten he owed Hastein his life for his skill in dealing with arrow wounds – as well as using needles and silks. 'Besides,' Hastein added with a grin, 'I know you'll be pleased to see those two again. Odin knows when another chance will come along. In my opinion Freydis is little changed, though I doubt you'll recognise Yrsa unless someone points her out to you. And I'm sure Bjorn will be happy to take you back to Elston once Hamid has had some much-needed care.'

Eadwulf wondered just how keen Bjorn would be on an idea that would involve delaying his return to his own family at Aros for a few more weeks. But it seemed that Bjorn had no objection to the plan, and Jorund was delighted to be visiting his old home, so it was to Ribe they'd headed.

In truth, Hamid was not causing anyone too much concern. Although his leg was undoubtedly painful, it showed no signs of festering and he'd managed to stay cheerful. Ameena kept the wound cleansed, though it was obvious to everyone the gash needed properly stitching and binding. Yet for the past day the tangled knot in Eadwulf's stomach had refused to unwind and the closer he got to Ribe, the tighter it became.

It was twelve years since he and Freydis last met – so briefly – just before Bjorn's plans for his thrall's return to Mercia had become reality. But in all that time, her image had been jealously locked in Eadwulf's heart. In his dreams Freydis became real, holding him close as he breathed in the fragrance he'd once known so well. And though his love for Leoflaed had been strong and true, that love had been different to the overwhelming passion and longing he felt for Freydis. He would never stop loving her.

But would Freydis still think fondly of him, or have simply reduced his memory to that of a thrall she'd known when she was young?

That question tormented his thoughts, though he knew it would be best if she had forgotten him years ago. Freydis was still Hastein's wife, after all, and Eadwulf would never do anything to hurt a man he'd come to love as a brother.

He turned his thoughts from Freydis to Yrsa. It would be good to see his half-sister again and he smiled at the memory of her as a chubby-faced two-year-old. But, at fifteen, Yrsa would probably look every bit the young woman. He wondered if she still remembered him at all… then chided himself, knowing that Freydis and Hastein would have kept his memory alive for her, just as Jorund would have done before he'd left Ribe. On his arrival at Elston seven years ago, Jorund had amused Eadwulf with his descriptions of their nine-year-old half-sister's incredible temper tantrums, and he could not help another smile.

'It's good to see you looking cheerful,' Bjorn said, squatting down beside Eadwulf's oar port. 'You've looked downright miserable for the last couple of days. I know Hamid's wound must be worrying you, but your father tells me he's bearing up well. The wound is in desperate need of further treatment, including a few stitches, and Hastein thinks Ribe's the best place for that. It seems Yrsa's pretty good with a needle.'

'I was thinking about Yrsa just now,' Eadwulf admitted. 'Somehow the thought of Jorund's tantrum-throwing "little vixen" struck me as funny.'

'Yrsa's grown up since Jorund last saw her, Ulf, and the temper tantrums are a thing of the past. My sister loves the girl as her own and the feeling is mutual. The two are almost inseparable, and they're as headstrong as each other.

'As for your meeting Freydis again,' Bjorn added, his voice no more than a whisper, 'I think both you and she will find this reunion difficult. I beg you to keep all signs of your feelings hidden. I'm not sure what's behind Hastein's suggestion to come to Ribe instead of sailing on to Elston. It would probably have been better to get you all straight home, but my cousin convinced me that no one could be as clever as Yrsa with a needle, and that you may never have chance to see your sister or Freydis again.'

Bjorn patted Eadwulf's arm. 'Just take care, Ulf,' he said as he rose. 'Don't let Hastein catch so much as an over-long look between you. It's not hard to recognise a longing in someone's eyes, and I've a feeling Hastein might be expecting to see just that.'

* * *

The long summer day was drawing to a close and night-time shadows were creeping across the spacious hall. Carefree voices and occasional laughter drifted through the open shutters and Freydis headed for the door to call the children in for the night, ordering servants to light a few more candles and oil lamps on her way. She paused for a final glance round to ensure that preparations for the evening meal were almost complete.

Flatbreads were already stacked on a trestle table alongside a wall, together with bowls of summer fruits soaked in honey and jugs of creamy white skyr for the desert. Mounds of sweet honey cakes had been baked as an additional treat. She popped her head into the fireroom off the main hall, where Yrsa was stirring a cauldron of thick pea soup as it simmered nicely on the edge of the meal-fire. Platefuls of skewered mutton steaks were piled on a table ready for taking through to the hall for roasting.

'Time to get the meats started,' Freydis informed her adopted daughter, smiling as she tilted her head in the direction of a couple of seemingly idle serving girls. 'Everything else is ready, so I'll leave you to organise these two to carry the skewers through to the hearth while I round up the children.'

'I'll do that,' Yrsa replied, smiling back. 'And I warned Dainn and Aguti earlier not to wander off. They've taken to practising their battle skills around the cemetery. It seems the whole group of lads go out there and take part, and most of the girls go along to cheer them on. Dainn's determined to be good enough to sail with his father next time he goes off raiding.'

'Oh, is he now?' Freydis said with a mock scowl. 'He'll have me to contend with first. If Dainn thinks he's old enough at eleven to fight against grown men, he can think again. I'll have words with Hastein, too, when he gets back. Dainn sailing with him when he's trading is one thing, but raids are a different matter. But right now, I believe the children are outside because I could hear them through the hall windows. In fact, I can still hear them from in here. They sound excited about something. Time to calm them down, I think. '

* * *

The *Eagle* sailed on past the port of Ribe for a further couple of miles and moored alongside a small jetty on the edge of Hastein's lands. The sun had left Midgard for the night and dusk was falling as they followed Hastein through the field of grazing cattle towards his imposing reed-thatched hall. Memories of the last time he'd been here flashed across Eadwulf's mind. He'd had little chance to speak with Freydis on that occasion and he was leaving his younger brother and baby sister behind.

A group of children stopped in their tracks as they neared, their chasing game forgotten. As recognition of familiar faces dawned, they surged forward, their joyful shrieks of welcome bringing adults out of the hall.

Leif and Jorund helped the limping Hamid along between them, leaving Eadwulf and Bjorn to walk with Beorhtwulf and Ameena. The lump in Eadwulf's throat felt large and constricting and his breathing quickened as he watched Freydis heading towards Hastein with a smile on her face. He drank in the sight of her, his memories aflame, and hoped she wouldn't notice him just yet.

As Hastein had said, Freydis was little changed, at least from a distance. Her long flaxen hair still tumbled free of the head veil around her lovely face, just as Eadwulf remembered it, and her youthful figure had not thickened at all. But the air of self-confidence and authority about her could not be denied.

Two boys suddenly darted from Freydis' side, heading straight for Hastein, their arms flailing wildly as they shouted his name. Both were as ginger-headed as Hastein and it seemed obvious to Eadwulf that the pair must be Dainn and his young brother, Aguti. Hastein had spoken proudly of his sons on many occasions.

It was then that Freydis spotted Bjorn and she gave him a happy wave – just before she realised who was walking with him. Her face registered her shock and confusion as she momentarily stared at Eadwulf before returning her attention to Hastein.

Eadwulf averted his eyes and Bjorn dug him in the ribs with his elbow. 'You can't avoid her until we leave,' he whispered. 'Shall we greet my sister together?'

Bjorn hurried over to Freydis with Eadwulf trailing in his wake. She chatted with her husband and sons as they approached, and Eadwulf could see she was avoiding catching his eye. Bjorn gave her a brotherly hug and turned to speak with Dainn and Aguti, leaving Hastein to break the evident awkwardness felt by his wife and friend.

'Well,' Hastein started, his grinning face moving from one to the other. 'After twelve years I'd have thought the least you two could do was to greet each other.'

'You're right,' Freydis said with a nervous smile as she

held out her hand to Eadwulf. 'Forgive me my bad manners, Eadwulf – or is it Ulf? It's been many years since we saw you in our lands and I'm sure you have much to tell us. So I hope you'll be staying here a little longer than just one night.'

Eadwulf smiled, savouring the feel of her hand in his. 'We'll likely be here for a few days, my lady. As for my name, I am both Eadwulf and Ulf… depending on the company I'm keeping,' he added with a sidelong grin at Hastein. 'Your husband and brother still call me Ulf, and in Mercia, I am Eadwulf.'

'Our friends will be with us until the young man in their company recovers from an arrow wound,' Hastein put in, gesturing to the guests to his hall. Beorhtwulf responded with a raised hand and the little group of four made their way over.

'Jorund!' Freydis exclaimed as the group drew close. She rushed over and flung her arms around him in a welcoming hug before moving back to look him up and down at arm's length. 'I can scarce believe how you've changed… You've filled out perfectly. I think your brother must be feeding you too well.'

Laughter erupted. 'That was my first thought, too, when I arrived in Elston some weeks ago,' Hastein admitted. 'I'm over the shock now, and I can tell you that Jorund has the same knack of getting himself into scrapes as his brother. And if Eadwulf thinks I'll keep their escapades in Cordoba to myself, he's wrong.' He slapped Eadwulf and Jorund on the back. 'But on this occasion I can confirm that those escapades couldn't have been in a better cause.'

Hastein turned to the three strangers and Eadwulf stood back as introductions were made and Freydis fussed over Hamid's wound.

'I'll ask Yrsa to stitch that up for you as soon as we're indoors,' she insisted, as Hamid nodded. 'It looks painful and I fear it will not heal well unless we draw the edges of the gash together. And you've done well to keep it so clean, Ameena,' she added, smiling at the red-haired girl. 'That couldn't have been easy while you were sailing.'

'We had plenty of salt water, Lady Freydis,' Ameena replied, but little to use for bandaging. I used most of the spare cloth we had soon after the injury happened and the blood flow was at its worst.'

Freydis patted Ameena's arm in a knowing gesture. 'I had guessed from the ragged edges of your tunic that was the case. I'd say Hamid is lucky to have you to nurse him.

'I can see I have much to hear from all of you,' Freydis continued, gazing round, and I'm eager to learn about your lives so far away in Iberia. But now, come inside and refresh yourselves with a mug of ale while the meal is set out and Yrsa and I tend Hamid's wound.'

She gestured at the *Eagle's* crewmen, grouped together close by, and grinned at her brother. 'A crew of thirty or so men, I'd say. Not the number we expected to be feeding tonight, but I'm sure we can roast more meat to feed everyone here. Yrsa and I have been baking bread and honey cakes all day with our serving women, so I think we'll have enough of everything else ready prepared.'

'Where *is* Yrsa?' Jorund suddenly blurted. 'I haven't seen her yet.'

Eadwulf had been wondering the same thing himself, but hadn't wanted to interrupt Freydis' flow. He smiled as he watched Freydis pat his brother's arm in a consolatory sort of way, as one would a child.

'You will see your sister very soon, Jorund,' she assured. 'Yrsa offered to stay inside and oversee the cooking while I came out to see what all the fuss was about. And now I know… and how pleased I am to see you all!'

Freydis' gaze momentarily fixed on Eadwulf before she seemed to collect herself and favour them all with a beaming smile. 'Now, I'm sure you'll all relish that mug of ale.'

* * *

Though his face twitched a time or two, Hamid remained silent as Yrsa stitched his gaping wound, his gaze determinedly fixed on the rafters, high in the thatch above. Freydis declared she was truly impressed with his fortitude as she stood by to assist and the young man beamed on hearing her words. His smiles continued as further compliments flowed and Hastein presented him with a new pair of breeks.

Yrsa was overjoyed to see her two half-brothers again and insisted on sitting between the two of them for the meal. As he'd expected, Eadwulf was both surprised and impressed by the way Yrsa had blossomed and was pleased he could see no resemblance to Rorik other than the darker hair and eyes and more rounded chin than Jorund's – which was so like Morwenna's had been.

Eadwulf savoured the freshly cooked food, listening to Yrsa's happy chatter about her life in Ribe. It was obvious she felt relaxed when addressed by Jorund, but a little shy when speaking directly to him. This was only to be expected, he knew. Yrsa would have no memory of her elder half-brother, despite hearing so much about him from others. On their initial meeting, Yrsa's first words to Eadwulf made everyone laugh. 'By Freya, I wish someone had told me Bjorn had a twin!'

As he gazed round the hall, admiring the colourful wall hangings and shields, Eadwulf wondered whether anyone at Ribe had guessed it was he who had sent the loathsome Jarl Rorik to Helheim. As far as he knew, only Bjorn and Leif had known of his intentions to kill the man responsible for his mother's death. But if Bjorn had confided in Hastein, it was possible that Freydis – and perhaps Yrsa – also knew. Rorik had been her father after all, and it was possible she wouldn't view Eadwulf's actions so kindly.

He put such thoughts from his mind, though his eyes constantly strayed to Freydis as she supervised the serving of the meal. Suddenly recalling Bjorn's warning, his attention swung to Hastein sitting diagonally across the table, to be met with a calculating stare that even Eadwulf's smile did not alter.

Alarmed by Hastein's strange reaction, Eadwulf fought the urge to even glance at Freydis as she eventually ordered servants to clear the tables and serve the mead. He took a few sips from one of the drinking horns and passed it along as Beorhtwulf entertained them all with tales of his life in Cordoba.

Pride swelled Eadwulf's chest as his father attributed no praise to himself, but simply described incidents as they happened, as though he were telling any other story. His descriptions of the stifling heat in the quarries and the exquisite designs of the Moorish buildings held them rapt. But his account of life in the emir's palace left all but the youngsters speechless.

At Beorhtwulf's sides, Ameena and Hamid remained silent, sipping their goat's milk, happy to let the confident, older man tell their story and smiling at each other as he embellished tales of their mother and their childhood escapades. Listeners were awed to learn that Hamid was no less than the son of a great emir, and uttered heartfelt condolences on hearing of the plots against the young man's life.

Eadwulf could see how proud of his second family his father was and was annoyed with himself for allowing a tinge of envy to sully his thoughts. After all, he'd found happiness in a strange land himself, amongst those he'd once condemned as his bitter enemies. He, too, had been forced to accept that when the old life has gone forever, the only way to find peace of mind is to embrace what the new one has to offer.

It was nearing midnight as Hastein brought the gathering to a close, his grey gaze sweeping the room. 'It has been a long day, my friends, and we all need to find our beds.' He summoned one of the servants from his task of stacking the trestles. 'Show Jarl Bjorn's men to the byre, Erland,' he said, gesturing to the *Eagle's* weary-looking crew. 'The hayloft is large enough for at least thirty to sleep soundly without being kicked in the groin by someone snoring next to them.

'I can offer you, my friends, the comfort of my hall,' Hastein continued, addressing Bjorn and Eadwulf and their Iberian guests. 'We have several unused sleeping areas along our walls. But I must apologise for having no spare sleeping chamber available for you, Ameena. I know you are used to privacy.'

'I am happy to sleep in your warm hall, Lord Hastein, close to my father and three brothers,' Ameena replied, smiling at her two recently found siblings. 'After sleeping on the ship, any bed will seem perfect.'

'Then that's settled. Some of the women will bring furs, or woollen blankets, if you prefer, then we can all get some much-needed sleep.'

* * *

Surrounded by his newly united family, the next few days at Hastein's hall passed pleasantly for Eadwulf. Hamid's thigh showed every sign of healing and the pain was gradually lessening. He even managed to limp around unaided well enough, though Ameena was never far from his side. And, surprisingly to Eadwulf, nor was Yrsa. His young half-sister seemed to have taken Hamid's recovery as a personal task.

Being so close to Freydis, yet unable to even smile at her too often or for too long, let alone show his feelings, took every shred of Eadwulf's willpower. But Bjorn's warning resounded inside his head, as did the look on Hastein's face on the night of their arrival at his hall. Eadwulf had no intention of jeopardising the friendship of a man he'd both admired and respected for so long. So all he could do was snatch glances at her as she worked, or casually speak to her when they were part of a group. He was surprised one afternoon to catch Yrsa staring at him as he replied to Freydis's question regarding the day of their leaving. The expression on his half-sister's face resembled the one he'd seen on Hastein's.

The crew of the *Sea Eagle* had taken themselves into Ribe, with Leif along to keep an eye on them and instructions from Bjorn to be back ready to sail in four days' time. After all, Bjorn had explained to Eadwulf, the men deserved some time to themselves to enjoy the port's ale houses and brothels before setting off across the Northern Sea.

Beorhtwulf was generally content to sit in the hall during those days, chatting with whoever was around. He was especially fond of listening to Jorund's childhood memories of Morwenna. Eadwulf had been prepared for this, and had warned both Jorund and Yrsa never to divulge the manner of their mother's death. It would serve no purpose other than to distress the ageing man; best he believed the wife he'd loved had died of illness. Bjorn had repeated a similar request to Freydis, who readily agreed with the wisdom of hiding the awful truth.

On the day before the men were due back from Ribe, Hastein and Bjorn joined Beorhtwulf and Hamid around the hearth, leaving Eadwulf and Jorund to finish their game of *hnefatafl*. Ameena had joined the women, keen to help in the preparation of the evening meal and continue chatting to her new friends, Freydis and Yrsa. During conversation, Hamid asked about the role of a Danish jarl.

Hastein was happy to explain the complexities of responsibility, allegiance and loyalty involved in his position, as well as his role as priest and upholder of the law. Hamid listened intently, at times nodding, at others showing surprise. 'In my country, the emir's word is absolute,' he said. 'His people must obey his commands or they are punished. Some of our emirs have been wise and generous and did much to improve the living conditions of their subjects, but others have thought only of amassing wealth for themselves.'

Hamid was quiet for some moments and Eadwulf could see his thoughts were on his homeland and the life he'd been forced to leave behind.

'My father, Muhammad, is not the wisest of emirs we have had, but by no means is he the worst. He has brought justice to our lands, as Lord Beorhtwulf can testify, and done much to stop wanton killing and thieving going unpunished. He demands loyalty from his people, just as do you, Hastein – and you, Bjorn – but he feels little need to care for their welfare. Yet, in many ways he's made al-Andalus a better and safer place for those people to live in than it had been during the reign of his father before him. Muhammad has also made the country more beautiful than ever; the many new buildings in cities like Cordoba and Seville will be marvelled at by countless generations to come…

'But his treatment of traitors will also be remembered – and probably condemned – for a long, long time. His crucifixions have become the most feared things in the whole of al-Andalus.'

'Well said, Hamid,' Beorhtwulf remarked, patting the young man's arm, 'but remember, your father's crucifixions are only for those who betray their country – or their religion.' Beorhtwulf shuddered, evidently realising what he'd just said. He glanced at Eadwulf, the shared look imparting all. If they'd been caught fleeing from Cordoba, Emir Muhammad would have had them all crucified upside down, including Hamid, his own bastard son.

A short discussion about the Islamic faith followed, and it

was clear to Eadwulf that Hamid was a true believer.

'Well, Hamid,' Hastein said as the conversation drew to an end, 'we have many gods in our lands, but I understand that different peoples each have their own.' He turned his attention to Beorhtwulf. 'I realise, too, my lord, that you were once a believer in the Christ-god. But I won't pry into your beliefs now, after so long in Iberia. It's no business of mine, and tomorrow you'll be sailing back to your own lands. I can't imagine the feelings you have about that.'

Beorhtwulf nodded and smiled but gave nothing away, and Hastein did not push for an answer.

'And now, my friends,' the Ribean jarl declared, turning to include Eadwulf, Jorund and Ameena in his address, 'we have time to take a look at my lands before the men return, if you wish. It will give you some idea of the area under my control.'

Ameena was the first to reply. 'I would love to see your lands, Lord Hastein, and I thank you for inviting me. It's been too long since I rode anywhere. Besides,' she added with an impish grin, 'someone has to make sure Hamid doesn't fall off his horse.'

Everyone chuckled at Hamid's feeble protestations and Hastein turned to his cousin. 'I imagine you and Ulf would prefer to stay and check over the *Eagle* before you sail?'

'I'm not sure Jorund needs to ride out, either,' Bjorn replied, flashing a grin at Eadwulf's brother. 'As far as I can see, your lands haven't changed much since Ulf was last here, let alone Jorund…

'But you may well enjoy the ride out, Jorund, and Ulf can check out the ship with me.'

'I'd like to go,' Jorund replied, 'if only to impress my father with my riding skills.'

Once the laughter had died down the group of four headed to the stables with Hastein, and Bjorn fixed serious green eyes on Eadwulf. 'I'm heading to the river in order to give you time to talk to Freydis. I've no idea what she's planned for the rest of the day, so it will be up to you to pick your time. Just don't leave it too late – and don't do anything that could harm my cousin in any way.'

Eadwulf stayed in his seat, finishing his ale while watching Freydis and Yrsa from the corner of his eye. He also realised that both women were only too aware of his presence and caught their eyes on him on several occasions. It wasn't long before he noticed Yrsa gesture to Freydis, tilting her head first at him, then at the oaken door.

'I'd best get into the fireroom now,' she said. 'I'll take the women with me to prepare the vegetables for the soup. And if you've a spare moment, Freydis, we could do with another sack of onions fetching from the store.'

'Then I'll probably need someone to help carry it,' Freydis replied, flashing Yrsa a look that Eadwulf could only interpret as one of appreciation mingled with humour.

'You'll carry the sack for Freydis, won't you, brother?' Yrsa called over to him. 'She can show you where the vegetables are stored, if you'd be kind enough to provide the necessary muscle.'

'My muscles are at your command,' Eadwulf said, flexing his biceps, which set the women giggling as he headed for the door.

Yrsa disappeared into the fireroom with the women and Eadwulf escorted Freydis towards the wattle and daub hut behind the towering byre. It was agony being so close to her and his tongue suddenly felt as though it were tied up in knots. Freydis, too, was silent and stared down at her feet as they walked.

The shutters of the single window in the large hut were open, throwing afternoon light on the many sacks and jars that held produce from the land and spices acquired from the market at nearby Ribe. Freydis knew exactly where to look, and headed over to a corner, from which the pungent aroma of garlic and onions emanated as they neared. Suddenly she turned to face him and he could see her eyes were moist with unshed tears.

'Now we're alone together, I find I don't know what to say,' she whispered, echoing Eadwulf's thoughts. 'I've pondered on the words I'd use so many times over the years, hoping and praying I'd see you again before we both left Midgard.'

Emotion swelled Eadwulf's throat. 'I've never forgotten you, Freydis, not for a single moment. I loved Leoflaed, and grieved for many months after her death; a better wife and mother would be hard to find. But I married her knowing I could never have you. You've always held my heart, and always will.'

'Hold me, Eadwulf,' Freydis begged, taking his hand and stepping well away from the open window. 'The memory of your embrace will bring me great comfort when we are far apart again. I hardly dared hope you still cared for me. I have never stopped loving you, either, no matter how good a husband Hastein has been.'

She reached up to touch his cheek and Eadwulf pulled her close. Their kiss held insatiable fervour, tinged with the urgency of the snatched moment and the sadness of the hopelessness of their abiding love. Tears ran down their cheeks as they clung to each other as though they would never let go. Eadwulf drank in the scent of her hair, a scent he'd never forgotten, basking in the sensations aroused by her body next to his.

But Freydis was still Hastein's wife, and he duly pulled away, taking her hands and gazing into her eyes from arm's length. 'I've dreamt about having you in my arms for so long, Freydis, but have always known we could share no more than a loving embrace. The memories of just holding you will stay with me as I carry on my life back in Mercia.'

Freydis gave a wan smile. 'Our embrace is more than I could have hoped for, dear one. Knowing you still love me has given me reason to hope.'

Eadwulf squeezed his eyes shut as emotion welled anew. Though unwilling to destroy her dreams, he could only accept the hopelessness of them himself. Whilst Freydis was still married to Hastein, it would never be possible for them to be together.

'I truly believe Hastein does not love me any more,' she continued, her voice holding a strange combination of sadness and resignation. Eadwulf stiffened, amazed by such an assertion. Wasn't it the look of a suspicious or even a jealous husband he'd seen in Hastein's face the other night? Hastein had always loved Freydis dearly, so what could have caused such a change of heart?

'Hastein hasn't yet suggested divorce,' Freydis continued,

'and I've no grounds on which to demand divorce from him. He is still respectful, and he loves our sons very much, but, when we are alone he has become cold and distant toward me. And there's something else… He has taken to listening to the teachings of Ansgar and –'

'The Christian preacher! That's hard to imagine after all the times he and Bjorn have teased me about the Christ-god of my people.'

'I was shocked at first, too,' Freydis confessed. 'But he's become almost obsessed by the idea of bringing peace and love to his fellow countrymen. Ansgar died seven years ago, of course, but his followers try desperately to keep his teachings going. Though I fear they're fighting a losing battle in these lands. The Christ-god finds little favour with true followers of our own gods. I, for one, could never forsake my faith in Freya. It has brought great comfort to me over the years.'

'So, are you saying that Hastein's newfound beliefs might make him release you from your wedding vows?'

'I'm not sure what I believe, Eadwulf, but he's hinted at sailing to the northern lands to take the teachings of the Christ to the Norwegians. Only days before he sailed on this venture with Bjorn, he laughingly mentioned that our lives seemed to have taken separate paths. He even hinted that we'd both be better going our separate ways. How that could be possible, I really don't know. I could never stay in this hall if Hastein divorced me, though I'm sure Bjorn wouldn't object to me and our sons living at Aros…

'So you see, my love, there is a glimmer of hope for us yet, though how far into the future that may be remains to be seen. And, when all's said and done, I doubt you'll still want me when I'm old and stooped.'

Eadwulf pulled her close for one last emotional embrace. 'You forget, Freydis, I'll be old and stooped too.' And on that cheerful note, he threw the sack of onions over his shoulder and they headed back to the hall.

'What does Yrsa believe about us?' Eadwulf asked as they walked. 'She gave me a strange look the other day when she caught me watching you, a little like Hastein did at that first meal we shared. And just now, she deliberately set this situation up, didn't she?'

Freydis gave a small sigh. 'I think Yrsa realised how I felt about you some years ago, when she heard me talking in my sleep. I tried to convince her it was no more than a troubled dream about the day you saved Ubbi from drowning, and I thought she'd believed me. Though I know I've called out in my dreams many times since then. It wakes me up, you see. So it is likely that Hastein has heard me, too. He's said nothing, of course, though it must have caused him distress at the time.

'As for this "situation", as you call it, Yrsa's been telling me since you arrived that you and I need to talk, alone. Perhaps she thinks it will help us put our past behind us. Or perhaps, knowing of Hastein's plans to go preaching, she senses that divorce could be the outcome of that, leaving me free to be with you.'

They said no more, but Freydis's words bounced inside Eadwulf's head. That small ray of hope would warm his heart throughout the months – perhaps years – to come, as he trudged the path he knew he was destined to follow.

Nine

Elston, Mercia: late July 871

Bjorn and his crew stayed overnight at Elston and shared the happy reunions and greetings of new acquaintances. Aethelnoth was overjoyed to see Beorhtwulf again and greeted Hamid and Ameena with a mixture of amazement and delight. Eadwulf's two children – Aethelred, a strapping lad of almost ten, and five-year-old Leofwynn – were simply nonplussed by it all, although Aethelred was overawed to meet his newfound grandfather who had once been King of Mercia. Little Leofwynn was shy of the strangers at first and hid behind Odella, who was now blossoming in the advanced months of her pregnancy. But the child soon responded to the fuss made over her by Jorund, as well as her new aunt, Ameena.

For Eadwulf the homecoming brought both happiness and pride: the enormous joy at being with his children and friends again and great pride in their achievements in finding Beorhtwulf.

His fondness and respect for Bjorn, and the gratitude he owed him for making the venture possible, would never die. Yet beneath it all, the feeling of sadness at leaving Freydis and Yrsa behind was lodged resolutely in his heart, where he knew it would stay for a long, long time.

The following morning, fond farewells were made to Bjorn and Leif and the rest of the *Eagle's* crew, who had all done their best to help Eadwulf and Jorund in Cordoba. With promises to visit again in the not-too-distant future, the *Sea Eagle* pulled away from the banks of the Trent to begin its homeward journey, first towards the Humber estuary before continuing north-east across the Northern Sea to the Danish lands.

Once again the emptiness of loss gripped Eadwulf's chest. So much of what he loved and admired would be across that wide grey sea, perhaps for years to come.

In the mid-afternoon, he and Jorund accompanied Beorhtwulf, Hamid and Ameena on a ride out to view the land over which Eadwulf was ealdorman. Whilst Jorund chatted to the younger man and woman about trading ships that sailed upriver to Nottingham, Eadwulf focused his attentions on Beorhtwulf.

'I hope you'll find peace in our hall, Father, and not miss your big stone house in Cordoba. It's a long time since you lived in a wooden hall and it could take a while for you to get used to it again. The three of you will probably find Mercian winters hard, too.'

'Believe me, winters in parts of al-Andalus can be very cold, especially in the mountains, deep inland. We get used to extremes between summer and winter down there. I'm relieved to be able to enjoy a pleasantly warm summer in Mercia instead of dripping away in Cordoba.'

They both laughed at that and Beorhtwulf went on, 'As for your hall, I'll be more than content, and equally happy to be of use to you around your lands. And just knowing I'm in my beloved Mercia, with the family I didn't know I had until a few weeks ago, means more to me than I can say. All those years I'd thought you dead, Eadwulf…'

'As I did you, Father, and if not for Bjorn, we'd both be thinking that still.'

Jorund and the two others raced ahead, allowing their horses to stretch their legs in a good gallop, and Eadwulf pointed out villages, woodlands and fields of corn ripening in the August sun. Soon the harvest would be upon them.

As yet, neither of them had broached the subject of Burgred. It had been on the tip of Eadwulf's tongue when Beorhtwulf said, 'What are your plans for killing my treacherous brother?'

Taken aback by the directness of the question, Eadwulf gawked at him before replying, 'I aim to make another attempt as soon as I've been back here long enough to find out where he is. It would suit me best if he were to come up to Nottingham again, or perhaps Tamworth or Stamford. Any of his northerly estates would be good, and preferably not with the Wessex king in tow this time.'

Beorhtwulf nodded. 'I agree, but now I need to ask you something. I never thought I'd see the day when I'd be saying this, Eadwulf, but I want to be with you when Burgred dies. I realise I wouldn't have a chance of killing him myself in any one-to-one, whereas you are young and strong. I doubt many warriors could best you in a fight. But I want to see you overpower and humiliate the cur. Then I want to be the one to plunge my sword through his black heart. Or perhaps we could both plunge our swords in together.'

Eadwulf was silent for some moments as he thought about that. For so many years he'd visualised himself alone being the one to put an end to Burgred miserable existence. Would revenge feel less satisfying if shared with someone else? Deep down, he knew his father's grievances against Burgred were just as great as his own, if not more so.

But there were the practicalities of working together to consider. Moving about unseen in a city would not be so easy with an old man by his side. But on the other hand, helping a rickety old man to move around may well throw suspicion away.

'I understand how you must long to do that,' he said, at length, 'and when the time comes we need to make our plans very carefully. But right now, I need to spend some time finding out what the situation is in Wessex. From what Aethelnoth tells me, King Alfred paid the Danes to leave his kingdom. So what I want to know is where they'll be moving to from there. If it's back to Northumbria or the East Angle lands, we may have a chance to move in on Burgred. But if the Danes head back into Mercia in the hope that Burgred will pay them geld again, we probably won't have a chance for some time.'

Ten

Worcester, Mercia: Early November 871

Burgred was at howling point. 'Curses on Wessex!' he shrieked at a handful of his councillors as they sat around a table at his Worcester hall. The meeting had been called once news had flooded in that the Danes were back in Mercia and aimed to make their new base in London. He rubbed his throbbing brow, taking some moments to calm himself before continuing. 'The Danes' return can mean only one thing. The snivelling boy-king, Alfred, has paid to get rid of them. And I wouldn't be surprised to hear it was him who'd suggested they move back to Mercia.'

Councillors glanced at each other, their unease at such unproven, accusatory talk apparent, and the spokesman of the group, Ealdorman Irwyn, spoke up. 'My lord, paying tribute to be rid of invaders is the obvious answer for any kingdom's leaders. Didn't we do exactly the same at Nottingham?' He held out his upturned hands with a tilt of his head to accentuate his question. 'But as to the accusations you direct at Alfred of Wessex, I believe I speak for all Council members when I say we cannot accept them as truth. Danish leaders are clever enough to decide for themselves which kingdom will offer them the best pickings.'

Burgred glowered at the ageing man, knowing him to be the wisest of his advisors, but livid with him for the implications embedded in his words. Grudgingly, he admitted to himself that openly blaming Alfred would not help their plight. The Danes were already here, and he was helpless to stop them taking over Mercia. His kingdom would have great difficulty in finding tribute to buy peace for a second time, and he couldn't go grovelling to Wessex for help as he'd done once before at Nottingham. After his own refusal to give aid to Wessex in her time of need, Mercia must stand on her own. Even sending Aethelswith to plead with her snivelling brother for help was out of the question.

He closed his eyes in an effort to ease his pounding head, opening them abruptly when Ealdorman Irwyn coughed.

'My lord, it is the Council's opinion that we meet with the Norse leaders and negotiate terms by which Mercia can remain at peace while they are here.'

'How in blazes can we do that when we have no coin to bargain with?'

'For all we know, my lord, the pagan horde may simply wish to remain in Mercia for a while before moving elsewhere for more lucrative takings. Although, I fear that may be wishful thinking on my behalf.' He gestured round the nodding councillors. 'We're all more inclined to suggest that we make every effort to obtain coin. Our people would surely prefer to be poor and alive than wealthy and dead!'

Burgred nodded, loath to pursue this discussion further. He knew full well that the vast army of Norsemen would not leave Mercia without further tribute. Nor would they leave his kingdom unscathed, no matter how short a time they stayed. Just to keep the pagans fed and housed would tear into Mercia's resources far more than it could afford. And how many

Mercians would die, protecting their wives and families from lust-filled, pillaging Vikings? Not that he'd lose sleep over the fate of the lowborn ceorls, but he had his abbeys, monasteries and noblemen's estates to consider.

'We wait for a demand for a meeting from one of their so-called "kings"', Burgred threw over his shoulder as he headed for the door. 'Then we'll do our best to negotiate the easiest terms for Mercia. In the meantime, I suggest you come up with some ideas regarding how in God's name we can squeeze more coin from our dutiful subjects.'

'My lord, my suggestion is that we follow the lead of King Alfred. When he found himself in this same position, it was largely to his bishops he turned.'

Burgred hovered in the doorway, scowling. The thought of finding anything praiseworthy about his wife's upstart brother always set his temper off. But on this occasion, he was clutching at straws when it came to raising further tribute, and he nodded at Irwyn to continue.

'We should first try visiting the bishops, and while we're here in Worcester, Bishop Waerferth would be a good starting point. You could call on him yourself while we travel out to other clerics in the kingdom.'

Burgred nodded, considering the idea.

'I'm told King Alfred insisted his bishops and abbots should cede church land back to him in return for his paying their share of the tribute. Oh, the Wessex clergy protested fiercely at the idea of losing land to pay the pagans off – as, no doubt, our Mercian clerics will do – but since their king insisted, they had no choice in the matter. There's enough coin in our coffers to cover such a move, and I can't see us needing it for anything as vital as this.

'Think on it, my lord.'

Burgred needed no time to think about the proposal. He had no choice in the matter, either.

* * *

London, Mercia: Mid-March 872

Guthrum threw back his head and roared, his laughter causing the warriors in the London hall to chortle along with him. They didn't need to ask what he found so funny. On the table before him, mounds of Mercian silver gleamed in the light of the blazing hearthfire.

At Guthrum's side Halfdan shared the jovial mood. 'It seems Burgred's got a better hold over his people than that upstart in Wessex,' he said. 'It took Alfred months to collect what the Mercian's have managed in a few weeks.'

'Likely because Burgred's terrified of what we'll do to him if he didn't pay up.' Guthrum's bitter sneer was enough to silence the hall. 'He's not a man I could trust, I'll tell you that. He's a shifty-eyed sycophant… His pathetic grovelling would shame his own mother. He couldn't look me in the eye for more than a few seconds when he spoke to me.'

Halfdan grunted. 'I'd say that'll make things easier for us. A coward like him will give in to our demands for geld without trying to haggle for less – or a later date of payment, as Alfred did. Perhaps we could even leave Burgred as "king" once we've secured our hold over his kingdom – on our terms and with our men to make sure there's no treachery.'

'Let's just see how things go over the summer, Halfdan. By next winter we'll demand more tribute, and see how quickly Burgred comes up with it then. Now that Wessex king, Alfred, young as he is, he locked his eyes with mine and I'll tell you this. I could feel him weighing me up as much as I was doing to him.

'And I'll tell you something else,' Guthrum added, 'we'll be coming up against him a lot more in the years to come. Alfred knows we won't stop until we've conquered his kingdom as well as we do. But I've a feeling that taking Wessex isn't going to be easy.'

Four weeks later, three Danes arrived in London after a gruelling five-day ride from the Northumbrian city of York, a journey of two hundred and ten miles. The leaders of the Norse army ensconced in the London hall erupted at what they had to say.

'The Northumbrians have done *what*!' Halfdan shrieked, surging to his feet, his expression thunderous. 'And where were the men we left in charge up there while they were doing it? Well…? *You* explain,' he demanded, stabbing his finger at the chest of the nearest man.

The messenger squared his shoulders and looked levelly at Halfdan. 'The Northumbrians are devious bastards and must have been organising a rebellion for months. We got no wind of it until a two hundred strong army was heading for York. The pathetic puppet king, Ecgberht, and Archbishop Wulfhere fled the city before they were slaughtered. Last thing we heard, they were heading south.'

'I expect our men eventually put an end to the uprising?' Guthrum cut in before Halfdan could rant further.

'We caught some of the Northumbrian scum, lord, and they paid dearly for their actions. But over half of them fled back into the forests and will doubtless be gathering more men as we speak.'

The messenger turned to face Halfdan. 'As for your question, Lord Halfdan, our men are always on the lookout for signs of rebellion, but in the villages and towns, all is generally quiet. These rebels must meet out in the wilds, probably at night, where we cannot see or hear them.'

Halfdan took a deep breath to calm his rising temper. 'So are you here now just to inform us of events?'

'No, lord,' the same messenger responded. 'We've come for help. If the uprising's going to be as big as we think, we've nowhere near enough men to stop it. Many of the Northumbrians we'd thought were working with us to keep the rest of the dogs in their place turned out to be some of the ringleaders.'

'Then there's only one thing we can do,' Guthrum said. 'We head north at first light tomorrow.'

'What, all of us? If we all head back to Northumbria, it'll give the Mercians time to get their armies together, maybe bring in help from Wessex. We may not take this kingdom so easily a third time.'

Guthrum grinned. 'I doubt Burgred would even think of that. He'll be too worried not knowing what we're doing up in the north of his own kingdom. No, Halfdan, we won't be leaving Mercia for long for some time yet.'

Halfdan had no idea what Guthrum was talking about, but he nodded. He'd only make himself look more of a fool by admitting he didn't understand this new idea.

* * *

April was drawing to a close when the Great Norse Army left London, intent on stamping out the Northumbrian revolt. Almost half the men rode north along the old Roman road of Ermine Street, the rest sailing their ships out of the Thames and heading north towards the Humber estuary. From there they would veer inland along the Trent to meet up with their comrades at a place proposed by Guthrum.

Halfdan's mood was light as he rode. The spring weather was fine and bright and he savoured the time he could spend delving into his thoughts. Though he missed Ivar's strict command of the men, he and Guthrum had achieved much over the past year. Their hold over Mercia was something to be proud of, and despite not yet having gained control of Wessex, the fact that King Alfred had been reduced to paying them off was a sign that the kingdom would be ready for the picking within a year or so. Until that time, once they had re-established their hold on the Northumbrians, they had Mercia to play with.

News that the Great Army had left London for Northumbria would soon reach Burgred. Halfdan smiled as he thought of the look of relief that would spread across the sycophant's face. The look of anguish that would replace it a few days later made him laugh out loud.

Riding at his side at the head of their army, Guthrum

flashed him a puzzled look. 'Do you find the idea of a long ride funny, Halfdan? I'll feel happier once we get there.'

'No, the ride is something we have to do, like it or not. I'm just amusing myself with thoughts of that grovelling king's face when he realises we're still in Mercia. I just hope we can find a well-placed base.'

Guthrum grunted. 'A few villages in the north of this kingdom are close enough to Northumbria to provide us with a suitable base. From any of them we could move out and put an end to this revolt – without losing our hold over Mercia. But the town we're heading to sounds ideal. It's right on the northern edge of Mercia, and before you ask, it couldn't be better placed for waterways. It sits on the banks of the Mercian river, the Trent, before it flows into the Humber and out to the Northern Sea. And once we're on the Humber, we also have a clear route to York along the River Ouse.

Halfdan nodded. Guthrum was not telling him anything he didn't already know about the settlements and rivers of this region.

'Not only that,' Guthrum went on, 'this town happens to be at a point where the old Roman canal, the Fosse Dyke, meets the Trent. That's an added bonus when we consider that the canal links the Trent with the Witham – which flows obligingly all the way to East Anglia before heading out to the Northern Sea. Another route home if we need it…'

Guthrum shifted in his saddle, his brow creased in thought. 'If the East Angles get ideas about rebellion once they hear the news from Northumbria, we could have another uprising on our hands. In which case–'

'The Witham could prove a quick route down there for us. Yes, that's all plain enough,' Halfdan snapped, annoyed at not having been involved in the decision making for the choice of base. 'So has this town we're heading for got a name?'

'Torksey,' Guthrum relied. 'Which is where I've told our men to moor the ships.'

* * *

In the early afternoon in the first week of May, Burgred had some unwelcome visitors. With an escort of only four men, the fleeing Ecgberht, the Norse army's puppet-king of Northumbria, and his fellow-countryman, Archbishop Wulfhere, arrived at Worcester, weary of riding and desperately seeking shelter.

Aethelswith ordered servants to bring food and wine and seated herself with her daughter, Mildrede, at an inconspicuous corner table as Burgred requested the reason for the impromptu visit.

As Aethelswith had expected, her husband was in no mood to be burdened with other people's problems and only half-listened while Ecgberht and the archbishop relayed the story of their flight from York. 'You must realise, my lords,' Burgred responded, his irritation evident, 'that Mercia is in no position to help you. Northumbria must deal with her own problems. You will, of course, stay with us and rest overnight; as you see, we have space in here to offer all six of you beds. But tomorrow I suggest you ride on to the Wessex court at Winchester. King Alfred's kingdom is not presently overrun with Danes, and is in a better position to offer you sanctuary than we are.'

As the hall quietened and stilled for the night and Aethelswith and her husband headed for their separate sleeping chambers, Burgred surprised her by sharing his thoughts.

'I've had time to think this request for shelter through and realise I was too hasty in my refusal. I now believe that welcoming these two men into our hall could prove my own loyalty to the Norsemen's cause. I imagine their leaders will be pleased with such thoughtfulness on their behalf. After all, Ecgberht and Wulfhere were chosen by them to rule over Northumbria in their stead, and it isn't *Danes* these two men are fleeing from but their own countrymen. I'm hopeful that my actions will encourage Guthrum and Halfdan to overlook the need to demand more tribute from Mercia.'

Aethelswith stared at her loathsome husband as he turned away, grinning like a simpleton. Offering the men shelter was the courteous thing to do, and she could find no fault in that. But if Burgred seriously thought the Danes could be so easily impressed, he was a bigger fool than she'd realised during the nineteen years of their miserable marriage.

* * *

The Norse army quickly made Torksey its own and by the middle of May, a vast encampment spread out across Mercian land. Villagers in the region too slow or unable to flee were shown no mercy. Those few spared were forced into thralldom, most of them women who were degraded and humiliated as warriors' satisfied their lust. All soon wished they had died with the rest.

Within a week of establishing themselves in their new base, the Norse leaders were keen to deal with the Northumbrian rebels, and as the next day dawned, over half of the vast Norse army under Halfdan and Oscetel's leadership, rode out for York. Guthrum and Anwend remained at Torksey with the rest of the men to hold the Mercian region in check.

Halfdan relished the sight of the Northumbrian scum attempting to flee from their path as they rode. Hearing their screams as his warriors torched their hovels and cut down anyone within their reach helped to satisfy his overwhelming need to wreak revenge on the kingdom that had dared to rebel against Danish rule. And once the Great Army reached York, this kingdom would be given a lesson it would never forget on what Danish wrath really looked like.

Then they'd head back to Mercia and drive that message home to the snivelling Burgred.

* * *

It was September by the time Burgred received news of the Danes' success in putting down the Northumbrian rebellion. The Mercian court was at Tamworth when the small group of riders arrived. It seemed the news had simply travelled by word of mouth, and a local thegn had taken it upon himself to ensure his king was aware of events.

'The Danes were merciless to anyone involved in the revolt, no matter how small a part they played,' Sweyn said, bowing before Burgred, who was downing his third mug of ale of the morning. 'Many in the rebel army met their end during the conflict, and most of those who fled were rounded up and dealt with later. But it wasn't an easy task for the Danes. It took many weeks to root out the rebels from their hideouts in the hills and forests. In the end Halfdan decided those still at large wouldn't dare risk a second uprising when news of the executions reached them.'

'Go on,' Burgred ordered, putting his ale mug down. He was impatient to hear the rest and what it would mean for himself and Mercia.

'Thirty of the captured rebels were beheaded, my lord, just chosen randomly as a warning to the Northumbrians of the consequences of defying Danish control. Thankfully, only three of their leaders suffered the blood eagle. At least most of the deaths were quick.'

'A godsend indeed,' Burgred murmured, his mind on his own position in Mercia. 'Did anything relating to the Danes' intentions for Northumbria travel with this news? I mean, do they intend to reinstate King Ecgberht here to the throne?' He gestured at the pasty-faced old man, silent beside the younger Archbishop Wulfhere further along the table. 'And do we assume the Norse army will now be at least overwintering in Northumbria to ensure the kingdom is securely theirs this time?'

'We heard nothing of their plans for the future of Northumbria, or Mercia, lord. But they do intend to move back to Torksey for the winter. If we hear anything else, I'll be certain to ride here to make sure you know.'

Burgred withdrew into his black thoughts, leaving Aethelswith to arrange refreshment for the good-natured thegn before he rode back to his hall. News of the entire Danish army being back in Mercia was the last thing he'd wanted to hear.

Eleven

Mercia: March - September 873

Burgred spent the rest of the winter in a state of constant agitation, which intensified as rumours from the north began to increase with the onset of March. News now confirmed that the Danes had regained full control of Northumbria, and their leaders expected to reinstate King Ecgberht and Archbishop Wulfhere to their former roles once spring arrived.

Not that Burgred would be sorry to see the backs of these two whinging Northumbrians. He couldn't stand the sanctimonious, god-fearing Wulfhere, nor could he take much more of the ailing old king. The man had looked close to death since he'd arrived last May, but now he had actually taken to his bed. Physicians declared the old king's lungs would not hold out much longer and he would soon leave this world. And when that happened, Burgred could only hope that Halfdan and Guthrum would not hold him responsible.

Now at his Nottingham manor for the approaching Eastertide, Burgred's dread of a demand for more tribute resulted in sleepless nights and days spent in an ale-filled daze. He knew too well that even his abbots and bishops would struggle to provide more silver so soon after the last time, and most of his thegns had already been bled almost dry.

He downed a few more mouthfuls of ale and massaged his pounding temples, aware of his wife's scornful eyes on him.

"I know what you're thinking, woman, so don't bother to

say it!' Burgred yelled, unable to bear hearing her repeat what she'd thrown at him many times before. He already regretted failing to honour his alliance with Wessex. Together, Mercia and Wessex could have stood a chance of withstanding the heathen army. Too late now… Mercia was no longer his to control.

He watched in silence as Aethelswith shook her head with a look of utter disdain on her face before she turned and headed to her room with Mildrede.

* * *

In the middle of May, Burgred's fears became reality when a group of Danes arrived at Nottingham demanding another huge payment of geld. The frantic task of collecting it took almost three months, the effort almost bringing Burgred to a state of collapse. His only consolation was that Guthrum and Halfdan allowed him to remain as king, albeit in name only. Nor did they blame him for Ecgberht's death, simply sending word to their men in Northumbria to replace the old man with another as compliant as he had been. News filtered back that a thegn by the name of Ricsige had been selected.

But, in mid- September, barely a month after the tribute had been handed over and a further peace treaty negotiated, Burgred was dealt a further unexpected blow. The Great Army left their camp at Torksey and sailed up the Trent, past Nottingham under his very nose, and seized the town of Repton, some twenty-six miles to the south-west, and in the very heartlands of Mercia.

Burgred finally accepted that no amount of tribute would ever be enough to keep the Danes from taking whatever they wanted from his kingdom. His kingship meant nothing. His shrieked profanities rang round the Nottingham hall and his advisors had a hard time calming him. His face glowed red with outrage, fuelled by the many cups of ale he'd been downing all day. 'How could they do this to me when we've only just paid more geld! We're finished. Mercia's finished. Our sacred city is in their greedy clutches.'

'That is surely the greatest of blows to our kingdom, my lord,' Ealdorman Irwyn agreed, voicing the opinion shared by the dozen advisors present. 'The church of Saint Wynstan is Mercia's most sacred shrine, the burial place of our kings since the days of the mighty Offa. I fear the heathens will desecrate the crypt and raze the church, and they'll undoubtedly sack the rest of the town. May God have mercy on the townsfolk.'

Burgred hung his head in shame and despair as he listened to his own fears put into words. Repton would have been his burial place, too. But there was nothing he could do to change a thing. Nothing he had done in his entire life had ever turned out the way he'd planned.

* * *

'This isn't somewhere I'd choose to linger in for long,' Guthrum grumbled as he and Halfdan inspected the eerie crypt beneath the stone floor of the Repton church. Light from a couple of torches carried amidst their men cast wraithlike shadows across the cavities in the walls of the dark chamber, in which rested the ancient burial caskets. 'I can feel the spirits of the dead watching us, condemning us for disturbing their sacred place.'

Halfdan guffawed to hide his own sense of unease, pleased that he hadn't been the one to voice those thoughts. Though not yet the end of September, down here it seemed like mid-January and he sensed the presence of spirits as much as Guthrum did. But it felt good to throw scorn on the usually well-composed man.

The half-dozen men accompanying them joined in the laughter, although Halfdan was well aware of their nervousness, too. He'd noted their wide-eyed faces as they'd entered the realm of the long-buried dead and tried to hide his own telling face from the torchlight's glare. 'I feel only the need to wreck this Christian shrine,' he crowed. 'It'd show these pig-faced Mercians what our Norse gods think of the weak, people-loving Christ-god.'

'Not a good idea to do that…' Guthrum said, shaking his head and climbing back up the steps to the daylight of the church. 'We had little trouble taking this town, but if we desecrate the people's sacred mausoleum, we'll be facing confrontation. And no matter how feeble their forces may be, I'd prefer not to risk losing any more of our men. Besides,' he added, his hand swinging out to the town beyond St Wynstan's stone walls, 'tomorrow we need the men to start digging ditches and building fortifications. I won't feel safe in my bed until Repton is impregnable to outside forces.'

Halfdan shrugged, realising that Guthrum had a point, but unwilling to say so. 'So far, Mercia has been the easiest of these kingdoms to take,' he said, 'and we can thank the snivelling king, Burgred, for that. A blind man would make a stronger leader. But Northumbria wasn't much different to start with, thanks to that pathetic war between those two rival kings. Yet three years later, there are Northumbrians who refuse to bow to our command and continuously plot against us. I can tell you, Guthrum, we haven't seen the last revolt up there. And we can't risk them gaining the upper hand a second time…

'Then there's still Wessex to be conquered,' Halfdan went on. 'The Saxons have given us a rough ride so far, and it's a long way from being over yet. Once all's settled in Mercia, our army needs to take Wessex.'

'I need no reminder about Wessex, or the determination of its young king,' Guthrum growled, momentarily glaring at Halfdan. 'We'll deal with Wessex once I'm satisfied Mercia is well and truly docile – which, with an ale-sop like Burgred as her king, shouldn't be too far in the future. Whatever we demand, Burgred meekly complies. But you're right, if our conquest of these lands is to be total, we must take Wessex.'

He paused, a frown crinkling his brow. 'You think it likely the Northumbrians will rebel again? Our punishments were not severe enough, perhaps?'

'Could be that, or it may just be there are still a lot of free men willing to try their luck against us. Whatever, I intend to make sure they don't get that chance. Any hint of rebellion will be gouged out before it has chance to fester further.'

'Guthrum nodded as understanding dawned. 'You're going back up there?'

Halfdan grunted. 'And I'll be taking my army, or what's left of it. Of the thousands of men who came over with Ivar and me nine years ago, I can count barely two hundred now. The battles have taken the lion's share of them, and others have chosen to settle in Anglia or Northumbria over the years. I'm thinking it's time the rest of us helped ourselves to a piece of Northumbrian land and settled down. It would also be easy for me to sail over to Dublin from up there, if I decide the peaceful life's not for me. Whatever, your army's likely to keep swelling, considering the number of ships arriving each year, so my two hundred men won't be missed. And those of us who settle up there can help keep the rebels in check if they decide to rise up again.

'We'll be here until the defences are up, but I want to be on the move by next spring. Then you, Guthrum, can plan how you'll deal with Wessex and that young upstart, Alfred.'

Twelve

Elston and Nottingham, Mercia: 873

The first half of the year passed uneventfully at Elston, although Eadwulf made sure he kept himself updated on the movements of the Norse army, as well as the whereabouts of Burgred. The newcomers had settled in well over the last two years, adjusting to the way of life with relative ease, and Eadwulf had done all he could to help Hamid and Ameena adapt to the different customs of Mercia.

Ameena loved her new life and welcomed the fact that her status as an unmarried woman in Mercia did not require her to cover her head. She relished the freedom of walking outdoors with her long red hair blowing in the breeze and only in the depths of winter did she resort to covering it with the hood of her coat. Little Leofwynn adored her new aunt and Odella, now with child for the second time, was happy to have another female companion with whom to spend her time.

With Hamid, Eadwulf had thought that the change from a life of luxury in a land of warmth and sunshine to the simple life and cooler weather of Mercia would be hard to accept – not to mention his status as son of the emir, albeit a bastard one. Yet Hamid was no stranger to hard work and had soon put his practical abilities to good use. Trained to high standards as a stonemason, he was initially disappointed to learn that stone was not a favoured building material in Mercia. But he simply turned his designing and carving skills to wood and created strong furniture and household goods, and not only for the Elston hall. He even taught Jorund a thing or two and Eadwulf's brother soon became Hamid's willing apprentice.

Hamid's reputation as a master carpenter had spread, and it wasn't long before people from nearby villages were requesting his skills. He and Jorund enjoyed the rides out as well as the work, and though payment was little, they were content with whatever the villagers could manage, even if that payment was in the form of food or wool.

A strong and fit young man, Hamid loved the forest hunts during the winter months and his ability with bow and spear impressed them all. Eadwulf began to realise that the emir's son would be a good man to have at his side in battle.

The late August day was hot and muggy and Eadwulf swept his sleeve across his wet brow, noting the grin on Beorhtwulf's face. After years in Cordoba, his father had found the Mercian summers pleasantly cool. 'Hamid's a fine young man,' he said as they strolled across the outer compound where they could speak without interruption from young Ethelred, 'and would have made a great emir, had his status in his family been different.'

'As is too often the case,' Beorhtwulf replied. 'I've been proud of Hamid since he was a boy, even though he wasn't my own. He favours Muhammad in looks, though his skin is a shade or two paler. But he hasn't got his mother's flaxen hair and blue eyes.' He chuckled. 'But nor has Ameena. She couldn't look more like you and me if she tried.'

Eadwulf nodded, wanting to get to the point of this conversation. 'As you know, the Danes took Repton in May and seem to be settled there, at least for a while. They may even decide to overwinter there.'

'I imagine they will have already ransacked the mausoleum in Saint Wynstan's Church in search of holy relics. The church has been a Mercian shrine for so long…' The once well-loved king of Mercia shook his head, emotions of anger and sadness vying for supremacy. 'Burgred must surely realise his kingship is over – not that I feel any sympathy for him. The Mercian throne was never his to claim, and now he's paying for his traitorous actions. Killing him would give him a way out, but kill him we must. I'll die a happier man after savouring the sweet taste of revenge.'

'That's what I wanted to talk to you about,' Eadwulf said, nodding. 'With Burgred in Nottingham and the Danes in Repton, it's a perfect time for us to move. Jorund will be coming with us, and possibly Aethelnoth, although I'd feel easier leaving him to watch over things here. But his father's death in the London raid gives him good reason to want Burgred dead.'

'Thrydwulf was one of the finest warriors to have ever served Mercia,' Beorhtwulf agreed, 'and his son has every right to play a part in my brother's death.'

'Aethelnoth will make his own decision in this, Father. Odella's nearing the time for birthing their second child, so he may want to stay here. But if he wants to come with us, I was wondering whether Hamid would stay to watch over the hall.'

'I think he'd be happy to do that, and I imagine he'd have Selwyn to help him...?' Eadwulf nodded. 'Hamid's come to think of you as a brother and he tells me he's learned much about swordsmanship from you and Aethelnoth.'

Eadwulf shrugged. 'He already handled himself well, so took little teaching in weaponry. Hamid's used to having authority, too. The servants here have become fond of him – as well as holding him in awe. To have an emir's son in their midst must seem unreal to them.'

'I can understand that. Hamid has an air of grandeur about him, and I can promise you, he'll take no slacking from the servants. If their work is shoddy they'll answer to him for it.' Burgred paused, his next words seeming to hover on his lips. 'About this trip to Nottingham… You didn't seem too keen on the idea of taking me along when I suggested it three years ago, and now our number has doubled. Why the change of heart?'

'I've been thinking a lot about things recently. Jorund and Aethelnoth being with me when I went after Ivar had its advantages. It's always good to have your back covered, which Aethelnoth does willingly. But if he chooses to stay here, I'll respect his decision.'

Beorhtwulf nodded. 'When have you in mind for this venture?'

'We'll leave in a couple of weeks.'

* * *

In the days following the seizing of Repton, a pall of shame hung over the Mercian hall at Nottingham. Most of Burgred's closest supporters deserted him, leaving him alone to face the Danes and their continuing demands for tribute. Only the dozen thegns currently serving at his Nottingham residence stood by him.

Fraught with despair at the hopelessness of his situation, Burgred's decision to flee had come as no surprise to Aethelswith. He was a self-centred coward who would always put his own wellbeing above that of others. His Mercian subjects meant nothing to him.

Having little choice other than to accept his ultimatum that she and Mildrede would go with him, Aethelswith was now packing travel chests with clothes and a few of her prize belongings. Although it would be a great relief to take her beloved daughter away from this beleaguered kingdom, the thought of starting a new life in a strange land, away from all she knew and loved, was not easy to accept.

'I'm sure we'll be happier in the Holy City, Mother,' Mildrede said, coming up behind her and giving her a hug. 'We just have to face the journey there, which I don't think should be too great a hardship. Uncle Alfred travelled there and back twice when he was very young, so it can't be all that bad.'

'He did,' Aethelswith agreed, her memories of her precocious five-year-old brother bringing a smile to her lips. 'And he never forgot those visits, especially the building of the wall around the Leonine City. Rome certainly impressed my little brother – and my father. King Aethelwulf donated a hefty sum towards the upkeep of the Saxon School, or the *Scola Saxonum,* as the Romans call it. He spoke many times of the contentment he'd felt when he was there.'

'And I truly hope Father finds the peace he seeks in Rome. He's been a tormented man for most of my life and I'm hoping the Holy City will help him to find the contented and loving person buried deep inside him.'

Aethelswith squeezed her daughter's arm. How could she tell her that Burgred hadn't a grain of goodness in his entire body? Somewhere in his distant past, Burgred's heart had irrevocably hardened. But perhaps... just perhaps... the Holy City would find a way of softening it.

'I also hope he can rest on the journey,' Mildrede added, looking pointedly at her mother. 'Although you haven't told me, I can see Father isn't well, is he?'

'Your father isn't at all well, Mildred. The pains in his chest have become stronger since the Danes returned to Mercia. Worry and anxiety, as well as drinking too much ale, have done him no favours.' Aethelswith could find no sympathy in her heart for Burgred and promptly changed the subject. 'We leave at first light, dear one, so tonight we must pray for the loved ones we'll be leaving behind. We won't see any of them again.'

Aethelswith's voice caught in her throat as her thoughts again turned to Alfred and his lovely young family. Mildrede held her in her arms in a comforting embrace. 'I know, Mother, but I also know there's no place for us here now that Mercia belongs to the Danes. And I doubt that Guthrum and Halfdan will have trouble finding a replacement "puppet" to do their bidding.'

* * *

It was late afternoon when Burgred came into the hall after speaking with his thegns outside. Aethelswith could not help a frown as he strutted over to sit with her and their daughter, the usual sensation of loathing engulfing her. If only she and Mildrede were leaving without him.

'My men have arranged passage for us aboard a ship bound for Quentovic in West Francia,' Burgred started, pouring himself a mug of ale, 'a good place from which to begin our journey.' Aethelswith nodded, recalling the name of Quentovic from her father and Alfred's journeys to Rome. 'Half a dozen of them have agreed to ride with us as escort. The rest of my men are preparing to return to their own halls as we speak, and I've told the servants to leave here as soon as they've cooked our meal.'

He looked levelly at Aethelswith. 'You and Mildrede will need to serve the food, which I'm sure you're capable of.'

Aethelswith bristled. Although she had no objection to serving the meal, it was the tone in which the demand was delivered that jarred. Burgred had constantly treated her as a servant, which had earned her many sympathetic glances from Mercian nobles over the years.

Oblivious to his wife's umbrage, Burgred pushed on. 'We sail from Dover in Kent, which means we'll have a trek of two hundred and forty miles to get there, and with the wagons it will be a slow journey. But the route will keep us away from the regions the Danes presently hold.'

Aethelswith watched her husband as his fingers circled his temples, and felt not a shred of pity for him, or for the loss of his throne. He deserved no better.

'From Nottingham we'll travel along rough tracks until we reach Ermine Street,' he continued, 'which we'll stay on all the way south to Dover where our chests will be loaded aboard ship and the wagons and horses will be sold. Once we've crossed the Narrow Seas to Quentovic, we'll stay for a day or two at the nearby hostel of Saint Judoc while we buy more horses and food for the next stage of the journey.'

'Will it take many weeks to reach Rome from there?' Mildrede asked, her blue eyes wide at the thought.

Burgred shrugged. 'Between two and three months, depending on the weather and how the horses bear up. It's mid-September already, far too late for starting on such a journey. I doubt we'll be crossing the Alps before next spring. And replacing lamed horses could considerably slow us down – as could sickness amongst us, if we are unfortunate enough to pick any up.'

'And we will be sleeping out in the open on most nights?'

'Hopefully not at this time of year,' Aethelswith put in, looking at Mildrede. 'I know from your grandfather and Alfred there are hostels for travellers at a number of places along the pilgrim route, so we'll have some nights of comfort. But, for the most part, we'll be sleeping in the wagon.'

'Make sure everything's ready for loading before sunset,' Burgred said as he started towards his bed chamber. 'At sunrise tomorrow I want nothing more to do than move out.'

* * *

The meal was eaten in frosty silence. Even Burgred's half dozen thegns said little, other than to thank Aethelswith and Mildrede for the food they served. Burgred said nothing at all, choosing to remain seated, cradling his ale mug, as the work of clearing the trestles continued around him. He absently watched his wife and daughter packing the remnants of food for the first part of the journey before heading out to the chapel to pray, leaving the men to carry the packed crates and chests out to the wagons. His self-pity and shame had gradually ebbed away to be replaced by the relentless remorse that had so often overwhelmed him during the past twenty-two years.

Why must the Christ-god continue to punish him? Burgred was forever doomed to remember his own deplorable actions… his unforgivable betrayal of his own family, as well as the very people he now attempted to rule. No amount of remorse made God forgive him. Shame and self-loathing burned inside his head until he'd downed so much ale he could think no more. There'd be no sleep for him this night, unless he succumbed to drinking himself senseless, but with the long journey ahead he knew that to do so would be more than foolish.

The September nights were drawing in and by the time the wagons were eventually loaded the last glimmers of daylight were fading. Aethelswith and Mildrede retired to their chambers to rest before the early-morning start, leaving Burgred's thegns playing tabula and other dicing games to while away the time before they, too, snatched a few hours of sleep.

For the first time in years, Burgred felt the need to pray, to repent his sins to the God he'd rejected for so long. He made his way out to the solitude of the small wooden building that served as chapel for the royal residents at Nottingham.

* * *

'That's him,' Eadwulf whispered, peering through the cracks in the palisade surrounding the Nottingham hall at the figure momentarily silhouetted in the light streaming through the opened door. At his side, Beorhtwulf seemed to have ceased to breathe as he took in the sight of the brother he had once loved; the brother who had ordered his death.

They watched in silence as Burgred headed across the compound towards a small building set against the cliff face at the far side of the stables, some fifty yards from the hall. Then Aethelnoth said, 'All those people leaving earlier seems odd, but for all we know there may still be plenty more inside than the six men who just loaded the carts.' He scratched his head in thought. 'But we can't miss this chance of getting at that bastard while he's out here alone.'

'I agree,' Beorhtwulf said. 'Let's do it.'

'If someone gives me a leg up over this fence, I'll open the gates,' Jorund offered, lifting his left leg in readiness.

* * *

Burgred peered into the single room of the dingy chapel, his eyes drawn to the halos of light cast by six burnt-down beeswax candles in their simple clay pots. Four of these stood on the beaten earth of the room's corners, the other two at either side of a wide table along the opposite wall to the doorway. Between these two candles and reflecting their warm orange glow, was a white marble statue of the Virgin and her child.

He knelt before the table and stared at the statue, reminding himself of the time he'd turned his back on the Christian God – the time when he'd become the worst kind of monster: one that betrays the love and trust of those who had held him dear. Perhaps if his early life had been different he would have become a better person…

All Burgred had wanted throughout his childhood was a share of his father's love, but every drop of that love was showered on his firstborn, Beorhtwulf. A second-born was of no consequence as far as his father was concerned. Not once had Burgred heard a word of encouragement or praise for his progress. His intelligence and battle skills were simply ignored.

Burgred convinced himself he was unworthy of his father's love. But over the years he turned the blame for his rejection in a different direction. His envy of Beorhtwulf had gradually evolved into a searing hatred that had burnt away any shred of goodness he'd ever had. He'd become obsessed with the desire to see his brother dead. Even now he didn't regret having Beorhtwulf killed – or of ridding himself of that brat, Eadwulf. Deep down Burgred knew that was why God still hadn't forgiven him. He wasn't truly repentant.

Yet Morwenna's fate had been a different matter. Burgred had never intended to do her harm and had really thought he loved her, then. Though, on reflection, it could simply have been that he'd wanted to take her from Beorhtwulf.

He suddenly sensed death hovering close. The crushing pain in his chest told him that God's hand was reaching out to toss him into the fiery pits of hell, denying him the chance of ever getting to the holy city of Rome. He pulled himself to his feet, his eyes fixed on the statue and his rage against the God who had never helped him suddenly erupted. With a roar he swept his arm across the table, sending the statue crashing to the floor.

'It seems you never learned to control that temper of yours.'

Burgred spun round, gasping as another pain seared his chest. He could make out the shadowy shapes of two men, one either side of the doorway. The voice sounded vaguely familiar, though he couldn't place it. He pulled himself to his full height, and attempted a sneer. 'If you're looking for things to steal, you're unlucky. The Danes have taken everything of value, even the blasted candlesticks!'

'We aren't here to rob you.'

Burgred squinted through the semi-darkness. The faces of the men were partly hidden by their loose hoods but the stance of the one who'd spoken suggested someone of advanced years. He guessed they'd both be armed beneath their cloaks and fought down his rising panic. He was wearing a sword himself – but there were two of them. 'Then why are you here?'

The older man took a few paces towards him, pushing back his hood as he did. 'Do you recognise me, Burgred?'

Burgred stared, taking in the steel-grey hair and beard, but was still no wiser. 'Are you one of my thegns?'

The younger man shoved his hood back and came to stand at the older man's side. 'Enough of this, Father. Let's do what we came for and be gone.'

Burgred gasped as red hair glinted in the candlelight and his eyes fixed on the face with a square jaw that reminded him of…

Another glance at the older man's face and he knew.

'Beorhtwulf! Egil said…' Burgred did not finish what he'd started to say and his attentions swung to the younger man. 'Eadwulf?' He stepped back, suddenly very aware of their purpose.

'Yes, *Uncle.* I am Eadwulf. We both survived your betrayal, though others did not.'

Another two men entered the chapel, halting Burgred's intended question.

'What's going on?' Eadwulf demanded. 'You two were supposed to keep watch.'

'Which we did, long enough to know there's no one about. Now we're here to do business.'

Burgred eyed the wild hair and thickset build of the warrior who'd replied, his mind racing. 'Do I know you?'

'You knew my father well enough before your treachery led to you becoming *king.* Thrydwulf died in the raid *you* set up with Rorik.'

Burgred knew exactly who Thrydwulf had been and looked away, not daring to speak of that day. 'And you?' he asked, focusing on a much younger man. 'Was your father killed in London?'

'My father's right here in front of you, Scum.'

Burgred glanced at his brother and back to the young man. 'I don't understand… Beorhtwulf had only one son.'

'Morwenna gave birth to me in Rorik's hall soon after they reached the Danish lands.'

'Is…is Morwenna still alive?'

'Enough talk!' Eadwulf snapped. 'Traitors don't deserve to be given answers before they die.'

Burgred launched himself at Beorhtwulf, sliding his sword from its scabbard and striking out at his brother's side, only to have the thrust parried by Eadwulf.

Crushing pains shot across Burgred's chest and he sank

to the earthen floor, gasping for breath. Eadwulf reared over him, his sword poised.

'God's punishment…' Burgred panted, his voice barely a whisper as the others closed in. His hand reached out for Beorhtwulf. 'I'm dying, brother; no need for my death to be on your conscience. I beg forgiveness.' He clasped at his chest, his eyes locked with Beorhtwulf's. 'I won't live much longer now.'

'I will not be denied the pleasure of killing you,' Eadwulf growled. 'I've waited for this day for too long to show lenience now.'

'No! I beg you, my lord. Burgred is right, he is already a dying man, so killing him now would serve little purpose. Our doctors have declared him unfit for travel and he'll likely die before we reach Rome. His heart will not withstand the rigours of the journey.'

Burgred became aware of his wife's voice, unable to understand her presence, though it seemed she was pleading for his life.

Eadwulf's sword arm remained poised. 'Lady, do you have any idea just how much harm this *animal* has inflicted upon each of us here, how many deaths are on his head? He betrayed us, his own family and friends, to the Danes. He destroyed our family, our home and took my father's throne. And you ask us to spare him?'

Aethelswith gasped and moved from the doorway to stand beside them. 'My lords, I did not know. I am Burgred's wife, daughter of King Aethelwulf of Wessex and sister of King Alfred. I confess, I never knew how mortally my husband wronged his own brother.' She turned to face Beorhtwulf. 'I saw you once at my father's court when I was a girl, and I know he thought you an honourable man. So I beseech you to show mercy in this, however much pain Burgred has caused you. He has wronged many amongst us and has not ruled Mercia wisely, or honoured our alliance with Wessex. But I tell you this: he has suffered for it over the years and has always known God would punish him in the end.'

Burgred let out a moan – a combination of shame and physical pain – and suddenly longed for death to release him from his torment. 'I am ready to face God, so do what you must.'

Eadwulf did not need a second telling and drew back his arm for a strike. This time it was Beorhtwulf who stayed him. 'We will not sink to the same level as him, Eadwulf. I am content to know that Burgred is already dying. Let him head for Rome and beg forgiveness from God.'

'I've lived for the day I could wring the life out of this gutless cur for over twenty years, Father, and when I get the chance you ask me to walk away. I can't do it.'

In the silence, Burgred held his breath, anticipating the strike. But moments went by. In many ways, it would be better to get it done with. Death was following him and would likely claim him on the way to Rome, denying him the chance of finding the forgiveness he craved.

'Do this for me, Eadwulf. Like you, I can never forgive Burgred, but I'm ready to show mercy. It's God's forgiveness he needs before he dies.'

Eadwulf turned on his heels and stalked from the church, followed by the two other men. Beorhtwulf knelt beside Burgred and, too ashamed to look his brother in the eye,

Burgred stared at the beaten earth. 'Listen to me,' Beorhtwulf said, 'once we've gone from here, Aethelswith will call your men to carry you into your hall. Tomorrow you will leave for Rome, as planned, and for the sake of your immortal soul, I hope you reach the Holy City. God alone can forgive the sins you've committed in this life. I cannot, and Eadwulf would have seen you dead.'

Beorhtwulf rubbed his brow, a habit Burgred recalled well from his childhood. 'Your actions caused such suffering, as well as the death of the woman I dearly loved. How could you do it?

Burgred groaned. 'Deep down, I always knew Morwenna would not survive for long as Rorik's concubine. She loved you, and I hated you even more for it, although I never intended her harm. I admired her too much for that.'

Relieved his brother didn't demand explanations about his true intentions regarding Morwenna, Burgred watched him push himself stiffly to his feet, casting a glance at Aethelswith standing mute since her initial request.

'It would serve no purpose to drag all this up now, Burgred, and I'm sure you've thought about it often over the years. But do you have one shred of remorse for what you did to us – or how much misery you've caused to so many others?'

Burgred could not reply. How could he tell the brother he'd wanted dead that he felt no remorse for that? All that mattered to him now was God's forgiveness, but how could he expect any when he still felt no regret for his sins? Beorhtwulf had always known of his churning dread of hell fire and he could not speak of that now.

Aethelswith stepped closer to Beorhtwulf, and Burgred

squirmed beneath her stare. 'I already despised you as a domineering man and a coward, she said, 'and I do not speak of your shameful bullying and heartless treatment of Mildrede and myself. Your refusal to honour your alliance with Wessex and help my brother at a time of such desperate need made me realise the depth of your selfishness. I will never forgive you for that.'

She paused as emotion welled but Burgred knew there would be no tears. His wife was strong and proud, the main reason why he'd always found it hard to accept her as a wife: that, and the fact that she had never loved him.

'But the true depth of your wickedness was unknown to me until now, and I readily understand Beorhtwulf's son's desire to kill you. You are truly depraved and will find no forgiveness from anyone on this earth. Like Beorhtwulf, the *true* king of Mercia,' she sneered, 'I hope God can forgive you. For the sake of our daughter, I am prepared to take care of you on the journey, in the hope that you reach the Holy City. If you do not, you will be buried wherever you die. Mildrede will be told nothing of tonight's encounter, nor will our men. They will believe you collapsed in the church and nothing more.'

Burgred watched as his wife turned to face Beorhtwulf. 'I am honoured to have met you again, my lord,' she said, 'though I know your life cannot have been easy since we last met each other. My heart goes out to you and your family for the anguish caused you by this man. I can only hope he clings to life until we reach Rome and finds it in himself to feel deep regret for his heinous sins. Only then can he seek God's forgiveness.'

'Your kindness does you credit, Aethelswith, and I wish

you God speed on your journey. And although it's probably of little consolation to you, my son, Eadwulf, intends to ride to Wessex and join King Alfred's army. He knows much about Danish tactics, having been a thrall in their lands for many years. Others may well join him, too.

'Now we must leave. Give us time to get clear of the palisade before you fetch your men from the hall.'

Burgred watched his brother leave the church, knowing he'd never feel sorry for what he'd done. His hatred of Beorhtwulf was too deeply rooted to be unearthed and tossed away now.

Thirteen

Winchester, Wessex: January 874

'Have you told the king yet, my lady? I mean, it won't be many more weeks before you'll have no need to tell him and–'

'I know that Agnes,' Ealhswith interrupted, smiling at the serious expression on the nurse's face as she lifted Edward from her lap and sent him over to play with Aethelflaed. 'I'll tell Alfred when I find the right moment. I've seen so little of him since the Danes left Wessex, and when he's here in Winchester, he's so tired after all the travelling, especially now the weather's turned so cold. I swear he intends to visit every major town in every Wessex shire, and he won't stop until he's satisfied his nobles have followed his orders. But if we have heavy snows this year, things will simply be put on hold until spring, and Alfred will not be a happy man.'

Ealhswith smiled as she thought of the passion in Alfred's voice when he spoke of his plans for his beloved Wessex. 'He's obsessed with the need to strengthen our kingdom's defences before the Danes come back. And rightly so: we all know they're bound to come back. But we can't even guess when that will be. It could be within the next few months, next year, or…

'The point is, Agnes, that Wessex has to be ready next time, and being the man he is Alfred won't rest until he sees the fortifications built exactly how he wants them. So you see, I don't want to worry him with anything else when he gets home because he desperately needs to sleep.'

'Well, my lady, King Alfred will be here for a few days now, at least until this latest bout of his illness passes. I know you can't say much while he's in such pain, but maybe once he feels a little better? I'm sure he'll be happy about it. At least the Norsemen aren't in Wessex now, so we won't need to go off to Wedmore for the birthing this time, unless they come back before then.'

'I'm praying the cursed Danes will *never* come back,' Ealhswith snapped, her emotions getting the better of her. 'Why can't they just leave our lands alone! How can any of us plan for the future?

'Oh, Agnes, I'm sorry. I didn't mean to burden you with my worries. I trust Alfred and, whatever happens, I know he'll fight for Wessex until the end. The Danes will not find Wessex easy to take, as they did our neighbours.'

'We all know that, my lady. Our young king has the wisest head on his shoulders that I've ever come across.'

* * *

Alfred roused from the first night of comfortable sleep he'd had in three days, thankful the griping spasms that had clawed at his gut for what seemed like weeks had eventually eased. He reached out for Ealhswith, only to find an empty space beside him, and from the light squeezing through the still-closed shutters, realised she would probably have risen some time ago. Having been taken ill on his way home from Sussex, he'd had little chance to speak with her and felt in desperate need of her company.

He rose and dressed slowly, his body weak from enforced idleness, and he knew it would be a day or two before agility returned to normal. A strong gust of wind whistled through the thatch and he shivered violently, despite the warmth from the glowing brazier. Not for the first time, he cursed the fact that winter dictated the need for his building plans to slow down – or rather, winter decreed he could not be there too often to ensure those plans were implemented properly. All he could do was trust his ealdormen to do that in his stead.

The mid-morning meal was being cleared from the trestles as Alfred entered the hall. Busy talking with the women at the looms, Ealhswith did not notice him – but Aethelflaed did. The robust five-year-old hurtled towards him.

'Papa's here!' the small whirlwind shrieked.

Alfred bent to hug his daughter as Ealhswith hurried over. In the presence of servants they greeted each other with only a discreet embrace, but as Ealhswith led him to his chair by the hearthfire, the look of concern on her face made his heart swell with love for her. Not to be outdone, Aethelflaed climbed up to nestle beside him.

'Well, I can see I've been missed, and I've only been in the next room.'

'You were poorly, Papa, and I didn't see you.'

'As you can see, little one, I'm better now, and in need of food and drink before I fade away.'

'I'll arrange for one of the servants to bring you a bowl of pottage and some goat's milk,' Ealhswith said, heading to the kitchens.

Now displaying a comical pout, Aethelflaed pointed at

her dark-headed three-year-old brother drawing shapes on a parchment with Agnes, oblivious to anything happening around him. 'I'm not little, Papa! It's Edward who's little.'

'You're right,' Alfred soothed, admiring his daughter's blue-green eyes, identical to her mother's. 'You're bigger every time I see you.'

The serving woman arrived and placed a bowl of meaty pottage and a chunk of warm bread on the table, followed by Ealhswith bearing a cup of goat's milk and evidently trying not to smile. Alfred murmured his thanks and lifted his daughter down from his chair.

'Now, Aethelflaed, let your poorly papa eat, before–'

'–before he fades away,' the child finished for her mother, turning to skip across the hall back to Edward and Agnes.

Alfred and Ealhswith shared a smile as she seated herself beside him. 'I'm sorry you've had to spend so much time caring for me,' Alfred started. 'I hate being a burden to you. I'm also frustrated that this illness always flares up at times when I need to be active.'

'Perhaps that's the answer. Your body is telling you you're doing too much to cope with. The pains are a warning that you need to take time to build up your strength. '

Alfred responded with a grimace. 'If that's the case I'd prefer a less painful warning – though I'd probably take little notice of a mere twinge. But I can't afford to spend three days in my bed right now. There's still so much to be done.'

Ealhswith nodded, her expression suddenly crestfallen. 'Don't you think it likely the Danes will stay in Mercia until they're convinced the kingdom is fully suppressed? Surely they wouldn't leave yet, risking another uprising like the one they had to deal with in Northumbria.'

A stab of pain shot through Alfred's chest as he thought of the plight of his beloved sister, probably now in Rome. Chances of him ever seeing Aethelswith again were slight, and he sent a silent prayer that she'd be kept safe. 'You're probably right,' he replied, 'but we need at least a couple of years to build all the defences Wessex needs and I doubt we'll get that long.

'What good are towns with simple wooden fences at keeping besieging armies out?' he ranted on. 'High stone walls, and in some places, encircling ditches or trenches, are what we need for keeping the Danes out. But the first thing I need to do once I'm on my feet again is get down to the south coast. I set a shipbuilding plan in motion last September and the shipwrights and fishermen of the towns and ports along the coast are already working on building a number of vessels to my own design.'

Ealhswith nodded, but did not interrupt as his words poured out.

'Our long southern coastline provides invading armies too many places easy access into Wessex and we need to be able to stop at least some of them from making landfall. To do that, our vessels need to be fast enough to challenge the Norse longships. Our first attempts at that may well be unsuccessful.'

'Then you have much work ahead of you,' Ealhswith said, 'though I know it will keep you away from home for so long. And we do miss you…'

Alfred squeezed her hand, silently thanking God for giving him such an understanding wife.

Ealhswith smiled. 'Now you need to finish your milk and let your mind as well as your body rest. And I can tell you, husband, you won't be riding out anywhere for some time.'

'What makes you say that?'

'It's been snowing since before midnight last night and travel anywhere is out of the question. So you'll just have to be content to stay with me every night for a while.'

Alfred threw back his head and laughed. 'I'd like nothing more than to stay with you permanently, and I suspect Aethelflaed would like that too.'

'Well, my love, I think now might be the time to tell you. I'm carrying another child. It should be born in late June, when you'll most likely be away overseeing the building of your ships.' Ealhswith took her husband's hand. 'And when all's considered that might be a good thing – for you, at least. If this babe is anything like Aethelflaed was, no one here will get any sleep before next Christmastide.'

* * *

Heavy frosts and snows persisted throughout January and early February, but once they had lessened enough to render main roads and trackways usable, Alfred decided to ride out to the villages with Radulf, the Hampshire ealdorman. It was still bitterly cold, and the strong north-easterlies made it seem even more so, but he knew this may well be his only chance to rally the ceorls to readiness as part of the Hampshire fyrd.

Village life hummed with activity as people busied themselves with winter chores. Despite the bitter cold, people worked tirelessly for the welfare of their village. The unmistakable sounds of smiths rang out; men sat atop the simple houses repairing thatched roofs and carpenters created or repaired items of furniture. Others tended livestock in the barns, while women scurried back and forth to storage sheds for remaining scraps of meat and vegetables for the pottage. Indoors, other women worked hard at their looms, creating new cloth for tunics and cloaks.

Alfred was impressed by the villagers' determination and energy, and how life in these settlements was precious, and not something to be wiped out by pagan invaders. He was also pleased to find most of them eager to fight for their kingdom should the Danes return, and promptly sent orders to the ealdormen of all his shires to instruct the fyrds to remain in a constant state of readiness. Spring was a mere few weeks away and Alfred couldn't risk his armies wasting valuable time searching for suitable weapons or being unfit when the call to arms came.

In late April, Alfred left Winchester for Kent, keen to check on the progress of his shipbuilders. The shipwrights and fishermen of these southerly ports were skilled at their trade, and although Alfred's requested design for his ships was different to their usual style they had evidently not been idle over the winter months. He strolled along the Folkestone quayside with them, congratulating them heartily on the nine sleek ships ready for launching. The workmanship was second to none. And sitting high on the prow of each towered the carved head of the Wyvern of Wessex.

Within a week of his arrival in Kent, Alfred's spies sent

news that the Danes had left Repton around the same time as Alfred had left Winchester and were now camped at the Mercian town of Cambridge. At least, most of them were. It seemed that Halfdan and his force of some two hundred men had split from Guthrum's army and headed north, intent on returning to Northumbria.

'So,' Alfred said to Radulf and Kentish ealdorman, Anlaf, once the messengers were enjoying refreshment, 'word around Repton is that after nine years in the Angle and Saxon kingdoms, Halfdan's men have grown weary of battle. And since Northumbria is already under Danish control, they see it as a good place to settle down. The loss of two hundred men is unlikely to cause Guthrum sleepless nights; those numbers will doubtless be replaced many times over during the next few months – and for some years to come!'

Alfred took a few deep breaths, determined to keep his anger and frustration at that thought under control. 'Guthrum and the two kings are now in Cambridge, which is, thankfully, still in Mercia. And it isn't such an immediate threat to Wessex as London would have been, right on our borders. But it's still a step closer than either Torksey or Repton.'

'That's true,' Radulf agreed, 'and Halfdan's men being tired of battles suggests to me that Guthrum *is* planning on further battles at some stage. It's unlikely Halfdan believes there'll be large-scale uprisings in Mercia in the near future, so I'm guessing he's leaving for a quiet life because Guthrum has set his sights on Wessex.'

'But we've still no way of knowing when he'll make a move. It could be any time from now on,' Anlaf put in.

Alfred's brow wrinkled in thought. 'I doubt it will be within the next few months, but my spies will follow wherever Guthrum goes. As soon as he starts to ready his army we'll know about it. It could be later this year, but something tells me he'll wait until even more of his countrymen arrive next year. He won't want to strike at Wessex until he's confident enough in his power to outnumber and defeat our armies…

'About what you said, Radulf: Guthrum may or may not believe rebellions will break out in Mercia, but he'll want to be sure Ceolwulf is keeping control and not inciting rebellion behind his back. If Guthrum *is* intending to take Wessex, he can't risk any kind of trouble in Mercia calling him back, as happened with the Northumbrians. So all in all, I don't think Guthrum will rush into an invasion of Wessex. But I'm pretty sure he won't be satisfied until Wessex is his.'

* * *

Sussex Coast: Late July 874

'Ships to the east, my lord! Six – no seven – perhaps a mile off and less than a half mile from the coast. Sails are down… They'll be rowing hard with this westerly hitting them straight on.'

From the prow of his own new ship, *Wyvern*, Alfred peered through the gap in the rocks, the sight of the small fleet of longships sending a jolt of anticipation through him. 'Signal our ships, Radulf,' he yelled in reply. 'We move eastward any time now. Sails hoisted as soon as we push away.'

Alfred glanced at his newly built ships in the small cove behind the *Wyvern*: fifteen of them, each with a crew of twenty men, all well-muscled and trained for battle at sea. Though similar in design, the Wessex ships were heavier than those of the enemy, but still sleeker and faster than anything the Saxons had known before. Alfred knew he owed much to the skills of the seafaring men of Dorset and Sussex.

He thanked God that their first encounter with the Danes would be with a fleet of only seven. Added to that, the wind would be in their own sails as soon as they rounded the cove to block the enemy path. It would be Wessex ships doing the attacking – not something the skilled Danes would be prepared for. But the timing had to be right. If Saxon ships showed themselves too soon, the Danes could turn tail and flee – and Alfred knew that Norse longships could still outrun his own any day.

'Now!' he yelled.

Morning sunlight hit the backs of Wessex oarsmen as they rounded the cove. The strong westerly filled the ships' sails, and they sped across the coastal waters straight at the approaching Danes.

Though the Norsemen must have panicked at the sudden appearance of Wessex ships heading straight for them, Alfred saw no sign of it aboard their ships. The longships simply changed direction, but not in the awkward way that he'd expected. Norse crewmen simply turned at their oar ports and rowed back the way they'd come.

By the time Danish sails were hoisted – at a speed Alfred could only envy – Wessex ships were moving alongside them.

Yet, as he'd expected, once the speed of the enemy ships was up, Saxon vessels simply couldn't keep up and most sped out of their reach.

'Aim for the ships at the rear, Radulf!' Alfred yelled, desperate to capture at least a few of the Norsemen. He didn't want the Danes to see his new fleet as totally ineffective and contemptible. At the very least he needed them to know that sailing across the south coast of Wessex would not be so easy in future.

The *Wyvern* and another of Alfred's fleet veered across the last three of the seven ships. Deftly the Norsemen swerved, two of them managing to escape their grasp. The rest of the Saxon ships closed in on the lone Dane, and evidently realising the hopelessness of their position, none of the Norse crew drew sword.

'We head to Southampton, Radulf,' Alfred said, once the ship was powered by Saxon oarsmen and the Danes securely bound. 'Though small it may seem, I'm hoping our victory today will give the rest of these marauders something to talk about.'

* * *

The year had not been kind to Ealhswith. By the onset of summer she had lost the child she was carrying, leaving her feeling wretchedly weak and prone to bouts of tears. For the first few weeks following the loss she rarely ventured from her room, preferring to spend her time in prayer, desperately needing to understand why God had let this happen. She'd tried so hard to protect the growing babe and did not overtax herself physically. She hadn't ridden out for weeks and had even allowed Agnes to assume full responsibility of caring for Aethelflaed and Edward. Yet still, the pregnancy was abruptly ended.

Ealhswith came to believe it was merely God's will that the babe should not survive and accepted that she would not question further. Many women suffered the same misfortune and most recovered well and went on to birth healthy babes in the future. In a few months' time she may even feel ready to face another pregnancy herself, but for now she needed time to heal and besides, Alfred was rarely home.

At the start of August, news filtered through to Winchester that Alfred had been given the chance to put his new navy to the test. Initially stricken to hear of her husband's confrontation with the Danes at sea, Ealhswith almost collapsed in relief when the outcome of the encounter was delivered.

'Didn't I tell you not to fret so, my lady?' Agnes said, once the messenger had left. 'The king knows what he's doing, and has been determined for years that our kingdom needs a good fleet of ships.' The old nurse nodded, in accord with her words 'This win will probably make him determined to build more vessels.'

'Perhaps,' Ealhswith replied, frowning as she thought about that. 'But there's still so much to be done in our towns, so Alfred must decide which is of more importance. He knows the Danes won't stay in Mercia for ever, and now that Burgred and Aethelswith have been forced to flee, he worries they may set their sights on Wessex again.'

"Don't say that, my lady, or it may come true sooner than

you think. But it's a sad tale for the king's sister and her husband, that's for sure.'

'I'm upset about never seeing Aethelswith again, Agnes, and Alfred is devastated. He loved his sister dearly, and loathed Burgred for treating her so badly. I hope they find comfort in the Holy City.

'We must also hope that Alfred will see Ceolwulf as a more acceptable king of Mercia than Burgred, even though the man can do no more than dance to the enemy's tune.'

* * *

Alfred was back in Winchester by the end of September after securing the two dozen captured Danes at estates of trusted noblemen across Wessex. It would pose too much of a risk to hold them together, and even as individuals, they could not be trusted to make compliant slaves. The newly acquired longship took pride of place with Alfred's small fleet, where his shipwrights would study every detail of its design as they continued their work for him.

It felt good to be home and Alfred needed a short rest before riding out to order the building of new fortifications at his towns along the Mercian border. Oxford and Abingdon were high on his list. He hoped to have at least a few weeks before winter swept in again and put a halt on that much-needed building work.

Alfred could not shake off the feeling that the time of peace in Wessex was nearing its end. He'd known for the past few years that Guthrum would eventually set his sights on his kingdom again. And there was nothing to hold him back now that Mercia was completely under Norse control, just as much as was Northumbria.

Though news had reached Alfred that the two kings, Anwend and Oscetel, had now followed Halfdan up to Northumbria, taking their own forces with them, it did little to counter his growing worries. Those losses were trivial compared to the dozens of longships that had arrived during the summer. The crewmen from those ships had now joined Guthrum in Cambridge, and come the following spring, Norse numbers would start to swell yet again. By which time, as far as Alfred could see, the shrewd and calculating leader would be ready to make his move into Wessex.

Fourteen

Elston, Mercia: Late 873 - 874

Following his thwarted attempt to kill Burgred in Nottingham, Eadwulf sank into a state of silent, smouldering rage, mingled with a desperate frustration at the opportunity missed. The only opportunity he'd had in twenty years…wasted! All those years of planning and imagining how his treacherous uncle would die had come to nothing. If he hadn't agreed to take Beorhtwulf with him to Nottingham, Burgred would now be dead. He should have listened to his own reasoning instead of being swayed by his father's request to play a part in the kill.

It had taken almost a month before Eadwulf could bring himself to speak to his father without scowling. But as the cold days of winter drew in, his rage ebbed and he realised how petulant he must seem to everyone in his hall. He also took consolation in knowing that Burgred was dying anyway – could already be dead, for all he knew. No doubt word of the former Mercian king's passing would eventually reach his homelands. Aethelswith would surely send news to her brother, Alfred, at very least, and the news would soon spread throughout the kingdoms. Perhaps then, Eadwulf would be able to bury his aching desire for revenge.

As winter became spring, Eadwulf became obsessed with the need to hear of his uncle's death. Messengers arrived now and then with news of the whereabouts of the Danes in their kingdom and opinions on the new king, Ceolwulf. It was late April when news reached Elston of the Danes' shift to Cambridge, but since they already dominated Mercia, it made little difference to Eadwulf whether they were in Repton or Cambridge. So far, they hadn't caused problems in Elston, despite having been camped so close at both Nottingham and Torksey over the past couple of years. But one piece of news sent possibilities whirling through Eadwulf's head: Halfdan had taken his army back to Northumbria.

Eadwulf agonised over whether killing Halfdan would ease his frustration of not killing Burgred. And would chasing Ivar's brother across Northumbria – even killing him – make any difference to the way he felt?

Perhaps the main thing holding Eadwulf back was the thought of leaving Elston again. His father was an old man, and one whose life had not been easy. Having lost each other for so many years, Eadwulf couldn't bear the thought of Beorhtwulf dying while he was gone.

At last, in mid-August, his longing to hear word of Burgred was satisfied. Three riders arrived at Elston with news from the new Mercian Court and once they were seated in the hall with mugs of ale, the spokesman for the group explained, 'King Ceolwulf received news from Queen Aethelswith two days ago, my lords, and wished to make it known to his ealdormen.'

Eadwulf's heartbeat quickened and, at his side, Beorhtwulf shuffled. Aethelnoth and Jorund remained statue-still. 'Go on,' he urged. 'We know King Burgred and Queen Aethelswith left for Rome last autumn, and we've often wondered whether they arrived there safely.'

The messenger nodded. 'They did, but the letter revealed

that the long, slow trek during the winter months had been too much for King Burgred and he'd become gravely ill during the journey. On nearing the Alps in late November, they'd decided to stay at a hostel until the spring rather than attempt the ice and snows of the passes through the high Alps. They were unable to continue their journey until mid-April.'

'So all is now well with King Burgred and his family?'

The spokesman's eyes fixed on Beorhtwulf. 'Queen Aethelswith and Lady Mildrede are well, lord, but King Burgred passed away two weeks after their arrival in Rome. The queen assured Ceolwulf that her husband had found comfort in the Holy City and had asked God's forgiveness for his sins. He was buried in the church of Saint Maria in the *Schola Saxonum.*'

'My brother is at peace,' Beorhtwulf murmured, once the messengers had left.

Eadwulf surged to his feet, anger and disappointment rising anew. 'Yes, he's at peace, Father. But I am not. Traitors to their people should pay for their sins!'

Beorhtwulf stared down at his hands, and in the silence of the hall, Eadwulf stormed out.

* * *

Daylight was fading and Eadwulf's empty stomach growled. Having had all afternoon to dwell on his childish outburst, he now felt too ashamed to return and face anyone. Even his children must think him a fool. At thirteen, Aethelred was as astute as they come and even nine-year-old Leofwynn was proving to be as perceptive as her mother had been.

Deep down, Eadwulf realised that the longer he spent wandering aimlessly around his estate, the harder it would be to face people when he eventually returned. He'd just resolutely turned about when he noticed Aethelred crossing the meadow towards him.

'Father!' the boy yelled as he drew close. 'Odella sent me to find you. She was worried you'd be hungry by now and none of us want to start the evening meal without you.'

Eadwulf smiled at the look of concern on his son's face. 'I was just about to head back. I was also thinking how stupid I was to make such a fuss – and that I owe Beorhtwulf an apology.'

'Grandfather isn't angry. He just hopes you'll forgive him for asking you to spare Burgred's life. So I think you just need to give each other a hug and move on.'

Such words of wisdom coming from his son made Eadwulf laugh and he pulled Aethelred close to him. 'You're right,' he said, 'a good hug can often take the place of words. And do you know what?' Aethelred shook his head. 'I'm absolutely starving.'

* * *

'You're not intending to go after Halfdan, then?' Aethelnoth asked as they ate. 'I've been half expecting you to make a move for weeks now.'

Conversation around the trestle ceased and Eadwulf glanced at the expectant faces. His eyes locked with Aethelnoth's and he knew his friend would be riding with him if he did decide to head north. Jorund's raised eyebrows confirmed that he, too, wouldn't be left behind.

Beorhtwulf drew breath to speak but it was young Aethelred who said, 'You aren't going anywhere, are you, Father.' It wasn't a question. 'When news of Haldan's move to Northumbria reached us in April, you definitely said you wouldn't be going after him.'

Aethelnoth grunted. 'I heard him say that, too, Aethelred, but your father has a habit of changing his mind when he's had time to brood on things.'

Beorhtwulf remained silent but Eadwulf didn't miss the small sigh of relief.

'Please don't go away again, Papa. We get lonely when you aren't here.'

Eadwulf smiled at the worried look on his young daughter's face. Leofwynn was seated at the end of the table next to Aethelnoth's wife, Odella, and her two young children. And it seemed that Odella shared the same concern as Leofwynn.

'I can tell you all,' he said with an assuring smile, 'I will not be chasing after Halfdan. I intend to stay in Elston for a while. But I can't promise I won't need to go away again at some stage in the future.'

Again all eyes fixed on Eadwulf, but he refused to say more on the subject. From the faces of those who'd been present before he and Jorund had left with Bjorn in search of Beorhtwulf, it was apparent they remembered his intentions to offer his services to Alfred of Wessex. But Wessex was not under attack by the Danes right now – although that could change at any time. It was too late to fight for Mercia, but Wessex had not yet been subjugated. And when that time arrived, Eadwulf intended to seek Alfred out.

He glanced at his father, convincing himself still further that Mercia owed a debt to Wessex. King Aethelwulf had readily offered aid to Beorhtwulf when the Danes invaded Mercia twenty-four years ago: the time that had changed Eadwulf's life forever, as well as the lives of his parents, of Aethelnoth and even of the then unborn Jorund.

Eadwulf mulled things over as he finished his ale. If Wessex could withstand Danish conquest, perhaps…just perhaps, at some stage in the future, all Saxon and Angle kingdoms could be persuaded to band together against the Danes. He realised such thoughts were no more than his own hopes for the future, but he also knew, without doubt, that he'd rather die trying to oust the Danes than succumb to their rule. And although Eadwulf was just one man, when the need arose – as he knew it inevitably would – he would offer his sword arm to the army of Alfred of Wessex.

* * *

Winter swept into Mercia early that year. Although the snows had not yet fallen, a bitter north-easterly rendered November an uncomfortable month, especially for working outdoors. Wind rattled the shutters of the Elston hall, determined to gain entry, and despite the extra thick woollen tapestries draped over most of the wood-planked walls, icy draughts continued to seep through. Young and healthy, Hamid and Ameena took it all in their stride but, ageing and less robust, Beorhtwulf rarely ventured from the hall and seemed to grow more frail as the days passed.

Eadwulf became increasingly worried about him, and from the way they fussed around him, it was evident that Hamid and Ameena felt the same. Vigilant as ever, despite her many chores and the children to care for, Odella kept the old man well supplied with drinks and food as he sat close to the hearth-fire, contentedly watching his grandchildren amuse themselves with board games while daytime chores continued around the hall. During the long, dark winter evenings, he took pleasure in sharing memories and stories with them all.

As December came in with a less ferocious blast, Beorhtwulf passed away in his sleep. Despite his death being anticipated by all, it cast a shroud of deep-felt sorrow and grief over the household. For the first few days, Ameena was inconsolable.

'Why couldn't God have granted my father just a little more time in the land he'd pined to return to for so long!' she wailed. 'What sense is there in taking him now?"

Sunk in his own grief, Eadwulf had no answers to Ameena's questions, and nor, it seemed, did anyone else.

It was decided between them that despite his claims to have forsaken Christian beliefs in order to marry in Muslim Cordoba, in reality Beorhtwulf had never lost faith in the Christian god. Eadwulf knew that to be true from the words his father had spoken to Burgred on the night he had begged Eadwulf to allow his treacherous uncle live. And Ameena admitted she'd heard her father praying on many occasions. So the final resting place of a former proud Mercian king would be in the graveyard of the little Elston chapel, close to where Eadwulf's wife and stillborn son lay, and Wigstan, his father-by marriage. It would be a quiet and simple affair for the occupants of the Elston hall alone.

As they ate their mid-morning meal on the day before the burial, Eadwulf announced, 'I'm heading out with the servants soon to help dig Beorhtwulf's grave. I told Father Eboric of my plans two days ago so he wouldn't send out his own gravediggers. He's marked the spot where the grave will be.'

He let his words hang in the momentary silence of the hall before continuing, 'I'm doing this in honour of my father and the deep love and respect I had for him. And for all the years when we thought each other dead…' Eadwulf's voice caught in his throat and he swallowed hard.

'I'm coming with you,' Jorund declared, 'for all the years my father and I didn't even know of each other's existence.'

'Count me in, too,' Aethelnoth put in, 'for the respect I had for Beorhtwulf as both man and king.'

'You may think my request odd, since I am not of your faith,' Hamid started, 'but I also wish to accompany you in bestowing this honour on the man who adopted and cared for me as his own. I came to love and respect Beorhtwulf far more than I did my real father.'

Eadwulf's gaze moved between the three determined faces and he couldn't help smiling. 'Then it seems the servants can get on with their usual chores this afternoon. Four diggers are more than enough and we can take turns with the task. Two's easily enough digging at any one time.'

'What can I do, then?' Aethelred piped up. 'Beorhtwulf was my grandfather, even though I've known him for such a short time. I really liked him and he told such wonderful stories about the days when he was king, and about Cordoba.'

'You can keep the diggers supplied with watered ale,' Eadwulf replied, grinning at his son's affronted expression. 'It's thirsty work, digging, and you can fetch a couple of jugs of ale, one at a time… It's a short enough walk over to the chapel. And it might be an idea for you to take a turn at digging, too.'

'Thanks!' Aethelred yelled, punching the air in a gesture that made the others chuckle. Eadwulf felt no guilt about that. Grief would leave no room for smiles when they said farewell to Beorhtwulf tomorrow, let alone laughter.

Fifteen

Winchester, Wessex: Christmastide 875

Ealhswith and her women had lovingly decorated the Winchester hall for the Christmastide. Boughs of holly and other forest greenery bedecked the walls, a huge Yule log smouldered in the hearth and trestle tables were permanently laden with a variety of mouth-watering foods. Game was plentiful, including wild boar and venison, as were cheeses and flatbreads, and the cauldron of simmering pottage was repeatedly filled. Honey cakes were stacked alongside bowls of nuts and syrupy fruits that had been preserved throughout the summer and autumn. All was perfect for the Wessex king and his guests.

At the start of the Christmastide the endless supplies from the kitchens had delighted them all. Between the daily gatherings at the hall's own chapel and major services in Winchester's imposing cathedral, they had all abandoned themselves to what Alfred could only describe as sheer gluttony.

There was no shortage of adults present with healthy appetites. In addition to Alfred's family were the many household servants and dozen resident thegns. Hampshire ealdorman, Radulf, was also here for the Christmastide with half a dozen of his men, and as a gesture of goodwill to those in holy orders who had been enraged by his demand for silver a few years ago, Alfred had invited fifteen clerics from various Wessex shires, along with Ethelred, the pompous archbishop of Canterbury.

Much as Alfred disliked entertaining the hostile clerics,

on this occasion he enjoyed observing their antics. Despite gorging themselves on the food he'd generously provided they frequently glared at him as though anticipating a sudden demand for more silver. Alfred said nothing and watched them squirm as he simply smiled in return. He would not be requesting silver on this occasion, but there would undoubtedly come a time in the future when he would need to.

Feasting had begun on the day before Christ's Mass and now, on December 27, the second day after that holy day, Alfred longed for the season to be over and normality to return. For one thing, he had new building plans to set in motion and he was desperate to get down to the coast to check the progress of his shipbuilders. He gazed around the hall, noting that few were still indulging in the spreads of food, or even the ale or mead. Thankfully, the archbishop and most of the clerics had already left for their respective churches or abbeys, whilst those of his thegns and Radulf's men not on guard outside played board games or dice, or simply chatted amongst themselves.

Surrounded by a small group of her women, Ealhswith was busy working on a new wall hanging to replace an old one that was now looking rather worn. Metal needles flicked back and forth to a rhythm set by swiftly moving fingers. Thankfully, Agnes had taken Aethelflaed and Edward outside for a breath of fresh air before their bickering drove everyone mad.

Alfred sat alone, musing on the current state of Wessex and the chances of another year free of Danish attack. His kingdom had now had four years of peace, but should the Danes return during the coming year, he wanted to be ready. As many of his towns as possible must be well-fortified and the shire fyrds in a state of permanent readiness to be called. Guthrum's ever-expanding army had been in Cambridge for almost a year, and Alfred suspected they could be on the move again come spring, and possibly into Wessex.

So deep was he in thought, he hadn't noticed Ealhswith's approach. 'You look troubled,' she said, sitting by his side and nestling close. 'I hope you're not about to tell me the pains have started again. This often happens when you have too much rich food and drink.'

Alfred patted her hand. 'Not this time, though. I've needed a level head on my shoulders and a dignified appearance with all those clerics glaring at me. Besides, I learnt my lesson regarding rich foods a long time ago. So no, I haven't been eating like a pig recently, and I have no pains, other than the ones that trouble my thoughts.'

Gently, he took hold of Ealhswith's chin and turned her head to face him, his eyes searching deep into hers. 'But don't think I haven't noticed you eating like a sparrow since well before Christ's Mass. And decorating this hall sapped your strength sooner than usual. I'm guessing you have news for me…?'

'I was hoping I wouldn't need to tell you for another month or two, and I didn't want to give you anything else to worry about. But yes, I am with child again, although little more than two months into my term. I can't eat a great deal, as the sickness overwhelms me at times. But things were no different with the other babes and the nausea should soon pass.'

She snuggled closer into Alfred's side as he kissed her cheek. He knew just how ill his wife felt during these early weeks of pregnancy. Sometimes just the smell of food sent her hurtling outside.

'But it seems you guessed my secret,' Ealhswith added with a small smile. 'If all goes well this time, the child should be born in June.'

'Then we'll look forward to June together. I've been hoping you had good news for me all month, and I couldn't be more pleased to hear it. And I don't want to hear any more morbid thoughts. All *will* go well this time, I'm sure of it.'

By mid-morning the following day the last few bishops and abbots had left. Radulf and his men were still at Winchester, although he, too, would need to return to his home near Southampton within the next few days. The hall seemed much larger without the sixteen clerics in their voluminous attire. It was also pleasantly quiet, a state that Alfred savoured when he needed to make plans for the coming months. Since Radulf was still around they sat together and listed the Wessex towns most in need of fortifying, and the order in which they would ride out to them.

As daylight began to fade in mid-afternoon, four men arrived at Winchester on well-lathered horses. They were ushered into the hall by the thegns on duty and, recognising them, Alfred shot to his feet, his heart pounding. There was only one reason why his scouts from Cambridge should have ridden to Winchester with such speed.

The group's spokesman fell to his knees and poured out his garbled tale.

'Half of Guthrum's army left Cambridge three days ago, lord, heading south-west and crossing Wessex south of the

Berkshire Downs before circling down to Wareham. We followed from a distance so we wouldn't be seen.'

Alfred momentarily stared at the man, wondering whether he'd heard him correctly and motioned for him to stand. 'Half of Guthrum's army, Sigebert…? What about the rest? Are they still in Cambridge?'

'Yes, lord. We thought they'd likely stay there until early spring when they could sail their ships round the south coast to join the others.' Sigebert looked a little sheepish. 'But that was just our thoughts…

'The whole Norse army is huge now lord, though the force in Wareham looks small without the warriors who stayed in Cambridge. So many ships came…'

'We got your reports of arrivals over the summer, and I thank you for them,' Alfred said, his stomach lurching at the realisation that Guthrum's army had suddenly become *his* problem.

'What I want to know,' he murmured, as though thinking aloud, 'is how this army managed to travel through Wessex without a single challenge from our towns….'

'They stayed clear of important towns. Most of the settlements along their route were small places, with no way of challenging them. The Danes didn't bother many of them anyway, they just rode past.'

'And they're now settled in Wareham?'

'They are, lord. We left as soon as they'd taken the town. There was little fighting, as far as we could see. Wareham folk must've given little resistance because the bloody Danes just rode calmly in... Excuse my venom, lord; it was hard to watch without the bile rising. But we didn't want to be in the area once they sent out foraging parties, so we rode straight here.'

'You have my sincere thanks,' Alfred said, gesturing to the four scouts. 'Get your horses over to the stables then refresh yourselves in here. As you see, there's plenty of food and drink about.'

'There's only one thing we can do,' Alfred said, his anger rising to take the place of dread as he turned to Radulf. 'Come tomorrow morning, we get word to our ealdormen to call up the fyrds. We need armies from as many shires as possible – and the sooner we reach Wareham, the better.'

'I'll leave for Southampton at first light and get word to our Hampshire thegns to call up the fyrd. And if you send men to some of the other shires, I'll send men out to the rest. I suggest we decide which we'll cover between us.'

Alfred nodded grateful thanks. 'Gathering an army will take time we can't afford but that's the way it always is!' he yelled, struggling to control his rising anger. Now wasn't the time to rant about the inefficient age-old Saxon custom of relying on shire fyrds instead of a regular force. 'All armies will head to Dorset as soon as is humanly possible and rally at Wimborne. The town's a good thirteen miles from Wareham – close enough for our army to cover when the time comes, and, hopefully, far enough away to muster without Guthrum knowing. Whatever happens, we arrive at Wareham as a complete force and the more men we have, the better. '

Radulf nodded. 'If Daegmund's as wise an ealdorman as I think he is, he'll already be rallying the Dorset fyrd. I'll send word to prepare him for a Wimborne muster.'

For the rest of the day, the Winchester hall buzzed with plans to be put into motion with the forthcoming dawn. Other than Alfred's small force camped outside Winchester, the Hampshire fyrd, like those of all other shires, would still be enjoying the Christmastide. It was not the ceorls that Alfred was worried about, but the thegns who would need to rapidly snap out of their revelry. The poorer folk had little means of providing rich food and drink for such a lengthy period. But still, heading to likely battle in the freezing weather of early January wasn't a pleasing prospect to anyone.

Alfred was reminded of the battle at Ashdown four years ago. How close the Saxon armies had come to defeat that day. A harsh wind and freezing rain had made a gruelling battle seem even worse. Memories of Aethelred filled his mind, along with regrets of the harsh words he'd thrown at his beloved brother once the battle was won.

How events would play out at Wareham remained to be seen but Alfred knew, without doubt, that this was to be the beginning of a long and bitter struggle to keep the Danes from taking Wessex.

* * *

Alfred had little sleep that night. He sat with Radulf as candles and oil lamps burned low, pouring out what he saw as his own failings over his four years of kingship. Radulf had become his closest confidant during that time and Alfred trusted no one more. Of all his ealdormen, Radulf alone addressed him as Alfred when not in the company of others.

'I should have given more thought to defending the routes through Wessex, Radulf. All I could think of was fortifying the towns where defences were poor, no matter where they stood in the kingdom. Four years wasted... Guthrum just rode across our lands without finding an obstacle in his way. I should have made sure the towns – and even the smaller settlements – along roads and rivers were the first to have their defences improved. Forts along roads and rivers should also have been built and permanently manned. How could I have overlooked something so vital?'

'You alone aren't to blame for that, Alfred. Many of us advised you on defences for Wessex, agreeing that our main towns were in a sorry state and needed looking at first. Besides, where would we have got the coin from to pay for so much building work? We had enough problems prising coin from those fat clerics when we needed to get the pagans out of Wessex four years ago.

'The thing we all overlooked is that Guthrum's a clever bastard. From what Sigebert said, he chose his route well, keeping to little-used tracks where there were no towns to give resistance - which in itself tells me Guthrum was in a big hurry to get to Wareham. So even if we'd strengthened towns and built forts along our main routes, it wouldn't have made a blind bit of difference.'

Alfred shook his head. 'I'm still the one responsible. I'm the king and final decisions rest with me – just as blame rests with me when anything goes wrong. When I think of how well Charles the Bald used his time after paying the Danes to leave Francia, I feel ashamed. His defences along main routes did him credit. But it's too late to think of more building work now, or even expanding our naval fleet. The Danes are here and there'll be battles to face. Wessex may well be torn to shreds and many of our people will die. We just have to do all we can to limit that.

'And you're right about Guthrum seeming in a rush to get down to Wareham. I'm wondering what makes that particular town seem so attractive.'

Sixteen

Wessex: January - June 876

Before the twelve days of Christmastide ended the Hampshire and Dorset fyrds had assembled at Wimborne, with the men of Berkshire, Wiltshire, Somerset and Devon arriving over the next few days. Surrey and Sussex warriors showed up during the middle of the second week of January, leaving only Kent and Cornwall to appear. The numbers were impressive enough and Alfred prayed they would be at least a match for Guthrum's half force.

Alfred had not expected help from Cornwall, the only one of his shires that still refused to acknowledge it was a part of Wessex. He'd also anticipated the late arrival of the Kentish fyrd but, as the days passed, he began to wonder whether they would come at all. From previous dealings with Kentish nobility, he knew only too well how they begrudged aiding the western shires, repeatedly claiming they had raiding Danes to deal with and could not afford to send warriors to help elsewhere. Knowing that to be half true, Alfred generally left Kent alone and the shire had not requested help from their king for some years.

By the end of the week the Saxon army was heading for Wareham. The thirteen-mile journey took a little under three hours, the pace determined by the fyrds who were mostly on foot. Alfred led from the front on his ageing black stallion Caesar, with Radulf and Daegmund riding on his flanks. He cursed as he saw how brutally the land around the town had already been pillaged. Surviving villagers were burying their dead beside homesteads burnt to a crisp. Makeshift shelters constructed from branches of winter-bare trees and shrubs provided their only protection from bitter January winds and frosts. The Wessex presence would put a stop to more pillaging but it was evident to Alfred that the Danes had already taken everything from these people. Wareham would likely be stocked with enough food to last for some time, while Saxon villagers would need to hunt if they were to survive.

Eventually they forded a narrow river to gather within three hundred yards of the town. Being familiar with the area, Alfred knew this river to be the Piddle, a chalk stream that flowed across the northern side of Wareham on its way to Poole Bay. To the south of the town, and also flowing towards the bay, was the River Frome. Just east of Wareham, these two rivers merged, becoming the wider channel that eventually reached Poole Bay. The town itself sat on a wedge of dry land between the Piddle and the Frome and was an excellent defensible position.

Only the western side, where the Wessex army now waited, was not protected by a river, although the remnants of an earlier earthen rampart were visible. It was also apparent that Guthrum had impressively reinforced the town's fortifications. A stab of guilt shot through Alfred at the realisation that if he'd got round to doing that himself, Wareham may not have been taken.

'All weak spots seem to have been strengthened,' he said, his outstretched finger moving to indicate a number of sections along the outer walls where stonework stood out, bright and new. Clustered around him, his ealdormen nodded. Alfred knew he was stating the obvious, but he needed to work through his thoughts. 'And there'll be lookouts patrolling the ramparts as we speak. An attack by us would be futile and we'd lose too many of our men.' He looked from one man to another. 'It seems we have no other choice than to pitch our tents and prepare for a siege. If we can't get into Wareham, we make sure Guthrum can't get men out to forage and no other Danes can join him. We place archers along the banks of the two rivers as well as the channel into the bay, leaving no way in or out of Wareham unwatched, day or night.'

During the first few days at Wareham, Alfred continuously patrolled his army to ensure that nowhere around the town had been left unwatched. It was hard to resign himself to facing the long, cold weeks of siege but he knew his army must hold its ground until starvation threatened, forcing one side or the other to surrender. A big worry was that by spring he'd be unable to hold the fyrd any longer. The ceorls would need to be back on their lands, planting the corn – without which, people across Wessex would face starvation during the following winter.

Bloody Nottingham all over again! Alfred rubbed his aching brow, trying to block his memories of that wasted winter siege of seven years ago. The outcome of that had been stalemate, which resulted in Burgred paying the Danes enormous sums of tribute before they agreed to leave his kingdom. Alfred knew he could eventually be facing the same situation here.

So much about Guthrum's sudden move to Wareham puzzled him and by the end of the first week of the siege, once satisfied his men were organised for the night watch, he talked over his fears with Radulf and Daegmund as they shared a mug of ale in his tent.

'Why would Guthrum move to the coast when he's brought only land forces with him?' he started, knowing the two ealdormen would have wondered the same thing themselves. But now was the time to put thoughts into words and hopefully, find some answers. It was warm in the tent but he absently rose and placed another log on the already glowing brazier. 'There are no Norse ships in Poole Harbour, although from what Sigebert said, that could change before long. Guthrum could also be hoping that even more ships join his own with the spring, or sooner if the seas begin to calm.'

'That's more than likely what he's waiting for,' Daegmund said. 'We've had Norse ships along this coast for some years and every year their numbers have grown. If a sizeable fleet arrives at Wareham, there could be thousands more Danes joining Guthrum's army. And we'd have fat chance of stopping them moving out and taking the rest of Wessex. The sooner we get the bastards out of Wareham the better.'

Alfred nodded. 'My thoughts exactly. But we all know there's only one thing that could persuade Guthrum to leave. We pay him off again. Our nobles will baulk at a request for more silver, especially the ecclesiastical orders, but they'll be given no choice.'

He scratched his head as his thoughts whirled. 'We'll keep on with the siege for a few more weeks in the hope of starving them out. They're probably well stocked for some time yet, although they'll get through a hefty amount of food every week… But I still say we persevere until at least the end of February.'

He looked intently at the two men. 'I'll send out a couple of thegns from each shire with a parchment from me authorising the collection of silver. They'll need to be back here as soon as they can with whatever they collect so we have it to bargain with, if need be. I'll leave it to you two to speak with the other ealdormen. They'll need to pick suitable men and have them ready to leave first thing tomorrow. Two or three from each shire is all I can spare. If Guthrum chooses to attack, I don't want our army to be too outnumbered.'

Radulf and Daegmund rose to head out and Radulf added, 'It might be an idea for me to take a couple of Hampshire thegns and ride to Kent. I don't see why Kent should escape giving us any help at all.' Radulf's opinion of Kent was evident from his scowl and Alfred knew he would be thinking about the last time Kentish nobles refused to give tribute on Radulf's request, forcing an unnecessary visit by Alfred himself. Even then, the haughty Archbishop of Canterbury only agreed to cooperate when Alfred threatened him.

'I agree, the least Kent can do is cough up some tribute, considering they ignored our request for an army from them. Take the parchment from me straight to that pompous Ethelred. I'll add a few extra words of "encouragement" to it– a little reminder of how continuing his role as archbishop depends entirely on my goodwill.'

Radulf's scowl morphed into a toothy grin. 'That should do the trick nicely, Alfred. Thanks for that.'

* * *

By the end of February it became obvious that the Danes were not going to be starved out of Wareham any day soon. It also became clear to Alfred that his own army's supplies were running dangerously low and it was Saxons facing starvation unless he made a move. Many of his ceorls were already complaining of having too little to eat, despite hunting parties providing wildfowl and small game. Icy weather and bitter easterlies were beginning to fray men's tempers and too often, brawls were breaking out. To make matters worse, murmurs of the need to be home in time for spring sowing already buzzed through the camp.

Daylight hours were gradually lengthening and although it was still bitterly cold, spring was drawing near. But Alfred knew well that storms could still sweep in during early spring, although travel by sea would become more frequent as the weeks passed. Guthrum's army must be out of Wareham before a Danish fleet had chance to berth, or Wessex was lost.

Thegns who had been sent out to their shires had been trickling back to Wareham over the past week, some having had more success than others. All in all, Alfred was pleased with the bulging bags of silver they presented – and delighted with Radulf's success in Kent. Not only had the Hampshire ealdorman persuaded Archbishop Ethelred that Alfred really needed silver from the shire, he had also managed to acquire a dozen mounted thegns and eighty men of the Kentish fyrd.

The time for negotiations had arrived.

'Now that we have enough tribute, it's time I paid Guthrum

a visit,' he started, his gaze sweeping the nobles squatted on the sparse grass between the tents. 'I need volunteers to approach the town with my request for a meeting. They will carry a white flag, which I hope the Danes will recognise: they did at Nottingham and Reading, so I've no reason to believe they wouldn't here.'

Daegmund rose to his feet. 'As ealdorman of Dorset, I'm responsible for Wareham, and willingly volunteer to carry your request, lord. I'll take two Dorsetshire thegns with me and we'll head over there before noon.'

Alfred smiled at the ealdorman, knowing him to be an experienced warrior and one used to speaking at meetings. 'Sincere thanks, Daegmund. I can think of no one better suited to this task.'

* * *

Daegmund returned within an hour of leaving the Saxon camp. He and the two thegns had been escorted directly to Guthrum inside the Wareham hall. 'Tell your king I'd be happy to see him again,' the Dane replied when Daegmund repeated Alfred's request. 'It's been a few years since I had the pleasure. I'll hear his offer in this hall at noon tomorrow. No more than two must accompany him.'

Now Alfred himself, with Radulf and the young Hampshire thegn, Osrid, were inside Wareham's gates and entering the sizeable hall in which Guthrum had taken residence. The Danish leader greeted them with a perfunctory nod and ushered them to a table where two other men were already seated and on which sat a wine jug and six silver goblets. Alfred guessed the two must be Guthrum's chosen advisors now that Halfdan and the other two kings had returned to Northumbria.

A buxom Saxon girl with long auburn braids hurried across, filling the goblets with rich, red wine before disappearing from view. Alfred kept his eyes focused on Guthrum who, in turn, was watching the three of them closely. Perhaps the Dane hoped for some reaction to the fact that many of Wareham's women had become slaves to himself and his warriors. But, although Alfred baulked at the thought of his people being so badly used, he refused to give Guthrum the opportunity to sneer at his Christian values. Fortunately, Radulf and Osrid also stayed mute.

Alfred cleared his throat. 'I thank you for agreeing to this meeting, Lord Guthrum. I'm sure Daegmund made clear to you that I wish to discuss terms for tribute.' Guthrum nodded, flashing that infuriating wolverine grin again but saying nothing.

Alfred returned a curt nod. 'It seems our siege would have to continue for some time if we want to starve you out of Wareham. And much as I'd be willing to oblige, I'm sure you and your men would prefer to be somewhere where… where you are free to move out and about, shall we say?'

Guthrum threw back his head and roared. He was a handsome man, Alfred considered, and one who would stand out among his warriors. His collar-length black hair, wide dark eyes and tall muscular build would doubtless appeal to many women.

'I see your sense of humour has improved since we last met, Alfred. Whatever gave you the idea we were unhappy being in Wareham? After all, it has everything we could need for some time yet. Whereas your men aren't enjoying being out there in those tents… Besides, your villagers will need to get back to their farming soon.'

'That's true enough,' Alfred admitted, 'so a treaty now would be beneficial to us both. You could leave Wessex for somewhere you could raid without a Saxon army to stop you, and we could get back to our daily lives. You realise, you'll never be free to raid in Wessex as you please. Our kingdom is too proud and well organised to let you to do that.'

Guthrum grinned and glanced at his two companions who were also smiling, though seemingly more at Guthrum's amusement than their own. 'A nice little speech, King of Wessex – though not totally convincing as yet. But I'm all ears for the part which just might persuade me there are better places out there than Wareham. Danegeld is very useful to us, so we're always in need of it. My men really like the look of bright, shiny silver.'

Eventually an amount for the tribute was fixed that was acceptable to Guthrum and just manageable to Alfred. But Alfred had not yet finished.

'I want assurances you won't break your word and refuse to leave once we've paid you,' he said bluntly, all humour now done with. 'Since you aren't Christians, it would be pointless to request you to swear an oath on the Bible. So, this is what I want. Over there I see one of your holy arm rings of Thor.' He tilted his head towards a sturdy wooden chest along the far wall with the amulet resting on top. 'Since Thor is one of your most powerful gods, I would not expect you to break an oath sworn on his sacred ring.'

'You've thought this out carefully, I see. Yes, I'll swear an oath.'

Alfred nodded. 'I also want an exchange of hostages. You will choose six of my men and I'll take six of yours.'

Guthrum turned to speak quietly to his two men. Alfred had already discussed this strategy with his ealdormen and thegns, and all had agreed that if they were chosen, they would honour their duty to Wessex.

Guthrum rose to indicate the meeting was over. 'Noon tomorrow, we make peace outside the city walls. Six hostages will be exchanged to ensure we both keep to our word. I will swear on Thor's arm ring and you on your Christian Bible. You will also hand over the silver. Then my army will begin preparations to leave Wessex within the week.'

* * *

The gathering the following day went smoothly enough. Oaths were sworn and Alfred picked some of the most distinguished Danish warriors as his hostages, certain that Guthrum would not risk those men's lives by breaking his pledge. Guthrum showed no surprise at Alfred's choice, but made certain his hostages were from amongst the Saxon elite. Ealdorman Brihtnoth of Wiltshire, along with five sturdy young thegns stepped forward, their heads held high. Alfred prayed the Danes would honour the agreement to treat their hostages well.

A feeling of relief swept through the camp that night and the fyrds were in jubilant mood, knowing they'd soon be going home. Even though Alfred made it clear that no one would leave until the Danes had left Wareham, their high spirits did not abate.

Three days later, as the black skies of night lightened with the pre-dawn, chaos erupted. The city gates burst open and mounted Danes streamed out. The Saxon watch raised the alarm and bewildered warriors poured from their tents, grabbing shields and weapons as they went. But attack was evidently not the Danes' intention and against thundering hordes of mounted men, the Saxons could do little but keep out of their way as they galloped towards the Exeter road.

Alfred fumed, realising that Guthrum had never had any intention of leaving Wessex. Tribute had been handed over for nothing – and it seemed that Guthrum had intended to head elsewhere all along. Once again, pursuit was his only option. The fyrd would not be going home just yet.

Yells suddenly erupted from the roadside, outraged cries taking the place of alarm. Crowds parted, allowing Alfred to walk through… but in his heart he already knew what he would see.

The bodies of the six warriors taken as Guthrum's hostages lay strewn along the road, the gaping wounds across their throats dripping dark pools of blood. Alfred fell to his knees, praying for the souls of his friends and comrades and berating himself for not seeing the slyness of the serpent in the pagan Guthrum.

* * *

Alfred felt no desire to be merciful to the six Danish hostages despite admiring the way they accepted the inevitability of death without pleas for mercy. Their executions were swift, performed in torchlight by comrades of the six slain Saxons, and in the same manner. Although unwilling to leave the bodies for the townsfolk to deal with, Alfred refused them the honour of a Norse funeral pyre. They were unceremoniously buried in a rapidly dug pit.

As soon as dawn light enabled, the Saxon hostages were buried in the grounds of a small wooden church inside Wareham's walls. Surprisingly, the church had evaded being burnt to the ground, but it had been ransacked of all relics, statues and ornaments and the old priest slaughtered. But, priest or no priest, Alfred insisted his men deserved burial in consecrated ground, and said the words of a few well-known prayers over the graves himself.

By noon he was anxious to be in pursuit of the Danes. It was almost seventy-five miles from Wareham to Exeter, which could take more than two days for a mounted army, unless horses were pushed to dropping point. With the fyrd on foot, it would take much longer. Then there was the possibility that Exeter was not Guthrum's intended destination. The Norse army could well veer inland and target important Saxon cities in the west of Wessex. But, unable to shake off the feeling that the coast was where Guthrum wanted to be, Alfred dismissed the likelihood of that.

Whatever the reason for Guthrum's night-time flight, Alfred had the feeling it had been pre-arranged long before his offer of tribute had been made. Guthrum had simply played him for an inexperienced fool.

* * *

By the time the Saxon army reached Exeter four days later, the Danes had not only taken the town, they had stripped surrounding homesteads of foodstuffs and strengthened the defences along the town's outer walls and gates. Although Alfred realised the extra men from Kent meant his army now outnumbered Guthrum's, attacking the fortified town would result in the loss of far too many of them.

Reluctantly, Alfred admired Guthrum's ability to plan his moves so well and could readily understand why the Danish leader had fled to Exeter – especially considering the likely arrival of a fleet of ships bringing hundreds more warriors. Situated on the banks of the River Exe eleven miles from its mouth on the south coast of Devon, Exeter was a perfect place from which the Norse army could move into Wessex. Guthrum would almost certainly advance in a north-westerly direction, towards the major towns of the kingdom. Sherborne, with its beautiful cathedral could be targeted, as could Wilton, Chippenham and even Winchester. His stomach lurched when he thought of Ealhswith and his children in Winchester…

Nowhere in Wessex would be safe.

Alfred prayed he was wrong in believing Danish ships were on their way to Exeter. If that dread materialised, only a miracle would save his kingdom.

* * *

Morale was low among the fyrd as the men pitched their tents outside Exeter, facing untold more weeks of siege conditions. Tomorrow they would need to hunt and forage for food. Alfred could see no way out of a situation for which he rigidly blamed himself. He should have seen through Guthrum's ready acceptance of peace and recognised that wolverine expression for what it was: a mockery of everything Alfred stood for. Guthrum was a dishonourable, oath-breaking bastard, and Alfred would deal with him as such in future. A man who dishonoured a vow made on the holy amulet of his god would not give second thoughts to breaking treaties with Wessex.

Three days later Alfred's worst nightmare was being played out and he could see no way of waking from it. A huge Norse fleet was reported to be heading west along the coast of Sussex and would soon be approaching the Isle of Wight. A further two days sailing from there would see it veering into the estuary of the Exe and on to Exeter.

Alfred resorted to the only thing he could. He prayed. He prayed that God would send a miracle that would save his Christian kingdom from the clutches of the heathens from across the seas.

* * *

The small group of_horsemen galloping towards the camp had the Saxons s wielding their weapons, though it was soon apparent that attack was not on these riders' minds.

'We've news for the king!' one of the men yelled, leaping from his horse and scanning the sea of faces.

'Then let's be hearing it, Oswald,' Alfred said, stepping out from amidst his men as he recognised the group as his shipbuilders from Swanage.

'The Danish fleet is sunk, lord!'

Alfred sucked in a rapid breath, holding it as he savoured those few sweet words. God had truly sent the miracle he had prayed for.

'A great storm struck the ships as they reached the Swanage coast,' the shipbuilder went on. 'It's a treacherous stretch of coastline at the best of times, as you know, but two days ago a tempest seemed to roll in from nowhere, masked in some kind of unholy fog.' He crossed himself at the memory. 'We watched, agog, as it swallowed up the ships, carrying them awhile before spitting them out on the rocks. Over a hundred and twenty ships there were, all smashed to pieces.'

Alfred's tongue seemed momentarily in knots as he tried to visualise the scene and he gaped at the shipbuilder. The event may well have seemed 'unholy' to the Danes – as well as to the Saxons watching from the shore – but to him, it was heaven sent.

Oswald's voice brought Alfred back to the present. 'We've seen many of those dragonships along our coasts and most had around thirty men at the oars, so we reckon more than three and a half thousand Danes were lost that day.'

'It's a huge number of deaths,' Alfred murmured, considering the implications of that. To him it meant only one thing: the Norse army would not be blessed with the reinforcements they'd been waiting for. 'I'll take our happy news to Guthrum myself,' he added with a grim smile. 'He'll be wondering where his ships are by now. Let's hope the glad tidings leave the Dane's stomach heaving and him grovelling for a way out of Exeter.'

* * *

Motionless at a table in the Exeter hall, Guthrum stared at his wine cup, his vision a little blurred. He'd already drunk more than his usual quota for one night and he knew he should stop and focus on how to play things from here. News of the loss of the ships had shattered his plans and left him in a state of near desperation as to what to do next. And the smug look on that young king's face as he delivered the news made him want to punch it right off. The wine had simply calmed him and offered solace for a while.

Over the past few days, Guthrum had watched the Saxons from the battlements of Exeter's walls and realised how much Alfred's army had grown since leaving Wareham. His own army was now outnumbered and without reinforcements had little chance of successfully fighting its way out of the city. To make matters worse, Alfred's warriors were on the lookout for any signs of a night-time bolt, their horses saddled and ready…

As king of the *hnefatafl* board, Guthrum had failed – on this occasion.

Although the hall was filled with warriors, the mood was unusually strained. They played their dicing and board games in muted tones, their attentions too often wandering. He knew they were watching him; the heat of their stares seemed to bore right through his hair and heavy woollen tunic. They wanted to hear his orders, to know what they would do next in this fiasco that had become a failed attempt to take Wessex. Guthrum also knew that any sign of weakness and indecision on his behalf now could spell the end of his leadership – and he could name several who would happily take his place, Sveinn and Ornolf amongst them.

'Tomorrow we request a further treaty with Wessex,' he said, bluntly. 'I've thought deeply on this and see no other option.' He gestured at Sveinn and Ornolf. 'You two… pick three men to take my request to the Wessex king and I want a reply by noon with arrangements for a meeting the following day. This time I'll offer Alfred as many hostages as he wants and I'll swear oaths on any damned thing he chooses! I'll write the details into the request, so see that the men don't go without it.'

Guthrum acknowledged the nodding heads and stood to leave the hall, signalling to the buxom Saxon girl to come to him. 'But if the young king thinks he's seen the back of us he couldn't be more wrong. This is only a setback, my friends, and not the end. More of our ships will reach the eastern coast over the summer and make us strong again.' He nodded at his own determination. 'Let Alfred think he's kept his kingdom… for now. It will suit us best if he believes Wessex is free of us for good. When we next strike, he'll be totally unprepared for it.'

* * *

In mid-June, Ealhswith gave birth to a daughter in her bed-chamber at the Winchester hall. The tiny but robust babe, who was given the name of Aethelgifu, was helped into the world by two experienced midwives and Ealhswith's loyal nurse, Agnes. The new arrival displayed a head of downy fair hair and had vocal cords to rival those of her elder sister, Aethelflaed.

Ealhswith wept with joy at having delivered a healthy babe

and Alfred was simply relieved that both his wife and child had survived the birthing ordeal. He had purposely stayed within reach of Winchester during Ealhswith's confinement, leaving his ealdormen to deal with the new fortifications he'd ordered around his kingdom.

'So, Edward now has two sisters to bully him,' he jested, perching on the edge of the bed as Ealhswith cradled the sleeping babe. 'The poor lad rarely gets a word in when Aethelflaed's in full spate.'

Ealhswith flashed him a smile. 'And we must hope Aethelgifu grows to be a little more subtle than her older sister. Aethelflaed says whatever's on her mind without a thought that it might offend. She reminds me a lot of someone I know…'

Alfred nodded. 'I admit, she is much like I was as a child. It took some years for me to learn to keep my tongue in check.' He stroked Aethelgifu's dimpled cheek, his thoughts veering to the fragility of life and how it must be protected by the strong. Feeling the touch of Ealhswith's fingers on his own cheek he grasped her hand and kissed it with vehemence. 'But on a different note, Aethelflaed has the good fortune of looking like her mother, which any woman would envy.'

'Then, my lord, I sincerely hope that one day, Aethelflaed will find as much happiness in a marriage as I have in mine.'

Alfred reluctantly left the bedchamber when Agnes declared her mistress in dire need of sleep before the babe wakened and demanded feeding again. He headed back to the hall to enjoy a mug of ale and mull over his thoughts.

Wessex was once more at peace and he prayed that the thirty, high-ranking Danish hostages and the many oaths sworn by Guthrum and two others who called themselves 'kings' would be enough to keep it that way, at least for a while. Having already had several dealings with this duplicitous Dane, Alfred knew that the peace would only be a temporary one. Guthrum was unlikely to abandon his craving to control Wessex and would try again at some stage in the future. But he hoped for a year or two – just long enough to secure Wessex from the Dane's greedy fingers.'

Seventeen

Wessex: August 876 - November 877

Guthrum had requested to remain in Exeter until late summer to allow time for his army to prepare for the move back to Mercia. Although not happy with that, Alfred agreed, if only as a gesture of goodwill. True to his word for once, in mid-August, Guthrum notified Odda, the Devonshire ealdorman, that his army would be leaving the city the following day.

By the time news reached Winchester three days later, Guthrum was on his way, and Alfred sent out his own scouts to check that the Danish army really did leave Wessex and the move was not another of Guthrum's tricks. After almost another two weeks the scouts sent word that the Norsemen had ridden north along the old Roman road known as the Fosse Way, and were now in the Mercian town of Gloucester. Guthrum had shown no mercy to the people of that region, driving many of them out and ransacking the land.

The merciless Dane seemed to be taking revenge for his failure in Wessex on those innocent people of Gloucester.

A further worry for Alfred was that Gloucester was barely forty miles from the Wessex border and he feared that Guthrum could use the town as a base from which to plan his next move into Wessex. But as the winter months neared, his scouts informed him that the Norse army had moved east, back to Cambridge, and Guthrum was now busy dividing the entire eastern half of Mercia between his warriors for settlement. The puppet king of Mercia, Ceolwulf, whom Alfred had found to be a far more competent king than Burgred, was left in control of only the west, and even that excluded the area around Gloucester, which was already under Danish control. Though Alfred's heart went out to the Mercian people, he could only hope that Guthrum would now be content with what he had and would leave Wessex alone.

* * *

Chippenham, Wessex: Christmastide, December 877- January 878

'I'm so glad to be here for Christmastide, Alfred,' Ealhswith declared as she paced the floor of the hall in an effort to help Aethelgifu to nod off. 'I've seen nowhere other than Winchester this year.'

Her old nurse, Agnes, was busy arranging pine cones, ribbons and woodland evergreens into decorations for the walls and tabletops with Aethelflaed and Edward, and Ealhswith had been glad of their interest in the task while she tended Aethelgifu. Now all she needed was for the demanding eighteen-month-old to sleep awhile so she could join them in their preparations for the twelve days, the first of which was now only three days away. 'It's more than four years since we were here and I've really missed it.'

Alfred glanced up from his parchments and Ealhswith chided herself for distracting him from his work. They'd only arrived in Chippenham two days ago and she knew her husband wanted to finalise the plans he had been making for reinforcing the vill with Thunar, the Chippenham reeve.

'It's a pretty settlement, especially with the River Avon so close,' Alfred agreed, seeming unbothered about being drawn from his work. It's especially beautiful in summer when the forest's in full leaf. But even in winter the woodland has a stark beauty that can take the breath away. There are plenty of deer in there, and wild boar. It was my father's favourite hunting lodge, so I came here many times as a child. In fact, Thunar led a hunt the day before we arrived. The couple of deer and young boar they took will add to the Christmastide meats.'

Ealhswith laid the now sleeping child in her crib and came to sit beside him. 'I hope we can enjoy this season after all that has happened these past two years,' she started. 'You've been away so much and I've feared for your life too often. I hope you can rest and enjoy our guests and the food while we're here, at least. But Alfred, please don't think I don't know why we've really come to Chippenham.'

'Am I really so easy to read?' Alfred said, and smiled at his wife's affirmative nod. 'I haven't said anything because I'm praying my fears will be unfounded, but–'

'You still don't trust Guthrum to keep his word,' Ealhswith finished for him.

'No, I don't. The fact that he's recently moved back to Gloucester bothers me. He wants Wessex, it's as simple as that. And he's already proved how little he cares for the lives of hostages we take, so there's nothing to stop him. On top of which, my spies tell me that since he moved back to Mercia sixteen months ago, he's recruited enough men to his army to more than replace those lost on the ships that went down…

'That's a big worry, I confess, and I hope that while we're this close to the Mercian border, if Guthrum decides to invade Wessex again, we'll hear about it long before he actually makes his move. My spies are watching things Gloucester and will inform me if anything seems amiss.'

Ealhswith simply nodded, but her heart reached out to him. She had hoped Alfred could put all thoughts of invading Danes out of his mind this Christmastide.

'Our guests should start arriving over the next couple of days,' Alfred went on. 'The hall will be heaving if they all get here, just like Winchester was two years ago. I've invited the entire witan, so it will be interesting to see who actually comes. Archbishop Ethelred's already sent word that he'll be here with a small retinue. I've heard from a couple of ealdormen, including Radulf, Unwine and Wulfhere, but I'm hoping to see as many as possible, as well as a good number of thegns and clerics, including the Abbot of Malmesbury. We missed the gift-giving completely the year Guthrum took Wareham, and last year our coffers were too low to do justice at the ceremony. So it's time some of my most faithful men were properly rewarded.'

Ealhswith smiled. 'I can remember what you said that year about fat, greedy clerics staring at you. Are you likely to enjoy their company on this occasion, do you think?'

'Probably not, but I promise not to stare back this time.'

'What about the thirty warriors you have camped outside? I mean, will they come in to enjoy the feasting over the twelve days? We can't expect them to stay out in the cold while we're all enjoying the warmth and good food in here.'

'I've told them they can come in and out at any time, so don't worry on their account, Ealhswith. Thunar's certain we have enough foods of every description to feed everyone for the twelve days, and the women will continue to collect eggs and bake bread and suchlike on most mornings. But the men will have to sleep outside; there just aren't enough sleeping benches in here for them. Most of them have moved into the warmer barns and byres and some have been given shelter by Chippenham villagers for the twelve days.

Ealhswith nodded, savouring her visions of the days ahead and determined to put thoughts of invading Danes out of her mind. Alfred was right: peace may not last for ever, and who could say what the new year would bring? But for now she was content to enjoy a peaceful Christ's Mass with the people she loved most in all the world.

* * *

'My lords!' Alfred yelled, rising to his feet and lifting the mead-filled drinking horn to salute his guests in the Chippenham hall, 'I'm sure I don't need to remind any of you that today is the sixth day of January and the twelfth and last day of Christmastide. And tonight is Twelfth Night – the night on which we enjoy the wassail feast and remember the gifts given to the infant Jesus by the three magi. Amongst our Saxon forbears, the act of gift-giving became the role of kings – a role I gladly undertake.'

He gestured at the central hearth. 'Tomorrow the yule log's charred remains will be dragged outside along with the decorative evergreens, and we will spend the seventh day of January like any other winter's day. Some of you will even begin your long journeys home. But tonight the celebrations are to be enjoyed by all.'

Some of the elite of Wessex had been given pride of place with him at the high table, with the arrogant Archbishop Ethelred immediately to his right in respect of his holy office, and Abbot Hunfrith to his left. Others were seated at tables positioned around the hearthfire, while still others perched on stools, or on the edge of the sleeping benches around the walls. The wives and children of prominent Wessex men occupied tables at the side of the hall, Alfred's own family amongst them.

Alfred took a sip of mead and passed the drinking horn along. He needed his wits about him for the ceremony and had no intention of getting drunk tonight. 'This Christmastide our lands are free of the pagan Danes,' he went on, 'for which we have given our thanks to God many times over. On Twelfth Night two years ago we were gathering in Dorset ready to confront the Danes in Wareham, and our wassail tradition of gift-giving was abandoned. Last year, Wessex resources were simply insufficient to do justice to our age-old Saxon custom. But tonight, here at Chippenham, I intend to make up for that.' He selected a scroll from the table in front of him and held it up. 'No one who has served Wessex well will go unrewarded. Those absent tonight will be informed over the next few weeks, among them Ealdorman Wulfhere of Wiltshire, who, as you all know, had need to leave our celebrations three days' ago on news of his wife's imminent childbirth.'

Although many of the men were enjoying the gathering, Alfred could not help noticing others who were sour-faced and silent. Among them was Archbishop Ethelred.

'I owe you all much for your efforts in defending our kingdom,' he continued, 'and although our stores of silver are still low after payments of tribute, I still have gifts of land to bestow. And,' he added, lifting a sack up from beneath the table, 'arm rings and other pieces of jewellery I've kept for these occasions. So now I'll make a start, then we can get on with the serious business of mead drinking!'

Whistles and cheers and hammering on tables showed what the men thought of downing mead. 'I'll begin by naming those who remained steadfast throughout the events at Wareham and Exeter: Radulf of Hampshire, Daegmund of Dorset, Paega of Berkshire, Unwine of Sussex, Odda of Devon, Aethelnoth of Somerset and Ceneric of Surrey. Nor have I forgotten Wulfhere of Wiltshire, our newest ealdorman since Brihtnoth's death at Wareham –'

The door was suddenly thrown open and one of the half-dozen guards Alfred had placed on watch burst in. 'King Alfred! Your four spies are here from Gloucester.'

Sigebert pushed past him and fell to one knee. 'Guthrum's army is in Malmesbury, lord, and will be here before daylight.'

Alfred surged to his feet, his heart pounding, as the room broke into an uproar of outraged cries. Malmesbury was barely ten miles away. He held up his hand for silence. 'You know this for certain…?'

'Aye, lord. They took Malmesbury mid-afternoon, but only as a place to rest on the way here. They'd ridden hard over the thirty-five miles from Gloucester and we followed at a distance. We were hard pushed to keep up with them until they stopped at the town.'

'And the Malmesbury people...?' Abbot Hunfrith's blanched face reflected his anguish. 'Pray God few have been harmed.'

'There was no resistance as far as we could see, lord, and the Danes did no damage to the town,' Sigebert assured the now trembling abbot. 'Most of the townsfolk seemed to have fled, probably into the forest, though the old and bedridden may have been still inside their homes. We just watched Guthrum's army ride in and tend to their horses before setting about feeding themselves.'

Abbot Hunfrith sank to his seat, and Alfred focused on Sigebert. 'You haven't yet said how you know they're aiming for Chippenham.'

Sigebert glanced at his three companions. 'Once the Danes left Gloucester, the people were abuzz with things they'd heard about where Guthrum was heading. Norse warriors like to brag, they said. It seems Guthrum knows you're in Chippenham, and he wants you dead. He believes Wessex won't hold together once you're gone.'

Alfred's head reeled and he struggled to pull his thoughts into focus. 'I would have hoped for an earlier warning!' he yelled as Sigebert cowered. 'If Gloucester people knew of these plans, why didn't you? An army can't just mount up and leave without preparation, so where were you three when they were doing it?'

Calls of agreement with Alfred's words rang around the

room and the four spies hung their heads in shame. Sigebert eventually confessed, 'We paid little heed because it was Christmastide and midwinter... and we didn't think Guthrum would make a move until spring.'

'You didn't think *at all*!' Alfred yelled, his temper boiling. 'Guthrum took Wareham at this time of year, so why wouldn't he try the same thing with Chippenham? And if the Danes hadn't stopped at Malmesbury, we would have had no warning at all!'

But he had no time to waste on berating his scouts. 'We'll speak of this another time and pray God this late warning gives us time to get well away.' He gestured to a score or so of his men. 'Load up the wagons with food and drink and get the women and children to Wilton with all haste. And take the sack over there,' he added, his arm sweeping the trestles. Guthrum's greedy hands won't get anything of value from this hall. Keep going, other than stopping to rest the horses. Pray to God you lose no wheels due to potholes. The rest of us will catch up with you before long.'

Ealhswith didn't need any second telling and was up with Agnes and the servants collecting thick coats and boots and furs and blankets, as well as the remnants of the night's food and drinks, to take to the wagons. It was thirty-five-miles from Chippenham to Wilton, and with slow-moving wagons, the journey could take almost two days. Although Alfred could see the need for these goods, he was impatient to see his family as far away from Chippenham as possible by the time Guthrum arrived, and hurried them all on their way.

He watched the wagons pull out, sending an extra dozen

of his warriors as further escort, and it wouldn't be long before the rest of them caught them up. Then, once they reached Wilton, it would be a case of calling up the shire fyrds again.

Alfred returned to the hall and yelled for silence above the chaos of confusion and concern. 'Other than my resident thegns and the warriors here with us for protection, I ask none of you to come with me to Wilton. Some of you face long journeys home, so I suggest you leave very soon.' He turned to focus on the sour-faced archbishop. 'My lord, Ethelred, you have the furthest of all to travel, and I'm glad you came with a large an escort, but you need to be setting out now.'

'Do you think me afraid to face the heathens?' the archbishop retorted. 'God will protect me, and we will leave only after I have spent time in prayer – so you will likely leave before me. You must do as you see fit, King Alfred, and flee to Wilton, since that is your closest place of refuge. May God give you strength when the Danes do catch up with you.'

Though Alfred found the archbishop's words strange, he nodded and turned to the rest of his nobles. 'I'll be glad to have all of you back in your shires and ready to raise the fyrds as soon as I send word.' The men agreed with the logic of that. 'As soon as I reach Wilton, Ealdorman Wulfhere will be raising the Wiltshire fyrd, so my messengers should reach you all within the next week or so. Guthrum's army has grown since we last met, so we need as many able-bodied men as possible. I don't want to be laying siege at Chippenham as we did at Wareham –'

'– which did not turn out in our favour and cost the kingdom coin it could ill afford. So no, we don't want a repeat of

Wareham,' Daegmund agreed. 'We need to face the Danes head on, and win – which is possible, if we raise enough men.'

Alfred nodded his thanks to the Dorset ealdorman but did not comment. Raising enough men had been the problem all along. 'The sooner you all leave Chippenham the better,' he said. 'We should be gathering close to here in the next few weeks to confront Guthrum. And, hopefully, this time will be the last.'

* * *

Guthrum could barely contain his rage. Having reached Chippenham some time before the January night lightened with the pre-dawn, he had found his quarry flown. A menacing presence in helmet and chainmail byrnie, he stormed round the hall, noting the signs of rapid departure – and turned his venom on the man he held responsible.

'You swore to me that Alfred would be here… yet what do I find? The place is empty, and my men can find very little food around! Give me a believable explanation or die where you stand.'

Archbishop Ethelred's face registered alarm but his voice was calm. 'The king had warning from the spies he'd had watching your movements in Gloucester. Their arrival took us by surprise in the middle of a feast and gift giving ceremony. Had there been no alert, Alfred's men would have been mead-sodden and snoring by the time you got here. Taking them in that state would have been easy. Perhaps if you hadn't stopped at Malmesbury, Lord Guthrum, the spies following you could not have got here first.'

The warlord's chest heaved and he took a threatening step towards Ethelred, his hand on his sword hilt. Yet somehow he managed to control his temper at the blatant criticism of his decision to rest the horses. This man would be more use to him alive than dead. 'Stopping at Malmesbury seems to have been a mistake in that case, as does the fact that we failed to see we were being followed…

'So now we make alternative plans. I'm hoping you're about to tell me that Alfred headed for Wilton.'

Ethelred nodded. 'He did, lord, with his family, a dozen thegns and a band of thirty or so hired warriors. They're unlikely to reach Wilton until late tomorrow, perhaps the morning after that, even if they have no hold-ups on the way. They have wagons with them –'

'I've no intention of charging after them tonight, if that's what you're thinking,' Guthrum snapped. 'Whenever Alfred reaches Wilton, I'm relying on Wulfhere to hold him until we get there. The fifty warriors I left with him will remind him who his new overlord is and our men should have no problem in taking such a small number.'

Guthrum smiled to himself, imagining Alfred's reaction when he realised his newest ealdorman had betrayed him and accepted Guthrum's rule over Wessex. Alfred's reactions would be even more amusing when he discovered that the powerful Archbishop of Canterbury had also lost trust in his kingship. But what did Alfred expect? So far, his kingship had relied almost wholly on his nobles repeatedly digging into their coffers to pay tribute to the Danes following the battles he had lost.

All Guthrum needed to do now was convince a few more of them they'd be better off paying *him* directly, eliminating the battles and bloodshed in between.

No, things weren't as bleak as he'd originally thought. Alfred may still be free, but that freedom would soon come to an end. Before long he'd have no supporters left to be able to raise an army. Besides, Guthrum now had another good hall to call his own, and once Alfred was dealt with, his men could start rounding up thralls and pillaging local settlements for foods.

Whatever happened now, Alfred was no longer King of Wessex. And at that thought, Guthrum's laughter rang out – just in time to welcome the first glimmers of daylight on the seventh day of January.

* * *

It was approaching noon as Alfred's party crested a rise four or five miles north of Wilton. Their journey from Chippenham had been unbearably slow, despite spending two nights with very few stops. Alfred fretted they may not reach Wilton before Guthrum's men picked up their trail and caught up with them. Yet the rumbling wagons and carts could go no faster and he bit back his frustrated curses.

He shielded his tired eyes against the glare of the watery, January sun, still low in the sky despite the hour, and gestured to three of his men. 'Wulfric, Raulf and you, Edgar, ride ahead and let Wulfhere know we'll be in Wilton soon. We need food and somewhere to sleep… and I want Wulfhere to start raising the Wiltshire fyrd. We've no time to waste in this. We'll keep moving at our own pace and meet up with you there.'

Alfred watched his men ride off, and turned his mount to see Ealhswith and Aethelflaed heading his way.

'Papa, will we be there soon? It's boring sitting in that wagon all the time.'

'We haven't far to go now,' Alfred replied, amused by his daughter's disgruntled face. 'But you do know why we had to get away from Chippenham?'

'Yes, and we've all been scared in case the Danes caught us. They won't be able to get near us in Wilton… will they?'

'Aethelflaed, don't pester your father about such matters now,' Ealhswith scolded.

'It's all right,' Alfred assured his wife before answering Aethelflaed's question. 'Once we're inside Wilton, with Wulfhere's men we'll be well able to defend the place if the Danes find out where we've gone – at least until some of the shire fyrds get here. But now we just need to get there.'

Aethelflaed nodded, seeming to think about that before turning to pull her mother back to the wagon.'

They had covered little over a mile before the three thegns came hurtling back, gesturing wildly for the party to stop. It didn't take much to work out that something was very wrong and Alfred didn't need to ask for explanation since Wulfric just blurted it out.

'The place is crawling with Danes. A couple of dozen of them were patrolling outside, guarding the gates and there were others atop the walls. We were fortunate to hear some of them laughing and stayed behind the trees. But lord, we also saw…'

Wulfric faltered, as though unwilling to finish what he'd started to say.

'Saw what?' Alfred demanded.

'Ealdorman Wulfhere was there, just strolling about and laughing with them.'

Alfred's spirits plummeted but his mind was working fast as his family gathered round him. He'd think about the implications of Wulfhere's evident betrayal later. Right now, getting his wife and children away from danger was his foremost concern. Sherborne was a possibility, although, as a major ecclesiastical centre it could be one of the first Wessex towns to be targeted by Guthrum. What he needed was somewhere quiet and out of the way… like the place in Somerset where his father had often retreated to.

'Then we head into Somerset, somewhere away from the coast where more Danes could still land. The village of Muchelney is as good as anywhere while I make my final decision. It's almost fifty miles from here, so be prepared for another few days of travel. Have we enough food to last?' Ealhswith nodded and Alfred motioned for the party to head west.

* * *

Dusk was falling as the wagons pulled up beside a small wood-planked hall amidst a cluster of wattle-walled houses and a simple chapel that constituted the village of Muchelney. The settlement sat on the edge of an expanse of dark, foreboding fenland and was backed by dense woodland, and Ealhswith wondered at Alfred's decision to come to this place. Yet after almost a week of travelling and sleeping in a wagon since leaving Chippenham, thoughts of the comforts found inside a hall – no matter how small – lifted her spirits. The children were becoming unbearable, cooped up in the wagon day after day, and Ealhswith's pretence at cheerfulness was wearing thin. As always, Agnes had been a gem, keeping Aethelflaed and Edward occupied with guessing games, especially when Ealhswith had needed to tend Aethelgifu.

She was thankful the January weather had not been mercilessly icy. A few snowflakes had fallen two days ago but had not settled. Fortunately for Alfred, the extra men he'd hired for their security at Chippenham were equipped with tents for sleeping outdoors, which provided protection for them all during the cold nights, and guards on the watch kept the campfires burning all night.

Yet still, for Ealhswith, the underlying worries for the future persisted. She had no idea how long they'd be in Somerset, or what Alfred would decide to do tomorrow. But for tonight she would try to put it from her mind as she snuggled into Alfred's warmth, hopefully in something that resembled a bed.

* * *

Two days later, Ealhswith was enjoying a moment's peace outside the hall while Aethelgifu slept when Alfred hurried over to her from the stables. She smiled as he approached, but that smile soon dropped when she heard what he had to say.

'I'm sending you and the children to Wedmore tomorrow. I want you well away from here so that if Guthrum comes after me again, I can take comfort in knowing that at least my family is not in immediate danger.'

But to Ealhswith, thoughts of a separation stabbed hard at her heart. 'Alfred, I don't want to go to Wedmore! I'll do nothing but worry about how you are, so please, let us stay here with you. And Aethelflaed and Edward will be so miserable.' She turned away to hide the welling tears, searching for something to say that would make him change his mind.

'Look at me, Ealhswith,' he said, turning her to face him. 'You know as well as I do, I'll have to face Guthrum eventually. Right now, I can't see further than today, so how that will come about I've no idea. But the last thing I want is to be constantly fretting over yours and our children's safety. Wedmore's some distance from central Wessex, which is where I believe Guthrum will target. I also think he'll know before long that I've gone into hiding into the marshes –'

'The marshes… You mean that boggy fenland?' Ealhswith almost choked on the words as she pointed at the foreboding landscape beyond the village. How can you possibly survive in there? Surely, there's no way anyone can get in and out of that place. It frightens me just to look at it. It's bog, Alfred. You'd sink, and –'

She stopped suddenly, realising Alfred was smiling at her.

'The fens are only a danger to those who don't know them. I came here many times with my father and know most of their secrets – though not as many as those who dwell on the isles that rise out of the marsh. There are odd pathways to be found, but they aren't in obvious places and are obscured by shrubby trees and thick reed growth. Few strangers to these lands find their way through. Many have stepped off the paths, to be sucked down, deep into the bog…

'Don't look so worried. I know the pathways well and many of the Fen Folk will remember my father, if not me. I'm hopeful they'll also help us to set up a quick camp somewhere. We need to be protected from the weather at this time of year; I had enough of sleeping in a tent at Wareham two winters ago. Some of the dry areas are of reasonable size – but knowing how to get out to them is the problem. The Fen Folk spend their whole lives in these marshes, growing their crops and rearing a few livestock around their simple wattle-and-daub homes. They're skilful fishermen, too, poling their little boats along the narrow channels between the reeds in search of places to cast their lines. There are some fair-sized lakes and they're well stocked with fish.' He shook his head. 'But I'll speak no more of all this. You'll be safe in Wedmore. I know you like it there. After all, Edward was born there.'

Ealhswith sighed, realising the futility of trying to persuade Alfred to change his mind. And when she thought about it with her head instead of her heart, she knew Wedmore would be better for the children. 'Yes, I like Wedmore, and Erwig and his wife. Goda is such a caring soul. We'll be content enough there, Alfred, so you'll have no need to worry.'

'Good. I'll send a score of my men to escort you and they'll stay at Wedmore to add to Reeve Erwig's guard. At the first hint of Guthrum's men heading his way, Erwig will have you away, in some place of concealment they'll never find. He knows Somerset better than most and I trust him to keep you all out of harm's way.'

There was nothing more Ealhswith could say on the decision and she vowed to stay strong, for Alfred's sake. Tomorrow, she'd give him a cheery smile as the wagons pulled out, carrying her and the children to Wedmore. Then she'd pray constantly that God keep her beloved husband safe.

Eighteen

Elston, Mercia: mid-January, 878

'My mind's made up, Aethelred, so don't think you can talk me out of it. The Wessex king needs as much help as he can get. It's common knowledge he was forced to flee with only a small band of men. Rumour has it they've gone to ground out in the Somerset marshes.'

Eadwulf shared a glance with his son, but neither broke the momentum of their wood cutting. The day was bitter and they needed to keep moving. Besides, the sky was heavy with snow clouds and having a good supply of logs for the hearthfire was vital before the snows fell again.

'I've heard all that, too, Father, and I've been wondering when you'd get round to telling us you'd be heading down there. Your mind's been far away since the last travellers came through here a week ago. But what I want to know is how King Alfred and his men can expect to survive in the marshes. People say fenlands aren't places to go near, let alone live in, and the only way into them is on a boat.'

'I couldn't say if that's true, but in the Danish lands, people lived on higher patches of solid ground in the central fenlands. There are also reports of people living in the stretch of fen where our Mercian lands border those of East Anglia. I imagine people find some way of surviving in there.

'But wherever Alfred is, I need to get away from here, son. And before you open your mouth again, no, you can't come with me. If you were a couple of years older, I might say yes, but you're not properly battle-trained and believe me, there'll be battles to face before long. I think Jorund will want to come, and so might Hamid, but I'm not sure about Aethelnoth. He might not want to leave his family.'

It was obvious to Eadwulf that Aethelred was weighing up plausible objections and the boy eventually said, 'I haven't yet taken part in a battle, or even a raid, but I've had plenty of practice with a sword and shield with Aethelnoth, and I've had lessons in using a bow from Hamid. He says I'm a really good shot. I'm also pretty good with a spear. So I'm probably older and better trained than many of King Alfred's fyrd!'

Eadwulf had no answer to that, knowing his son's words to be true. Aethelnoth and Hamid kept him well informed regarding the lad's progress and he knew that Aethelred's swordsmanship was already admirable. He just needed a little more practice to perfect a few moves.

'And who's going to take charge around here if you all disappear?' Aethelred persisted. 'Selwyn's too old, and if you think I'm too young to ride with you then you evidently think I'm too young to run a hall and estate.'

'Eadwulf put down his axe and looked levelly at his sixteen-year-old son, trying hard not to laugh at his indignant expression. 'As I said, Aethelnoth will probably be staying here – and, yes, you're a little too young to run the estate on your own. But that doesn't mean you and Selwyn can't work on things together. And contrary to what you seem to think, Selwyn's mind works as well as ever and he knows the estate inside out. He's lived here all his life, after all. There are also plenty of hardy male servants around the place to continue the physical work…'

He paused, realising he was giving Aethelred more reasons for going with him to Somerset than staying behind in Elston. 'And to add to my objections, just think how upset your sister would be if you left here as well as me.'

Aethelred frowned as he thought about that and eventually said, 'Leofwynn wouldn't even notice I'd left! All she does all day is play with Odella and Aethelnoth's children, fussing over them like a mother hen.'

Eadwulf rolled his eyes skyward, realising he'd run out of reasons to leave Aethelred behind. He cast his mind back to when he was sixteen, sailing with Bjorn to faraway places and keeping the *Sea Eagle* ready for pushing off once the raids were over. His life was fraught with danger, so how could he justify treating his son like a child? Deep down he knew he just wanted to keep Aethelred safe. But, thinking on it, Aethelred wasn't likely to be standing in a shield wall…

'We'll say no more about all this until after I've spoken to the others and see what they think about you tagging along. But I want to be leaving before the end of this month whether you're coming with us or not.'

* * *

Somerset, Wessex: 878

Ealhswith's arrival at Wedmore was unexpected, as she had known it would be, but Reeve Erwig's frosty welcome suggested there was more to it than that.

“Lady Ealhswith… you come alone?’ he said, offering his hand to help her down from the covered wagon. ‘The king is not with you?’

‘He isn’t, Lord Erwig. My husband was needed elsewhere.’ Ealhswith did not miss the scowl on the reeve’s face as he took in the twenty men in her escort and wondered what had happened to the amiable man she remembered. Erwig had aged much in the seven years since she’d stayed here and his once dark hair was now liberally threaded with grey. His tunic seemed to hang from his thin frame and his formerly round face was gaunt and sallow.

‘These are difficult times for Wessex, as you know,’ she continued, feeling wary now, ‘and it was thought best that we come here. King Alfred doesn’t know where he’ll be from one day to the next over the coming weeks and his constant need to travel would only be hindered by our presence. Our wagons move slowly at the best of times.’

She glanced around, trying not to look guilty at the lie she’d just told. Yet something told her to say nothing of Alfred’s precise whereabouts and she felt distinctly uncomfortable about that. She’d come to know this royal vill so well during the time of Edward’s birth and hoped she could rekindle her fondness for the place. ‘I trust Goda is well?’ she said, registering her absence.

‘She is well enough,’ Erwig replied, inclining his head towards the hall. ‘At this time of day, my wife will either be organising the weaving, or starting preparations for the evening meal. That’s her usual pattern in the early afternoons. But she’ll be happy to see you again, Lady Ealhswith. We'd heard you'd birthed another child since we'd last seen you,' he added, his attention fixing on Agnes cradling the babe with Aethelflaed and Edward close to her. 'Allow me to congratulate you before we enter the hall. Then I must leave my wife to order food and drinks for you all while I finish my chores before darkness falls.'

Hoping to find Goda in good spirits, Ealhswith entered the hall. Perhaps the maternal woman would offer some explanation for Erwig's unfriendly welcome.

'You're a sight for sore eyes,' Goda gushed, rushing over once she'd ordered servants to bring refreshments. She clasped Ealhswith to her substantial body before stepping back to look her up and down. Ealhswith smiled back at her, realising that Goda did not seem to have aged as much as her husband – but then, little of her fair hair was visible beneath her head veil and her smiling face distracted the eye from any wrinkles. 'It's been too long since we've seen you, my lady, but you look as lovely as ever. Hearty congratulations on the birth of your new babe', she added, smiling at Agnes and indicating she should sit down with the squirming infant. 'I'll take the tot off your hands for a while once you've all refreshed yourselves. I can see she's a bit of a handful.'

Goda moved toward the older children and ruffled Edward's mop of dark hair. 'You were a tiny babe the last time I saw you, and now you're a big lad of seven. And just look at little Aethelflaed,' she said, taking the girl's hands. 'Not so little any more. Why, you're up to my shoulders already and with such a pretty face you're sure to make young men's heads turn before long.'

Aethelflaed's appalled expression at such a thought made everyone laugh. 'Are you keeping well, Goda?' Ealhswith asked, keen to find out if anything was troubling the family.

'As well as can be expected at this time of year, my lady, though the cold punishes my aches and pains. I'm not as young as I was and find I tire more easily now. But all in all, I can't grumble.'

'And Erwig is well, too? We had no time to enquire after each other's health just now. He was in a hurry to complete his work before daylight failed.'

Goda's brow crinkled and she gave a small sigh. 'My husband worries much these days, if I'm honest, my lady, and rarely comes into the hall, other than to eat and sleep. We exchange few words, but whenever I ask what bothers him, he becomes irritable and tells me not to fuss. I can't think what has him in such a state, other than the presence of the Danes in Wessex. Perhaps he fears they'll come here.'

Ealhswith patted the kindly woman's arm. 'I didn't mean to upset you, Goda, and would not have asked except that Erwig's welcome was… well, a little cooler than I expected. I remember him as a cheerful man with a ready smile, but I saw none of that today. Perhaps it was just the surprise of seeing us, or the fact that my escort presented him with so many more mouths to feed. Unfortunately, we couldn't let you know in advance. King Alfred has been –'

'I know, Lady Ealhswith, and my heart bleeds for you all. But if anything is certain about your husband, it's that he won't give up trying to get his kingdom back. So let's not speak more of dismal things. Seat yourselves at the table close to the hearthfire,' she said, leading them to a trestle table, now bearing food and drink. I'll send someone out to ask your escort in, too. I imagine they will be hungry.'

Goda suddenly chuckled and Ealhswith smiled, happy to see her friend in cheerful mood. 'Big strapping men like them are permanently hungry in my experience, my lady. And it's up to us women to keep their bellies full if we expect them to be at ease and not resort to brawling with each other.' She shook her head, serious again. 'I just wish I could use that tactic on Erwig. I can't get through to him, whatever I try. Food's the last thing he wants most of the time and he's starting to look like a bag of bones. There's something weighing him down, but I can't find out what it is.'

For a week, Ealhswith was content at Wedmore, spending much of her time with Goda as she entertained little Aethelgifu with her many songs and rhymes. Agnes often found herself with much-needed time on her hands, which enabled her to pay more attention to Aethelflaed and Edward, whose desire to explore their new surroundings was boundless. But Ealhswith saw little of Erwig. He'd left two days after her arrival with a few of his men, bound for Wells, just ten miles away. It seemed his brother in the town had been ill for some months, and Ealhswith wondered whether that was the cause of the reeve's unfriendly welcome on her arrival.

On his return in the middle of her second week at Wedmore, Erwig brought with him that same aura of discourtesy he'd carried before he'd left, despite proclaiming his brother to be recovering well. Ealhswith was thankful he came little into the hall, although she admitted to herself that, as a royal reeve, his incivility towards her – the king's wife – was unacceptable and Alfred would be sure to relieve him of the role if he knew about it.

Erwig had been home for a mere day when Goda scuttled through the doorway of Ealhswith's bed chamber. The January morn was barely light and Ealhswith was about to join Agnes and the children in the hall as they broke their fast on the usual oatmeal and buttermilk.

'My lady,' the reeve's wife croaked, twisting her hands in agitation, 'what I'm going to say will distress you, but say it I must. It's my husband…' Goda seemed to choke on the words and Ealhswith feared that Erwig had suffered some kind of accident. 'I know why he's been behaving so rudely towards you. He… he…'

Ealhswith patted her arm. 'Take your time, Goda. The right words will come to you soon. I'm in no hurry to go anywhere.'

'Oh but you are, my lady. That's just the point! Erwig has betrayed you… betrayed us all. He's given his allegiance to the Danes and sworn to serve their leader, Guthrum. It seems he's been thinking of doing so for weeks, and you coming here finally helped him to make his decision'

Ealhswith gasped and her heart pounded as she realised the danger she and her children were in. 'How did you discover all this?'

'My husband didn't go to Wells last week; he went to see Guthrum, at Chippenham. Two of the men he took with him aren't at all happy about what he's done and came to warn me. Wassa and Chad are loyal to King Alfred and will not side with the Danes. They said Erwig believes King Alfred will never be a match for a leader like Guthrum, and he wants to be on the winning side. Oh, my lady, I hate being the one to tell you all this…'

The woman's sobs touched Ealhswith. 'None of this is your fault,' she said gently. 'I know you believed Erwig went to Wells last week, and you could never betray anyone. But Goda, are you saying that Danes are already on the way here?'

'From what Wassa and Chad told me, Erwig was to be given time to get back to Wedmore before Guthrum started out from Chippenham. If the Dane keeps to his word, he and his men could be here later today, so the sooner you're away from here the better. I was told Guthrum roared with laughter on hearing of your presence here, and said Alfred's family would make a perfect bargaining tool for drawing him out of hiding.'

'Erwig doesn't know you've come here to warm me, does he?'

Goda shook her head. 'He was up well before dawn and left for Wells, wanting to check his brother was recovering well – or so he said. How true that is, I don't know, and I'm not sure I'll ever believe anything he tells me again. It could be he's gone to meet Guthrum on his way here. But he did say he wouldn't be back before dusk and only took three of his men with him, which is how Wassa and Chad managed to come to see me.'

'Listen to me, Goda. I have to get my children away from here as soon as our belongings are back on the wagons. I'll let our men know we'll be leaving soon after sunrise. And, Goda, please come with us. I couldn't bear the thought of anything happening to you when Erwig gets back, or worse still, when the Danes get here and find we've gone. Perhaps Wassa and Chad should come with us, too. Erwig will know that *someone* betrayed him. Promise me you'll think about it.'

'I'll do that as we get things on the wagon, my lady. But I can't promise anything else.'

The scurry around the Wedmore hall took the servants by surprise, but it didn't take long before Ealhswith was ready to leave. Agnes settled the children into the wagon as Ealhswith spoke with Goda in the hall doorway.

'You won't change your mind and come with us?'

Goda smiled but shook her head. 'No, my lady, but I know Wassa and Chad are only too glad to be joining King Alfred. They're true Wessex men and when Erwig knows they've gone, he'll realise it was they who warned you. So don't you go worrying on my behalf because Erwig will have no cause to suspect me. As far as he's concerned, I didn't know about his betrayal. Besides, he's been my husband for over thirty years, and whatever foolish thing he's done, I'll stay with him until the end.'

'But when the Danes come, you could all be –'

'I know what the future could hold, dear one, but I'll stay all the same. Now you must be off. At least I'll feel happy knowing you'll be miles away when Erwig gets back. And since I don't know where you're bound, I can't let it slip out unintentionally.'

* * *

At the end of the first week in February, Eadwulf and his four companions drew rein outside the hall in the village of Muchelney in Somerset. It was late afternoon and they were cold, hungry and travel-worn, and desperately seeking somewhere that could offer them a bed for the night. Aethelnoth rapped on the hall door and they were invited inside, only to find themselves surrounded and a dozen swords aimed at their throats.

Eadwulf took in the group of twenty or so armed men, and the two women with three children standing as far from the doorway as possible. It didn't take him long to work out who these people were, or that the armed men were their bodyguards. 'If you're Wessex men, we are not your enemy,' he said to the sword wielders. 'We are Mercians, and have come to offer ourselves to the service of King Alfred.'

None of the men spoke, but Eadwulf wasn't surprised to see the younger of the two women approach and speak as though she had every authority to do so. 'Lower your swords,' she said to the swordsmen, 'but stay ready to move if our visitors should prove to be unfriendly.'

Eadwulf watched her give the five of them close scrutiny before she replied to his declaration. 'If you are sincere in what you say, I'm sure that four of you would be of use to the Wessex king. But it appears that one of your party is a little young for the kind of warrior King Alfred has need of.' Her gaze shifted from Eadwulf to Aethelred and back again. 'From the look of him and his colouring, I'd say he was your son…?'

'He is, Lady Ealhswith, and he's only here with us to watch and learn the ways of warriors. I'm sure he'll also be very useful around your husband's camp.'

Ealhswith's giggle brought a smile to everyone's lips. 'It seems you have admirable powers of deduction, or else you had prior knowledge of our presence here.'

'It wasn't too difficult to guess who you were, my lady. It's common knowledge that King Alfred is in Somerset so it seemed obvious. I also knew you had three children and that the youngest would still be an infant. Then there's the children's nurse and this substantial bodyguard.'

Ealhswith nodded. 'As for King Alfred's camp, just where do you think that might be?'

'It's in those fenlands,' Aethelred blurted. 'That's what travellers through our lands said, anyway. My father is Ealdorman Eadwulf from Elston, and I'm his son, Aethelred. My grandfather was –'

'Enough, Aethelred,' Eadwulf snapped. 'Now isn't the time for that. But you're right to remind me we haven't introduced ourselves to Lady Ealhswith.' He gestured in turn at the others. 'Our three companions are my brother, Jorund, and our friends Aethelnoth and Hamid...

'Hamid is from al-Andalus in Iberia and he is like a brother to Jorund and me,' he explained, noticing Ealhswith's scrutiny of the young man. 'Other than my son, we are all skilled in weaponry, and Aethelred will continue to practise while we are here.'

'I think you mean, *if* my husband accepts you into his army, Lord Eadwulf. If you believe King Alfred to be in those marshes, how did you intend to make contact with him? Did you plan to simply wait here until he emerged, perhaps in need of something from this village? Or were you intending to try your luck at finding the right pathways through the boggy land?'

'We had hoped to find at least one person who knew the

fens well enough to guide us to Alfred's camp, my lady.'

The babe in the older woman's arms began to bawl and Ealhswith hurried over to take the child herself. 'Then you're in luck, Lord Eadwulf,' she said, rocking the infant back and forth to quieten her. 'We've already organised a guide to take us to King Alfred tomorrow. The man has a brother living on one of the isles in the fens and knows exactly where my husband has built his camp. You would be welcome to come with us tomorrow, but as for staying here overnight…' Ealhswith swept out her arm, drawing attention to the room. 'As you see, this is a small hall and there are no more available sleeping places. I'm afraid the five of you would have to sleep in the barn along with my men.'

'You are gracious, Lady Ealhswith, and we can't thank you enough,' Eadwulf replied, wondering why Alfred's family wasn't with him in the first place. But he kept his thoughts to himself. 'And sleeping in a barn is all we could have hoped for anywhere.'

'Good. Then I'll order food and ale to refresh you after your journey, and once you've stabled your horses and prepared your sleeping places for the night, you'd be welcome back here until we've had the evening meal. Perhaps then you will tell us a little more about yourselves and why Mercians should feel the need to help the King of Wessex.'

* * *

Their guide was a good-natured, Muchelney man called Ina. He appeared to be of late-middling years, with wiry brown hair that was just beginning to recede at the temples. Despite his relatively lowly status of ceorl, his tunic hung well on his muscled frame and he had an air of authority about him. He served as the village iron smith, and was not a man to be argued with regarding their trek into the fens.

'There'll be no horses taken into the marshes if I'm to be your guide,' he made clear to Eadwulf's party as they prepared to set off the next day. 'We ride as far as the village of Burrowbridge, nigh on nine miles north-west of here, and your horses will be stabled there till you're in need of them again. My sister's husband and his family will make sure they're well cared for. They'll be exercised daily and out in the paddock for some of the daylight hours, but back in the stables these cold nights. King Alfred's horses are there as well, and he's happy with the arrangement – paid my brother-by-marriage well for caring for his company's mounts. Lady Ealhswith's done the same for hers, so perhaps you might find a few coins…?'

Eadwulf agreed, thanking the guide for his thoughtfulness, and Ina's commanding tones became more genial now that his most crucial demand had been accepted. 'I'd also advise you to walk in a single line along these paths, my lord. I've led enough folks through these marshes to know that even walking in pairs is risky. If you keep to the middle of the paths no one need fear sidestepping off the edge and plummeting into the bog.'

The guide shook his head, his face grim. 'It's a terrible sight to see someone being sucked into the marsh, I can tell you. You'd best believe it, lad,' he added, noticing Aethelred's horrified expression, 'and make sure you walk behind each other. I've told Lady Ealhswith the same, and that big wagon of hers would never make it along some of these paths. As for the horses pulling it… I saw a horse panic once, when a marsh bird shrieked. It reared up, then bolted straight off the path, taking everything on the wagon into the bog with it, including the other horse and the wagon's passengers.

'Well, once we get to Burrowbridge, we'll unload Lady Ealhswith's baggage into packs that her men can carry between them. As luck would have it, the lady has nothing too heavy with her. And you've just got your saddle packs with you, so they'll be easy enough to carry. Now we seem to be almost ready for off.

'I'm not bragging when I say I know the paths through these fens as well as I know the lines on my own face and my rules are for the good of folks I take in there. So, although my words may sound harsh, they're spoken with your safety in mind.'

'You have our trust, Ina, and we'll gladly follow your advice,' Eadwulf said. 'Were you King Alfred's guide into the marshes?'

Ina chuckled. 'I was with him, but in truth, the young king needs no one to guide him in there. He knows which paths to take and which ones lead to disaster almost as well as I do.' He smiled, and Eadwulf could see how fond the smith was of the Wessex king. 'Alfred's loved this place since he was a lad. He'd spend whole days in there watching the wildfowl and visiting the folks on the isles when he came here with King Aethelwulf. He would often borrow one of the isle folks' little boats and take himself across the stretches of river and lakes, too. In truth, the only way to reach some of the isles is by boat

– which you'll see for yourself before long. Most of the folks remember Alfred and his father well and will see he doesn't go short of food and such like until his camp is running well.'

'King Alfred sounds like a man I'd admire,' Aethelnoth said, helping Hamid to adjust his stirrup straps before mounting himself.

'Most people like him – except perhaps the Danes,' Ina jested. 'He's straightforward and honest and says what he thinks, even if it means offending folk. He's no time for fools or idlers, either, but he's kind and just to those he sees as the same. And I'll tell you all something else. Alfred isn't beaten yet. I know him well enough to know he won't be giving up on Wessex till the day he dies. And my wife, who calls herself a bit of a seer, says he won't be dying for some years yet…

'Now we'd best make a start. It's a miserable day, and I can't see the sun breaking through this dark cloud somehow. And gloomy weather like this can make the fens seem more sinister than they really are. But I suppose, to those who don't know them, marshlands are rarely safe places in which to venture without a guide.'

Ina nodded to the five of them and headed to the front of the column to lead them out.

By late morning they had reached Burrowbridge, where they stopped to settle the horses into the stables and eat some bread and cheese bought from the villagers. In the early afternoon they set out on foot to their fenland destination, which Ina assured them was a mere mile and a half away.

The paths were every bit as perilous as Ina had warned and Eadwulf was thankful the February day was ice-free and dry. A slippery path would add to the dangers along this forbidding route. Aethelred walked in front of him behind Lady Ealhswith's escort, while Jorund, Hamid and Aethelnoth brought up the rear behind him. Eadwulf watched his son like a hawk. Should the boy take a false step, he would be there to catch him.

In many places, marshlands became lakes alongside their paths, and before long they were following the banks of one of the more extensive ones. Views across it were obscured by dense reedbeds and bulrushes, and copses of willows dotted amongst them, seemingly on isles of dry land that enabled roots to take hold. An ensemble of calls, squawks and wing beats rose from the many marsh birds; reedbeds in turn rapidly silenced as the threat of human predators passed close by. Eadwulf guessed the Fen Folk would be skilled hunters in this place, hidden away from the rest of the world. Water fowl would be a vital addition to fish for meals.

A few miles on they halted where a group of Fen Folk were gathered beside a collection of small, narrow boats tied up at the water's edge. To Eadwulf, navigating craft even as slim as these between the reeds seemed impossible. But there, in front of them, the boats waited…

Ina greeted the gathered folk before addressing Lady Ealhswith. 'King Alfred's been told of your arrival sometime today, my lady, and we're almost there now.'

Eadwulf glanced around, but could see no signs of any camp. Ahead of him, Ealhswith was doing the same. 'Just where is it?' he heard her ask, relieving the nurse of the weighty infant. 'If it's much further, Agnes and I will need to ask the help of our escort in carrying Aethelgifu, and she can become very noisy when she realises she's being held by a stranger.'

Ina chuckled at that thought. 'You'll be glad to know the king is less than a couple of hundred yards from us, my lady,' he said pointing across the lake. 'We can't see his camp because of the reeds and willows but it's out there on one of the bigger isles. When the wind blows this way we can smell the smoke from his camp fires, and sometimes, even what he's cooking. Today, the wind will carry those smells across the river that flows beside the far side of this lake.'

Eadwulf wondered again how anyone could find their way through the reeds. Even in February the growth was dense enough to obscure any channels of water. And Ealhswith's perplexed face mirrored his thoughts.

'The Fen Folk will take you to the king,' the guide explained. 'They've got half a dozen boats lined up here, and each will carry three of you as well as the person doing the poling, so a second journey will be needed to get you all across. Daylight will soon be fading so we need to make our move.'

Eadwulf and his companions were among the second group to be ferried out to the isle. Eadwulf shared a boat with Jorund and Aethelred, while Aethelnoth and Hamid were in another. The cheery young man deftly steered the boat through the reedbeds using his long pole to keep the boat moving, and although Eadwulf watched every twist and turn, he knew he'd never remember the route back unaided. It was like groping through the fog and the sensation of being totally lost was a weird and unsettling experience.

'Do you bring your boats onto the lake often?' Jorund asked as the youth concentrated on steering out of the reeds into an open stretch of lake.

The lad nodded. 'Most of us come out to fish more than anything else. These lakes are full of them – bream, roach, tench and perch, to name just a few. Then there's pike, some of the biggest you'll find anywhere. If I can catch one of those, my mother's happy for days. Just one pike can feed a few of us.'

'I can fish,' Aethelred chipped in. 'Well, I've had a few goes at it with Selwyn back in Elston. There's plenty of perch and bream in the River Trent, and carp and pike. But we just sat on the riverbank to fish, which was boring. It must be much better from a boat.'

'It is,' the lad agreed. 'Perhaps you should try it sometime. I'll bring a boat across in a few days and you can come out with me, if you like.'

Aethelred glanced at Eadwulf. 'Sounds like a good idea to me,' Eadwulf said, 'as long as you can borrow some fishing gear from…?'

'It's Garth, lord, and I've got plenty of kit, so I'll sort some out tomorrow. We'll just fish, this time. Sometimes we go out for waterfowl, and I can show you how to do that, too. We catch plenty of birds for our pot, different kinds of ducks mostly, but also geese and swans. But right now, we've reached the island. I'll take the boat as close to the beach as I can so you can step straight onto dry land and not get too wet.'

'We thank you,' Eadwulf said, stepping out of the boat. He handed Garth a couple of silver coins, knowing it was probably more than the lad had ever seen. Aethelnoth and Hamid's boat was just pulling ashore as Eadwulf turned to view the camp… and noticed the Wessex king coming towards them.

Nineteen

'Welcome to Athelney,' Alfred said, grasping Eadwulf's arm in a gesture of friendship before welcoming the other four as they drew round. 'I'm glad to have the five of you here. We need every man we can get, though I admit, you're the first Mercians to join us. But come, let's be seated away from the beach and you can refresh yourselves as we speak.'

Alfred led them up the gentle rise to where his makeshift camp was set up. The day had continued cloudy, though mild for early February, and Alfred's men were still busy at their various chores, making the most of the daylight before darkness fell. And from up here, Eadwulf admired the views across the lake.

'Ealhswith tells me you're an ealdorman, from Elston,' Alfred started, refocusing on Eadwulf once they were seated on sections of upturned logs and drinking watered ale. 'Elston's a mere fifteen miles or so from Nottingham, I believe, so you hadn't travelled too far on that day we met in Nottingham. I'm glad to see you haven't daubed your hair with river mud on this occasion.'

Eadwulf grinned at Alfred's sardonic expression, recalling how those piercing amber eyes had disconcerted him all those years ago in Nottingham. 'I knew you'd remember me and I'd have known you anywhere. I've met few men with eyes as searching as yours.' He held up his hands in a placatory way. 'No offence, lord, but your eyes seemed to bore right through me that day. And I remembered your hair because its colour reminded me of wheat.'

'Well, Eadwulf, your hair and eyes are pretty memorable, too, and I'm guessing that's why you chose to disguise your appearance. Though why you felt the need to do that, I don't yet know. Perhaps you can enlighten me later, along with your reasons for joining us.'

Eadwulf nodded. 'All five of us have our reasons, lord, although parts of our story may well have you wondering whether you can trust us. But each of us will swear to stand with you against the Danes.'

'Hmmm,' Alfred murmured, scratching his head. 'So far, Eadwulf, you've succeeded in confusing me with your unexpected arrival and now your riddled reply. I see I'll need my wits about me when speaking with you. But at least we won't be short of entertainment around our camp fires.

'What do you think of our camp, by the way? We plan to make some improvements, but we've managed with this until now. We catch our own fish and water birds, and there are wild goats and deer on the isle, including a few handsome stags. The Fen Folk fetch us fresh bread and a few turnips and suchlike every couple of days, plus a few hares and the occasional half pig – for which we're all grateful. They've also brought us some sturdy yew logs. As you probably all know, yew is ideal for making bows.'

Alfred gestured to the cluster of tents and shelters, the latter created from branches of trees and shrubs, while his men were dotted about, still engaged in their tasks. A few were chopping wood for camp fires and pieces of simple furniture, while others skinned hares or gutted fish. Still others were sharpening weapons or stringing bows and fletching arrows. One group worked on the beginnings of a barricading fence and another appeared to be in the process of building a few small boats.

What Eadwulf perceived was an ordered unit, a group of individuals working for the good of the whole. Despite agreeing with Alfred about the need for improvements, he was already impressed and said so.

Lady Ealhswith and her nurse and children disappeared into one of the shrub-built structures as they talked and, following Eadwulf's gaze, Alfred said, 'I've given my family one of the larger shelters we've built so far. There's enough space for the five of them to sleep and walk around, if need be. Once we get the new fortress built, I hope we'll have something resembling a small wood-planked hall, which should improve things. As you see, the island isn't short of trees, and although they're mostly willow and alder, some are of substantial girth.'

'You mean to build a fortress, lord?' Aethelnoth's expression reflected his surprise. 'Are such strong defences needed out here in the lake? Surely no great number of Danes could get to the island unless they managed to steal enough boats and force locals to guide them through those reeds. And even if that happened, they'd only get here a few at a time and could be easily struck down as they landed.'

Alfred nodded. 'But there's always the possibility of something like that happening and we must be prepared. Though as you say, their arrival in batches would give us a big advantage. You've probably noticed some of my men have bows…?' Alfred acknowledged their nods and went on, 'Well-aimed arrows could deal effectively with any Danes who attempt to approach

Athelney, even before they land. At very least, arrows could seriously lessen their numbers. My archers practise daily and I can tell you, their aims are remarkably accurate.'

'Yet you still feel the need for a fortress?' Aethelnoth persisted.

'We do, and for a reason none of us realised until we'd been here a week.' He smiled at the puzzled faces and even Eadwulf couldn't guess what he was about to say. 'Athelney is not always a completely disconnected island,' Alfred said. 'When water levels are low in the lake, a causeway appears, linking our isle to the village of East Lyng, about a mile to the west of here. This sometimes happens when the tide is out along the Somerset coast or when there's been little rain, especially in summer after long periods of dry weather.'

Aethelred whistled. 'So the Danes would just need to wait for low tide and ride across! That means you could probably bring your own horses here, too.'

Alfred focused on the lad for a moment. 'Your first observation is spot on,' Alfred complimented, causing the boy to grin widely, 'but as to the possibility of bringing our horses here, unfortunately, I can see problems in doing that.'

Aethelred's grin dropped. 'With our horses here on the isle,' Alfred explained, 'when the causeway is underwater – which is for much of the time during winter and spring – we could face long waits whenever we needed to leave here. And we aim to be out in Somerset and Wiltshire a great deal in the coming weeks, causing havoc at Danish camps and the halls of treacherous Saxons. So our horses are best left at Burrowbridge and we'll continue to row across the lake. We should have enough boats of our own before long, so we won't need to rely on our Fen Folk friends.

'Yes, I did say Saxons,' he said, in response to their puzzled faces, 'although it pains me to admit it. Ealhswith tells me that even some of my once loyal Somerset men are pledging allegiance to the Danes. And from what my spies have reported back, there are also a number of traitors in Wiltshire, Ealdorman Wulfhere being the worst of them.'

Alfred's voice was edged with bitterness. 'Wulfhere's betrayal means I have no way of raising the Wiltshire fyrd, so we need to win back the trust and loyalty of the Wiltshire thegns as well as the people in the villages. And by making frequent attacks on Danish camps and their raiding parties we can show them the fight for Wessex hasn't been abandoned. I'm also hoping the continued plundering of our settlements by Danish warriors will make Wessex people realise their mistake in giving them their loyalty.'

'Are there Danish camps close to here?' Alfred's words seemed to have sparked Jorund's interest and Eadwulf shared a knowing glance with Aethelnoth. Possibilities of seeing his childhood friend again were never far from Jorund's thoughts.

'Guthrum knows we're in these marshes,' Alfred replied, 'but he's made no move to come after us yet, other than having men camped in a few places not too far away. And thanks again to my spies, we know exactly where most of those camps are.'

Alfred's amber gaze swept the five of them. 'From what we've gathered, Guthrum's control of Wessex hasn't yet spread beyond Wiltshire and Somerset, and he and the bulk of his army are still at Chippenham. But until we have enough men and feel ready to confront the Danes in battle, I plan to start attacking as many of their camps and raiding parties across those shires as we can. We have some fine warriors with us here, and between us we can show Guthrum we'll never give up on Wessex. Our first foray into Wiltshire will be four days from now, so you couldn't have chosen a better time to join us. From what Ealhswith told me, Eadwulf, I'm guessing your son won't be coming with us?'

Eadwulf glanced at his son. 'Aethelred will stay here, lord – at least to start with. I've told him I'll think about him joining us later on. He's already found a friend amongst the Fen Folk, and will probably be going out on the lake fishing with him in the next couple of days… Garth's the lad who rowed us across the lake earlier,' he added, in response to Alfred's questioning look.

'Garth's a fine young man,' Alfred assured them, 'and if his family wasn't so dependent on him to supply them with food, he'd be here with us now. I'm still hoping he might join us, especially now his younger brother's old enough to take over his chores.'

Eadwulf nodded. 'He's a strong lad, and would be a good addition to your band. Have you spoken to his parents about it?'

'Not yet, though I intend to soon. But, I don't want anyone mentioning that to Garth before I've had time to speak to his father.' Alfred focused on Aethelred. 'So I'm counting on you to keep things to yourself when you go fishing.'

'Yes, lord, I'll keep my mouth shut – at least about that.'

'Thank you, Aethelred,' Alfred managed to say, pulling

himself to his feet once the chuckles died down. 'Now, it's growing dark and time to find a shelter big enough for the five of you. Later on you will join us for our meal, which we have round the camp fires if the weather suits – which isn't too often at this time of year.' He pointed towards what appeared to be the largest shelter, an expression of amusement on his face. 'If not, we cook on a hearthfire in what we laughingly call our "hall" and eat in there, too. We're roasting a goat tonight. And after that, I think you've got some stories to tell me about exactly who you all are.'

* * *

The following morning, Garth came across to Athelney with a message from Odda, the ealdorman of Devon. The parchment had reached Muchelney the previous afternoon, in the hope that someone in the village knew of Alfred's whereabouts. Ina had delivered it to his brother-by-marriage at Burrowbridge who, in turn, had trekked into the fens to Garth's home. The message was intended to notify King Alfred of recent events in Devon and assure him that the situation had been effectively dealt with so no further action was needed.

Alfred seated himself on a log to read Odda's words himself before gathering his men and sharing the information with them.

'Odda has sent word of another group of Danes that planned to cause havoc in Wessex,' he started, his gaze moving round the faces, Eadwulf and his group amongst them. 'And we have Odda and the men of Devon to thank for putting a stop to those plans.'

Vocal praise of Odda followed and Alfred paused until it quietened. 'This band came across the Bristol Channel from Dyfed, landing their twenty-three ships near Countisbury on the North Devon coast. They'd been raiding and pillaging in Dyfed for most of last year, causing hardship and loss of life to the people there. Odda managed to raise over two hundred of the Devonshire fyrd and a dozen thegns, plus he had thirty able-bodied men from Countisbury and its surroundings.'

He held out his hands in a questioning manner. 'When I tell you those twenty-three Danish ships carried a good five hundred men, I'm sure you'll agree that it must have seemed our men were doomed…?'

Nods and murmurs confirmed agreement. 'At first it looked that way to Odda, too, and they prepared themselves to face attack, and began fortifying the village as best they could. But no strike came. Instead, the Danes laid siege to the place.'

'Why would they do that, lord?' Hamid asked. 'From what my friends have told me of Danish tactics, they usually raid as soon as they land and move on – unless they were intending to ride inland and join other invading groups.'

'That's true,' Alfred agreed, 'and this band may well have been intending to join Guthrum in Chippenham. But the reason they didn't attack the village straight away was simply because it would have been too difficult. Odda claims that Countisbury has some of the best natural defences of any town he's seen. The land surrounding it is wild and craggy, rising and dipping in a way that would obstruct any raiding force. So, these raiders decided to surround the village beyond these defences and lay siege until the people ran out of food and surrendered.

'And this was where Odda's quick thinking paid off. Though greatly outnumbered, his army launched a surprise attack while the enemy slept. And it worked. The arrogant Danes would have believed the relatively small Wessex force incapable of attacking an army far greater than their own. A mistake that cost them dear…

'Villagers knew of ways through the craggy terrain and could reach the enemy camp unseen. Most of the Danes were hacked down as they slept. Odda describes the attack as vicious and rapid and that no lives were spared. Even captives were later slain, including their leader, who enraged Odda's men by flaunting their Raven banner and yelling of Valhalla, even after most of his men were dead.

'Unfortunately, Odda's men also torched the ships – all twenty-three of them,' Alfred added, shaking his head. 'No doubt they were driven by blood lust, but those ships could have been useful to me and my growing fleet.'

'Is this the same Norse fleet that raided along the south coast of Wessex and around Cornwall for some years?' Jorund probed. 'I ask, lord, because we'd heard it was under the command of one of the sons of Ragnar Lothbrok.' He flashed a look at Eadwulf, who had wondered that himself.

Alfred shrugged. 'The only name Odda mentioned was that of its leader, but whether he was a son of the notorious Ragnar, I couldn't say. Odda simply called him Ubbi, and that he struck the man dead himself, claiming the Raven banner as a trophy.'

* * *

Jorund's grief over the death of his childhood friend took him to the far side of Athelney throughout their third day on the island. He needed solitude, and Eadwulf warned his companions to leave him alone while he mourned.

Eadwulf spent the day helping around the camp with Aethelnoth, Hamid and Aethelred, learning how things worked in Alfred's small army and getting to know the men. His own heart ached for the boy he'd once pulled from the clutches of a fast-flowing river. Ubbi had idolised him for years after that, and had taken the young Jorund under his wing following Morwenna's death.

Alfred joined them as they ate their morning meal, and Eadwulf knew he would want to hear of their connections to Ubbi. The name hadn't arisen when they'd shared their memories of life with the Danes on their first night on the isle. But after hearing Odda's message yesterday, Jorund had gone very quiet, holding his grief inside. That Alfred was aware of Jorund's distress had not escaped Eadwulf's notice, but the Wessex king had not pressed for reasons, then. But now, with Jorund's withdrawal, Alfred wanted to know.

'Jorund and Ubbi became firm friends when we were in Aros', Eadwulf started. 'Ubbi was the youngest of Ragnar's sons, and only two years older than Jorund. It was Ragnar's firstborn, Bjorn, who befriended me and gave me the freedom of sailing with him,' he added, 'and Ivar and Halfdan were the two middle sons, who hated and tormented me before Bjorn put a stop to it. It was they who organised the Great Summer

Army thirteen years ago and we'd heard that Ubbi had insisted on joining them.'

'Yes, you told us some of this the other night,' Alfred said, nodding, 'but now I appreciate your brother's sadness. Hearing of Ubbi's death would have hit him hard. I can only commiserate with his grief, and will tell him that when he comes back to camp.' Alfred's chuckle made the four of them smile, and Eadwulf wondered what he would say next.

'You were right when you said your story would confuse me as to your loyalty to Wessex,' Alfred went on, 'but I know that lasting friendships were made between you all and certain Danes, and despite your differences, it stands to reason that you still feel connected to them in some ways.'

Alfred looked levelly at Eadwulf. 'From what you told me about your journey to al-Andalus, I know your friendship with Bjorn is a strong one. The fact that he is Ragnar's firstborn, yet played no part in the original invasion, is interesting. I know you said he was away in the Middle Sea when Ivar and Halfdan organised it, but he could have joined them later on… And to think he sailed up and down the Trent to Elston while his brothers were taking our lands seems unbelievable. The man is daring, I'll give him that – and someone I'd like to meet.'

'Bjorn is a rare mix of daring, courage and honour, and he holds loyalty to those he respects or feels indebted to, highly. He would never break his word. As for raiding…' Eadwulf shook his head. 'Bjorn takes more pleasure in trading nowadays,' he added, the half-lie scorching his lips. 'He has lands and villages under his care and a family he dearly loves. He wouldn't want to risk losing all that –' He halted, realising that Bjorn would be devastated to hear of Ubbi's death. His youngest brother meant so much to him.

'I never had the pleasure of meeting Ivar,' Alfred said, a derisive smile on his lips, 'though I heard much about him and the power he had over his men. When the Danes took Nottingham ten years ago, Ivar kept behind the city walls. Only Burgred got to meet him when he took the Mercian tribute to him… But, since you were also at the camp, you'll know that already.'

Alfred shot Eadwulf an amused look. 'I rarely forget a face, or someone with deliberately muddied hair; although, it wasn't black with mud on that occasion. '

'I knew you recognised me during the siege, but I realised there was no opportunity to stop and speak. It was a humiliating time, especially for Burgred. And the less said about him, the better.'

'I couldn't agree more,' Alfred murmured. 'As for Ragnar's sons, I've met Halfdan a number of times now, and I wounded him in the thigh during our last face-to-face in the shield wall. Just a stroke of luck on my behalf,' he added modestly. Halfdan's strong and quick on his feet, and the clash was gruelling. Only a slip on his behalf enabled me to make the strike that finished our fight.'

Eadwulf nodded, old memories rekindled. 'Halfdan spent hours in battle training when he was young, and prided himself on his skills. Pity he didn't have a brain to match the rest of his well-toned body.'

'I'd thought the same thing myself,' Alfred admitted with a smirk. 'He let Bagsecg walk in and take control a few years ago, and probably went back to Northumbria to get away from Guthrum. I can't say I was sorry to see the back of him, though.'

'But now you have Guthrum.'

'Yes, Eadwulf, now I have Guthrum. And I swear by all that is holy, he will not hold Wessex for much longer.'

Twenty

Athelney and Wiltshire: Mid-February 878

Aethelred felt almost abandoned when Alfred's warriors left the isle, his father and friends among them. But the men staying behind as Lady Ealhswith's bodyguards were a jovial bunch, who readily took him into their group, allowing him to join in with their arms and archery practice. Aethelred's pride soared when he heard them praising his skills and he practised long hours to further improve. And four days after the king's raiding party had gone, Garth turned up, inviting him out to a day of fishing.

'I've brought you a rod and line,' the cheery lad said as Aethelred boarded the small boat. 'The rods are just wooden poles, but they're well strong enough to take the weight of a pike, if we're lucky enough to catch one.'

Aethelred seated himself on a board fixed across one end of the boat, and examined the rods, which were similar to the one he'd used with Selwyn in the Trent. 'The line's made of nettle hemp, by the look of it,' he remarked, as much to impress Garth with his knowledge as to satisfy his own interest.

'Yeah, that's right,' Garth replied. 'Nettles are easy to get, especially in summer. We collect heaps of them then, and after we've stripped the leaves for our soup, the stems are given a good soaking and pulped until we get separate strands.'

'I know about that,' Aethelred said, watching his new friend push the boat away from the beach before splashing through the shallow water to leap aboard and stand at the opposite end of the vessel to himself. Picking up his long pole, Garth pushed it against the bed of the lake and they glided smoothly away from the isle. 'I didn't until a couple of days ago when I had archery practice with some of King Alfred's men,' Aethelred continued. 'They told me it's what they use for their bowstrings.'

Garth nodded. 'Some folks use animal sinew for bowstrings, but for us, nettle hemp's just easier to come by. Right then, in the buckets over there, you'll see I've collected enough bait to last as long as we feel like staying out...

'Best not rock the boat too much though,' he added with a grin as Aethelred leaned over to inspect the buckets' contents. 'The lake's not too warm at this time of year. You can see we've got plenty of leeches and worms, as well as tiddlers, including minnows. Pike'll go for most of those and some of the minnows are still alive, so they'll wriggle well when we hook them. Some insects, like crickets, would have been good, but it *is* winter, when all's said and done.'

Aethelred loved the freedom of being out on the lake and was happy to listen to Garth's cheerful chatter, as well as his explanations about fishing techniques and different species of fish and water birds. Born and raised in the fens, there was little Garth didn't know about them, and he skilfully poled his boat through the reedbeds to locate pockets of different fish species. He showed Aethelred how to attach his bait to the hook at the end of the line and cast it out into the water, and soon, Aethelred was doing everything himself with ease.

'You make a good tutor,' he said as Garth handed him a

chunk of flatbread and some hard cheese from a leather bag. It was mid-afternoon and they were both ready for something to fill their rumbling bellies. 'And you seem to think of everything,' he added, washing down the welcomed food with watered ale from the skins also produced by Garth.

The young man flashed a broad smile. 'I can't take credit for the food, Aethelred. We've my mam to thank for that. She always makes sure I don't go hungry when I'm out and about.' He gestured at the two bulging sacks in the stern. 'I'd say we've had a successful day, wouldn't you? Your sack's almost as full of fish as mine and I think your friends on the isle will be pleased to cook them. I told you these lakes are full of fish, didn't I? Pity we didn't catch a pike, but we can't be lucky every time out. But now it's time we got you back before it starts getting dark. We'll come out here again in a few days, if you like.'

Aethelred couldn't sing Garth's praises highly enough that night as he enjoyed the products of his first day of fishing with those on the isle. Even Lady Ealhswith complimented him on his success as she enjoyed a platter of bream. It felt good to be praised, and Aethelred promised himself that until his father allowed him to ride out with him and King Alfred, he would impress everyone on Athelney with his skills in fenland survival.

The following week passed quietly and Aethelred spent much of his time helping Alfred's men working about the island, as well as continuing his arms practice. He found he enjoyed helping to build another boat, similar to the one in which Garth had taken him fishing, and even enjoyed helping with the construction of the fortifying fence. And, only three days after the last outing, he spent another day on the lake with

Garth – and prided himself in bringing back a pike.

Lady Ealhswith was again the first to congratulate him and she and her family group relished the fish. Even Aethelflaed and Edward came over and thanked him for such a delicious meal. Aethelred was only too glad to have been of use, even though the cooking had been nothing at all to do with him.

* * *

Alfred and his thirty warriors tethered their mounts to woodland trees and crouched at the top of the gentle slope, shields slung across their backs, swords hanging from the baldrics of the nobles and spears gripped tight by the rest. Taut as bowstrings, they waited for Alfred's signal to move.

Eadwulf willed his pounding heart to slow, though he knew it would not. They had already made two raids on Danish camps and four on patrols since leaving the isle a week ago and he knew the tension in the moments before conflict would never lessen. It was what kept warriors alert, and would continue until the blood lust rose to carry them through the heat of the action.

But this was their first raid in the blackness of night and, somehow, the shadows created by the glow from the thin wedge of moon sharpened his unease.

Beyond the slope, the vale stretched for two hundred yards before rising to a wooded ridge. Along the foot of that ridge, remnants of watch-fires threw muted light on the edge of the camp, where almost fifty of Guthrum's Danes slept. With Odda's night-time success in mind, Eadwulf hoped the guards would be too drowsy at this hour to be vigilant.

An owl screeched its alarm, flapping from a low branch to glide like a spectre between the leafless trees behind. One of the horses whinnied in response to the harsh cry and Eadwulf held his breath, fearful the sound would carry to the Danes below. But, nothing stirred across the vale and Alfred raised his arm, the signal to advance down the slope.

Stooping low, they moved in silence, crouching at intervals behind scrubby gorse and leafless bramble, panted breaths evidence of heightened tensions as conflict neared. They inched across the open ground, spread out and wary of being seen. But it seemed the guards were nodding, or else intent on thoughts of their own. With only five yards to go, one of the guards roused and opened his mouth to yell, only to have sound stopped dead by a stab through his throat from Eadwulf's sword.

Alfred's warriors swept through the camp, cutting down unarmed Danes as they slept. Those who woke snatched up swords and shields, but were no match for Alfred's fired-up warriors. Engrossed in his own grim task, Eadwulf lost sight and thought of his companions. His blood lust was up and he became the fearless and ruthless warrior he had once been.

Bodies soon littered the site, the earth slick with blood and gore. Like Odda, Alfred took no captives, his rage at the invaders to his kingdom evident to all. And Eadwulf admired him for it.

'Gather the horses,' Alfred yelled. 'Bury our dead and take whatever we can use from the tents. Then toss the rest of the corpses into them before we fire them.'

* * *

For another two weeks, Alfred's band of raiders continued their relentless purge on Danes across Wiltshire and Somerset, ensuring their tactics varied each time they struck. Some raids were made at night, others just as enemy warriors emerged from their tents in the greying light of the pre-dawn. At times, his army ambushed foraging bands on the move, his own mounted men suddenly appearing from the concealment of woodland or from around some hill or ridge.

Alfred was pleased with his army's success, and even more so with the support they'd had from villagers they had saved from Danish raids. Many provided bread and cheese and a few of last years' wizened fruits to supplement the foods they'd retrieved from defeated Danes, or the hares and other small mammals caught in their well-laid snares. But, before they returned to the concealment of the marshes, they had one more raid to make. And this one, Alfred would take the greatest of pleasure in executing.

'Wilton was my father's favourite vill,' he explained, twisting in his saddle to face Eadwulf and squinting into the pale, early-morning sun. It had been an easy ride from their camp, just three miles to the north, despite the hard frost nipping at noses and exposed fingers. 'Aethelwulf felt more at peace here than at any other manor in Wessex, and I stayed here with him on many occasion.'

Eadwulf nodded but said nothing and Alfred knew he would have many such memories of his own. 'It grieved me to think of Wilton in the hands of traitors,' he went on, 'and by all that is holy, Wulfhere will pay for what he's done. But I'm reluctant to slay everyone here. Most of Wilton's occupants would have had no choice in the betrayal: fifty or so Danes posted here would have made sure they sided with Wulfhere in supporting Guthrum.'

'Tell me what you intend for the vill, Alfred, and we can get the men in place, ready to move as soon as you give the order.'

'We'll spend time watching it, although at this time of year few people will be in and out of the gates unless it's to hunt or fish. But there's an embankment behind the outer palisade which allows them to post lookouts. They were always vigilant in the past, especially with Reeve Hunlaf to oversee things and Ealdorman Brihtnoth keeping an eye on events in the shire. So unless the Danes have changed things, we'll need to be careful not to be seen: which is why our attack would best be made at night.'

Alfred sighed, his memories of Brihtnoth and Hunlaf filling his mind. 'I'm praying Guthrum's called his men back, otherwise the odds won't be in our favour – even with you four Mercian lions. You've all impressed us with your fighting skills, and Wessex is in your debt.'

Eadwulf smiled at Alfred's choice of words. 'Well, we've never been called lions before, but I can only stress that you owe us no debt, Alfred. As Mercians, we were shamed by my uncle's refusal to help Wessex. My father held dear the alliance he made with King Aethelwulf, and his greatest aim was that our kingdoms would make a united stand against the Danes. We are merely honouring his wishes. Despite having respect and affection for individual Danes, we are still proud Mercians.

And Hamid has become a part of my family and vows that our battles are now also his.'

'Hamid certainly knows how to use that pair of scimitars to deadly effect.'

'He was taught the arts of warfare by masters – paid for by the great Emir Muhammad himself. He'd never handled a sword until he came to Mercia, but a couple of lessons from Aethelnoth were enough to rectify that. Hamid's also a master with a bow and I've yet to see a more accurate aim. You've noticed the long sheath attached to the side of his saddle…?' Alfred nodded. 'He made that bow back in Elston, but so far, he's only used it for hunting.'

'We may well make use of Hamid's archery skills in the coming months,' Alfred replied, 'though not in a shield wall. But during raids and sieges, I can think of several instances when skilled archers could prove invaluable.

'And what can I say about the rest of you? Aethelnoth is a fine warrior, as are you and Jorund. I am more than fortunate to have you at my side. Lions indeed.'

Alfred mused on things awhile before he remarked, 'As for the emir… Such wealth is a fine thing, as long as it is used for the good of all and the betterment of the kingdom. Although, from what you've told me, that isn't how Muhammad sees things. Do you know what I want to do, Eadwulf, once Wessex is rid of the Danes?' Eadwulf shook his head. 'I want to make reading accessible to as many of our people as I can. Learning is a wonderful thing and I'll encourage it until my dying day.

'Unfortunately, such plans are for the future, and I'll probably be old and grey by the time the Danes are ousted. But they will be ousted… eventually. And now, our punishment of Wulfhere will stand as an example of our contempt of those who would betray their kingdom.'

A dense patch of forest came into view and Alfred ordered his men to dismount and tether their horses. The royal vill of Wilton stood beyond these woods and Alfred was only too aware that the whinnying of their horses could give them away. They continued on foot through the trees, the greens of hollies and ivies and occasional fir vibrant against the winter-bare boles and branches of the rest. Keeping low, they halted behind the shield of shrubby growth along the forest's edge, some eighty or so paces from the vill's palisade.

For some time, Alfred watched, expecting to see lookouts pacing the embankment behind and needing to determine whether the Danes were still here. But none appeared. He found it odd that Wulfhere paid such little heed to the safety of the vill. Posting constant lookouts had always been of utmost importance to Hunlaf. Was Wulfhere so secure in his belief that allying himself to the Danes would keep him safe? Surely word of Alfred's raiding Saxons would have reached Wilton by now.

To Alfred, the absence of a continuous watch from the vill made finding tactical methods of attack seem pointless. Using a ram to get the gates open, followed by a full-on assault of the vill appeared the obvious things to do. Yet there was always the possibility that things were not as lax as they looked…

Alfred weighed up the possibilities and made his decision.

'Now!' he yelled, urging half a dozen of his men forward with the thick trunk they'd stripped of branches and fashioned into a battering ram. 'Archers in position!' he continued, and

Hamid and three others with bows spread out to take aim at the top of the palisade across the front of the vill.

The pounding on the gates pulsed loud on the evening air – but no guards appeared. Nor did it take long for the gates to give way and swing inward. Wary now, Alfred motioned his men to follow him inside – and Eadwulf, Jorund and Aethelnoth stepped into position at his sides.

The scene that greeted them was of a place that had been abandoned in a hurry. The expansive yard was empty: doors to the stables and storage huts swung open, revealing emptiness within. And yet, logic told Alfred that the gates must have been barred from inside… or had they been barred at all? Was he basing that assumption on his experiences of past time in this vill? The rams had taken little time to crash through the gates, after all.

The hall seemed just as deserted as they pushed open the heavy, oak door. Trestle tables were set up, the remnants of a meal still in place. He shared a glance with Eadwulf, who looked as puzzled as himself. He knew the rooms to the rear of the building were simply sleeping chambers, and despite telling himself there would be nothing there to find, his logical mind would not agree. To leave a single nook unsearched could prove irresponsible – or even ruinous to his cause.

Eadwulf pushed open the nearest door and stepped into a room that Alfred knew to be the reeve's. Eadwulf's yell brought them all running…

Ealdorman Wulfhere's mutilated body was sprawled across the wide bed. It was a gruesome sight, since little of him had been spared the knife. His eyes had been gouged out and stab wounds covered most of the rest of him, as though a host of malicious elves had taken revenge for past wrongs committed. Alfred knew too well that traitors often met with grisly deaths, but he felt no pity for Wulfhere: after all, he'd intended killing the man himself. He could not help the fleeting sensation of rage that *he* hadn't been the one to inflict those wounds. He also wondered whether Wulfhere's death had been at Danish or Saxon hands.

A movement beyond the door caught their attention, and, as Aethelnoth was closest he yanked it back and hauled the scrap of a man inside.

'Hunlaf…?' Alfred said, unsure whether this scrawny and ragged creature was the reeve he'd admired not so long ago.

'Yes, lord, it's Hunlaf.' He bowed his head, unable to look Alfred in the eye. 'Wulfhere brought shame on us! He betrayed you and forced everyone here to grovel to the Danes. We had no choice while the Norsemen were here but Guthrum called them back to Chippenham a couple of weeks since. And news of your success across Wiltshire made me and other loyal Wessex men get together and make plans.'

'And this was the result of those plans…?' Alfred said, gesturing at the carnage. 'If so, why are you alone here? Where are all those loyal men now?'

'Still close to Wilton, lord, but in the homes of family and friends. I haven't set foot in this room since we… we did *this* two days ago.

'If I've done wrong, lord, kill me now!' Hunlaf cried, falling to his knees before Alfred, his sobs filling the room. 'I couldn't bear to see the Danes taking our kingdom – and Wulfhere was no more than a treacherous dog. He couldn't see how that Norseman… Guthrum… was playing him for a fool.'

'There's no blame on you, Hunlaf,' Alfred said, holding out his hands and helping the man to his feet. 'I can only commend your actions. I would have killed Wulfhere myself if we'd found him alive. My army will stay here for tonight, and tomorrow we'll dispose of Wulfhere's body while you let the rest of our household know that all is well and ask them to come back. Wulfhere will get no Christian burial. He'll burn along with everything we toss out of this room. Everything the man touched is tainted with his treachery, and I want no reminder of him in my vill.'

'But lord, what if the Danes come back?'

'I'll leave a dozen men with you so you can make the vill secure and set up a regular watch. I also ask that once the vill is running well, you start sending men to the villages to rally the fyrd to our cause. The day when we confront Guthrum isn't too far away, and when I call for an army, I want men to be ready.'

* * *

Aethelred stared at the target hanging from a thick bough of a leafless alder on the outer edge of the camp. It was a large sack, well-stuffed with straw and marked with a circle of white daub to indicate where he should aim.

He lined himself up to the sack, his bow pointing at the ground, just as Hamid had taught him back in Elston. He nocked the arrow and slowly raised the bow, pointing it at the target. Concentrating hard, he drew back the bowstring and aimed the arrow at the white circle.

'Why are you practising on your own today?' a voice blurted from behind, causing him to jump and lose his grip on the arrow. It flew across the twenty yard gap to become embedded in the trunk of a spindly willow three yards to the right of the sack.

'What are you thinking!' Aethelred yelped, spinning round to confront young Aethelflaed. 'I could have hit someone – and it would have been *your* fault! *Never* creep up on anyone in the middle of firing arrows! Are you stupid, or something?'

Aethelflaed looked momentarily crestfallen and Aethelred berated himself for allowing his anger to get the better of him. But then the girl pulled back her shoulders, her pride seeming to conquer her distress at being shouted at. 'It wasn't just *my* fault!' she hurled at him, her face now a picture of outrage. 'And it couldn't have killed anyone – there's no one around! Anyway, how was I to know you didn't have a good hold on the arrow? My father's men don't make such a scene when I come out to watch them in archery practice. In fact, they usually let me join in – and I can probably shoot better than you can, anyway.'

Aethelred scoffed at the boastful words of a girl who didn't even reach up to his shoulders and could not have been more than nine or ten years old. 'Don't talk nonsense… er… Lady Aethelflaed,' he added, suddenly remembering whose daughter she was. 'I mean, even drawing back the bowstring takes some doing.'

'Yes, and I'm good at it.'

'Here, then,' Aethelred said, thrusting his bow at her. 'Show me.'

Aethelflaed glared at him, then at the bow, but eventually she took hold of it. 'It's longer than the bow Cena made for me,' she said. 'But I'll have a go.'

Aethelred handed her an arrow and watched as she made ready to fire, positioning herself perfectly as far as he could see. It was suddenly evident she had done this more than a few times, and he watched her arrow fly… straight to the white circle in the middle of the sack.

'I told you I was good,' Aethelflaed bragged, handing the bow back to Aethelred. 'Your turn now.'

Aethelred took aim once again and this time his arrow joined Aethelflaed's inside the circle. 'Shall we just call it a draw?' he said, wondering how long this girl had been practising with a bow.

Alfred's daughter suddenly laughed, her blue-green eyes shining. 'That's what Papa always says when he can't beat me at tabula,' she declared, causing Aethelred's own smile to drop. Now she was insinuating he couldn't beat her at archery – just when he was trying to be nice.

'We'll see who's best if we set up a proper contest. That shot of yours was probably just a fluke.'

'It was not! You're just a poor loser, Aethelred of Mercia. My shot was as good as your… your *second* attempt.'

Aethelred shook his head. There was no way he could defeat this girl in an argument. 'I'll set up a match for us tomorrow and you'll see how good I really am.'

'Very well,' Aethelflaed agreed with a smile, 'but I'll be

using my own bow. It would be unfair to make me use yours. Look how big you are compared to me. My bow was made to suit my size.'

And with that, Aethelflaed headed back to the makeshift hall, leaving Aethelred wondering just whether the outcome of this contest tomorrow would be in his favour.

* * *

Congratulating himself on setting up an impressive set of targets, Aethelred turned to head back to the hall and let Aethelflaed know all was ready for the contest, only to see her less than twenty paces away. In her hand, she carried a small bow and the wide strap across her shoulders suggested a quiver of arrows hung down her back.

'You've found so many things to shoot at!' Aethelflaed enthused, surveying the range of items hanging from two sturdy boughs extending from either side of the alder's trunk – on which a white circle was marked. She inspected the variously sized straw-stuffed sacks, the lengths of bark, the old boots and large turnips. She wrinkled her nose at the hogs' heads and giggled at Aethelred's attempts to create a pair of straw-stuffed men. 'This is going to be fun.'

Aethelred wasn't at all sure the contest would be fun. He'd spent hours finding pairs of almost identical objects, and had been careful not to tell anyone why he wanted them, despite their reactions when he'd asked for the bits and pieces. He'd asked Aethelflaed to keep quiet about the contest, too, and could only hope she had done. He wanted no audience for this. If he lost, he'd never live it down.

'The turnips were in a sack in one of the food stores, and I'll have to get them back before they're needed for the pottage.' He gave a one-shouldered shrug. 'They could be in bits by the time we've finished with them but they should still be usable. And those straw men took me ages to make,' he admitted. 'I had to borrow a big needle and some wool from Agnes. She looked at me in a funny way, but didn't ask why I wanted them. She probably thought I was going to mend my clothes!'

Aethelflaed's laugh was infectious and Aethelred laughed with her. 'As you see,' he said, once the laughter stopped, 'I've marked the heads and chests with blobs of white daub. We can aim for either head or chest, although if we hit the arms or legs we'll still count it as a hit. And we'll finish off with one shot each at the circle I've marked on the tree trunk.

'So let's get started or Lady Ealhswith will have Agnes out here looking for you. Which side of the tree do you want?' Aethelflaed shrugged her indifference but finally decided to take the bough to the right of the trunk.

'We'll start with the bigger targets and finish with the smaller pieces of bark and the turnips before we have a shot at the trunk. Then we'll retrieve the arrows and decide whether we want to go start again.'

They headed to the shooting lines and the contest began. None of the targets caused either of them much difficulty, although one of Aethelflaed's arrows only skimmed her turnip and one of Aethelred's hung uncertainly from a piece of bark. Aethelred struck his straw man in the head and Aethelflaed struck hers in the chest.

'I'd say the first round was a draw,' he said at the end. 'Want another round?'

'Aethelflaed nodded. 'Just one more, then I'll have to get –'

Sounds of a commotion in the camp cut Aethelflaed's words short. Dropping their bows, they sped back to find the place in uproar.

Alfred's raiding band was back on Athelney.

Twenty One

After spending only three days on the isle, Alfred and his army headed back to Somerset and Wiltshire to continue the raids. Alfred had long since realised that by keeping Guthrum busy dealing with his continuous assaults, the Danish warlord was unable to further extend his control of Wessex. So far, Hampshire remained untouched, as did Dorset and Devon, other than Ubbi's seaborne attempt on the Devon coast. Alfred was pleased, as well as relieved, that his own raids had worked so well. It seemed that Guthrum was a man more used to leading attacks than countering them, and Danish numbers suffered as a consequence. Guthrum never knew where Alfred would strike next, so could not send forces to challenge him.

Their well-planned attacks continued throughout the rest of March and it was early April by the time they returned to Athelney. The drab garb of winter was, at last, being cast off by the isle, presenting a welcoming sight to the returning raiders. Catkins hung on the alders and willows, and leaf buds were beginning to open. Celandines and anemones dotted grasses and greening woods and a few early bluebells and orchids added such colour and fragrance that Alfred felt his spirits lift. His determination to regain his kingdom took on renewed urgency.

Work on the new fortress was almost complete. The island hummed with activity as men fetched and carried materials to and fro, chopped, sawed and hammered in the April sunshine. 'Guthrum's temper must be frayed by being unable to meet us in battle,' Alfred said, voicing his thoughts as he raised another plank of wood with Eadwulf in the construction of the new hall. 'He'd probably feel a lot better if he knew just how close we are to obliging him, but it's good to think of him venting his frustration on his men.'

Eadwulf smiled at Alfred's sneer. 'So you think we'll have enough men to face Guthrum soon? I know the news from Radulf was good. If he can raise over a thousand of the Hampshire fyrd, as he believes, those numbers would be invaluable. But what about your other shires?'

Alfred inserted a wooden peg into one of the holes in the plank and Eadwulf hammered it through to attach it to the adjacent timber. 'From what we've seen in Wiltshire, I'd say we'll have no problem raising a lot more men than Radulf. Wiltshire people want their old lives back, with a king who doesn't treat them like vermin and whose armies don't rape their women and leave them without food.'

He took a steadying breath, needing to dismiss visions of Danes ravaging Wessex villages. 'I'm also hoping that Ealdorman Aethelnoth will equal Radulf's numbers. Like Wiltshire, Somerset is sick of Danish oppression and Aethelnoth has stayed loyal to me throughout, despite others in Somerset – like my own reeve! – turning against me.'

Alfred paused, recalling the news that greeted them when they'd ridden to Wedmore during their raids in Somerset. Though his sole purpose had been that of killing Reeve Erwig himself, discovering that Guthrum had slaughtered most in the vill was hard to stomach. No one had been given a chance to explain and Guthrum's warriors butchered any who had not had time to flee. Survivors spent days digging the graves.

Alfred felt no sorrow over his treacherous reeve's death, but his sadness over Goda's fate was real. He owed the kindly lady much for enabling Ealhswith to escape Guthrum's clutches. On hearing the sad news, Ealhswith had wept till her tears ran dry.

He pulled his thoughts back to the present. 'If we can count on the armies of Hampshire and Somerset, and rally the Wiltshire fyrd, we stand every chance of beating Guthrum. So all we can do is hope all goes to plan.'

Jorund suddenly put down the small auger he'd been using to bore holes along the edges of wooden planks. 'What about Devon and Dorset, lord? Won't the fyrds of those shires rally to our cause? You said they've always been a part of your army in the past.'

'It's true, Wessex has never gone to battle without those shires before,' Alfred replied, feeling a stab of regret that this occasion would be different. 'And if I asked Daegmund and Odda to raise armies for us tomorrow, I know they'd do their best to comply. But, as events at Countisbury have shown, there are still Danish fleets out there plaguing our coasts. Some of them may even be planning to join Guthrum's army. I can't risk our coastal shires being left undefended in case further attacks occur and Guthrum gets reinforcements.'

Jorund nodded and resumed his work, but Alfred hadn't missed his crestfallen expression at the mention of Countisbury. It would take some time for Jorund to get over Ubbi's death.

'So our friends Aethelnoth and Hamid are out at Burrow Mump again?' Alfred knew full well they were, but wanted to take Jorund's attention away from Ubbi. The pair had volunteered for the task every day for the past week.

'Yes, lord,' Jorund replied, his face brightening a little. 'Aethelnoth isn't a man to enjoy building things. He'd much prefer to be out there, keeping an eye on Danish movements. It's a useful place, so close to Athelney. Aethelnoth says that on a nice day, he can see across the countryside for hundreds of miles from up there.'

Alfred laughed. 'Well, I'm not sure he could see quite that far, but the peak of Burrow Mump rises a few hundred feet above the surrounding land and we can see well into Wiltshire from the top. Campfires are easy to spot, so are patrols on the move. I'm planning a couple more raids now the hall is almost finished, so their information over the next day or two will be useful.'

Alfred suddenly focused on Eadwulf. 'Will Aethelred be with us next time we ride out? Aethelflaed tells me he's desperate to take part in the raids, but the decision is yours, so I'll leave things with you.'

* * *

It was obvious to Eadwulf that Aethelred's first experiences of raiding elated him. He wielded his sword with confidence and, like Hamid, his aim with a bow was commendable.

Although he kept a wary eye on his son, Eadwulf realised he had no real need. He was pleased to see how Aethelred handled himself, despite the worry he felt for his safety. Had she lived, Leoflaed would have been so proud of him. Though not seventeen for another few months, Aethelred had grown tall this past year and his daily arms training on Athelney had made him strong and sturdy. So much so, he'd been mistaken for Eadwulf on a few occasions, albeit from a distance.

Yet, performing well in ambushes and raids wasn't the same as facing enemy warriors in battle formation. The time for confronting the Danes was drawing close and Eadwulf knew it wasn't only Aethelred who needed training in shield wall combat.

* * *

After a week of successful raiding, Alfred's warriors were again back on Athelney. It was the middle of April and the urgency of facing Guthrum before reinforcements reached his army now consumed Alfred's thoughts and deprived him of sleep. It was time to act.

Messengers were sent to Radulf of Hampshire and Aethelnoth of Somerset to begin preparations with their fyrds and he knew his two loyal ealdormen would not fail him. But, since Wulfhere's betrayal, Wiltshire had no ealdorman, and Alfred was relying on Hunlaf to alert the thegns to ready the fyrd. Realising the stupidity of depending on one old man to perform this crucial task, he sent four of his men to visit a handful of Wiltshire thegns who would carry the order to the rest.

Alfred planned the gathering of his armies for early May, which meant they had less than a month to prepare villagers in shield wall tactics and give them time to have suitable weapons and armour to hand. Many of them had fought with Alfred at Ashdown and several battles since, and were already skilled in procedure. But others were young or, like his Mercian allies, had no idea what to expect.

This time, Alfred had no intention of facing Guthrum with unprepared or unskilled warriors. Village smiths would be busy forging helms and spears, and mail shirts for those who could afford them, and battle training would be in earnest. This would not be easy in either Somerset or northern Wiltshire with Danes still moving about, but he hoped that focusing a few more raids in northern Wiltshire over the next couple of weeks would deter the enemy from venturing far from Chippenham.

'Radulf and Aethelnoth agree that Whit Sunday would be a good day for our armies to muster,' Alfred told his men as they ate their meal around the camp fire. The spring evening was warm and days had lengthened enough to give them time to talk and enjoy each other's company. 'Guthrum won't be expecting trouble on one of our holy days, but it's still vital that we move to our assembly place quickly and along little used routes wherever possible. We meet at Egbert's Stone, which, for those who've never heard of it, is on Wiltshire's southern border with Somerset, to the east of the great forest of Selwood. It's almost fifty miles from here, and even if we leave before sunrise, we'll only manage to cover thirty miles by late afternoon…

'I *know* our horses aren't all old nags,' he jested, looking round at the questioning faces, 'but we'll be meeting Ealdorman Aethelnoth and the Somerset fyrd in Burrowbridge at dawn, and most of his men will be on foot. So we'll make camp for one night on the way, and should reach Egbert's

Stone early the next day.

'But, before that time arrives, our latest recruits need some battle training,' he added gesturing at Eadwulf's group. 'Their worth as warriors can't be doubted, but standing in a shield wall for the first time is a daunting thing. So, I'll rely on the rest of you to set up a few training sessions.'

'There's just one other thing, lord,' Eadwulf said. 'The five of us here have no mail shirts, and few Danes would go into battle without their chain byrnies. I've enough coin with me to have five made and wondered whether Ina over at Muchelney would oblige.'

Alfred nodded slowly. 'I've no doubt Ina would be happy to do that. And you're right, a mail shirt could well save your life. But, I can tell you, you've no need to go pestering Ina now. He and the two men he employs in his forge have been making mail shirts for the past month, so yours should be ready sometime soon. All six of them.'

'Six, lord? Is one of them for you?'

'No, Aethelred, it isn't. It's for your friend Garth.'

Aethelred's face lit up. 'So his parents agreed he could join us?'

'They did, and they were proud to know he'd be fighting for Wessex. Garth himself is more than pleased, especially as Ina's brother-by-marriage has offered to supply him with a horse. Your friend will be training with us in future, starting from tomorrow.'

* * *

In the early evening of Whit Sunday, the fourth day of May, the combined forces of Wiltshire, Somerset and Hampshire were eventually assembled at Egbert's Stone. Thirty of Alfred's warriors, with Ealdorman Aethelnoth and the Somerset fyrd, arrived soon after noon, having had only twenty miles to travel that day. Most of the Wiltshire fyrd were already there by then, and Radulf, with the forces of Hampshire, assembled at the site late in the afternoon.

Together they were a force of over four thousand men, spread like a closely woven blanket across the plain at the foot of Court Hill, reaching out to the great forest of Selwood.

From where he and his companions stood at the front of the impressive army of Saxons, Eadwulf gazed up at the Wessex king, standing proud beside a cluster of three large sarsen stones part-way up the hill. Together they were known as Egbert's Stone and Alfred had told them, they were named after his grandfather, the mighty bretwalda, Egbert.

It was obvious that Alfred was overcome with emotion at the appearance of such numbers and, as the cheers rang out, Eadwulf did not miss him sweeping the backs of his hands across his eyes. Radulf had raised well over a thousand of the Hampshire fyrd, and Aethelnoth almost equalled those numbers with Somerset men. But the Wiltshire fyrd had really done their king proud, their numbers reaching almost two thousand. Eadwulf knew that many had thought Alfred dead, that reports of his exploits were simply tales to keep his memory alive. Actually seeing him in the flesh, fit and commanding up on the hill next to the famous stone, renewed their patriotic zeal.

Alfred held out his arms and the cheers abated. 'I have

dreamt of this day for the past few months, my friends,' he yelled, although Eadwulf knew that many of the vast army would be unable to hear, needing to rely on those close to the front to pass Alfred's words on. 'But seeing you here before me, impressively armoured and armed and ready to fight for our kingdom, fills me with such pride that words falter in my throat. Yet I must calm my swelling heart and find voice to express my deepest thanks for believing in me… for believing in yourselves. We are warriors, and together we will drive the pagans from our lands!'

The resounding cheers were deafening, until Alfred again held up his hands. 'We'll spend tonight here in the shelter of the forest, and at dawn tomorrow, we head north-east for Chippenham and lay siege to the town. After a couple of weeks of starvation, Guthrum will be begging to make terms for peace…

'Although it wouldn't surprise me to find he has a welcoming party waiting for us on the way.'

* * *

Guthrum's rage had ebbed and in its place an overwhelming sense of despair washed in to trickle through his innards. He had listened in disbelief as reports of Alfred's raids came in, of his movements that none of his men could foresee or counter. The Wessex king had become an illusory wraith, silent and invisible until he struck.

But now, Guthrum's men brought news that Saxons were moving across Wiltshire in their hundreds. The young king, whom Guthrum had openly scorned as inadequate and inexperienced had, somehow, recovered from the loss of face and support at Chippenham and managed to rally the fyrds to his cause.

Guthrum had expected the Saxon people to hold Alfred in deepest scorn.

'Where are they mustering?'

The messenger shrugged, his hands upturned. 'It was hard to tell, lord. They were coming from different directions, and at different times. Our nearest guess is that they were heading to a place somewhere west of the great plain of Salisbury. So we rode straight here to let you know.'

'Today, you say?' The messenger nodded and Guthrum suddenly laughed, confusing his gathered men. 'Today, of all days… that does surprise me. Aren't good Saxons supposed to be grovelling to their Christ-god at this time? It's Pentecost, or some such pathetic festival, whatever that's all about.'

An uncertain twitter of amusement rippled round the Chippenham hall, and Guthrum knew they'd believe his jovial words to be feigned, signalling another outburst. But the news had had the opposite effect, lifting his spirits and giving him hope. At last he could meet the cursed Wessex king face-to-face. No more unheralded attacks his men could not avert. Alfred's untrained fyrds had never been a match for Norse warriors in a shield wall. And, despite the reports of hundreds of men on the move, Alfred was unlikely to raise more than a couple of thousand ceorls – whereas Guthrum had a good three thousand warriors, even without the five hundred he'd hoped for from Ubbi.

'Get our men ready to move out, Thorkell,' he yelled at a

beefy red-headed warrior who was watching him intently while drinking his ale. 'We're not giving the Saxon cur time to reach Chippenham. We meet him on open ground where our shield wall will best any number of his village rabble.

* * *

By early evening the next day, Saxon forces reached Iley Oak, a stretch of dense oak woodland that would again afford them cover for the night. It was twenty miles south of Chippenham, their destination for the following day. Most of the men were preparing their beds for the night, when Alfred's spies rode up. The news they delivered was no less than he'd expected and he immediately called a meeting with his nobles.

'Guthrum's made his move,' he said, his gaze sweeping the circle of ealdormen and thegns, Eadwulf and his companions amongst them. They were seated at the edge of the woods, where they would later eat the cold food from their saddle packs. 'And it seems he's been informed of our route and intentions. His forces are gathered at the old hillfort at Bratton Camp, up on the edge of the Wiltshire Downs just fourteen miles south of Chippenham. It's a good choice of site for an overnight camp, but what's left of the buildings wouldn't stand up to a prolonged attack. There's no water supply up there, either.'

Alfred nodded to himself as he thought of the times he'd visited Bratton Camp with his father and older brothers. 'There are remains of a settlement that must have been lived in a thousand years ago,' he explained for the benefit of those not familiar with Wiltshire. 'There's little left of it now, other than a few crumbling walls, but we found what looked like the remains of several roundhouses, as well as buildings that could have been food stores, stables and workshops. There's also a long barrow up there from even earlier times. The settlement must have been impressive in its day, as well as a forbidding and well defended fortress. It was surrounded by two rings of defensive ditches cut into the chalk, and beyond those, there are steep drops on three of its sides.

'But I'm pretty sure Guthrum isn't intending to hold the fortress. He wants full-scale battle because he'll believe it's his best chance of beating us. We can only guess where he'll form his lines but, if I were Guthrum, the open downland beyond the ditches on the south-western side would be my choice.'

'So we head straight there tomorrow?'

'We do, Radulf. And the best way from here is to move west for two or three miles, cross the River Wylie, then climb up onto Battlebury Hill. We'll continue north-east along the ridge for another four miles, which will take us straight to Bratton Camp. And if my guess is correct, the Danes will be expecting us.'

Again, Alfred swept them with his intense gaze. 'I'll leave it to you to inform the men of the likelihood of battle tomorrow. And that we move out at dawn.'

* * *

Guthrum chose the place to make his stand carefully. Stopping Alfred's forces from reaching Chippenham was vital to him, and he needed to consider which route they would travel. Despite not knowing where the Saxons had mustered, it was obvious they'd be heading north, so he could guess the likely path they'd take. And if Alfred should opt for a different route, Guthrum's spies, watching from surrounding hilltops, would alert him in good time to shift position.

Rays of early afternoon sunshine flooded the verdant downs as the Danes drew up in battle formation beyond the ditches of the old fort. On a pole planted firmly in the earth, the Raven banner fluttered, assuring the men of Odin's presence. Guthrum prayed to the god he'd too often rejected to grant his warriors strength and courage this day. A moment of panic seized him as he thought of the consequences of losing: the image of him, grovelling again to Alfred was more than he could bear.

Too late for such thoughts now…

'Saxons coming into sight,' the lookout's call rang out. 'I can make out the first dozen or so men with that red and white banner of theirs.'

'Stand firm until they draw near,' Guthrum yelled at his front lines. 'Then we'll welcome them in our usual way. And no one breaks rank until I give the signal.'

* * *

The Norse army reared into view as Alfred's warriors reached a hundred and fifty yards of the fort. Already in battle formation, the Danes stood silent and resolute, awesome and menacing in their shining helms and byrnies. Behind them, the tiered ditches of the old fort coursed like black scars across the rising green hillside.

Alfred estimated an enemy force of at least three thousand standing before them, and felt a film of sweat spreading across his skin. He'd anticipated a thousand less… Thanking God that, at least, the Danes were still outnumbered, he ordered his own shield wall to form up.

Four thousand Saxons now stood in eight orderly ranks, silent as Alfred took his place at the centre of his front line. To his left, his Mercian allies stared ahead, ready to face whatever came next. To his right, Radulf of Hampshire hoisted the Wessex banner, the fearsome white wyvern eliciting a resounding cheer as it rose. Alfred felt the men's patriotic fervour flow, the urge to kill an enemy that had threatened their kingdom for too long.

He stepped forward, taking the banner from Radulf as he did, and strode along the front line. 'Today we fight as we've never fought before!' he yelled, holding the flag high and waving it back and forth for all to see. 'We fight for our kingdom, our homes, and our Saxon way of life. We are better armed and armoured, and better prepared than ever, and we fight for what we hold dear. Trust in God to give us courage, and trust in your king to reward all who stand firm. The pagans will be smitten down this day and tomorrow, Wessex will again be ours!'

He thrust out his arm, gesturing at the waiting Danes. 'Before us, I see an army that is greatly outnumbered and knows it will lose. Guthrum will be trembling in his boots. We have the upper hand and we will not waste it. Odin will not prevail!'

Battle lust swept through the Saxon lines, and Alfred

welcomed its unyielding grip on his chest as he signalled the advance. Saxon shouts and taunts and drumming of spears on shields matched those of the Danes as the gap between the two forces closed. Twenty yards from the enemy, Alfred halted, and, like stones held in a catapult, his warriors awaited the order for which they'd been primed.

Before the volley of spears could fly from Norse lines, or Guthrum had time to step out to hurl the usual jeers and insults, Alfred yelled. 'Now'!

The Saxons charged, their tight shield wall ramming into the Danes before they had time to gather speed. Four thousand Saxons lent their might to the push and enemy lines were instantly driven back. Spears and swords struck out and men began to fall…

And Alfred focused on the man with whom he'd come face-to-face: the man who had done his utmost to turn good Wessex people against him; the man who had brought him so low.

Their eyes locked, the hatred in Guthrum's dark eyes reflecting Alfred's own. Alfred's sword arm could not hold back…

Guthrum was a little taller than him, but in strength they were equally matched, and Alfred was fit and agile from weeks of raiding. He ducked and sidestepped, and parried the warlord's stabs and lunges and made thrusts and jabs of his own, his one intent to kill the traitorous pagan who had failed to honour a single oath or treaty. He focused on Guthrum's every move, aware than the slightest loss of concentration would see him dead. The fight became a gruelling test of wills as well as battle skills. But it soon became clear that Guthrum was tiring, his thrusts becoming slower and less frequent, and Alfred realised he needed to keep the pace fast in order to defeat the warlord.

But then, a sudden powerful lunge from Guthrum caused Alfred to sidestep, and in that moment the Dane moved back, melding into his lines, his place instantly filled by a warrior from behind.

The battle raged on, both armies suffering countless losses. Screams of the wounded merged with the clash of hard steel. Dead or dying, men dropped to the earth, the nauseating stench of blood and gore pervading the field. But, as afternoon turned into evening, it became clear that Danes were falling faster than Saxons and their lines were continuously moving back towards the hillfort's ditches. The enemy could not hold the strength and determination of Wessex.

Alfred felt a sudden unyielding push surge through his men and Danish lines started to break. No longer holding together, the Norse army became a disorganised throng. Men slipped and stumbled on the greasy, blood-soaked turf. Saxons moved in, driven by rage and hatred for their pagan oppressors, cutting them down with spear, seax, sword and battleaxe. Danes were suddenly in flight, heading between the gateways of the fort towards the path that continued along the ridge, then down to the open countryside to Chippenham. Prepared for such a move, Alfred yelled, 'After them!' his words echoed by his men as they gave chase.

* * *

In the midst of Alfred's fired-up warriors, Eadwulf joined the pursuit, venting his fury on those who had taken the kingdoms of his homeland. In his heart, he fought for Mercia and his family, Rorik's leering face looming before him each time he cut down a fleeing Dane. He'd glimpsed Aethelnoth close by, but seen nothing of the others since the battle began, and prayed to every god he knew that they were alive, somewhere amidst this mayhem.

The fourteen-mile chase was gruelling and bloody as Danes too slow to escape Saxon grasp were mercilessly hacked down, leaving a severely depleted army to limp behind Chippenham's newly fortified walls. Darkness was closing in when Alfred's orders to circle the vill and camp outside its gates were in place. The men obeyed without question, despite suffering from the exhausting and punishing events of the day. Eadwulf understood that Alfred couldn't risk Guthrum escaping, and laying siege was the best way to ensure the warlord eventually surrendered.

Soon after reaching Chippenham, Eadwulf and Aethelnoth were reunited with Aethelred, Hamid and Garth, all uninjured other than a few cuts and bruises. Jorund was nowhere to be found and, as much as he tried, Eadwulf couldn't recall seeing his brother after they'd lined up in the shield wall. As the night wore on he lay awake, sick with worry and knowing he must prepare for the worst. But he also knew that deserting Alfred to look for Jorund was not an option.

* * *

Alfred's orders to his surviving nobles the following morning were absolute: 'Remove every source of food from the area around Chippenham, and that includes livestock – and horses, and anything else the Danes may have left around the place. Bring everything back to camp for our own use during the siege. If any of Guthrum's men do manage to get out to forage they must find nothing. It won't take long for supplies they have left in the vill to go, and I eagerly await the day when Guthrum crawls out and begs for terms.'

He paused, acknowledging the men's nods of agreement with a nod of his own. 'Each of you will send out half a dozen men to fulfil this order while the rest stay on watch here and construct a paddock ready for any livestock. Make sure all directions around the vill are covered and tomorrow, different groups of men will go out. I'm laying odds that Guthrum's supplies will run out soon – unlike what happened at Wareham where he'd had time to gather provisions.'

Alfred's amber gaze again moved from one man to the next, coming to rest on Eadwulf for a while. 'We, too, have lost men today and our dead still lie where they fell. But few Danes escaped our fury, and despite the small force Guthrum left behind to hold Chippenham, we still have many more men than he has. So, once all foodstuffs have been rounded up, we send, say, thirty men back to Bratton Camp to bury our dead…

'No, hear me out,' Alfred said, as men started to voice flaws in that idea. 'I realise we have no shovels, so the men can't be buried immediately. But our horses are still tethered in woods close to the fort and will need watering, anyway. So some of the men will ride down to villages in the plain and borrow picks and shovels, and anything else they could use for digging with. They'll also need a couple of carts to carry them in. The men staying at the fort will collect up our dead, ready for burial. It will take time, probably a couple of days, but, we *cannot* leave our men to feed the scavengers.'

* * *

Three days later, Eadwulf headed back to Bratton Camp with Aethelnoth, Hamid, Aethelred and Garth, along with two dozen of Alfred's men. Full of guilt and remorse for bringing his family and friends to face the perils of battle, Eadwulf barely spoke as they walked. They scanned the corpses along the fourteen-mile route, seeking Saxons from amidst the Danes, and finding few. Eadwulf hoped beyond hope that his brother would not be dead, that by some miracle he'd survived an injury and crawled away from the battlefield. Deep down he knew how impossible that sounded, but could not give up on hope.

They passed through the old hillfort, the harsh cawing of the crows testament to the location of the multitude of corpses; the reek of death assaulting their nostrils as they emerged on the battlefield moments later. A mad flapping of wings and more raucous cawing accompanied a rising swarm of black as scavenger birds voiced displeasure at being disturbed in their grisly feast.

The May sun was warm, and although only four days had passed since death had struck, decay was starting to set in. Clouds of buzzing flies gorged on open wounds or gaping holes from which eyeballs had been pecked away by greedy crows and jackdaws. Some corpses displayed gnawed, jagged wounds: evidence of the teeth of foxes, badgers, or the odd, lone wolf.

Eadwulf inwardly screamed at the images playing in his head. That his brother should suffer such indignity in death tore him to shreds, the dread of finding his body mounting as he stared at the gruesome scene. If only he'd insisted on coming to Wessex on his own. But he hadn't, and now, he'd live with the guilt of Jorund's death for the rest of his days.

Aethelnoth and Hamid rode down to the villages with the dozen men assigned to collect digging tools and drinking water, while Eadwulf joined the rest in the harrowing task of moving the Saxon dead and collecting their weapons and armour. At a time of battles and hostilities, they were too valuable to bury. Later, corpses of the Danes would be stripped of anything of use, including their chainmail byrnies.

It was hard to estimate the number of fallen, scattered as they were in parts of the battlefield and piled in heaps in others, but as they began moving their comrades' bodies to one side, it became clear that Norse dead doubled that of the Saxons. Of Alfred's initial four thousand men, Eadwulf guessed that almost a thousand would lie buried at Bratton Camp for all eternity.

It was mid-afternoon when Aethelred and Garth found Jorund's body. 'Father,' Aethelred said, laying a hand on Eadwulf's back as he bent to lift another fallen Saxon with one of Alfred's men. 'You need to go and look...'

Eadwulf glanced up, the tone of his son's voice and the sadness in his tear-filled eyes telling him what he'd so dreaded to hear. 'You're sure it's him?' was all he could think to say as he pulled himself up, still clinging to that last shred of hope.

Aethelred nodded and pointed toward the outer ditch. 'Over there…'

Too grief-stricken to reply, Eadwulf stumbled toward the ditch and knelt beside his beloved brother, now lost to him forever. Anger welled, so fierce and unyielding he could scarcely breathe – and, at that moment, it was directed at no one but himself.

Afternoon hovered on the edge of evening when the others returned with a couple of large carts filled with shovels as well as their refilled water skins and a little food. It was decided amongst them to bury their dead in a dozen or so deep pits since individual burials on this scale would be impossible in the short time Alfred expected them to be away from Chippenham. Eadwulf baulked at the thought of his brother's corpse lying mangled with so many others, but accepted it was the only practical way of doing things.

Daylight lingered long on clear May evenings, and they made a start as soon as they had eaten, creating three deep pits in the downland's green. The stony soil did not make for easy digging, clogged as it was with lumps of chalk and sharp pieces of flint. It was an exhausting task, despite taking the work in turns. But, as twilight closed in, the three pits each held a hundred bodies beneath the replaced soil and downland turf. Tomorrow, they would finish the rest.

Sleep did not come easy to any of the men that night, huddled as they were along the crumbling walls of the hillfort. The meagre bits of bread and cheese brought back by those who'd been down to the villages failed to fill the bellies of thirty hard-worked men. Unable to sleep, or even close his eyes, Eadwulf made his way to where Jorund's body awaited burial, the rays of a half-moon enough to light his way. He squatted at his brother's side, memories of the times they'd spent together playing in his head. He thought of Ubbi and how close Ragnar's youngest son and Jorund had become as boys. Eadwulf could still picture the two of them in Aros, shrieking with merriment as they soaked each other at the water trough…

Jorund had been inconsolable on hearing of Ubbi's death, and now he, too, was gone. Eadwulf could not imagine how he'd cope with his grief in the coming days, but knew for certain he must appear strong, if only for Aethelred's sake. To give in to his sorrows would be no example to set for his son.

Cursing Ivar and Halfdan for starting the invasion, Eadwulf lay next to his brother, curling into himself as he wept.

Twenty Two

As Alfred had predicted, the siege was a short one. After two weeks, Guthrum sent three of his men into the Saxon camp, requesting to speak with the king.

'Guthrum begs you to meet him to discuss conditions for our surrender, lord.' The red-headed spokesman shuffled, still clutching the white flag, evidently uncomfortable facing Alfred, and standing in the midst of the triumphant Saxon army. He was a burly warrior, although the days without food had left his face gaunt and pallid.

'Your name?' Alfred snapped. The time for pleasantries with the Danes had passed.

'Thorkell, lord. I'm a jarl from the island of Fyn.'

'Well, Jarl Thorkell, tell Guthrum I agree to meet him and two others here, in my camp, but any terms will be laid down by me alone. He can either agree to them or stay in the vill and starve.'

The following morning, Guthrum appeared with Thorkell and another of his men, the slump of his shoulders and dull eyes that of a man with nowhere left to turn. Nor could Alfred fail to miss the liberal streaking of grey in his once lustrous dark hair. The warlord was simply old and broken. 'I am here, as you asked, King Alfred,' Guthrum said, all arrogance and mockery gone from his voice.

'Then I suggest we get out of this wind,' Alfred replied, leading them to one of the makeshift shelters and indicating they should sit on a couple of hefty tree trunks. 'It goes without saying that you and what's left of your horde will eventually leave Wessex and never return.'

Guthrum heaved a sigh of relief. 'That is all I would have asked, Alfred, and I thank you. We can exchange as many hostages as you want, and I'll swear on whatever amulet or holy book you wish never to return to Wessex.'

'I haven't finished,' Alfred barked. Guthrum momentarily stared at him, evidently confused and probably wondering what other demands he could possibly ask. 'Yes, I want twenty hostages, but you'll get none from me. You've proved to be careless with my men's lives and I can't trust you with more.'

Guthrum looked down, unable to maintain eye contact, and nodded.

'You realise I could have you killed, don't you? You took my kingdom, pillaging and raping without mercy, yet you expect me to let you leave on promises of never returning – promises that no one in their right mind would trust. By rights, I should have you and your men executed. The blood eagle seems to be a favourite method with Danes for captured kings, and beheading for their warriors. Had you been the victor, the blood eagle would have doubtless been my fate … or perhaps I would have been pierced with arrows from head to foot as your people did to King Edmund in Anglia.'

Guthrum swallowed hard, taken aback by the vehemence in Alfred's words. He glanced at the wide-eyed faces of his men, then at Alfred's guards outside the shelter doorway, and was silent for a moment, before collecting himself. 'You've already said we must leave Wessex, King Alfred. You want hostages but not oaths from me, so what else do you want?'

Alfred glowered at the warlord. 'I'm told your blood eagle ceremony involves victims giving themselves to Odin, which they do by being barbarically sacrificed. Is that true?' Guthrum nodded. 'Well, I want you, and thirty of your men, to give yourselves to our Christian God. I'm no barbaric raider and this ceremony is a lot more civilized, and a lot less painful, for those on the receiving end. Nor will you end up dead. You and your men will be given to our God through the ceremony of baptism.

'The decision is yours and you have until late this afternoon to make it. I suggest you get back to the vill and discuss things with your men.'

* * *

It was mid-afternoon when Guthrum and his two men returned to Alfred's camp. Eadwulf and Aethelnoth watched the meeting with interest. That the Wessex king could actually trust someone who looked like the traitorous dog he was, amused and amazed them. They'd both lived and sailed with enough Danes to know what they thought of Christian baptism: simply a convenient way out of a tight situation. Norsemen mocked the pathetically pious Christians for thinking that warriors of Odin and Thor would keep their word, or put their faith in the Christ-god. Eadwulf could imagine Bjorn's face if he knew of Alfred's trust in this devious cur.

But Eadwulf also knew that Alfred was wise beyond his years and trusted he knew what he was doing. Only time would reveal the outcome of all this.

* * *

Following Guthrum's acceptance of the stipulated terms, Alfred sent the Hampshire and Somerset fyrds home with their ealdormen, Radulf and Aethelnoth, keeping only the Wiltshire fyrd and his loyal Athelney men at the Chippenham camp. The baptism ceremony was planned for three weeks' time, and he couldn't risk leaving the vill unguarded and giving the Danes the opportunity to escape. The score of hostages he'd demanded were taken to Hampshire with Radulf, where they would stay until Alfred returned to Winchester and decided how best to place them in his shires.

The three weeks proved to be long and tedious, with little else to do but wait, and Alfred's thoughts strayed often to his family still on the isle. He continued to send men out each day to hunt and buy food from local villages, and permitted Guthrum to do the same, but the gates of the vill remained vigilantly watched. He'd suffered enough of Guthrum's broken promises to make him disbelieve anything the man said. Yet still, on this occasion, he was hopeful that once Guthrum had been baptised, and heard Alfred's proposals for a newfound peace between them, he'd be more than willing to keep his word, and his Christian vows.

At the end of the second week, Alfred was stricken by the debilitating illness that had plagued him every so often since his wedding day. It had been some time since the last attack and this time it came with a vengeance. Retching his guts up and doubled over in pain, he beckoned two of his men over to carry him into his shelter, where he stayed until the unnatural sweating and sickness abated two days later. With every joint in his body screaming outrage, he dragged himself to his feet and into the open.

During these weeks, messengers were sent to members of his witan across Wessex, requesting their presence at Guthrum's baptism. Ealdorman Aethelnoth, who had returned to Somerset with his fyrd, was entrusted to prepare the royal vill at Wedmore for the celebratory feast that would follow the baptism. Since Reeve Erwig's death, no one at Wedmore was responsible for running the vill, and with the forthcoming arrival of the king, there was the collection of foods, ales and mead to oversee, cooks to organise, and huntsmen, fowlers and fishermen to send out to fill the stores – and even skalds to locate. Soon, a large number of guests would require feeding, and Alfred knew that Aethelnoth was not a man to disappoint his king.

On the appointed day of the baptism, Alfred and his band from Athelney, with a dozen members of the witan from various shires, gathered inside the small wooden church at Aller in Somerset. Beyond the church door, Guthrum and his thirty jarls donned the long white robes worn by all who sought acceptance to the Christian faith. Alfred gazed fondly round the little church. Less than a mile to the east of Athelney, it was the place he would come to be alone with his misery and shame during the early days of his exile. He'd prayed to God to help him find a way of regaining his kingdom – and God had listened and answered his prayer. The idea of a raiding band had come to him whilst he prayed.

In this church on the small island of Aller, surrounded by

the peaceful harmonies of the marsh, Alfred felt close to God: the reason he'd chosen it for the baptism of a pagan warlord.

* * *

Eadwulf stood with his son and friends amongst the Wessex guests waiting for the ceremony to start. Closely packed as the men were inside the small church, he felt hot and sweaty, and realised this lengthy ceremony would severely tax his patience. Having spent much of the past three weeks coping with his grief over Jorund's death, he was in no mood for enduring any worship of the Christ-god. But, having no desire to draw attention to himself, he resolutely turned to focus on the proceedings.

Before they'd left Chippenham, Alfred described the Christian baptism to them all, including Guthrum, so they knew what to expect. Eadwulf vaguely recalled watching babes being baptised when he was a child in Mercia, and found it hard to imagine grown men – many of them seasoned warriors at that – undergoing similar treatment. He wondered how Norsemen would react to being dressed in white robes and subjected to a number of symbolic rituals that sounded weird and humiliating.

Guthrum was the first of the Danes to be met by the priest inside the church door, where the first part of the service, the *cristnung*, would take place. Garbed in his flowing white alb and gold chasuble, the priest stood before the warlord and blew into his face. Guthrum's head jerked back in surprise, but he was otherwise still and composed. Eadwulf threw a glance at Aethelnoth, choking back a laugh at his friend's ridiculous smirk. This small act, according to Alfred, would blow away any evil spirits that might have resided in Guthrum.

The warlord was next anointed in the sign of the cross on his shoulders and breast, the earthy smells of the holy oils causing Eadwulf's nose to wrinkle. Guthrum stayed statue-still while the priest pushed the oil jar aside and wiped his hands on a small white cloth, but when he spat on his fingers to anoint his eyes, ears and nostrils with spittle, a small croak emerged from Guthrum's throat, stark in the silence of the church. Eadwulf strained to keep his face straight and could see Aethelnoth was doing the same. He also wondered how effective all this anointing would be keeping Satan from men's hearts –in other words, in stopping born-and-bred Danes from worshipping the gods of their ancestors. The gods were part of Norsemen's lives and what they believed about the world around them. Eadwulf knew of few Danes who would dare turn away from their powerful and vindictive gods. Brave warriors trembled beneath the watchful eyes of Odin's ravens. And who but mighty Thor could control the thunder and cause such storms at sea or determine the outcome of a battle?

Guthrum must be quaking in his boots for fear of his gods' wrath. Or perhaps, like Aethelnoth and himself, the warlord believed in no god at all.

A dab of salt was being placed on Guthrum's tongue as Eadwulf pulled his thoughts back to the ceremony. As with the oils, he found difficulty in accepting that a simple substance could be held in such high esteem. How could something as ordinary as salt be considered a food for the divine? Why would any god want to eat salt, anyway, no matter how hard it was to come by?

Alfred was now moving towards the end of the church opposite the door, where a wide, deep stone bowl filled with water stood on a stout pedestal. Eadwulf knew that this was the font and would be used in the main part of the baptism ceremony. Alfred stood by as Guthrum was brought before the font where he proclaimed his faith in Christ and renunciation of Satan for all in the church to hear. The priest anointed the Dane's chest and between his shoulders with the oils known as the holy chrism before plunging his head three times into the water. Each time, the priest made the sign of the cross on his forehead, his voice ringing out, 'In the name of the Father, the Son and the Holy Ghost'. On the third occasion it was Alfred who took Guthrum by the shoulders and lifted him from the water – an act that displayed to everyone that the Wessex king had accepted Guthrum as his own godson.

Having now been cleansed of former sins, the top of Guthrum's already drenched, dark head was anointed with holy chrism before being wrapped in white linen bands. Like the ceremonial baptismal robes, the head cloth would be worn for eight days, when it would be unbound with great ceremony during the feasting.

It seemed the former conniving and unscrupulous warlord was now a Christian, although Eadwulf wasn't convinced that a few rituals would make a man like Guthrum worship the Christ-god, or abandon his old ways. Only time would tell. For now, Alfred seemed pleased as he conferred the new, Christian name of Aethelstan on the formerly pagan warlord.

The rest of the ceremony dragged on, and Eadwulf shuffled, desperately needing to be out of the stifling church, and silently willing the priest to hurry. Guthrum's thirty warriors underwent the same rituals as Guthrum, only the conferral of godson status being omitted. Eadwulf's mind drifted from one thing to another throughout it all, and by the time it was over, his empty stomach was rumbling and he longed for a mug of ale to moisten his parched lips. Once they reached the little hall on the island of Aller, the ale was promptly served. But it was another three hours before he savoured the taste of food.

* * *

Soon after sunrise the following morning, the assortment of men from Aller set out on the day's ride to Wedmore, where the baptismal feast would be held. Alfred welcomed the warm sun on his face and spoke little as he rode beside his new godson. There would be plenty of time for speeches and proclamations of newfound comradeship at Wedmore, but for now he wanted to dwell on his thoughts.

Alfred had noted the amused faces of Eadwulf and Aethelnoth on a couple of occasions, and not for the first time wondered which god they actually believed in. He understood that spending much of their childhood with the Danes would have cut them off from Christian beliefs and practice, but refused to believe they could be outright pagans. As a devout Christian, Alfred's faith meant much to him. Perhaps after the twelve days at Wedmore were over, he'd ask them about it.

His thoughts strayed yet again to Ealhswith and his children still on Athelney; so close, yet still out of reach. He didn't want them at Wedmore where the festivities would consume his time, and had sent a message to the isle relaying that to Ealhswith. He just hoped she'd understand. In another two weeks, he'd return to the place he'd called home since January, before they all left to re-establish their lives and duties at Winchester.

Alfred's first task would be to confront those who'd betrayed him and turned to Guthrum – and Archbishop Ethelred would be first. Alfred would take great pleasure in publically reprimanding the traitorous cleric, though he realised he'd have no other choice than to show lenience and permit Ethelred to keep his position in the Church. To have the man executed, or even just exiled, would alienate Alfred with the pope, not to mention pompous clerics of every description in Wessex.

Ahead of him, Alfred saw years of work, making his kingdom strong and secure against raiders from across the seas. He would strengthen his towns, build up his naval fleet and create some kind of regular army that would be ready to act at the first hint of a threat to his kingdom. Events at Chippenham and his months of raiding during his exile in the fens had made Alfred realise he was strong and resourceful – and a king deserving of the loyalty and respect of his people.

* * *

Aethelflaed had not had a good day. Her mother and Agnes had kept her busy in the Athelney hall for most of it, doing things she hated, like sewing and preparing vegetables. How she hated being indoors, where the reek of simmering pottage filled her nostrils all day. Outside the May sunshine beckoned and she longed to practise with her bow, determined to beat

Aethelred the next time they had a contest. Even Edward was outside with Agnes now, while she was still stuck in here. And to make matters worse, her mother had just delivered another ultimatum.

'That isn't fair, Mother! Wedmore's only a day's ride away and we haven't been to a feast for ages. And I want to see Papa… and all the others. Why should Aethelred get to go there and not us?'

Ealhswith heaved a sigh. 'There'd be no place for us at Wedmore with the hall full of Danes. They'll be spending most nights swilling back ale and mead and singing raucous songs and spending their days out hunting, or playing games they like to call sports. Where do you think we'd fit into all that? As for Aethelred, at seventeen, he's almost a man, and after fighting in your father's army, he's earned his place with the warriors.'

Aethelflaed continued to sulk, her mind searching for reasons why they should go to Wedmore. 'I love hunting… well, I love riding, so I imagine hunting would be good, too. And playing games is fun. And my mouth waters at the thought of the lovely food we could be having instead of these… these turnips!' She dropped the turnip she was attempting to peel back on the table. 'I'm tired of eating goat and we haven't had any nice fish for weeks. At Wedmore they'll probably have all kinds of delicious meats and fish and honey ca –'

'That's enough!' Ealhswith snapped, rising to lift the howling Aethelgifu from her pen. 'You've succeeded in upsetting your sister, now I certainly can't do the vegetables. So I suggest you get on with them. Besides, if you want the truth, not going to Wedmore was not my decision. Your father thought we'd be better here while the baptismal feast is underway – and for the reasons I just gave you. He sends his apologies, but he'd simply be happier knowing we were safely here.

'We'll see him in a couple of weeks, Aethelflaed,' Ealhswith added, coming to stroke her daughter's gold-brown hair. 'Then we'll all return to Winchester, if everything goes to plan.'

'But what about the Mercians…? Will they be coming with us?'

Ealhswith grinned. Though Aethelflaed would never admit it, it was obvious she thought the world of a certain young Mercian. 'Oh, I think you'll have time for a few archery contests with Aethelred before he heads back to Elston. But, once they do go home, I'm not at all sure whether we'll ever see them again.'

* * *

For the first eight days at Wedmore, the newly baptised Danes continued to wear their white baptismal robes and keep their heads bound in the white linen bands of the chrism. Since their days were spent outdoors, hunting in the forests or enjoying sports like archery, horse racing and wrestling, it soon became clear that their ankle-length robes were an encumbrance. It caused great merriment when they hitched them up and held them that way with their belts. For dignity's sake, Alfred permitted them to don their breeks beneath the pulled-up skirts while the sports proceeded.

'I'm not sure what a priest would say to my decision,' he admitted, smirking at his new godson, Aethelstan, as they prepared to wrestle, 'but since no priest is here, I make the decision in his stead. I wouldn't want any accidents to befall you, after all. Although, I suppose you *could* just let your skirts hang and hold them up in your hands when you run. Women have been doing that for centuries and they manage not to fall flat on their faces.'

Aethelstan guffawed. 'And women are welcome to their skirts! I admit, we'll be glad to take these robes off, but we respect their meaning, and won't be doing that until the appointed time. Till then, using our belts suits us fine.'

At night, sumptuous spreads of food and drink were consumed around the hall's glowing hearthfire. Torches flared between the colourful shields, impressive weapons and drinking horns displayed across the walls. Supplies of roasted venison, beef and wild boar were supplemented by mutton, wildfowl and fish, and cauldrons of simmering, meaty pottage. Flatbreads, honey cakes, ripe cheeses and bowls of creamy white skyr were savoured as the mead and ale flowed and the skald played sweet music on his lyre. Saxon heroes mingled with Norse in their songs of brave warriors of long ago.

Alfred could only guess at how much time his loyal Somerset ealdorman, Aethelnoth, had spent organising it all, especially at such short notice.

As each night's feasting wore on and singing voices quietened, Alfred freely bestowed gifts on his new godson and Norse guests. Rings, brooches and other pieces of jewellery were retrieved from the large sack of treasures Alfred had taken with him from Chippenham on Twelfth Night, as well as larger, more desirable items like pattern-welded swords and helmets taken as spoils from fallen warriors at Edington. In his role as gift-giver, Alfred hoped that Aethelstan would recognise him as his overlord, and see the benefits of remaining an ally to Wessex. Yet he had his doubts, and finding himself next to Eadwulf and his fellow Mercian, Aethelnoth, one night as the skald thrummed his lyre, he quietly voiced them.

'I wish I could be certain our efforts to make these Danes our allies will work – in the long term, I mean.' He looked from Eadwulf to Aethelnoth but neither man spoke, so Alfred continued, 'I'm pretty sure Aethelstan will remain my godson for a while, at least, once he returns to Mercia or Anglia, or wherever he goes. But once other Norse bands come to join him with shiploads of warriors, will Aethelstan, godson of King Alfred revert to being Guthrum the Dane and try again to take Wessex?'

It was Aethelnoth who replied, his intense brown gaze fixing on Alfred. 'I know I speak for us both when I say that in our experience, Danes are no different to people from Wessex or Mercia, or anywhere else.' He gestured at Eadwulf, who nodded agreement. 'What one man does may well seem laughable or miscalculated, or just plain wrong to another.' He paused, smoothing down a strand of his wiry, straw-coloured hair, and Alfred could see he was embarrassed at speaking out. 'What I'm getting at,' Aethelnoth went on, 'is that most Danes we've met are faithful to what they believe in – their homes, their families and friends, their way of life and their gods, to name but a few. But, some Danes, just like some folk from our own kingdoms, are driven by selfishness and greed. I see Guthrum as one of those.'

'I can't disagree with anything you've said so far,' Alfred said, encouragingly. 'Human nature is difficult to understand.'

'That's true, lord,' Aethelnoth ploughed on, and although I don't think for one moment Guthrum will become a follower of Christ, he'll likely claim to be one because it suits his needs. He's wily enough to know what's best for him and will stay faithful to you and your kingdom because he knows that even if more Norsemen join him, he'll never take Wessex. By the time his army is big enough to try, your army will be even bigger. He's got the measure of you now and knows your people love and respect you and will rise to any trick he may try.'

'Well, my friend, you've bolstered what I was hoping myself and I sincerely thank you for it. We'll need to think more about the future in the weeks ahead, starting with the best place for Aethelstan and his men to go to. There are still Norse warriors at Chippenham beside those we have here, and I want them all out of Wessex.'

'That's understandable,' Eadwulf said, 'and I think Guthrum would feel at home in either Mercia or East Anglia. If he intends to settle peaceably, I doubt anyone in those kingdoms would have cause to object. Mercia may well be his first choice. After all, the eastern half of the kingdom is still under direct Danish control and his client king, Ceolwulf, still rules the west. But, then again, Anglia is ruled by Danes, too.'

Alfred nodded. 'We'll need to talk things over with him. Wherever Aethelstan goes, it's vital we find a way of keeping him as our ally. But for now,' he said, rising to distribute more gifts, 'we still have a few more days of celebrating to do, so let's make the most of them.'

The chrism-loosening ceremony took place in festive mood on the evening of the eighth day of the celebrations, as was customary. Aethelstan and his jarls discarded their white robes and unbound the linen bands of the chrism. The role of unbinding Aethelstan's chrism fell to Aethelnoth of Somerset, a role that, effectively, made Alfred's faithful ealdorman Aethelstan's second godfather. At last, amidst more feasting, the mead-filled drinking horns were passed round, finally welcoming Guthrum and his Danes into the Christian world.

Twenty Three

Ribe, Danish Lands: Mid-June 878

Bjorn stared at his sister, trying to take in what she'd just said. Having brought his wife on a long-overdue visit to Ribe, Freydis' words shocked him. 'What do you mean, they've gone? Do you know *where* they've gone?'

Freydis shrugged. 'We only know they were heading to Rome first. After that, they weren't yet sure themselves. They left in early May, on a knarr that was recruiting crewmen, so they'll probably have been there for a while by now. And they didn't intend to come back.'

'I'm surprised Hastein didn't take the *Jormungand*... although I don't suppose he'd have found enough crew to embark on a one-way trip. I imagine if either of them does decide to come back, they'll need to find another ship sailing this way.'

Freydis acknowledged her brother's remark with a nod and seated herself on a bench alongside a trestle table, indicating to Bjorn and Kata to do the same. Kata came to sit beside her as serving women placed cups of ale on the table before scurrying off to continue preparations for the morning meal.

'They'll be back by the end of summer, sister, I'm sure of it,' Kata said, taking Freydis' hand and giving it an encouraging squeeze. 'Hastein loves you, and Dainn won't want to stay away from you and Aguti forever.'

'Dainn claims he's as much a Christian as his father,' Freydis replied, touched by the concern in the dark eyes of her sister-by-marriage, 'and both of them were certain they'd spend the rest of their days spreading the teachings of the Christ-god. Goodness knows where they'll travel to after Rome, but it won't be here.'

Bjorn took a seat opposite the women. 'But you're Hastein's wife and Aguti's his son, so why didn't he take you both with him? How could he just abandon you?'

Freydis gave a small sigh. 'That's easy to answer. It was me who refused to go with him, not the other way round. I'm no Christian, though I wish no harm to any who choose to be so. But I could never abandon my goddess. Freya has been a source of comfort for too many years to do that. And Aguti wanted to stay here with me and Yrsa. Hastein and Dainn have agreed that the estate is now his and, in time, I believe he'll run it well. The *Jormungand* is Aguti's too, when he's old enough to sail it.'

'But sister, what about your marriage… or have you divorced?' Kata's concern for Freydis was obvious, and Bjorn was glad she was here with him.

Freydis' eyes glinted with unshed tears as she faced her sister-by-marriage. 'Yes, we are divorced, Kata. I had grounds for it as soon as Hastein became a Christ follower and set his mind on leaving Ribe. He couldn't force me to go, so we divorced. It was a friendly arrangement and I'll always love Hastein for being the kind and thoughtful husband he's been all these years. But I don't love him enough to forsake Freya for Christianity, or Ribe for Rome.'

'So, you're saying all is well here?' Bjorn asked, unconvinced. 'I've never seen you look so tired, for a start. I'm sure Yrsa will be working hard, as always, and imagine she's in the fire room, preparing food as we speak?' Freydis nodded, her face brightening at the thought of her adopted daughter. 'Is Aguti pulling his weight around the estate? I haven't seen him yet, either. If everything is his now, he'll have no time for running off with his friends.'

'Bjorn, Aguti is only just fourteen!' Freydis shook her head and chuckled at her brother's face. 'We can hardly expect him to take full responsibility of our lands and people for another few years. He works hard until mid-afternoon, but I allow him to enjoy himself with his friends after that. I'm only tired because I've slept little recently. I worry about things too much and by morning my overtaxed head throbs. It's the responsibility of it all that worries me, and I don't want Aguti inheriting a failing estate. Hastein and Dainn are greatly missed for the smooth running of things, and although I do my best and ride out every morning, it leaves Yrsa with too much to do in the hall. Eirik, one of our karls, does what he can but he has other chores to do, too. So we're all finding it a little difficult at the moment, but I know things will become easier in time.'

'What a nice surprise!' Yrsa's cheerful voice snapped them out of the sombre mood. 'It's over a year since we saw your smiling faces,' she went on, drying her hands on her apron and closing the fire room door before coming to sit by the two women. 'I imagine Freydis has brought you up to date with our news?' Bjorn nodded, trying not to laugh at the young woman's matter-of-fact manner. 'We're gradually getting used to things, though none of us would tell you it's been easy. To be honest, we've been expecting Hastein to leave for Rome for some time now, so we can't say it was a shock, but Dainn's decision to go with him was.'

'You didn't know of Dainn's interest in Christianity?'

Both Yrsa and Freydis shook their heads at Bjorn's question. 'He asked Hastein the odd question about it now and then,' Freydis replied, 'but he never seemed interested in following the Christ-god, or forsaking Odin.'

'If you ask me,' Yrsa put in, shoving her dark braids over her shoulders, 'Dainn just wanted to sail off in search of adventure. He was never keen on working around the estate and was at his happiest when he was off trading with his father. In my opinion, going off raiding would have suited Dainn better than spreading the teachings of Christ.'

'Perhaps Dainn will come back then, even if Hastein doesn't.'

'I've been wondering that myself, brother.' Freydis admitted. 'But I imagine it will depend on how much coin they have left by then. Spending time convincing people to follow Christ is not the best way of earning it. How they'll even manage to buy food and shelter in Rome once the silver they took with them has run out, I don't know.

Bjorn nodded. 'There's a lot to think about, but Hastein's a resourceful man, and I'm sure he'll come up with something. He might even decide to come back himself.'

'Maybe,' Freydis said, her tone lacking conviction. 'If he does return to the northern lands, it won't be to stay here with us. Hastein's new faith is far stronger than the love he has for his home and family. But, after seeing the Holy City for himself, he may come back to spread Christ's teachings to our people in the towns, as others have done in the past.'

Freydis' words suddenly hit, and Bjorn had no choice but to accept that he'd lost the cousin he'd loved so dearly all his life; the cousin who had continuously ridiculed Ulf of his people's faith in Christ; the cousin who had once been carried in a coffin to trick the pious Christians of Luna into opening their gates; the cousin who had ransacked and burnt down so many Frankish churches and monasteries and slain dozens of priests and monks…

Hastein, the once faithful follower of Odin, the All Father, was now a Christ-follower himself. And Bjorn would mourn his loss.

Twenty Four

Two days after the celebrations at Wedmore were over, Alfred and his men set out for Athelney where they would spend a short time before heading back to Winchester. Guthrum had requested that he and the remnants of his army remain in Chippenham until arrangements for leaving Wessex could be made, and Alfred had agreed.

'Can you trust this man enough to give him free rein around your vill?' Eadwulf asked, blinking into the drenching drizzle as they rode. The rain hadn't stopped since the previous day and the fresh tang in the air after a week of muggy heat was no consolation to riders huddled beneath their cloaks. 'In my experience seasoned warlords like Guthrum rarely change. Raiding's a way of life to most Danes and agreeing to become a Christian is something many of them often do to get themselves out of sticky situations. In Guthrum's case, he's got the feel for power. Having had control of both Mercia and Wessex, he won't be happy about staying loyal, or answerable, to anyone – especially once he leaves Wessex.'

Alfred nodded. 'I've thought of these things, too, and decided we'll only know what he intends once he's given the chance. I agree, by wanting to stay in Chippenham, Guthrum could just be playing for time. It's already mid-June and more Danes could be sailing up the Thames, or landing somewhere along our coasts as we speak. The hostages we took will mean nothing to him, although each one is a jarl in his own right. Guthrum may well leave us to kill them all if he's intending to betray our alliance. But as I said, we'll never know unless we put him to the test.'

He glanced behind at his warriors riding silently in the rain, Eadwulf's companions amongst them. Alfred would never forget the loyalty shown by these men and would ensure each was well rewarded at the next gift-giving. 'Besides,' he added, refocusing on Eadwulf, 'I still agree with your friend, Aethelnoth. Guthrum knows if he wants to take Wessex he'll need an enormous army to do it. Our people won't let him ravage their lands again and, knowing what's best for him, I think Guthrum will continue to play the role of my faithful godson, Aethelstan.

'But, I tell you this, Eadwulf: I don't believe for one moment the warlord has changed. Beneath the shell of newfound piety, he's still a pagan Dane. No,' he added, a wide grin creasing his face, 'Guthrum is no more a Christian than you and Aethelnoth are.'

Their laughter rang out, both men knowing that further pretence between them would now be unnecessary.

* * *

Eadwulf was glad to be back on Athelney after the constant noise and activity of the baptismal feasts. Once the initial reunions were over it was peaceful here, and he relished the return to a simple way of life, if only for a few days. Throughout the siege and celebrations he'd pushed Jorund's death to the back of his mind. Now the reality of it resurfaced.

At times, the grief and loss surged in, overriding all other thought, and he was forced to seek some place of solitude until the flood waters ebbed. He found himself wandering to the far side of the isle, where he could sit and watch the little River Tone winding its way to join the River Parrett, its joyful gurgling balm to his raging thoughts. Eadwulf could now understand why Jorund had spent so much time here after Ubbi's death. Being so close to the natural things of the Earth had a way of reminding him that life goes on, no matter what is lost along the way.

That his son and friends were mourning too, he could not deny, and he realised he'd need to speak with them soon. But, right now, he was so consumed with his own grief he felt helpless to offer comfort to anyone.

Aethelnoth had lived with Jorund for a long time in Ribe, when they were part of Hastein's household, and Eadwulf knew the big man was no harder than anyone else when it came to losing people he loved. His outer bravado was simply a cover for the pain he felt inside. Aethelnoth had come to love Jorund like a brother. Aethelred, too, would miss his uncle so much. Jorund had arrived in Aethelred's life thirteen years ago, taking his three-year-old nephew under his wing, teaching him riding and weaponry skills and generally spending time with the lad, particularly when Eadwulf was busy running the estate.

Thoughts of returning to Elston with the tragic news slammed into him anew. His twelve-year-old daughter, Leofwynn, would be heartbroken, as would his half-sister, Ameena, and Aethelnoth's wife, Odella. Jorund was a boy of fourteen when he and Aethelnoth had come to Elston. But thirteen years had passed since then, and Jorund's cheerful and willing manner had ensured him a permanent place in everyone's heart.

Eadwulf dared not even contemplate Yrsa's grief when she learned of her brother's death. Although they hadn't seen each other for some time, the bonds between the brother and sister were still strong.

Then there was Freydis, who had loved Jorund as her own son.

The hand on Eadwulf's shoulder took him by surprise and he sprang to his feet, reaching reflexively for his sword. He smiled at Hamid's placatory stance and upraised palms, and indicated they should sit together.

'My apologies for startling you,' Hamid said, seating himself opposite to Eadwulf. 'I should have kicked a few stones to alert you to my approach.'

'You have nothing to apologise for. I was lost in my thoughts and wouldn't have heard if a dozen people had approached.'

Hamid nodded. 'I respect your desire to grieve alone, but we are all stricken over your brother's death. In the six years since we met in Cordoba, Jorund became a dear friend to me and I can't praise his skill in our carpentry work highly enough. He was a fine man and will be greatly missed by us all.

'For some people, solitude is the only way to deal with the pain of loss,' he added, heaving himself up ready to return to the hall. 'But grieving alone is not Aethelred's way, and at this moment he needs his father.'

The emir's son left, his words still ringing in Eadwulf's ears. 'I know he does,' he murmured, convincing himself that the 'moment' Hamid had spoken of needed to be *now*. He pulled himself to his feet and followed his friend back to the hall.

It was early afternoon when Eadwulf and his little group headed to the narrow beach at the edge of the camp for the long-overdue talk about Jorund. They sat on the grass beyond the silty deposits, gazing out across the lake, savouring the warm sun on their cheeks and the soft breeze lifting their hair. Out on the lake, water birds squawked and honked, many swimming out of the reeds with broods of young in tow. Swarms of mosquitoes hovered over the water, reminding Eadwulf of Hastein in Francia all those years ago.

At first, grief-stricken words flowed as they shared their sorrow at facing the future without Jorund. But soon, the choking words of misery and loss evolved into memories of the past, of times when Jorund had brightened their lives with his good-natured cheerfulness, and blunt, outspoken ways. Eadwulf and Aethelnoth shared memories of Jorund following them to Anglia in pursuit of Ivar, his hair and face muddied and clothing tattered and grimy in imitation of Eadwulf's disguise in Nottingham some years before. Jorund's antics as a wine merchant brought an outright guffaw from Hamid, who hadn't heard the tale before.

'You mean he actually stole a cart full of wine and attempted to sell a few jars of it?'

Aethelnoth nodded. 'To be honest, he did return the cart, and the wine, later on. He'd just "borrowed it", he said, so he could follow us without arousing our suspicion. And it worked, too, although the cheeky young sod almost got my boot up his arse for eaves-dropping on our conversation. His disguise was good, I'll say that much. And he wasn't much older than you are now,' he added, glancing at Aethelred. 'It took some guts to ride alone all the way from Elston to Thetford with so many Danes about. But that was Jorund all over. I can think of two words that describe him really well: gutsy and impetuous.'

'You're right,' Eadwulf agreed, nodding at his friend. 'It was Jorund's guts and impetuosity that got the two of us locked up in Cordoba!'

Hamid grinned. 'That incident I do know about. It also nearly got you both executed, but it turned out to be the best way for you to find your father. So, it all worked out well in the end.

'Now, if I may, I'd like to add a few words to describe how I came to see Jorund.' Everyone nodded and Hamid continued, 'I knew Jorund for much shorter a time than any of you, but during our months of working together, I found him to be loyal, kind, good-humoured, funny, resourceful, witty, clever, brave and a wonderful brother, uncle and friend.'

'Is that all…?' Aethelnoth asked, bringing hoots of laughter from the others.

Eadwulf rose to his feet, signifying an end to their talks. 'Each of us has our memories of Jorund to help ease the pain over his death, and when we think of him, let's remember the joy he brought to our lives.'

* * *

It was a joint decision to return to Elston instead of travelling to Winchester with Alfred. They'd been away from home for over four months now, and five weeks had passed since Jorund's death. None of them wanted people they loved hearing the tragic news from the lips of strangers. Eadwulf must be the one to deliver it, and be there to comfort them all. Exactly how he'd do that, he had no idea.

It took five days for them to cover the two hundred miles from Burrowbridge, with overnight stops on the way, and they arrived at Elston in the early afternoon, travel-worn and hungry. They were just leaving the stables when Leofwynn spotted them.

'Father!' she shrieked, dropping the bucket she was carrying and running across to throw herself at him. 'We were wondering when you'd all get back. Travellers brought news of a battle some weeks ago and we thought you might come home after that.'

Eadwulf embraced his twelve-year-old daughter, the love he felt for her swelling his heart. Her flowing auburn hair reminded him so much of her mother, Leoflaed, the wife he'd lost to the perils of childbirth. The tiny body of their third child, a boy who had not survived the birthing, was buried beside her and his grandfather, Wigstan, at the little church close to the hall. Leoflaed had been raised a Christian, and Eadwulf had honoured her beliefs.

'I'm so glad to see you back,' Leofwynn continued, turning to give Aethelred a hug,' and once you've had a mug of ale, we'll expect to hear all about what you've been doing and what King Alfred and his family are like.'

She waved to Aethelnoth and Hamid and linked arms with her father and brother as they headed for the hall. 'Selwyn will be pleased to have you home,' she remarked. 'He's gone to Nottingham with a couple of the servants today, just for goods from the market, and won't be back until tomorrow. Don't tell him I told you this, but he's not in the best of health and has missed you all running things – even though Jorund spends more time with Hamid nowadays…' She twisted round, glancing at the stables. 'Is Jorund still tending your horses?'

'We'll catch up on our news once we're all in the hall,' Eadwulf said, evasively. 'Let's have that ale you mentioned first.'

Odella and Ameena were overjoyed to see them and hugs were shared all round. Odella embraced her husband before their two children had time to claim his attention. Ameena also remarked on Jorund's absence and was informed by Leofwynn that he was still in the stables dealing with the horses.

'We'd be grateful for something to eat,' Aethelnoth put in quickly, ending all talk about Jorund. 'We've had naught in our bellies since daybreak, and that was only a crust of stale bread apiece. And the pottage smells good…'

Odella scurried off to oblige, returning moments later with serving women carrying four bowls of steaming pottage and a mound of flatbreads. 'I'll fetch Jorund's when he gets here,' she said, 'otherwise it will go cold.'

Eadwulf nodded and tucked into his pottage to avoid further questioning. But he knew he couldn't stay mute forever.

'We need to talk,' he said, calling them all to him once the meal had been eaten.

Leofwynn headed for the door. 'I'll go and fetch Jorund. I can't think what he's doing all this time. You didn't have any horses go lame on the way home, did you?'

'Come and sit down, Leofwynn,' Eadwulf threw after her before she could leave the hall. 'That's the main thing we need to talk about.'

Leofwynn shrugged and came to join them around the table. 'Jorund must be starving by now, 'she went on, 'but he always made sure the horses were settled before thinking of his own needs and –'

'Before this pretence goes any further, I've got something to tell you,' Eadwulf cut in. 'I've put off saying anything until now because I didn't know how to. Well, I've decided the only way is to come straight out with it.' He glanced at the nodding heads of the three who had been to Athelney with him and took a breath.

'Jorund isn't in the stables. If fact he isn't with us at all. He was killed at the battle at Edington.'

A deathly hush descended for some moments as Eadwulf's words sank in.

'No!' Leofwynn screamed, jumping up. 'He was too good a warrior to die in battle. I've watched him teaching Aethelred to fight… and practising with Aethelnoth or Hamid. He was as good as the rest of you, so how could he have been killed?'

Leofwynn's sobs were heartbreaking and, at her side, Ameena wrapped the girl in her arms, her own tears flowing down her cheeks. Eadwulf felt his grief rising again and his eyes teared up. He'd known that delivering this news would be hard, but watching their stricken reactions made it even harder. Jorund had meant so much to all of them.

'Where is he buried?' Ameena asked. 'He *was* buried, wasn't he…?'

'Yes, sister, he was,' Hamid said, since Eadwulf didn't seem to have heard. 'Jorund lies with all King Alfred's warriors who died at Edington. The site of the battle up on the Wiltshire ridge will be beautiful again once the ravages of combat have healed. It is a pleasant spot for him to be at rest.'

'I've lost my father and one of my half-brothers since coming to Elston,' Ameena said. 'Father was ill, and his death was painful for us all, but it was easier to understand and accept than Jorund's. Jorund had many years ahead of him to be happy, and perhaps raise children of his own. I knew him for so little time, yet I felt as though I'd known him all my life. And now I just have you, Hamid, and Eadwulf and his children. I couldn't bear to lose anyone else.'

Leofwynn pulled away from Ameena's arms and sped round the table to snuggle into Eadwulf's side. 'You aren't going back to Wessex, are you, Father? Ameena's right, we couldn't bear to lose any more of our family. Can't you leave King Alfred to fight his own battles now?'

Eadwulf raised his head from between his hands and pulled his daughter close. 'I'm staying right here, at least for the time being. Alfred isn't facing battle at the moment. But I can't promise we won't be going back at some stage. It all depends on whether any more Norse armies try to take Wessex. Alfred's big enemy, Guthrum, could well try again, so it's a question of us waiting to see what happens.'

There was little left to say. News of Jorund's death had dampened all enthusiasm for talk of King Alfred and his family, or the men's exploits in Wessex since January. Jorund was dead and what they all needed now was time to adapt to that fact and learn to move on without him.

Twenty Five

Winchester: Early October 878

Alfred threw a sympathetic smile at his wife as she entered the Winchester hall with two-year-old Aethelgifu toddling at her side. 'Feeling better now?'

'A little,' Ealhswith said, hoisting the toddler up and sitting beside him at the hearthfire. It was early in the day and the light, autumn mist lent a chill to the air. But, at three months into her pregnancy, Ealhswith insisted that walking in the fresh air helped to ease the queasiness in her stomach.

'It promises to be a beautiful day once the mists have lifted,' she said. 'The colours are glorious this year and did you know, we watched a squirrel collecting walnuts, didn't we, Aethelgifu?'

The child nodded and giggled. 'Tell Papa what colour fur the squirrel had,' Ealhswith urged. But the little girl just gave a coy smile.

Alfred took his small daughter's hand. 'Was it red?'

'Red,' Aethelgifu repeated, pulling her hand away and burying her face in her mother's tunic.

'Good girl,' Ealhswith cooed, carrying the child over to Agnes. 'Red's a lovely bright colour, isn't it? If we're lucky, we might see another squirrel tomorrow. But now it's time you joined Aethelflaed and Edward for some nice oatmeal and buttermilk.

'So it's true, then? Guthrum's definitely gone back to Mercia?' she asked, her hand on Alfred's shoulder as she resumed her seat at his side.

'It's true, though I can't say I'm happy about where he's made his camp. I'm relieved to have him and his army out of Wessex, but Cirencester's too close to our northern border for comfort. It's also in the western half of Mercia where Ceolwulf still rules as the Danes' client king.'

'Ceolwulf must be an old man by now.'

'He is,' and the last time we heard from him, he wasn't in the best of health. It's possible Guthrum's hoping to take over the whole of Mercia once Ceolwulf dies. But, as always, we'll just have to wait and see.'

'It does seem odd that Guthrum didn't go back to eastern Mercia, or even Anglia. I'd have thought he'd feel more at home in a region completely under Danish rule.'

'Mmmm,' Alfred murmured, a frown on his brow, 'and the further away from Wessex, the better. He was never likely to go to Northumbria, but Anglia would have been my choice for him. Cirencester's not only too close to Wessex, it isn't far from the Welsh border. You know how many raids the Welsh have made into Mercia in the past and if Guthrum wanted to find an army to support another invasion of Wessex, I'm sure the Welsh would oblige.'

'Oh Alfred, will all this never end? The thought of bringing our children into such an uncertain and violent world causes me more worry than I can say. And I can't bear the thought of you going to battle. Losing you would be –'

Alfred reached for her hand and squeezed it gently. 'I've no intention of dying just yet. For one thing, we have another child to look forward to next spring, and for another, I have the inklings of a plan that might persuade Guthrum to move further east. I just can't do anything about it until I see what unfolds with Ceolwulf.

'You know, in some ways I'll be sorry to see the old king go. Ceolwulf's been a far better ruler of Mercia than Burgred, for a start, and more amenable to deal with. But I doubt he'll last much longer.'

Ealhswith nodded. 'Few kings could have been worse for Mercia that Burgred.'

'My biggest worry is that Guthrum has no intention of keeping his Christian vows,' Alfred went on, 'and is biding his time until he has an army large enough to invade Wessex again. Whether the extra men come from the Welsh, or from the arrival of more Danes, would be irrelevant to him, if that's what he intends. I have my spies watching his every move as well as movements around our coasts and estuaries. So far this year, the only Danes to come to these kingdoms have stayed in Northumbria or Anglia. But that doesn't mean things will stay that way.'

* * *

At the end of November, three riders arrived at Winchester with a message from Ealdorman Ceneric of Surrey. Alfred's focus shifted between the three, standing awkwardly inside the hall doorway between two of his guards. Their news caused his stomach to plummet.

'How many ships?'

The spokesman for the group shuffled, evidently uncomfortable at being the bearer of bad news. 'Around sixty, I'd say, lord. We had reports of them heading up the Thames, so we kept a careful watch. Lord Ceneric heard they'd sailed from Francia, carrying what's left of a large Norse band that had been raiding for some time over there. Word is they got a thrashing on the Loire from a couple of Louis the Stammerer's sons.'

'So they aren't in Wessex?'

'No, lord. They sailed past London and made camp at Fulham on the north bank of the river. If it had been on the Wessex bank, Ceneric would have called up the Surrey fyrd.'

Alfred held his head between his hands as the possible consequences for Wessex hit. 'That could mean close on two thousand men. If Guthrum joins with this fleet, and manages to gather another thousand or so men across Mercia, he'll have a sizeable army again. He could even try to raise men in Anglia.'

'Father!' Edward yelled, hurtling through the doorway. 'Come quickly. There's something happening to the sun. I think it's being swallowed up!'

Within less than a couple of months of his ninth birthday, Alfred's dark-headed son was a sensible lad, so Alfred had no reason to anticipate some jest, and by the time he joined the rest of his household outside, the sun had almost disappeared. A menacing black shadow was spreading across the land, taking away all light and warmth. Thegns and servants from the hall gawked at the terrifying sight and Alfred heard the murmurings of fear and dread pass through them…

This is surely an ill- omen.

Something bad will befall us now.

It must be a sign that God is angry and will punish us.

Alfred had read of such events, when the sun seemed to hide behind the moon, and he assured them all that the sun would return before long. He'd seen it happen before, when he was a boy, and knew that to be true. But what he couldn't explain, to them or himself, was what it meant. Like his people gathered here, he knew that the disappearance of the sun was a portent of *something.* Scholars of the past had declared it to be so, and he was in no position to say otherwise. Yet even the wisest scholars had been unable to say whether it was a portent of something good about to happen – or one of pending doom.

As the sun slowly emerged from its place of concealment, Alfred decided that this strange occurrence must be linked with the unsettling news he'd just received from Surrey. The future of Wessex hung in the balance.

Would Guthrum the warlord join with this new Norse group and bring the downfall of Alfred's beloved kingdom? Or would Aethelstan, Alfred's newly baptised godson, honour his Christian vows and stay loyal to Wessex?

Alfred would pray to God to help Aethelstan prevail.

* * *

Cirencester and Winchester: October 879

'I've seen cleaner looking pig yards than this,' Guthrum muttered, steering clear of piles of animal bones and remnants of inedible meals as he and Thorkell paced through their Cirencester camp. 'It reeks worse than one, too. Our men are living in filth and can't be arsed to get off their fat backsides and bury the stuff. They've had the same bored looks on their faces for weeks and spend their time playing board games! They only leave their tents to hunt or forage for food, especially now the weather's getting cold again.'

Thorkell shrugged. 'They look bored because they *are* bored, same as you and me.'

Guthrum glared at him, trying to decide whether the remark was a dig at his leadership, but let it pass. He couldn't deny that boredom was killing them all, bit by bit. 'A year we've been in this stinking hole and we'll all go crazy if we stay here much longer. It's time to move on.'

Thorkell held out upturned hands. 'Move to where... and for what? If you still intend trying your luck at taking Wessex again perhaps we should have joined our countrymen in Fulham last year instead of sending them packing.'

'As I explained at the time, it wouldn't have been in our best interests.' Guthrum scowled at Thorkell's amused face. 'I know what you're thinking, but I can't bring myself to...'

'...break your word to Alfred?'

Guthrum let out a sigh, bending to pick up a hefty chunk of rock and hurling it at an enormous rat emerging from another pile of rotting waste. 'It's partly that but, as I said, it wouldn't be in our interests to continue doing battle with Wessex. Look how many men we lost at Edington. Alfred's getting stronger by the year and a more astute leader I've yet to see. Sixty shiploads of men wouldn't be enough to face him.

'I know, I'm probably just getting old,' he added when Thorkell remained silent, 'and last year's events at Edington and on that island knocked the urge to fight right out of me.

I'm feeling the need to settle down. Some of our men won't like the idea, but there'll be no one making them stay with those of us who do.'

To Guthrum's surprise, Thorkell nodded in agreement. 'There must be something in this Christ-god worship that's affecting us. I admit, settling down and living in peace sounds good to me. I'd like to think my days of raiding are over.'

Guthrum threw back his head and roared. 'I couldn't give a toss about the Christ-god – or any other god, come to that. But it serves me best that Alfred still thinks I'm his bloody Christian godson, Aethelstan. You were right about me not wanting to betray him, but for the wrong reason. At one time I'd have spat at Alfred's attempts to make us allies. But now I can see benefit in it for us. And it makes sense for us to head to Anglia. Like eastern Mercia, it's still under our control, after all. Pity this western side isn't at present – at least not fully. We could just get rid of Ceolwulf, I suppose, but it might result in uprisings we aren't strong enough to deal with. No, we'll wait until our old puppet drops before we resume control. I'm just not sure what Alfred would think of that, although Mercia isn't his concern.'

Thorkell nodded but made no comment about Alfred, or what he might think. 'Then if we're heading to Anglia, we'd best make the move before the snows set in. At least once we've gone, all those rats you keep throwing things at can scavenge in peace and grow nice and fat.'

'We'll head out the day after tomorrow,' Guthrum said, 'which gives us tomorrow to pack up and make ready to ride.'

As it turned out, riding back to Anglia was put on hold for a few more days. In the early afternoon of the following day, four men rode into the Cirencester camp with a message from King Alfred. Although confused as to why the Wessex king should need to contact him now, Guthrum duly took the parchment, leaving the messengers to wait for his reply, and strode back to his tent with Thorkell in order to read it.

'So what does he want?' Thorkell asked when Guthrum eventually raised his head. 'From your face, I'd say it's something that needs some thought.'

Guthrum handed him the parchment. 'Take a look yourself and tell me what you make of it.'

'He wants us in Chippenham tomorrow… to talk about boundaries between our lands and his.' Thorkell's face creased in confusion. You don't think it's a trick to lure us into some kind of ambush?'

Guthrum shook his head. 'He wouldn't have gone to the trouble of having us baptised and feasted if he intended to kill us. He could have done that when we surrendered after the battle. No, it's not a trap, and the only way we can find out what this talk of boundaries is about is to head to Chippenham tomorrow. It's only a twenty-mile ride, and we'll be back here in a couple of days.'

'Alfred only wants you and the thirty men who were baptised to meet him,' Thorkell remarked. 'So the rest of our men will have to stay here and keep the rats company.'

* * *

'Thank you for coming,' Alfred said, reaching to embrace his godson as he slipped from his saddle in the fading late-afternoon light. 'You must be frozen to the bone. December's arrived with a nasty bite this year. There's ale and a glowing fire waiting for you and a hearty meal cooking for later on. I'll explain what this meeting's about as soon as you're refreshed after your journey.'

Aethelstan nodded. 'Ale and warmth will be welcome, though I can't deny I'm puzzled by your request. We were about to leave for Anglia tomorrow, so your message only just reached us in time.'

'Praise God it did,' Alfred said as they headed to the hall, 'because what I want to put to you should benefit us both. But I'll wait until you're warm before saying more.'

Aromas of ale and baking bread assailed their nostrils as the entered the hall and Alfred hoped the glow from the hearth-fire would give relief to near-frozen fingers and toes. Servants brought flatbreads and honey cakes with mugs of warm ale for the group of Danes before scurrying out of sight. A company of Alfred's men sat around the large room, playing dice and trying to look unconcerned about the arrival of thirty-one Danes, as Alfred had ordered. With his family close by, Alfred could not take the chance that it was Guthrum, not Aethelstan, he'd invited into his hall.

He retrieved a parchment from an old chest against the tapestried wall and summoned Aethelstan to join him at a vacant trestle.

'This is a map of the kingdoms of Wessex and Mercia,' he started, unfolding the parchment and laying it on the table top. Aethelstan nodded. 'I'm sure you're familiar with these territories, but there are some new boundaries marked here I'd like you to consider.'

Alfred stood by while Aethelstan bent to study the map, running his forefinger along unfamiliar boundaries. 'I can follow the new borders well enough but I'm not altogether clear how they affect me.' He flicked a glance up at Alfred and refocused on the map. 'The only thing I recognise is that the boundary cuts the kingdom of Mercia in half – the east and western regions…' He stopped, evidently considering what he'd just said. 'So the lands to the east of this boundary are those my people presently control: eastern Mercia and Anglia?'

'Right,' Alfred said, 'a region I've called the Danelaw. Although you and Halfdan conquered the entire Mercian kingdom, you agreed to have Ceolwulf ruling the west as your client king. I think we both know that Ceolwulf won't live much longer and, to put it bluntly, I don't want western Mercia under Danish control as well. You have more than enough land in these kingdoms to think about, with Northumbria, Anglia and eastern Mercia, without taking western Mercia. We also both know that if you tried, it would result in more battles and more bloodshed – which neither of us wants. Am I right?'

'You are. So you're saying that if I agree to rule all the land east of your boundary and make no claims or attempts to take the west – which, I'm guessing, you want control of yourself – you will agree to let us live in peace over there.'

Alfred nodded. 'That's about it, and we'll both sign a treaty to testify to our agreement and make it binding. It will bring peace to our peoples – although I'm certain there will be other fleets of Norsemen for Wessex to face in future.' He looked levelly into Guthrum's dark eyes. 'I'm sincerely hoping their arrival won't affect the treaty that you and I sign this day.'

Before Aethelstan could reply, Alfred went on, 'Let's take a closer look at where the boundary runs.' Like Aethelstan, he used his forefinger to trace the boundary's route. 'It follows the Thames inland to London before turning north to follow the River Lea toward Luton. It then continues across land to Bedford from where it follows the River Ouse to meet the old Roman road, Watling Street. It keeps to the road's north-westerly route for some distance, passing close to Northampton and Lichfield before eventually veering from the road and coming to an end a little to the north-east of Chester.'

Again he glanced at Aethelstan, pleased to see him nodding. 'I have a copy of the map ready for you if you're happy with what I propose.'

'London appears to be right on the boundary. Does that mean it will be open to both East and West Mercia?'

Alfred nodded. 'Since we're to be allies and live in peace with each other, I've no cause to make total claim on London. It's become an important port and trading city over the years and valuable to us all.'

'I'm taking my men back to Anglia,' Aethelstan stated, saying nothing more about the boundary, 'where those who want to can settle down to a peaceful life. It's fertile land and I'm sure most of them will be happy to farm and raise families. Those who don't will be free to leave.'

'You still have ships moored along the Anglian coasts?'

'A few, but I won't be sailing in any of them. Many of the men who sailed with me to these lands are gone, so it's time for the rest of us to finish our lives in peace.'

There was little left to say and the treaty was signed. Aethelstan would explain all to his men once they reached East Anglia and what they chose to do would be up to them. But Alfred remained hopeful that the former warlord would stay true to his Christian vows and become his loyal ally.

But, as always, that niggling doubt refused to leave his overwrought thoughts. And, despite what he said to Aethelstan, he wasn't certain he'd made the right decision regarding London.

* * *

Winchester, Wessex: January – Christmastide 880

Winter passed uneventfully in Wessex that year, and heavy snows in January rendered travel difficult. Alfred couldn't wait for spring to come, although he realised it would be some time before he could instigate the repairs his kingdom desperately needed after the ravages of the occupying Danes. Several huge payments of danegeld had left his coffers empty.

The movements of vast armies across the land had left roads ragged and pot-holed, a danger to travellers, especially those in wagons and carts, or on horseback. Trade was almost at a standstill and many of his great monasteries and abbeys, honeypots to rampaging Danes, had been burnt and pillaged. Farmland across some of his shires had been neglected, due to the number of times the fyrds had been called to battle, and Alfred knew that stocks of food in many villages would be dangerously low this year.

'At least we've had no more Danes arrive to cause concern

since those camped at Fulham left a year ago,' he said to Radulf as they rode back to Winchester with a small company of men after a day spent visiting local Hampshire villages. 'They've been causing havoc to the people of Ghent, but the Low Countries aren't our concern. And having Guthrum in Anglia, miles away from our borders, is a great relief.'

'Relief it might be, for now, but I still don't trust the traitorous cur,' the ealdorman said. 'I'll not forget in a hurry what he did to the hostages he took from us at Wareham.' A scowl darkened his face at recollection of the incident and Alfred patted his arm. It played heavily on his mind, too. 'Although I hear he's asking everyone to call him Aethelstan nowadays,' Radulf continued. 'He reckons his old name flew out the window at the Aller church.'

Alfred chuckled at the image as they dismounted at the hall and handed their reins to the grooms. 'Only time will tell if that's true, but we can't lose sight of the possibility of other Norse bands arriving at any time. If they do, let's hope they'll be small enough for us to deal with as soon as they make landfall. A peaceful year would enable us get a few repairs underway – at least as far as our limited reserves of coin will allow. And our people need time to get their lives and farmland back to normal, especially those in Wiltshire, Somerset and Berkshire. Thankfully, Hampshire and most of our eastern shires haven't been so savagely mauled.'

'It'll be good to see all our kingdom prospering again,' Radulf agreed. 'We've had a tough few years, that's for sure.'

In the last week of April, Ealhswith gave birth to another daughter, who was given the name of Aelfthryth. Like her brother, Edward, Aelfthryth was a placid babe, and Alfred was pleased that he and Ealhswith were able to sleep a little more this time round. It was good to see his wife so happy. Caring for their new daughter took her mind off what Guthrum may or may not do, and Alfred was glad of it.

Summer and autumn passed by without a single Norse raid and Alfred gave daily thanks to God. When Christmastide came round once again, nobles from across the kingdom gathered at Winchester to celebrate the peace they had now enjoyed for the past two years. It was a relaxed and happy occasion. Ealhswith, Agnes and Aethelflaed had bedecked the hall with red-berried holly and other bright evergreens, and Edward helped the men to drag in the hefty oak Yule log, lighting it to smoulder merrily in the hearth where it added its warmth and light to that emitted by torches flaring around the walls. Aromas of roasting boar, venison and mutton constantly pervaded the room, and guests crowded in to savour the vast assortment of delicacies throughout the twelve days.

As the old year prepared to depart on the last day of December, Alfred gave thanks to God for that peace, and prayed it would continue in the coming year. His children were thriving and Ealhswith had lost the look of deep anxiety that had become fixed on her lovely face.

Yet it grieved him that the gift-giving on Twelfth Night was, of necessity, a subdued affair. With promises of better rewards next year, he hoped his nobles would understand the need for any surplus coin to be used in the recovery of their kingdom. By way of consolation, he ensured they were lavishly fed and that ale, wine and mead flowed freely throughout the celebrations. And during the evening he took the opportunity of raising a number of issues regarding the future of Wessex with his most trusted advisors. Among those present were Ealdormen Aethelnoth of Somerset, Radulf of Hampshire and Unwine of Sussex.

'With Guthrum not being such a threat now, I want to plough on with some of the things I've needed to do for a while,' he started. 'And setting up a new witan is top of my list. There are at least seven long-standing council members I want out.'

Alfred scratched his head as he thought, determined to be ruthless in this. He needed a council he could trust, consisting of men who respected him and valued him as king. He had no intention of facing a constant barrage of hostility in future.

'I'll call the men I want to dismiss,' he said at length, 'and deal with those who opposed my kingship first. Many are too old to serve on my council anyway, and need dismissing on those grounds alone, so I may not have to raise the issue of past grievances. The old thegn, Milred, is the first to spring to mind. He served my father before I was even born, and was bitterly opposed to me succeeding Aethelred as king. He should have been relieved of his duties years ago. Then there's Bishop Tunberht of Winchester, another who has become incompetent in old age. I'm also sure he sided with Archbishop Ethelred in betraying me to Guthrum.'

Saddened, as he always was, at thoughts of traitors in Wessex, Alfred heaved a sigh. 'Believe me, I've considered banishing them from Wessex altogether, but decided that living with the scorn of their countrymen after being publically reprimanded for their betrayal will be punishment enough.

'Once the dismissals are dealt with, I'll summon the men chosen to sit on the new witan, and our first task will be to set down the wishes of my father concerning the succession of Wessex kings once and for all.'

Alfred's gaze shifted between the three ealdormen. 'There are members of the Wessex nobility who still believe my nephews, Aethelhelm and Aethelwold, should have inherited the throne when my brother, Aethelred, died. I'm determined that King Aethelwulf's wishes are clearly set out so that when I die – which, hopefully, won't be for some time yet – my son Edward will be crowned king without opposition from my nephews' supporters.'

Aethelnoth tweaked his short, dark beard. 'That sounds straightforward enough, although not being that young myself, I can only hope I'm not on the list of those to be booted out.' He grinned and gestured at Radulf and Unwine. 'All three of us served on King Aethelred's witan, didn't we?'

'We did,' Unwine affirmed, 'but as I recall, we were all in favour of the young aetheling succeeding his elder brother as king. After all, I was at Alfred's side at Ashdown and he showed real potential there, as well as battles following it. I always thought we should give him a chance to show how well he could rule…'

Alfred chuckled as the cheerful banter about him continued. 'I've always been grateful for your faith in me,' he said. 'It's little wonder I want my entire witan to consist of men like you: men who trust my judgement. Besides, I wouldn't call any of you old and incompetent just yet.'

Ealdorman Aethelnoth's smiling nod was reassuring, followed as it was by a pertinent question. 'Any more thoughts on which towns we fortify first? Not that we can do much before the spring, I realise, but I wondered if you'd decided where our priorities lie.'

'I've done little *but* think about that for the past few years, Aethelnoth,' Alfred replied, 'and hope to make a start on some of them as soon as the new witan is organised. There's so much to do that the question of where to start isn't an easy one to answer, but yes, I have listed the areas I see as priorities.'

He paused to collect his thoughts. 'The unexpected attack on Wareham three years ago served me well as a lesson in what Wessex needs. Guthrum not only faced little resistance to his taking the town, he managed to ride his army from Cambridge to Wareham without being challenged – a route of over a hundred and seventy miles. Yes, there are many inland towns that need better defences, but settlements around our coasts and borders must come first.'

Alfred's glance moved between the three men, and pleased to see their nods of agreement, he pushed on. 'The ealdormen of shires along our southerly coasts, from Kent to Cornwall, have dealt with numerous raids these past years, with islands like Thanet – and Sheppey, further into the Thames estuary – have been targeted time and time again. Exeter proved in great need of better defences three years ago, too, and more recently, our shires with western coastlines, like Devon and Somerset, have faced Norse raids – such as the one led by the Dane, Ubbi, at Countisbury in Devon.'

The mention of Ubbi made Alfred think of Eadwulf and

his little group, and he wondered whether he would see any of them again, now they'd returned to Elston. He could not help wondering how Eadwulf and Aethelnoth felt about living in Danish-controlled eastern Mercia. Then he laughed at the thought. After all, they were practically Danes themselves.

'So, friends, my guests will be leaving over the next day or two. I'll give them a few weeks in their halls before calling a meeting of the witan here in Winchester. Many of them won't like what I have to say, but they'll be given no chance to argue. And once I have a witan I can truly trust, we'll get to grips with the task of repairing and fortifying our kingdom. Our coffers have swelled nicely this year, so we're in a fortunate position to really get going.

'Now, let's enjoy our mead and look forward to progress in the year ahead.'

Twenty Six

Winchester: May 881

In the last week of February, Ceolwulf the Second, client king of Mercia, finally died. Alfred had neither liked nor disliked the man, but admitted he'd shown the unselfish good sense in ruling the kingdom that Burgred before him had lacked.

Following his treaty with Aethelstan, Alfred was now in control of western Mercia, and could not deny that things had played out perfectly for him. He'd dreamt of expanding his kingdom's borders for years – just as Wessex kings had done for generations. Taking over only half of the huge Mercian kingdom would make Wessex so much more powerful; so much better able to fend off future attacks by invaders.

But, in assuming control of Mercia, Alfred had also taken over dealings with the old, Celtic kingdoms of Wales, and he could only wonder whether that would be to his advantage.

'Relations between Mercia and the Welsh kingdoms on its borders have been far from peaceful over the years,' Alfred said for the umpteenth time as he and Radulf rode back to Winchester with a small group of thegns after visiting Eadred, the Basing reeve. 'Doing battle with the Welsh is the last thing we need while we're trying to make Wessex strong.'

'So you keep saying,' Radulf replied, feigning a weary sigh. 'But there's little point in worrying about it until the time arises. That is, *if* it arises.'

Alfred flashed an apologetic grin, realising the ealdorman

had a point. 'I'll say no more and let you enjoy the scenery for the rest of the ride.'

He settled in his saddle, his fingers raking his white stallion's mane as he mulled over what he knew of the relationship between Mercia and Wales. At times, Mercian strength had kept its borders safe; at others, the Welsh had raided Mercian lands at will. Over the years, west Mercian leaders had increasingly tried to gain more control in Wales, particularly in the northerly kingdoms of Gwynedd and Powys, where they'd come up against the powerful Welsh king, Rhodri Mawr. Following the Welsh leader's death in a battle with the Mercians three years ago, his sons were intent on vengeance, especially as Mercians continued to push further into Wales.

Doing battle with Rhodri Mawr's sons was not an idea that Alfred relished. For a start, he hadn't yet met with the west Mercian witan, and had no knowledge of the locations of the kingdom's ealdormen. Sending out orders to raise the various fyrds would not be easy. Besides, how they would all react to being ruled by the Wessex king remained to be seen.

* * *

On a blustery afternoon in mid-April, a small group of riders reined in outside the Winchester hall. Recognition was instant and Alfred hurried over from the stables where he'd been chatting with his grooms.

'You seem to make a habit of turning up out of the blue,' he said, grinning as he grasped Eadwulf's arm, then turning to welcome Aethelnoth, Hamid and Aethelred. 'I've often thought of you over the last three years and am heartily pleased to see you again. You can explain why you've come once you've had a mug of ale and something to eat. You must be weary after such a long journey.'

'More in need of a decent night's sleep than anything,' Eadwulf said shoving his hair back from his face, 'preferably on a softer bed than solid earth.'

Alfred sympathised as they entered the hall, knowing how true that was from journeys he'd made himself. 'If you can spare the time you must stay for a few nights before you head home. Ealhswith will be happy to have you here. In case you hadn't heard, we've had another daughter since we last met. Aelfthryth has just turned two and Ealhswith is due to give birth again this coming autumn.'

'Congratulations to you both. And the rest of the family are well?'

'You'll soon see that for yourself, my friend, but yes, they've all blossomed during the peace we've enjoyed since Edington. Aethelflaed will be twelve in a few months, and rapidly leaving childhood behind. She looks more like her mother as the weeks pass.'

Alfred glanced at Aethelred, noting how the years had changed him, too. As tall and broad as Eadwulf, the young man had the physique of a powerful warrior. 'I must warn you, Aethelred, my daughter has never lost her love of archery. Competing with you has made her determined to challenge anyone who carries a bow.'

'Well, lord, I can truthfully say I've rarely used a bow since I was on Athelney, so Aethelflaed would likely thrash me nowadays. I'll be sure to avoid giving her chance to humiliate me. Is… is your daughter still as outspoken and opinionated as she was?'

Alfred chuckled at Aethelred's question as he indicated they should sit opposite him at a trestle. 'She gets more so by the month, in my opinion. Unfortunately, she is much as I was at her age. But we won't get into that.

'Ale, fresh bread and cheese for my guests,' he said as serving women hurried to the table. 'Oh, and a mug of buttermilk,' he added with a nod at Hamid. 'And let Lady Ealhswith know we have visitors. I'm sure she'd like to welcome them herself.'

Ealhswith appeared with Aethelflaed and Edward once the food had been enjoyed and the men were relaxing with their drinks.

'Lady Ealhswith,' Eadwulf said, as they rose to greet her with a little bow and a smile at the two youngsters, 'it's good to see you again, especially in happier circumstances.'

Ealhswith flashed a broad smile. 'It's a delight to see you all, although I can only wonder what has brought you here on this occasion. We have no battles to face at present. But, whatever the reason, you are most welcome to Winchester and to stay as long as you wish. Perhaps you could do some fishing while you're here,' she added, focusing on Aethelred. 'We haven't tasted such delicious bream since you went out with Garth in the Fens.'

They all laughed at that as Ealhswith and the children sat beside Alfred. 'Have you seen anything of Garth since we left Wedmore, lord?' Aethelred asked.

Alfred nodded. 'Garth's often mentioned you, too, and I

know he was sorry to see you return to Mercia. As a matter of fact, he's become one of my regular bodyguards. He doesn't yet know it, but I'm also considering making him a thegn. He heads back to Athelney every so often to see his family, but he's always here when his turn for duty in my hall comes round. Much like you, he's a strapping young man, and has an impressive ability to instil trust in the others.'

'Garth always showed promise as a warrior,' Aethelnoth agreed, 'and his skills in the wild are impressive. He managed to make a good fisherman of Aethelred, which can't be bad. It's just a pity our young friend here won't have time to dally on the riverbank in future.'

Alfred's eyebrows rose. 'Oh, why is that? Could marriage be on the horizon?'

Aethelred let out such a snort that everyone laughed. 'I can tell you, I've no intention of marrying anyone just yet.'

'My son is now an ealdorman of Mercia,' Eadwulf explained. 'Although our side of the kingdom is still under Danish rule, we've had our own system of electing ealdormen and thegns since Burgred left. It's mostly hereditary, but not always. Old Selwyn, the brother of Wigstan, my deceased father-by-marriage, has taken it upon himself these past few years to spread the word that I am King Beorhtwulf's son and Aethelred, his grandson. Unfortunately, that also links us both to Burgred, who most Mercians were glad to see the back of, but the royal link is there. And few Mercians would deny either my or Aethelred's right to rule.'

'It's good to know your true positions in Mercia have been recognised,' Alfred said and meant it. 'But you must know there's unlikely to be another king of the Mercia you knew and loved.'

Alfred stared down at his hands resting on the table top, trying to decide how best to explain something they might not accept. 'I'm sure you realise that when Guthrum – Aethelstan – retreated to East Anglia, it was on the understanding that I'd be responsible for western Mercia in his place. Mercia, as a whole, was taken by the Danes while Burgred ruled and nothing had changed that, as far as Aethelstan was concerned. He had simply been allowing Ceolwulf to live out his life before taking over western Mercia himself.'

'We know of your treaty, Alfred,' Eadwulf said, 'and that western Mercia is now under your rule. That's the reason we're here.'

Alfred felt a sudden jolt of anxiety. He had no wish to make enemies of men he'd come to love and trust – but he had no intention of letting western Mercia go after waiting so long to have it.

'We realise the old Mercia has gone,' Aethelred said, continuing his father's words before Alfred felt composed enough to reply, 'but we have two things to talk over with you. The first is a proposal.'

Alfred shifted uncomfortably on the bench, recalling his own use of the word 'proposal' with Guthrum, and wondering what he would hear.

'The witan of western Mercia has elected me to oversee the west now that Ceolwulf has died,' Aethelred went on. 'But as an ealdorman.'

Alfred nodded slowly. 'I see… And how do you relate that

to my role in ruling the western kingdom?'

'Our councillors suggest I become the kingdom's overlord, something similar to a client king. I'll take care of affairs connected to governing western Mercia while you are busy dealing with affairs in your Wessex shires. I'll be answerable to you and follow your orders. I will also be on hand to mobilise and lead Mercian armies quickly should Guthrum attempt to take over again, or new Norse bands arrive.'

Alfred was momentarily lost for words, but couldn't deny the proposal seemed like a godsend. He'd wondered himself about sending Wessex nobles into Mercia to rally the various fyrds if attacks occurred. How much easier would it be if the Mercians were led by one of their own – and one whom Alfred knew he could trust?

'And you are happy to do that… defer to me, I mean?'

'I am, lord, and I've been living at the royal hall at Worcester for the past few weeks. If you have any objection to that, I'll move somewhere else.'

'I've no objection at all. Worcester's been a key Mercian town for years, so it's fitting you should have the hall there.'

'It's also not too far from the Welsh border,' Aethelred added, 'which brings me to the second thing I mentioned.'

Alfred's stomach plummeted. 'Are you saying the Welsh are raiding Mercian lands again?'

'They are, lord, and have been since mid-February. King Ceolwulf was on his deathbed by then and could do naught about it. The witan of west Mercia requested their ealdormen to call up their fyrdsmen, but the response was poor and none of the nobles felt able to take command. That was when the witan approached us at Elston. Knowing our heritage, they hoped that one of us would take over the leadership.'

'And it was you, Aethelred, who accepted?' Alfred flicked a questioning look at Eadwulf, but said nothing. There would be time to question his views on that over the next day or two.

'It was, lord. I felt I owed it to both my grandfather and father to prove my loyalty to Mercia. And by the middle of March, I was leading an army into Gwynedd to face the forces of Rhodri Mawr's sons.'

'Were you leading the army alone?'

'I had several Mercian ealdormen and thegns with me, but if you mean were my father and two friends with me then no, they weren't. I didn't want the men to think my father was in control, so I asked them not to come. But I didn't expect Mercian armies to be so unprepared for battle.'

'I can understand your decision. A leader should start as he means to go on. As for the Mercian fyrds, they're weak because they were rarely called during Burgred and Ceolwulf's time as king. Was the battle a total disaster?'

Aethelred nodded, his face downcast. 'To say we were thrashed would be putting it mildly. We were well outnumbered for a start, and the fyrds were ragged and untrained. Few had armour or suitable weapons, or any idea of combat. The Welsh may not fight in a shield wall, but they were all well-armed and helmeted, and carried long shields. Several even wore chain mail.

'But it's their skills in ambush that make Welsh warriors so formidable and they took us completely by surprise. When we reached the bridge to cross the river to Conwy, the place looked deserted. But, suddenly, warriors appeared out of nowhere – the settlement, the woods behind, and even along the riverbank. We were attacked from all sides by a screaming horde. Some of them rode their horses straight into our fyrd.

'It was a total rout, and many Mercians lost their lives. The rest of us fled, and fortunately for us, Welsh warriors did not pursue for long. As soon as we were away from the town they gave up the chase.'

Alfred didn't have to think too hard to realise what Aethelred's second request would be. 'You want me to raise a Wessex army and confront these sons of Rhodri Mawr?'

'I do, lord. The rout caused Mercia to lose control of northern Wales and now Rhodri's sons are trying to gain power in Welsh kingdoms further south, threatening our hold over those as well. Raids across the borders into Mercian towns have also become frequent again.'

'I can imagine,' Alfred said, frowning as he thought, 'and you have every right to ask for my help. When I was four, my father responded to Burgred's plea for help against the Welsh in Gwynedd. I only vaguely remember the Wessex army mustering, but I grew up hearing of the trek into the Welsh mountains during my father's many reminiscences. King Aethelwulf accepted Burgred's request on the grounds that it showed unity between our two kingdoms. He also gave my sister, Aethelswith, in marriage to Burgred to further cement our alliance.'

He paused as old hurts resurfaced, affecting a smile to disguise the feelings he knew would show on his face. 'So, yes, I'll honour my father's hopes for our kingdoms' unity. And since

I now rule western Mercia, to refuse would not reflect well on me or Wessex. I'll send messengers out to our ealdormen to raise their fyrds first thing tomorrow.

'And, if you want, Aethelred, you can send some of my men to your ealdormen to prepare them for a move on Gwynedd. Let's hope they'll raise at least a few hundred of the Mercian fyrd. The more warriors we have, the better. Wessex fyrds have seen plenty of action in recent years and should have weapons and armour to hand. And after that unsuccessful venture last time, let's hope Mercian villagers have seen the sense of having weapons and battle garb ready for when they're needed.'

Aethelred nodded. 'I hope I made that clear to the survivors, lord. But poor farmers…'

'I know,' Alfred said, nodding agreement, 'but it's our duty to make sure they understand. Sometimes, just carrying a shield can mean the difference between life and death.

'And, if we're likely to be ambushed on our way to Conwy, we'll have a battle plan to put into motion the moment the first Welshman shows himself.'

* * *

At the end of the first week in May, the joint Wessex and Mercian army of almost eight hundred strong moved out from where they'd mustered at the west Mercian town of Shrewsbury and headed north for Chester. It took two days to reach the old Roman town, after an overnight camp to break the forty-six-mile trek for the fyrds who were, as always, on foot. At Chester, they camped overnight again before heading west along the coast road on yet another forty-six-mile journey to Conwy.

Aethelred rode at Alfred's side, staring at the slate-grey waters of the Irish Sea. Angry waves crashed on the shore less than thirty yards from the road, while overhead, ragged black clouds raced inland. He braced himself against the strong westerly that seemed intent on infiltrating his mailshirt and tried not to think of the battle ahead. The shame he felt at his recent defeat was still tender and raw. Desperately wanting to impress his father, he now felt he'd let Eadwulf down.

Behind them, their army stretched out for what seemed like miles, a mix of mounted noblemen in chainmail shirts and metal helms and the various fyrds in their leather helmets and gambesons. Some of the most powerful ealdormen in Wessex were bringing up the rear, Radulf of Hampshire, Aethelnoth of Somerset and Paega of Berkshire amongst them and Aethelred suddenly felt overwhelmed at the privilege of leading the army next to the Wessex king.

Alfred continuously twisted in his saddle, his hawk-like amber eyes raking the road and open land to their left for signs of ambush. It was impossible to guess where the Welsh would strike. Alfred's scouts rode ahead, ready to alert them to the first signs of danger. Every bend was approached with caution. Neither Aethelred nor Alfred could see them, but their presence hovered on the briny air.

In the early afternoon their route veered inland and they continued across a wide, grassy plain broken by patches of woodland. After another three miles, Conwy came into sight, though distant as yet, sitting on the far side of the river of that name. The strange silence Aethelred remembered from the last time struck him again and he prayed Alfred's army would remember what they'd practised at Chester. He peered into the dense woods nearby, where many of the enemy had waited before, but could see or hear nothing to cause alarm. Yet with the Welsh that meant little and his screaming senses told him they were close. Too close…

Welsh warriors were suddenly streaming toward them from all directions – from across the bridge three hundred yards away and from hidden places in the woods behind. Others seemed to rear up from the depths of the earth itself along the river bank and any slight undulation of land. Screaming and shrieking they came, most on foot but flanked by at least a score on horseback on either side.

'Shield wall!' Alfred roared, struggling to control his white stallion amidst the chaos of noise and activity.

The fyrd swiftly formed into eight lines, shields locked together in an almost impenetrable wall. At the same time, Aethelred gave the signal for the mounted nobles to charge the Welsh horsemen, keeping them engaged and unable to ride into the warriors on foot.

'Charge!' Alfred yelled at his warriors, heeling his horse to join the mounted fracas as the shield wall rammed the enemy with a resounding, ear-piercing clash, pushing and heaving the loosely packed hordes and driving them back toward the river.

But the proud Welsh were not so easily defeated and soon rallied to strike back, the two armies becoming embroiled in a mêlée of close and gruelling conflict. Spears and seaxes stabbed and slashed at vulnerable spots of exposed flesh; men ducked and side-stepped, attacked and parried, while mounted warriors became intermixed with those on foot, held in a frenzy of slashing swords and fitfully sidling beasts. Dead or injured, men dropped to the earth to be trampled by humans and horses alike.

Aethelred was soon locked in battle with a wiry Welshman in chainmail, and though he was the stronger of the two, the man was no easy opponent. More used to combat than Aethelred's, his horse moved to the rider's advantage, and Aethelred struggled to counter a few well aimed strikes at his throat or thighs. But as the Welshman's sword again struck out, Aethelred brought his shield up beneath it, forcing it upwards and enabling him to plunge his sword deep into his opponent's throat. Blood gushed down the warrior's armour as he dropped from his horse, stone dead.

Aethelred turned his mount, just in time to deflect a sword thrust aimed at the back of his neck. The Welshman roared, lunging at Aethelred's chest, but the terrified Mercian-bred horse reared up, its forelegs striking the warrior's right arm and causing him to drop his sword. Aethelred slashed down on the man and though he wielded his long shield with skill, a sideways slash to the neck finished him off.

Losses to the outnumbered Welsh were taking their toll. Corpses littered the earth and the grass had become slippery with blood and gore, its acrid, nauseating stench mingling with the odour of sweat oozing from the skin of exhausted warriors. A group of Welshmen made a desperate run for the bridge but were cut down before they reached it. Aethelred felt a renewed energy surge through his army and, suddenly, pandemonium broke out.

Enemy warriors were being pushed or hurled, dead or wounded, into the river by Saxons and Angles fired by blood-lust. The fast-flowing, estuarine waters carried them past the town and out to sea.

The prolonged blast of a horn from across the river brought the battle to a tentative halt, though the lone rider responsible was too distant to make out. Anglo Saxons watched, non-plussed, as Welshmen backed away from the victors and laid swords and spears on the bloodied earth before them. Across the river, the horn-blast ceased and, in the silence, Alfred's warriors claimed the sacrificed weapons of the defeated Welsh.

'So, Alfred of Wessex, you have won,' a voice rang out from the midst of the battlefield. 'We stand before you, defeated, leaving me no option but to plead for terms of surrender. Let us speak civilly in my hall so we may part with an agreement my people can honour.'

Aethelred focused on a tall, dignified figure on a handsome bay, for whom warriors stepped back to make pathway through to the Wessex king, who was now surrounded by a group of his nobles. Alfred nodded stiffly and spoke quietly to the Welshman for a few moments before issuing orders to his men.

Radulf was suddenly at Aethelred's side. 'I'm sending fifty men as escort to Alfred, most of them well-trained thegns. As leader of the Mercians, you'll want to be with the king, especially if some kind of peace treaty is to be signed.'

The Wessex ealdorman flashed an encouraging smile at Aethelred's uncertain nod. 'It's all part of learning how to be a leader, lad. I've spent many years at Alfred's side to know how things are done. And you'll be the one dealing with these

Welshmen in future, should the need arise. So go and watch and listen. The rest of us will stay here to keep an eye on this lot.' He gestured to the defeated Welsh, now surrounded by the victors and being hustled away from the gore of the battlefield to wait.

Thanking Radulf, Aethelred made his way to be introduced to the Welshman he could only assume to be one of the sons of the famous Rhodri Mawr.

* * *

The Conwy hall was a large, circular, stone-built structure with a central firepit and a number of tables and benches set up around it, presently occupied by a score of Alfred's thegns, while the rest waited outside. Impressive tapestries covered the walls, disguising the coldness of the granite and radiating an aura of colour and warmth. Across the curved wall opposite the door was a stepped dais, the top of which stood three feet above the floor of beaten earth covered with rushes. A rectangular oak table stood on this platform with three, high-backed chairs behind it. Aethelred had seen similar arrangements in Mercian halls and knew the table would be used when the king sat in Council or presided over matters of law and the dispensing of penalties for crimes or injustices done.

But today, that table was not in use.

Alfred hailed him over to a smaller, round table set beneath one of hall's four windows and waited in silence beside the dignified spokesman from the battlefield. Two other Welshmen stood next to them, although Aethelred recognised neither.

One was a younger man of similar stature and dark colouring to the spokesman, the other a scowling, white-headed man whose craggy features looked as old as the Welsh hills themselves. Ealdorman Aethelnoth of Somerset stood behind his king.

'Lord Aethelred, this is Anarawd, king of Gwynedd and Powys, and his brother, Cadell,' Alfred said, his hand moving from the tall spokesman to the younger man. 'Both are sons of King Rhodri Mawr.' He shifted his attention to the ageing man. 'And this is Meurig, King Anarawd's chief advisor and the cousin of their mother, Lady Angharad.

Anarawd gestured at the chairs, of similar design to those on the dais, indicating they should sit.

'My lord,' the Welsh king said, his dark eyes fixing on Alfred, 'we are at your mercy and must abide by your decision regarding the future of our lands. I can only repeat myself and stress my hopes for an agreement between us that my people can accept without feeling… shall we say, belittled or degraded at your hands. I mean no disrespect to you in saying this,' he added, holding up a placatory hand as Alfred bristled, 'but we are a proud race, and if my people felt slighted in any way, I could not guarantee a peaceful future between us.'

Aethelred listened, wondering whether there would ever be true peace and acceptance between the Welsh and Mercian peoples. Supremacy had passed from one to the other for generations, and he could only think that any agreement reached today would be a temporary one.

'I have no intention of slighting you or your people, Anarawd,' Alfred assured, 'or of basing armed men here. I have no wish to become, or to be considered, a tyrant. I want only peace and your oath that the raids of Mercian lands will stop.' Alfred's owl-like gaze flicked to Aethelred and back. 'I have a proposal to put to you which I hope you will accept.'

Alfred held out his hand, gesturing at Aethelred. 'Western Mercia is now mine to rule and Lord Aethelred – a Mercian himself – is the kingdom's overlord.' Anarawd's puzzlement was evident on his face and Alfred added, 'Aethelred will explain how that works.'

Taken aback by being put on the spot, Aethelred blundered into a long-winded reply.

'King Anarawd, dire times have also fallen upon my own kingdom of Mercia. Conquered by the Danes it is now divided into two, the east still ruled by Norsemen, and rule of the west having recently fallen to King Alfred of Wess –'

'This I already know,' Anarawd cut in, with a dismissive flick of his hand. 'Explain, if you will, what your role as "overlord" involves, since it would seem that King Alfred has a similar role in mind for me in my own kingdoms.'

Aethelred could see that Alfred was trying hard to keep a straight face at Anarawd's air of affronted pride, which boosted his confidence to continue. 'As overlord of Gwynedd and Powys, you will be responsible for their smooth running and organisation, King Anarawd, just as you always have been. The only difference will be that King Alfred will rule over those kingdoms now, and you will be answerable to him and obey any commands he issues to you.'

Anarawd's face grew darker by the moment, but Aethelred pushed on. 'If you control your people justly and do not incite them to rebel against the Wessex king, there will be little change in your day-to-day role. But if the slightest hint of rebellion reaches him, you and your people will be shown no mercy. King Alfred's kingdom is vast now that he rules western Mercia, and he can rapidly raise a huge army of battle-ready men.'

'Thank you, Lord Aethelred,' Alfred said, with an appreciative smile. 'You explained the position of overlord well. I think King Anarawd understands what's expected of him.'

'What of our relations with Welsh kingdoms further south?' the white-haired Meurig asked. 'Are they to be severed or are we free to travel and trade at will?'

Alfred fixed the old man in his piercing gaze. 'That's a good question. If you think we know nothing of how you've tried to take control of those kingdoms, you can think again. I've already had requests for help in keeping you out of Ceredigion and Dyfed. You have not only tried to take Mercian lands, but also those of your own countrymen. So, the answer to that question, Lord Meurig, is yes, you will sever all relations with those kingdoms, including trade. And I will soon know if you do not comply.'

Meurig hung his head, remaining silent as King Anarawd accepted the terms and signed the treaty hastily drawn up by Alfred. There was little left to say and Aethelred accompanied Alfred and his men out of the hall. Tonight they would stay close by, setting a vigilant watch while they slept. Tomorrow they would bury their dead before setting off on the long trek home.

Twenty Seven

Ribe, Danish lands: August 881

'Dainn…!' Yrsa shrieked, leaving the flatbreads she'd been stacking and hurtling across the hall to clasp the young man in a sisterly hug. 'It's wonderful to see you again!' She stepped back apace, taking Dainn's hands and grinning up at him. 'I hardly recognised you behind that bushy beard, though I can't deny it suits you. And you look so fit and well. But in the name of all the gods, where have you been these past four years? We've all been so worried – and you've not sent a single word! Your mother will be overjoyed to see you. I take it Hastein's here, too?'

'No, it's just me. I'll explain about Hastein once Mother's in here.'

'She's in the fire room sorting out tonight's meal. Sit down and I'll fetch her,' she ordered, pulling him away from the doorway. 'What a surprise she'll get!'

Yrsa popped her head round the fireroom door. 'Have you got a moment, Freydis?'

Freydis glanced up from her scrutiny of the various meats on the table and tilted her head to one side. 'Is it urgent? I'm rather busy right now.'

'There's someone here, says he wants a word with you. He won't tell me what it's about.'

Freydis gave a weary sigh. 'I suppose I'd better hear what he has to say, then.' She turned to the group of serving women.

'Get the meats roasting, and check the fruits and cheeses are ready to serve. Oh, and we need another barrel of ale rolling in.'

Freydis' expression changed from one of confusion to absolute joy as she focused on the figure sitting at one of the trestles. She pulled her elder son to his feet and wrapped him in her arms, tears of joy flowing down her cheeks. 'I hardly recognised you,' she said between sniffles. 'You were little more than a gangly youth last time we saw you, and now you have the build of a warrior. And no one could doubt whose son you are with a beard of that colour. Hastein's hair was always a gingery shade.

'No,' she said, holding up a hand, 'you can tell us what you need to say about Hastein once Aguti gets back from Ribe. He planned to be home in time for the meal. I can see your father isn't here and would not have expected him to be. In truth, I never thought we'd see you again, either, but I thank Freya for giving me such a gift.'

Dainn hugged his mother close. 'I never wanted to hurt you but, as you said, I was a mere boy four years ago. The visit to Rome sounded like a dream when Father told me of his plans. It made life in Ribe seem so dull. Even becoming a Christian sounded like an adventure to me.'

'And did what you saw in Rome convince you to become a follower of the Christ-god?'

Dainn flashed Yrsa a look that confirmed her suspicions. 'I didn't think it would,' she said, coming to stand beside them. 'I told everyone you were more likely to be interested in raiding than turning the other cheek and living in poverty.'

'We did live in poverty, once all our money had gone. But

I'll wait until Aguti's here before I tell you the rest or I'll be saying it all twice.'

Freydis patted Dainn's arm and urged him to sit down again. 'One of the servants will bring you a cup of ale while we get the meal ready. After waiting four years to hear what you've been doing, we can wait a bit longer. But be warned, you'll have a lot of questions to answer later on.'

It wasn't long before Aguti returned and Freydis was delighted to see the closeness still there between her sons. She had feared Aguti may suspect Dainn of wanting to take over the lands and hall Hastein had bestowed to his younger son when he and Dainn left for Rome – with no intention of coming back. But if that thought had entered Aguti's head, he hid it well.

'What was the purpose of your trip to Ribe?' Dainn asked, tucking into the roasted goat at the evening meal. 'Was it a day trip, or have you had a few days there?'

'Just a one-night stop. We needed supplies and I wanted to sell some surplus goods from our trip to Kaupang a couple of months ago. If we don't rush back I can let the men have a night in the taverns, which I do now and then by way of thanking them for their hard work on the estate. We intend to sail up to Birka next year. So far, I've kept mostly to the Norwegian settlements, with the odd trip to Skåne.

'Is the *Jormungand* still in good shape? She wasn't exactly young when we were children.'

Aguti stretched across the trestle to spear a duck egg with his scramseax. 'Old lady she might be, but she's seaworthy and will last a good few years yet. I'll consider having another ship built as soon as I think *Jormungand's* days are numbered.'

'No raiding, then?'

'Not my style,' Aguti replied, biting into the egg and chewing it slowly before swallowing. 'I get to see some of the world when trading and it generally means I'll come back home in one piece. You?'

Dainn downed his last half-cup of ale and called a serving woman over for a refill. Freydis could see he was finding it hard to tell them something and began to fear the worst. And Yrsa's face reflected her thoughts.

'Raiding's what we've been doing for almost three years now. Father and me, I mean. Our money ran out after a few months and finding ways of earning coin wasn't easy for strangers in Rome. It didn't take long to decide the Christ-god wasn't for us, so we joined the crew of a Norwegian longship and stayed with them for the next two years.'

Dainn grinned at the open-mouthed faces around the table. 'At least Yrsa was right about me. I *do* love raiding. We spent most of our time round the Middle Sea, which was good for a while, but Father wanted to head back north. When a ship from our own lands berthed at Pisa, looking to recruit another half dozen men, we were in like an arrow shot. Well, that was a year ago, and much has happened since then.'

'So this ship sailed back here, yet you didn't think to visit us?'

'Didn't get the chance, Mother,' Dainn replied, shaking his head. 'The ship sailed north all right, but only as far as the Low Countries. We joined a large force of Danes already based there and spent almost a year raiding around Ghent.

But two months ago something happened and I don't know how to tell you.'

Freydis came to sit beside him, gently moving his hand away from across his eyes. 'Are you trying to say that Hastein was killed in Ghent?'

Dainn nodded, fixing Freydis in a tearful gaze. 'We were raiding a monastery when we were surrounded by a troop of Frankish warriors. We had to fight our way out and many of our men were killed, Father amongst them. We didn't even get chance to honour them with a funeral pyre and more of our men died on the way back to our ships.

'I'm so sorry, Mother. I know you and Hastein were divorced, but I also know you were still fond of each other. Hastein always spoke of you with affection.'

'Freydis smiled and patted her son's arm. 'That's true, but there's nothing for you to be sorry about, Dainn. Hastein's been on many raids in his life and even Bjorn tells stories of his daring and foolhardy escapades. To die in battle would have been his chosen way to leave Midgard. Hastein will always have a place in our hearts and I will weep for his death rather than my loss of him. I lost him four years ago.'

'Did you come here in the ship that took you to Ghent?' Aguti asked.

Dainn nodded. 'Jarl Logmar was heading north for the Limfjord, intending to sail down the Kattegat to the island of Fyn. The ship had to pass close to Ribe so I was dropped off on the coast and walked the rest of the way.'

'What are your plans now?' Aguti asked. 'I mean, are you intending to go off raiding again, or stay here with us?'

Freydis held her breath, desperately wanting Dainn to stay here but not daring to think how Aguti would react if he did.

'I'd like to stay here until next spring, if you've no objection, Aguti. I've no desire to settle down yet, but Jarl Logmar won't be sailing again until then.' He looked from Aguti to Freydis. 'I know you don't like the thought of me raiding, Mother, but it's the life I enjoy. Running the estate and farming aren't for me. Father left it all to Aguti and he made the right decision in that. Aguti is as good as married to these lands.'

They all laughed and Dainn looked on, puzzled. 'I wouldn't let Frida hear you saying that, if I were you,' Yrsa said. 'She's marrying Aguti next month and she might not like the idea of being a second wife.'

Dainn jumped up and grasped his brother in a bear hug. 'I couldn't be happier for you – and it looks like I chose the right time to come home – that is, if you'll allow me to stay until next spring. A wedding feast is what we all need before the winter sets in.'

* * *

Alone in her bed, Freydis wept long into the night for the death of her husband, a good and kind man who had loved her more than she could ever have loved him in return. But as the first glimmers of dawn light squeezed through the shutters, her tears became those of joy. Her outgoing, adventurous son had been returned to her, for now. What the future held for him, only the gods could say. She would pray to her goddess to keep Dainn safe and knew that Freya would listen, as she always had.

What the future held for herself and Yrsa was also in the hands of the gods. At twenty and five years, her adopted daughter should have been married by now, but had rejected every man to have shown interest. And over the past ten years, that had amounted to many. Freydis would never force Yrsa to take a husband she did not love. Having spent too many years herself in that situation, she could not inflict such heartache on Yrsa.

But for now, they had a wedding to look forward to and a young woman to welcome into their household. They also had Dainn to cherish for the next eight months. After that, Freydis knew she would need the help of her goddess to make the right decision regarding the future for herself and Yrsa.

Twenty Eight

Wantage, Berkshire: Early October 881

Alfred's patience was wearing thin, the ongoing silence of the men seated around the hearthfire before him dragging on needlessly. Ealhswith was in the birthing room and he needed this meeting over quickly in order to be there as soon as the babe arrived. But so far, the plans he'd just outlined had met with stony silence from the witan: plans which had been discussed and finalised over the past week with some of his most competent ealdormen, now at the high table beside him: Radulf of Hampshire, Aethelnoth of Somerset, Unwine of Sussex and Paega of Berkshire.

He swept the hall with an expectant look, hoping at least one of them would think of something useful to say. Alfred realised his schemes were vast, and would take many years to implement, but he was determined the building works started over the last two years would continue. And for that to happen he needed the witan's full approval of his plans, as well as their likely cost to the Wessex coffers.

But it seemed that simply asking for their opinions was not going to work and they needed a little prompting. This was only the second time the new witan had assembled since their formation earlier in the year, and some of the younger members were still reluctant to speak out in the presence of more seasoned councillors. At his side, Radulf's lips parted, ready to break the silence, but a discreetly raised finger from

Alfred stopped him.

He decided to try a more direct approach.

'Does anyone see problems arising from fortifying any of these towns?' He lifted the large piece of parchment from the table, on which he'd marked thirty cities and towns across Wessex and western Mercia that he intended to focus on. The men had been given time to study it prior to the meeting, so none could claim ignorance of the places he mentioned. The towns extended from Canterbury in Kent in the east, to Mercian Warwick in the north and Lydford in Devon to the west. Several towns and ports along the south coast were also included.

So far, no one ventured a question, so Alfred pushed on. 'As you all know, we've already started work on some of our coastal towns, like Rochester, and Wareham, and early next year I want to make a start on a few of the those further inland. The scheme will be ongoing for a number of years, but I can't stress strongly enough that in order to fend off Norse attacks in future this work is vital.'

A slightly built Dorsetshire thegn raised his hand, and Alfred invited him to speak.

'On what basis did you choose the towns to fortify, lord?'

Alfred smiled and nodded at the young man, whose question provided a perfect opening for his explanation. 'The answer to that is a simple one, Aldwyn. They are all certainly towns of some importance to our kingdom but, probably of more significance, they were chosen due to their location *in relation* to each other.'

He let them consider that point for a moment before continuing. 'As you know, in past years, the Danes have found no difficulty in entering and moving about our kingdom at will, either by road or along our many rivers. And should Norse bands attempt to invade in future, we can't afford to allow that to continue. These thirty towns are situated within twenty miles of each other – a day's march for the fyrd – and we will ensure the roads linking them are in good condition, enabling communications and supplies to move between them quickly. Each town will be constantly garrisoned by the new-style fyrd, something else I'm in the process of organising. So any invaders attempting to move through our lands would be unable to do so without being observed or opposed for long.'

'My lord, what do you mean by a "new-style fyrd"?'

Alfred nodded, acknowledging the question from the newly appointed Bishop of Sherborne, a man of late-middling years who he'd come to admire for the care he'd shown to those in his diocese. 'As I'm sure you all know, Wulfsige, I've been saying for years that our traditional way of calling up the fyrd only when the need arises is far too slow and ineffective. We need a better system in place well before the network of towns is complete. Our old system never worked. By the time our armies were mobilised and had travelled, *on foot*, to where they were needed, the cursed raiders had too often moved on elsewhere.'

The tonsured bishop rubbed his bald patch, his brow furrowed in thought. 'It seems to me that having troops permanently garrisoned at these fortified towns is your biggest problem.'

'It is,' Alfred replied. 'The problem has always been the

impossibility of taking our fighting men permanently away from their villages, where they are needed to work in their fields. Even taking our thegns away from the responsibilities on their estates has been difficult at times.'

'So you need a rotating system,' Wulfsige said, matter-of-factly, 'one that allows half the men to be on duty for a set period of time, while the rest are at home keeping their fields in production.'

Alfred smiled, impressed with the new bishop's perceptiveness. 'That's exactly the idea I came up with, and I was hoping to set up the system over the next few months. There's no reason why the fyrds within reach of each of the thirty towns can't be on active duty there, whether the towns are fortified or not. Once there, the men could construct defences well enough to keep attackers at bay until stronger ones are built.'

He held out his arms, indicating the ealdormen at his sides. 'Together, we have been working to organise the system of rotation and will make sure that every ealdorman and thegn in our kingdom becomes involved in dividing their fyrds into two halves. Each half will take its turn preparing for combat while the other half remain in their villages to work in their fields. It will still put a strain on village life and food production, but nowhere near as much as having all the men away for up to months at a time in times of need.

'Any questions about that?' he asked, noticing a few confused faces.

Again it was Wulfsige whose hand was raised and Alfred invited him to share his thoughts.

'My lord, when you say one half will spend time "preparing

for combat", do you mean they will do that while garrisoned in the thirty towns?'

'A good question,' Alfred replied, nodding. 'I intend to divide the half on duty in what I've called "the standing army" into two halves again. One half will be garrisoned in the thirty towns, ready to defend them should they come under attack. The other half will become a mobile army, camping in the open fields of our kingdom and able to move out at any time. They will provide their own horses, plus food to last up to sixty days, which will enable them to travel at speed to anywhere in the kingdom and meet attackers or invaders before they have time to move on elsewhere.

'We've spent many hours in devising these plans,' he admitted, gesturing again at the four ealdormen, 'and believe they will work. Our armies will no longer be unprepared, leaving the Danes to wreak havoc while they struggle to find weapons and armour and spend days travelling to the place of attack. No, my friends, in future, our armies will be ready!'

'Father!' Aethelflaed called from the doorway, bringing the hall to silence. 'Mother sent me to tell you that you have another son!'

Alfred laughed as the hall erupted in cheers and applause. 'I think that's my cue to bring the meeting to a close. It seems my family needs me. If anyone wishes to ask anything further, I'll be in Wantage for another five weeks before we move back to Winchester to prepare for the Christmastide. You are all welcome to stay here for a few more days, should you wish.

'Lead the way, Aethelflaed,' he said, the grin of a proud father fixed on his face.

* * *

By the time the midwives allowed Alfred into their bedchamber, Ealhswith was propped up in the marital bed cradling the sleeping babe.

'Aethelweard is a fine boy,' she said as Alfred perched on the bed beside them, 'and seemed in a hurry to get into the world. My pains had barely started when your witan gathered for the meeting, but before long they took me off my feet. Poor Agnes couldn't get the two midwives in here quickly enough. It's a good thing they were already in the women's bower or Agnes would have been delivering the babe herself.'

Alfred leaned over and gently stroked the tiny babe's cheek before kissing his wife on the brow. She felt hot, and her lovely gold-brown hair was a little tangled, but she looked happy and proud of the most recent addition to their family. 'I'm just relieved you are both in good health after the ordeal,' he said. 'And we now have another son – although I doubt he'll be company for Edward. I can't see a ten-year-old playing with a baby, somehow.'

They both laughed at that and Ealhswith said, 'Perhaps Aelfthryth will, though, when she and Aethelweard are a little older. Aethelgifu won't play with her. In fact, Aethelgifu rarely joins in with anything the others are doing and prefers to sit in some out-of-the-way place on her own. Perhaps she just doesn't enjoy the boisterous type of play that Aelfthryth revels in.'

Alfred nodded, ashamed to admit he hadn't noticed that. In truth, he'd seen little of any of his children since arriving in Wantage a month ago. Affairs of the kingdom had taken so much of his time. 'I'll make a point of having a chat with Aethelgifu tomorrow. Better still, I'll offer to take her out for a ride with me so we can talk then. Don't look so aghast, Ealhswith,' he said, chuckling at his wife's expression. 'I know the child can't ride her own pony yet but I think she'll enjoy sitting in front of me. Pegasus is s a placid creature and won't sidle or panic at the smallest noise like old Caesar used to do. It won't be a long ride, unfortunately. With many of the witan here for another day or two, I can't stay away from the hall for too long.'

'I think she might enjoy that. Just make it the two of you, though, and don't let Aethelflaed or Edward join you. I think Aethelgifu will like to feel special for a while. But I'll be happy if you could find out why she prefers her own company.'

Alfred grinned. 'I'll try to remember your orders, my lady. Have you enjoyed the month we've had in Wantage?' he asked, changing the subject. 'I'd live here permanently if I didn't have so many responsibilities elsewhere.'

'You mean if you weren't the king,' Ealhswith said with a mischievous grin. 'But, dear one, there's no one else could have kept Wessex free from Danish control as you have done. I'm so proud of you and so are our children. But to answer your question, yes, I have grown to love this vill as much as you do. The autumn colours across the vale lifted my spirits when I was feeling fat and frumpy. And we still have another few weeks before we go back to Winchester. Like you, I'd happily stay here forever, but Winchester is where you need to be so we'll make the most of it. I just hope Aethelweard will be a placid babe and allows us to get some sleep, or Christmastide won't be much fun.'

Agnes returned to the room, taking the sleeping babe from Ealhswith's arms and laying him in his crib. 'Now, my lord, Lady Ealhswith needs to rest before the babe wants feeding, so if you would kindly –'

'Yes, I'll leave, Agnes,' Alfred said, kissing Ealhswith on the cheek and squeezing her hand before standing. 'I'll come back once my wife is rested and Aethelweard isn't screaming to be fed. I'll be in the hall, so send a servant to fetch me.'

* * *

The southerly breeze did nothing to mar the pleasure of Alfred's ride with Aethelgifu across the Vale of White Horse ahead of their escort of a dozen armed thegns. The early October sun was warm and the look of delight on his daughter's face told Alfred she loved being out on her own with him. Sitting astride the proud stallion was a rare treat for the child.

'Why is he called Pegasus?' she asked, half twisting to peer up at Alfred's face as the horse picked its way across a shallow stream.

'Because he's white – and big and powerful,' Alfred replied, flexing his biceps and making her giggle.

'But he hasn't got wings, so he isn't really like Pegasus.'

'And how do you know the real Pegasus had wings?'

'Because I heard Aethelflaed and Edward's tutor reading them a story about him. Pegasus could fly because he was the son of a god – Poseidon, I think. And his mother was Medusa, who had snakes for hair! But Pegasus was very beautiful.' The child sighed. 'I wish I could have a tutor. I love stories like that… and I want to learn to read and write.'

'You'll start learning your letters in a year or so, Aethelgifu,' Alfred assured her. Aethelflaed and Edward were seven before they had a tutor and you are still only six.' He paused, thinking about it. His daughter evidently felt ready to commit herself to lessons and it would be so much better than sitting in a corner by herself. 'Would you like me to ask Wilfrid to give you a few lessons each week? I'm sure he'd be pleased to have such a keen pupil. Learning to read and write is very important, and I know he has lots of stories to tell you. You would probably be reading some for yourself before too long.'

'Oh, yes, Papa!' Aethelgifu squealed. 'I really don't like playing with Aelfthryth, you know. I like my little sister well enough, but she just wants to run about playing chase. I want to be able to read and write.'

'That's settled, then. I'll have a word with Wilfrid next time I see him, and you can start straight away.' He chuckled, and Aethelgifu stared up at him, her nose wrinkled in confusion. 'I was just thinking what a noisy babe you were, and now you just want to sit somewhere nice and quiet. I would have expected you to be more… well, more like Aelfthryth!'

'Perhaps I was just bored when I was little, Papa, and wanted someone to tell me a story about Pegasus.'

Alfred laughed and gave his small daughter a hug. 'You're probably right. Now, let's take a look at that little pond over there before we head back.'

Twenty Nine

Worcester, West Mercia: Mid May, 882

'What brings you here without a word of warning?' Aethelred asked, looking from his father and sister to Hamid and Ameena as they walked into his Worcester hall. 'I'm pleased to see you all, of course,' he added quickly as Leofwynn adopted an open-mouthed look of feigned indignation, 'but surprised, that's all. I only got back from Winchester last week after spending Eastertide with King Alfred and his family. If you'd arrived then, you'd have been entertaining yourselves.'

'It's good to see you, too,' Eadwulf said, a huge grin on his face as he strode forward to embrace his son before they sat around one of the trestles and Aethelred ordered refreshments. 'Having not seen you since Christmastide, we'd been wondering how you were and decided to find out for ourselves. So our visit was in no way planned. Perhaps we could stay for a day or two, unless you're needed elsewhere?'

'Your arrival this week is perfect, Father, so stay a whole week if you like. I take it Aethelnoth's still in Elston, helping to look after things there?'

Eadwulf nodded. 'Selwyn's too old to be expected to do things on his own. It's time he put his feet up. Aethelnoth's more than capable of running the estate on his own.'

'It just seems strange – him not being with you, I mean. You two have travelled everywhere together for as long as I can remember. I'll try to get over to Elston later this year, if I find the time. I seem to have the rest of the year already planned out for me,' he added with a shrug, 'but I'll be here in Worcester until the end of this month. I'm meeting with the West Mercian witan at the end of next week, and in the first week of June, I start visiting the shire's ealdormen to check the fyrds are keeping weapons and armour to hand and in good condition. Alfred's determined the fyrds should be ready in case of further attacks.'

Aethelred rubbed the bridge of his nose as he thought. 'You probably know that several of West Mercia's more southerly towns are to be fortified as part of King Alfred's new plans?' They all nodded. 'So the ealdormen in those regions will be responsible for dividing their fyrds into two halves in what Alfred calls his "new-style" fyrd. Perhaps you've heard of that, too?'

'We have,' Hamid said, 'and it's a good idea. My father had similar problems of raising armies when he first became emir, and for the same reason: men couldn't leave their homes and lands for too long or food production fell. He did exactly what King Alfred is doing and devised a rotating system.'

'There's something else Father wants to tell you,' Leofwynn said, glancing sidelong at Eadwulf.

Eadwulf gulped back a mouthful of watered ale and swept his sleeve across his lips. 'I was going to leave this until we'd been here a little longer,' he said, addressing his son. 'But it seems your sister is as impatient as your mother was.'

Leofwynn shot her father an apologetic look. 'Sorry, Father. I just want to know what my brother thinks of the idea.'

Aethelred chuckled. 'So, will you tell me what you're talking about, or not? Surely it's not something I'll object to?'

'I don't think you'll object to this, Aethelred. Leofwynn is to be married in September – in the little church at Elston. We were hoping you'd be able to come, but we'll understand if your many commitments mean you can't.'

Aethelred came round the table to hug his sister. 'I couldn't be happier for you, Leofwynn. He must be something special for you to have chosen him. Is he local to Elston?'

Leofwynn nodded. 'Oswin's a thegn from Farndon, less than four miles from our hall. He inherited the title and a small estate when his father died earlier this year. As our father is his closest ealdorman, he came to Elston to check that his taking over the estate was in order.'

'I had no objection to Oswin inheriting the title or estate,' Eadwulf confirmed. 'He's a capable young man and had been running things for some years while his father was ill. He has the respect of the ceorls, too, which says a lot for him. Leofwynn caught his eye during his visit, and he returned several times after that, on some excuse or other. And I'd have had to be blind to miss how Leofwynn felt about him.'

Leofwynn blushed and they all laughed. 'I'll be leaving Elston to live in Farndon after the marriage ceremony and feasting,' she said. 'Oswin's mother is old now and unable to do much work herself, but she's promised to help me become familiar with the household routines. There are several servants, too, of course.'

'Hearty congratulations, sister. I'll do my very best to come to your wedding.'

'Leofwynn will have the most beautiful gown you've ever seen, 'Ameena put in. 'I'll be making it myself, with lace and embroidery that would befit the most important lady in all of al-Andalus.'

'For which I am more than grateful,' Leofwynn said, turning to give her aunt a kiss on the cheek.

'Well, now we've got that out in the open, I'll tell you what else I intend to do, Aethelred.'

'I'm not sure you need to tell me. I've been expecting you to say you're leaving Elston for some time. With me here in Mercia and Leofwynn married, there'd be no real reason for you to stay, would there?'

Eadwulf looked away, seeming disconcerted by Aethelred's directness. 'I'll be leaving at some stage in the next couple of years, Aethelred, once I can be sure everything is well with you all here. But when I do go, Hamid and Ameena have chosen to come with me. And since you're not likely to return to Elston, I intend to pass the hall to Aethelnoth. He's run the place by himself many a time, and he and Odella are happy to raise their family there. His youngest is almost three now and I've a sneaking suspicion Odella's with child again.'

Aethelred smiled. 'I'm happy for them. Pass them my congratulations and my sincere wishes for a safe birthing. As for your plans, I find nothing to disagree with, other than the fact that I'll miss you all when you've gone. And you're right to pass the hall to Aethelnoth. There's little chance of me returning to eastern Mercia, and he's the ideal person to keep things going at Elston. My role as Alfred's overlord is in the west, and likely to be for life. Besides, I've known of your longing to return to the Danish lands for years and would never deny you that happiness. Will you go to Ribe?'

'No, I'll be heading to Aros,' Eadwulf replied. 'I'm not sure of the situation at Ribe, and Bjorn always said I'd be welcome back to his hall at any time. We'll need to find a homestead of our own, and Bjorn may be able to help us in that, too.

'But before then, Aethelred, we have a few days to enjoy with you and a wedding to look forward to in September. What more could a father ask than to see his children doing well in their lives?'

* * *

Surrey and the South Wessex Coast: Late July 882

Summer was glorious across Wessex that year, the promise of bountiful harvests lifting people's spirits and filling them with hope for a peaceful future. Alfred's building plans were underway in several cities and towns and the reorganisation of the fyrd was in place. And so far, the kingdom had been free of any major Norse raids. Alfred thanked God that Guthrum seemed to have settled peaceably in East Anglia and Anarawd ap Rhodri had made no move to regain control of Gwynedd and Powys. He could only hope that both situations continued.

Yet it worried him that small fleets of longships constantly plagued his coasts, making lightning strikes at ports and settlements that would yield easy spoils. So far, local thegns or port reeves had been able to deal with them, but there was always the possibility that larger fleets would follow.

In mid-August, Alfred rode down to Southampton with

Hampshire ealdorman, Radulf, and a dozen of his thegns to check on the progress of his shipbuilders. As the closest port to Winchester, Southampton had been the base for the Wessex fleet and its crew for a few years now. Though his shipbuilders worked in coastal towns across the south coast of Wessex, for the present, all completed ships were moored in Southampton harbour.

Alfred's fleet was growing steadily and could now boast thirty vessels he felt proud of. Other than a couple taken in successful encounters with pillaging Danes, all were built to his design – though he knew his skills fell a long way short of Norse craftsmen.

On the morning after their arrival in Southampton, Alfred and Radulf headed to the large warehouse on the quayside, now the workplace of his shipbuilders, to discuss Alfred's designs for another vessel. Talks had barely begun when the ageing port reeve brought news that set his mind abuzz.

'My lookouts are here, lord, with word of four longships off the Sussex coast.' Eadgar paused, breathless after hurrying to relay his news. 'They made landfall and camped a couple of miles this side of Hastings before dark yesterday. We don't yet know if they intend to raid in that area but I'm guessing they won't, unless they need food. Settlements along that stretch of coast are mostly small fishing villages and would offer little booty. They're more likely to have their sights set on Selsey Abbey.'

'I agree,' Radulf said. 'The abbey's been targeted a few times in the past. I just hope the new abbot's had sense enough to set up a watch along the coast and remove prized items from the church… unlike his predecessor.'

'He has, at least, as far as I know,' Eadgar replied. 'Hildred's a wise and thoughtful man who wouldn't risk raiders taking him by surprise and slaughtering his flock. He's also a lot younger and less set in his ways than Abbot Wynstan.'

Alfred grinned at that, recalling the old abbot, pretentious till his dying day. 'Yes, there's more to the role of abbot than being godly. Round up my crew, Eadgar. I want eight ships ready to sail in an hour, including the *Wyvern.*'

The port reeve scuttled off and Alfred and Radulf made their way along the quayside to where the ships were moored. 'We've around eighteen miles to sail before we reach the open waters of the Solent and roughly the same again to the tip of the Selsey headland,' Alfred said, mulling over his thoughts as they walked. 'There are no coves or craggy inlets where we can lie in wait along that stretch of coast so we'll be best staying to the west of the headland and relying on Abbot Hildred's lookouts to warn us when the ships are approaching.'

Radulf scratched his head. 'It's possible they'll get there before us, which won't be in the abbey's favour. If the ships left Hastings early this morning and kept sailing, they could be over half way there now. By my reckoning, it's roughly seventy miles from Hastings to Selsey around the coast. Even if the wind's against them and their crews need to row, they could easily cover forty miles or more by noon and the rest by mid-to-late afternoon.'

The ealdorman paused. 'Although… if they pull ashore for food, as Eadgar thought possible, or sail later than we're assuming, we could have a wait our hands.'

'That's true, Radulf, but a wait's preferable to getting there too late.'

A southerly wind kept Wessex crewmen rowing for the eighteen miles from Southampton harbour to the open waters of the Solent. Once they turned in a more south-easterly direction they tacked into the wind and the ships seemed to fly over the waves for the next fifteen or so miles to the tip of the Selsey headland. And there, perched less than a quarter of a mile from the shingle beach, Selsey Abbey reared tall and proud – and clearly visible from the sea. Alfred could only wonder why the monks of yesteryear should build their most holy place where it presented an open invitation to passing sea wolves. But evidently, on this occasion, the building was still unharmed.

It was late morning when they'd left Southampton and early afternoon as they rounded the peninsula. From his place at the *Wyvern's* prow, Alfred scanned the open waters ahead, unsurprised to see no ships on the horizon: they had made good time, which he intended to use to his advantage. For whatever reason, the Norsemen had not yet reached this point, though he had no doubts that they would get here, eventually.

'Keep moving,' he yelled to Radulf, master of the *Hampshire,* sailing at the *Wyvern's* side. 'Another twelve miles or so and we reach the chalk cliffs. We'll find concealment there.'

The wait seemed endless as the eight Wessex ships clung to the coast of a small, steep-sided cove, though Alfred was pleased to note that the wind had swung to the south-west. Then the master of the lookout ship yelled what Alfred wanted to hear: 'Four ships, five hundred yards east. No sails, so they're rowing.'

'Hold!' Alfred shouted. 'I want them closer. Be ready for my signal.'

Wessex ships pushed away from the cliffs as the lookout yelled, 'two hundred yards!' Crewmen rowed hard to the open sea, sails were hoisted as they rounded the cliff and the ships leapt forward to face the oncoming foe.

In a flurry of surprise, Norse sails were raised as oarsmen turned at their oar ports, rowing fast until the wind hit their sails. But Alfred's ships had already gathered speed and the gap between them quickly closed.

'Cut them off!' Alfred yelled as they reached the enemy's tail and his fury at the countless Norse raids on his kingdom suddenly erupted. 'Prepare to board – and show no mercy!'

Four Wessex ships arced out, moving up the Norsemen's sides and circling inwards at their head, effectively forcing a reduction of speed and eventual halt. The *Wyvern* and three others moved between them, drawing broadside and boarding them with ease.

Though outnumbered two to one, the Danes fought like men possessed, slaying and wounding a good two dozen Wessex men and ensuring the Valkyries deemed them fit to dwell in Valhalla. But Alfred's rage was afire and the crews of two of the ships were slaughtered before he accepted pleas for mercy and surrender from the rest.

Enemy dead were tossed overboard, food for the crabs and fish, while the three score remaining were bound at wrist and ankle to be taken back to the mainland. There they would be sent to the halls of Wessex nobles to spend the rest of their days in slavery.

'The ships come back to Southampton with us!' Alfred yelled. 'Secure them well and tow them in.'

* * *

Elston, Eastern Mercia: Late August 882

August sunshine felt hot on Eadwulf's face as he left the Elston hall in need of some moments alone with his thoughts. Leofwynn's wedding was less than a week away and seeing his daughter aglow with such happiness stirred memories of her mother and the many happy times they'd spent at Elston.

He swept his sleeve across his sweaty brow as he strolled over to sit on a bale of straw in a shaded place outside the stables. Leoflaed had been a loving wife, and a devoted mother to their children. That she had been taken from them so early in life filled Eadwulf with great sorrow, but also great guilt. He knew he could – *should* – have loved Leoflaed more. He could not deny he *had* loved her, as far as he was able, but he'd always known she could never take the place of Freydis.

Had Leoflaed lived to see her children grown, she would have been so proud of them. Aethelred's role as Overlord of West Mercia would have elated her, and right now, she would have been fussing over Leofwynn like a mother hen and spending hours preparing for her wedding.

Leofwynn had grown so much like Leoflaed, in both appearance and temperament. Her hair was the very same shade of auburn, and her hazel eyes reflected her emotions just the same. Eadwulf smiled to himself, imagining Oswin cringing beneath his young wife's acidic tones and unpredictable temper. Yet, as with Leoflaed, Leofwynn's temper was usually a cover for hurt or unhappiness she felt inside herself.

'What is it with women and marriages?' Aethelnoth said, seeming to appear from nowhere and plonking himself beside Eadwulf. 'If I stay in there much longer, listening to them all cackling on about lace and flowers, I'll go crazy!'

Eadwulf laughed out loud, realising his friend was spot on. 'Got to you, too, eh?' he said, throwing a consolatory arm round Aethelnoth's shoulders. 'Only a few more days, then at least we can enjoy the wedding feast. Leofwynn won't be here after that, and she won't have such attentive companions as Odella and Ameena in Oswin's hall. She'll have her work cut out with that moody old mother of his.'

'If you ask me, Leofwynn can hold her own against anyone. She'll find a way of keeping her mother-by-marriage in check. Besides, she's so hard-working the woman will have naught to whinge about anyway.'

'You're probably right. She's just like her mother in that.'

'So you're still determined to head back to Aros?' Aethelnoth said, changing the subject. 'Are you sure it's the right thing to do?'

'I'm not sure of anything right now. My children don't need me nowadays. They're both strong-minded and sensible, and have their own lives to lead. I just feel it's time to settle down somewhere I can live the rest of my life in peace.'

Aethelnoth guffawed. 'You sound like a decrepit old man, do you know that, Eadwulf? This is me you're talking to, and I'm not falling for that load of old crap. You're just feeling sorry for yourself. Yes, I understand how you feel about your children not needing you any more – I'll probably feel the same in a few years' time. But "old"…? Do me a favour! I'm forty and three, a year older than you, and I still feel like a lad. I'll tell you what, if it was winter right now, I'd challenge you to a snowball fight.'

They both collapsed in laughter, immersed in memories of days long gone.

Thirty

Ribe, Danish Lands: Late April 883

Yrsa headed back to the hall, cursing and muttering under her breath. In one hand she carried a basket of eggs, collected from wild hens and geese around the yard, and in the other, a three-quarter-full pail of buttermilk needed for the mid-morning meal. She trod carefully for fear of spilling the milk and making herself look a fool. Already fuming following yet another clash with Frida, she knew that if she tripped, she wouldn't be responsible for the outburst that followed.

At her wits' end, Yrsa knew she couldn't go on like this, but could see no way out of the situation. Aguti's new wife had gradually become more domineering and spiteful since moving into the hall eighteen months ago. Oh, Frida was polite enough to Freydis, at least, to her face. But Yrsa had caught the derisive sneers aimed at Freydis' back and the odd complaint about her to Aguti.

With Yrsa, Aguti's wife was openly cold and scathing, though always when Freydis and Aguti weren't around. As the daughter of a local karl, a free man like the rest of his class and answerable only to his jarl, Frida had enjoyed certain privileges all her life. But her newfound, exalted status since marrying a jarl had gone to her head. And knowing that Yrsa was the daughter of a thrall, Frida was determined to treat her as such.

Yrsa had never shirked hard work or rested while others did the chores. Yet over the months, Frida had given her the most unpleasant tasks to do, like sweeping out the vegetable sheds and clearing animal muck from the yard: jobs usually given to the most menial of thralls. But, not wanting to upset Freydis, Yrsa had simply done as she was told and said nothing. Until now. She'd given the girl a good piece of her mind on three occasions recently, though it didn't seem to make any difference.

'Let me open that for you,' a voice behind her said, making her jump as she reached the door. Some of the milk spilled from the pail as she spun round, a feeling of joy welling up.

'Bjorn!' she yelped, putting the pail and basket down and giving Bjorn a hug. 'It's wonderful to see you! Does Freydis know you're here?'

'Not yet,' Bjorn said, grinning from ear to ear, 'but I've a feeling she's about to any moment now.'

The door was flung back and Freydis threw herself at her brother. 'I knew that was your voice! You could have let us know you were coming. And Leif!' she called, giving the smiling old steersman a hug as he reached them. 'I'm guessing you've come in the *Sea Eagle* then?'

Bjorn nodded. 'I've let the crew take the ship back to Ribe to spend a night in the town. I just wanted to ask you something before we sail. I'll tell you what it is later,' he added, halting the question on Freydis' lips. 'That is, if you decide to invite us in.'

* * *

'Let me get this clear,' Aguti said, putting down his ale mug and looking directly at Bjorn. The morning meal had been cleared away and they all remained around the trestle to talk. 'You intend to sail across to Mercia to visit Eadwulf.' Bjorn nodded. 'And you'd like my mother and Yrsa to go with you.'

'I'd like that very much,' Bjorn replied, hoping Aguti wasn't going to be awkward about this. 'But more to the point, I think Freydis and Yrsa would love to come with me. I'm right, aren't I?' he said, his gaze moving between the two women as they nodded enthusiastically. 'And the decision is up to them. As far as I can see, there's no reason why they should need to stay here and miss the chance of sailing with us. You and your wife have servants and everything is running smoothly here.'

His attention fixed on the two women again. 'So I think the answer is yes…?'

'How could I not want to see my brothers?' Yrsa said. 'It's ages since I saw them both.'

'I'd love to go too,' Freydis admitted, smiling at Bjorn before facing her son, 'as long as you and Frida can manage here without us.'

Aguti nodded uncertainly. 'The journey will probably do you both good… but you will be coming back, won't you?'

'I think it's a wonderful idea they should go,' Frida cut in before Freydis could reply. 'We can manage perfectly well without them, Aguti. We have enough servants around the place, after all. And I *am* the mistress of the hall now and don't need any help in running it.'

Bjorn stared at the girl, his dislike of her growing with the passing moments. Her pretty face and the golden hair peeping from the sides of her head veil were just an outer veneer, perfected and polished to hide the canker inside. She certainly showed no concern for the feelings of her husband or his family.

'I suggest you show your mother-by-marriage some respect, Frida,' Bjorn snapped. 'Aguti's mother…my sister and the daughter of Jarl Ragnar Lothbrock… was running this hall efficiently for many years before either you or Aguti were even born!'

The brazen girl held his stare until Bjorn flashed his wolfish grin, which seemed to disconcert her enough to look away.

'Whether or not Freydis and Yrsa choose to come back to Ribe will be up to them once we return. They both know my hall is always open to family, and to have them living in Aros would make me very happy. But, as I said, that decision is not mine to make.'

They spent the rest of the day catching up with news of family and friends and generally enjoying each other's company. As always, talk of Hastein brought Bjorn close to tears. He'd been devastated by Hastein's death and knew that Eadwulf would be saddened to hear of it, too.

In the late-afternoon, Frida complained of a pounding headache and took herself off to her bedchamber. Bjorn fervently hoped she'd stay there until after they'd left the following morning. Freydis and Yrsa busied themselves with preparations for the evening meal while Bjorn and Leif continued to chat quietly with Aguti, mostly about his role as jarl. In his wife's absence, Aguti was a pleasant young man and Bjorn could not help thinking that unless Frida's attitude changed, Aguti would be divorcing her before long. There were plenty of agreeable women out there without tolerating one with a viperous bite. If Ragnar had realised that years ago and turfed Aslanga out of his hall, life in Aros would have been so much happier.

* * *

Elston, East Mercia: Early May 883

It had rained since early morning and Ameena felt in great need of being outside, away from the stuffy warmth of the hall. And from the constant squabbles that kept erupting, she was certain Odella and Aethelnoth's three older children were feeling the same. While their mother was busy caring for Durwyn, their six-month-old brother, the children were giving their nurses a hard time.

'I'm sure it's stopped raining now,' she declared, glancing through the open shutters. 'Would you three like to come for a walk before the morning meal – on your best behaviour, of course?'

Needing no second asking, the youngsters sped across to their adopted 'aunt' as their two weary nurses, both of late-middling years, flashed her smiles of gratitude. Ameena prided herself on being strict and the children knew better than to misbehave for her.

'Right then,' she said. 'Coats on first, in case it rains again. Be quick,' she called as they hastened to do as told, 'or I might change my mind and go on my own.'

'Now, Esme,' she said taking the four-year-old girl's hand, 'you will walk with me.' She looked intently at twelve-year-old

Raulf and nine-year-old Nelda. 'And you two will walk next to us. Is that clear? Good,' she said, acknowledging their nods. 'We'll probably find some bluebells in the wood. It's a little too early for poppies, but bluebells are lovely, too.'

They waved at Hamid, chiselling away at his latest piece of furniture in a hut Eadwulf had allocated as his workshop. The table looked beautiful and Ameena was suddenly reminded of such pieces in their home in Cordoba. Thoughts of her father caught her off guard and she blinked back the unshed tears.

Further across the yard, they peeped into one of the barns where Eadwulf and Aethelnoth had just dealt with a difficult lambing, then continued on to the bluebell wood.

'Just look at that,' Ameena said as they all gaped at the woodland floor with its carpet of purple-blue. The fragrance of damp earth and blossoms hung on the air and Ameena savoured its freshness after the mugginess of the hall. 'We'll pick a few just before we go back to the hall, or they'll wilt and –'

The sound of voices cut off what she had been about to say and, at the sight of the figures heading for the hall, Ameena almost gasped out loud. 'We have to get back. Now!' she said, silencing the children's protests with a raised hand and pulling little Esme along. 'Everyone's in for a nice surprise. Let's see if we can catch up with those people.'

The children looked on, bemused, as Ameena shared warm embraces and happy chatter with the two people she remembered so well, despite not having seen them for eleven years. Even Raulf had been a baby then, and too young to remember their visit to Elston, bringing Beorhtwulf, Hamid and Ameena back from Cordoba with Eadwulf and Jorund.

They reached the hall together, and Ameena smiled to herself as she envisaged the coming reunions.

* * *

At the sudden loud barking of the dogs, Eadwulf and Aethelnoth shot outside, just as Hamid emerged from his workshop. The three of them gaped, dumbfounded, and a few moments of silence reigned.

'Is this what you call a greeting in these parts?' Bjorn said, a grin spreading across his face. 'Well, I'm very pleased to see you three, too!'

Laughter erupted, followed by bear hugs and back-slapping. 'By Odin,' Leif said, 'I swear, none of you look a day older than you did the last time we saw you. Is it something in the water round here, do you think?'

Eadwulf smiled at the old steersman, realising he must be nearing sixty by now. 'You're looking well, too, my friend. If I look as good as you when I reach your age, I'll have no complaints. I imagine you've got used to being bald?'

Leif pulled a face. 'I don't have much choice, do I?'

Eadwulf chuckled. 'Still keeping busy?'

'You could say that – and Bjorn's planning a trip up to the Lofotens later this year. We heard Olaf'd passed away and the master here wants to pay his respects to the family.'

'I owed Olaf a lot,' Eadwulf said, nodding sadly, 'and I'm sorry to hear he's gone. But he was older than you, wasn't he, Leif?'

'A good five years or more. We'd heard he wasn't sailing

nowadays and thought he'd just called it a day. Seems he grew ill and died while he slept.'

'Well, I don't know about anyone else,' Bjorn cut in, looking pointedly at Eadwulf, 'but I could do with a mug of ale. Then we'll tell you exactly why we're here.'

'I'm sorry to hear about Hastein,' Eadwulf said for the umpteenth time once they'd brought each other up to date with their news. 'I'd thought it unusual he wasn't with you, but I never expected to hear of his death. I can only imagine how it upset you. You were always more like brothers than cousins. I hope Freydis is coping well, looking after the hall now Aguti's running it. It's a good thing she has Yrsa with her.'

Bjorn nodded. 'And I'm sorry to hear about Jorund. Yrsa will be devastated when we tell her. But the rest of your news is welcome. You must be proud of Aethelred, and to have your daughter married is perfect. My daughter, Astrid, is married, too, but neither of my sons has made a move in that direction yet. I'm in no hurry to give Thorgils a shove – he's only just seventeen – but Hrolf needs to get a move on. He's already twenty and five and claims he doesn't want burdening with a wife just yet.'

'He will, one day, Bjorn,' Leif chipped in. 'I still remember what you were like when Ragnar kept badgering you to marry. You dug your heels in and ignored him until you met Kata on Bornholm. Perhaps something like that'll happen to Hrolf.'

Bjorn just nodded and gazed round the room, the chunters of little Durwyn making him smile. 'And you, Aethelnoth, seem to be well settled and your family is growing steadily. Odella was always good with children, if I recall. I wish you all well.

'Two of my men should be arriving at your door very soon,' he added, focusing on Eadwulf. 'No doubt your hounds will let you know when they approach. They'll be delivering something we've brought for you before heading back to watch the ship.' He gestured at Leif. 'I was hoping we could stay in your hall…?'

Eadwulf smiled, pleased to know his friends wouldn't be rushing off. 'You're always welcome, you know that. In fact, I've been considering heading over to Aros sometime soon. I just needed to find passage on a ship sailing that way. But if you'll be away this summer, we'll leave it until next spring.'

'We?'

'Hamid and Ameena will be with me. We were hoping you might find us an empty dwelling on your land. I've a yearning to live back in Aros.'

Bjorn stared at him and glanced at Leif. 'You don't know how happy you've made me by saying that. To have you back in Aros is more than I could have hoped for, and Hamid and Ameena are more than welcome. Your children know of your plans?'

'They've known for a while, and are fine with the idea as long as I promise to visit them now and then.'

The barking of the dogs drew everyone's attention and Aethelnoth headed to investigate. 'You'd better come in,' he said, pulling back the door and stepping aside, his face a picture of surprise.

Bjorn's two men walked in, followed by two women.

Eadwulf's jaw dropped. 'Freydis… Yrsa! I don't know what to say.'

'Then don't say anything and give me a hug,' Yrsa said

hurrying across the room and flinging her arms around her half-brother. 'It's good to see you again. Eleven years is a long time, so we thought we'd come and see how you are. Didn't we, Freydis?'

Eadwulf's eyes locked with Freydis' as she came to greet him. 'I couldn't let Yrsa come without me. I hope you don't mind.'

'Mind! How could I mind? It's wonderful to see you both,' Eadwulf replied, taking her outstretched hand. He drank in the sight of her, still a lovely woman now she had turned forty, although she looked tired after the journey. He struggled to find words to say, not wanting to mention Hastein just yet. He glanced at Bjorn, whose grinning face helped put him at ease.

'Come and sit down and we'll speak further later. I can't tell you how pleased I am to see you looking so well.'

'Where's Jorund?' Yrsa suddenly asked, reminding Eadwulf of the time he'd returned to Elston to face the household with news of his brother's death. He didn't look forward to a repeat of that, but it had to be said.

Freydis held Yrsa close as she sobbed, and Eadwulf could see she was struggling to stop her own tears from flowing.

'Jorund made us all very proud,' he said, hoping they'd find comfort in knowing that. 'Even King Alfred praised him after the battle. But there's something else you need to know.'

Freydis' face seemed to crumple further. 'Not more bad news?'

Eadwulf nodded, glancing from Freydis to Bjorn. 'I wish I could say it wasn't, for both your sakes. Although you may already have heard.'

'We know Halfdan's dead, if that's what you're about to tell us. News of his death reached us… must be six years ago. In Ireland, we were told.'

'That's what we'd heard, too. But I'm not talking about Halfdan, Bjorn. It's Ubbi.'

Freydis' gasp told Eadwulf they hadn't known. 'Ubbi died the year after Halfdan, while he was raiding along the coast of Devon. He was proudly waving the Raven banner at the end, if that's any consolation to you. His death hit Jorund hard, and he hadn't really got over it before he was killed himself at Edington. My brother was hoping to be reunited with Ubbi one day. They were so close as boys, and Jorund never forgot Ubbi's kindness to him.'

Little was said until the two women composed themselves, but conversation lightened as they enjoyed the morning meal. Yet it wasn't until late afternoon that Eadwulf had chance to speak alone with Freydis.

'Bjorn told us about Hastein,' Eadwulf said as they strolled around outside.' I can't tell you how sorry I am to hear of his death. I realise you've known for a while now, but grief takes time to heal.'

Freydis gave a wan smile. 'It's two years since Dainn told us of Hastein's death, Eadwulf, and we hadn't seen or heard anything from either of them for three whole years before that. Hastein had not been my husband – or even part of my life – for so long that my grief was more for the fact that he'd lost his life than for his loss to me. Aguti has made an excellent jarl and will have been married for two years in September. There's no need for either me or Yrsa to stay at Ribe now and we were thinking of going back to Aros.'

'Have you mentioned that to Bjorn?'

Freydis nodded. 'He's happy with the idea. He really doesn't like Aguti's wife. If truth be told, I'm not fond of her, either, and Yrsa can't stand her.'

'No wonder he was pleased when I told him I intended to head there, too.'

'I believe Bjorn regrets forcing us apart all those years ago, Eadwulf, and is trying to get us back together. If you hadn't been planning to return to Aros, I'm sure he would have suggested that Yrsa and I stay here, with you.' Freydis looked away, seeming embarrassed by saying that.

'Bjorn did what he thought was right at the time, and we both know he had no other choice. He loved Hastein, too, and at the end of the day, he did what duty asked of him.'

'I know you're right, but I've wanted to be with you for so many years. I can scarcely believe that time has come. We'll be happy together, I know we will.'

Eadwulf held Freydis close. 'I've never doubted that for one moment,' he whispered.

* * *

Winchester, Wessex: Early May 883

The illness struck with particular venom this time, and barely three weeks after the last attack. Alfred was taken to his bed as pains threatened to grind his innards to shreds. As always, he felt sick and had lost control of his bowels, but on this occasion a fever took hold, sending him into periods of unnatural sleep from which he woke sweat-soaked and weak as a newborn babe.

During his more lucid moments Alfred thought about his plight, deciding that God must be punishing him for failing in some way. His own father, King Aethelwulf, had declared the Norse raids to be a punishment on Wessex people for falling away from the teachings of Christ and into a state of ignorance. Alfred had come to believe that people's ignorance – including his own – had resulted in such a lack of wisdom, they were unable to outthink and outmanoeuvre marauders in their lands.

Now that he was the king, Alfred realised that this failure rested on his shoulders. He'd done his utmost to stop the Danes from staying in his lands once they were here, but that had not been enough. He should have had the wisdom to *foresee* the invasions and made preparations in advance. Instead, he'd gloried in the peace he'd gained following victorious battles, or by paying the Danes tribute, and rested on his laurels until the next invading force moved in.

Alfred prayed for forgiveness, knowing that the increasing severity of his illness was punishment for his failure to keep learning alive in Wessex. It was time to rectify that.

Today, the first day of rising from his bed since illness took him, Alfred had been determined to make a start. Tucked away in a corner of the Winchester hall, he'd been sorting through heaps of scrolls since mid-afternoon. Now, at almost midnight, he was battling the overwhelming urge to sleep. The hearthfire was dying down and most of the lamps had been doused. The large room was dim and sleep-inducing and his resident thegns had already taken to their beds. Before long the servants would extinguish the last few lamps and do the same.

But Alfred still had work to do. Having spent many months retrieving these parchments and vellums from monasteries and abbeys fortunate enough to have escaped Danish wrath, he now knew why God had protected them. They were needed for a purpose.

He refocused on the scrolls before him, shifting the small candle to where it cast sufficient light for him to continue his scrutiny. Most were written in Latin, which, to Alfred's shame, he could not read, although he knew from their style that many were prayers and psalms. He placed the Latin texts at one side of the table and the rest, which had already been translated, at the other.

He stared at the candle's flickering flame, its mesmerising motion lulling him to a state of lethargy in which his thoughts strayed yet again.

Wessex had enjoyed peace for five years now, however uncertain it was. In East Anglia, Aethelstan remained true to his Christian vows and had not rebelled against Wessex; nor had Anarawd rebelled in Gwynedd. And Alfred had Eadwulf's capable son, Aethelred, effectively controlling western Mercia on his behalf. Odd coastal raids still occurred, but they continued to be small and easy to deal with by the local fyrds. Building works were continuing and Alfred felt certain that most Wessex towns would be able to withstand attacks and sieges well enough until the closest section of his standing army arrived.

Yes, Alfred was satisfied that all was progressing well in his kingdom, and at home he felt happy and content. He had a wife and five children he loved – children for whom he had such hopes. He smiled as he thought of their futures in a secure and prosperous Wessex. Edward would succeed him as Wessex king while his younger son, Aethelweard, would likely become a warrior and ealdorman or, should he so choose, a man of learning or member of the Church. And Alfred would ensure his three daughters made marriages that would benefit them and Wessex.

But before that time, the restoration of learning was foremost in his plans.

He rubbed his aching brow, recalling how many scholars and scribes there had been across the kingdom in his youth, and cursing the Danes for ransacking and burning so many great centres of learning. How many priceless scrolls had been torched in monasteries and abbeys; scrolls written by some of the greatest scholars of the past? Now there were few men left in Wessex with access to such treasures, and the interest in learning was dying.

He smiled as he thought of his father's erudite scribe, Felix. When Alfred was a child, Felix has seemed to him like a bottomless well of knowledge. So much so that he still held the scribe in the highest esteem. And Swithun, the highly respected and greatly loved Archbishop of Winchester, who had once been King Aethelwulf's mentor. It was men like these that Alfred wanted in Wessex now: men who could share their learning and wisdom with people who had neither – and could translate old Latin scripts into the Saxon tongue for all to understand. Alfred counted himself amongst those unfortunate ignorant and felt shamed by it. He yearned to be able to translate Latin prayers for his people to read.

So far, Alfred had located several scholars around the kingdoms of Britain as well as abroad, and tomorrow he would start sending out delegations of thegns to request their presence at his court. Among them was a certain Welsh monk at Saint David's Monastery in Dyfed whose reputation as a wise and godly man with a love of learning had spread far and wide. He went by the name of Asser.

Alfred had much work for this monk to do, including educating the Wessex king himself in the skill of reading and translating Latin scripts.

Relentless waves of fatigue washed over him and he yawned widely, unable to stop his heavy eyelids from drooping.

The gentle touch of Ealhwith's hand on his cheek roused Alfred from a fitful sleep. His neck was stiff from being twisted sideways on his crossed arms on the tabletop, and he rolled it a few times to ease movement back into it. The candle had burned out and Ealhswith stood at his side, a small oil lamp in her hand.

'Come to bed,' she said. 'You'll get no more work done now. You need sleep so you can face the new day with a smile.'

Alfred eased himself to his feet and took her hand. 'You're right. And I'm hoping we'll have much to smile about for many days to come.'

44895162R10239

Printed in Poland
by Amazon Fulfillment
Poland Sp. z o.o., Wrocław